"A BEAUTIFUL
HEARTFELT, RE
ELEGANT, BRAVE"

DREAD CENTRAL

"VOLK POSSESSES A QUESTING
MIND AND AN EXPANSIVE HEART
AND PAINTS DARK AND LIGHT
SIDES OF THE HUMAN EQUATION
LIKE FEW OTHERS"

*MICK GARRIS, PRODUCER & DIRECTOR,
"MASTERS OF HORROR"*

"BEAUTIFULLY WRITTEN.
PERFECTLY NUANCED.
I LOVED IT"

*NEIL SPRING, BEST-SELLING
AUTHOR OF "THE GHOST HUNTERS"*

"MESMERIC AND DEMONIC.
AN INSTANT CLASSIC"

*JOHNNY MAINS, SERIES EDITOR,
"BEST BRITISH HORROR"*

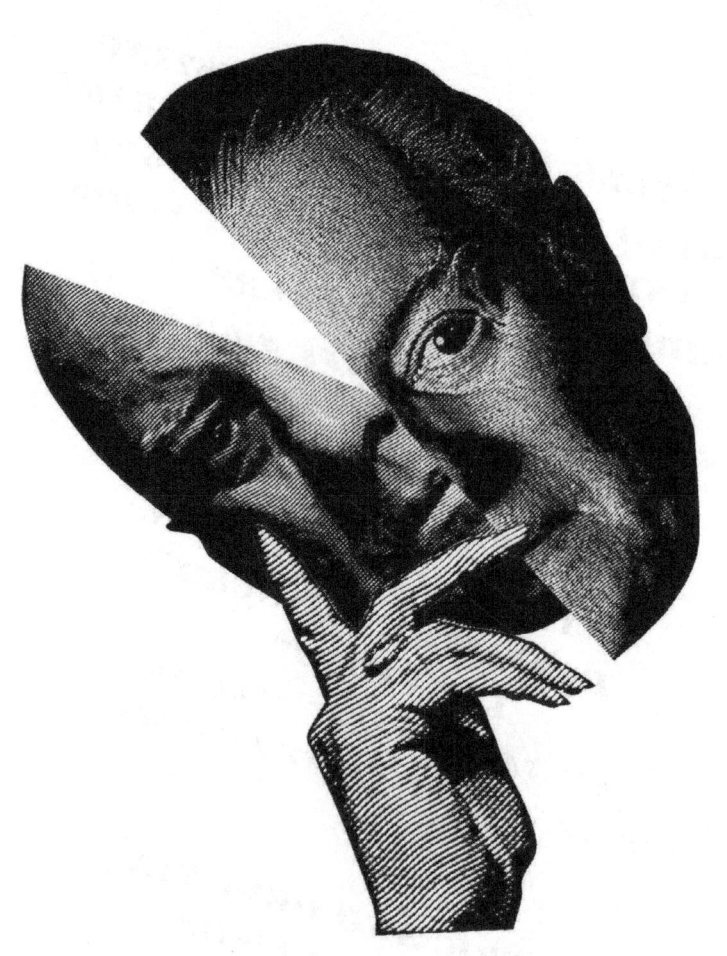

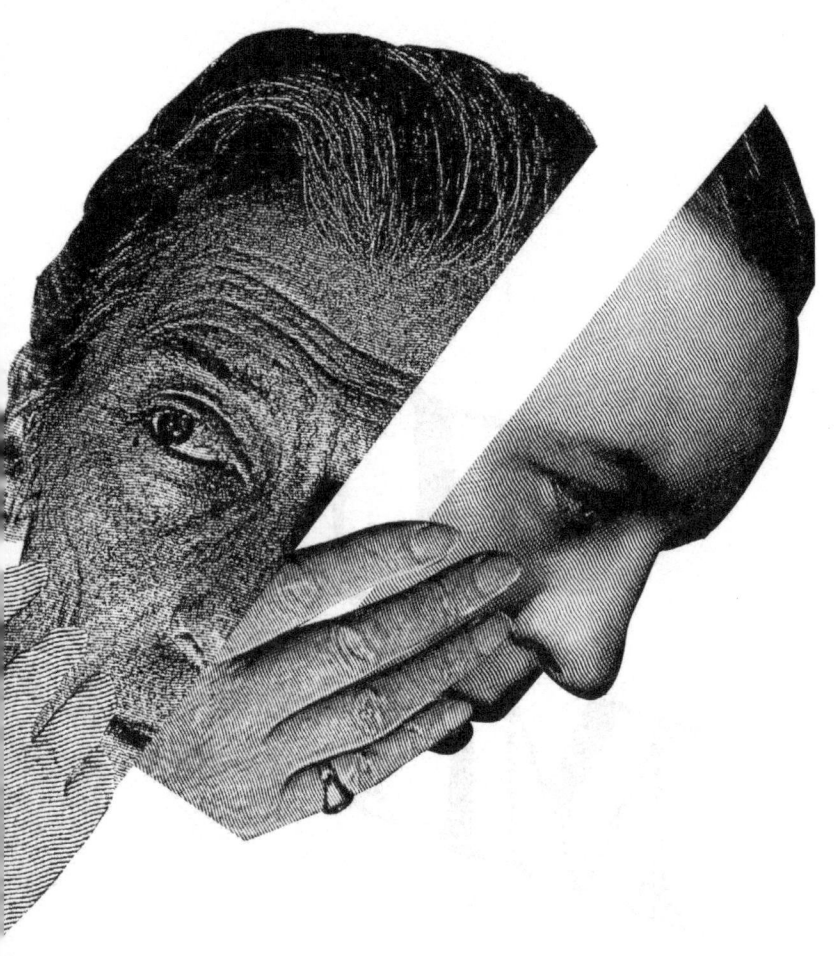

DA
MAS

THE DARK MASTERS TRILOGY

STEPHEN VOLK

DIP

First published in hardcover in 2018 by PS Publishing Ltd, this
trade paperback edition is published by Drugstore Indian Press, an
imprint of PS Publishing in April 2023 by arrangement with the
author. All rights reserved by the author.

ISBN
978-1-78636-990-1

2 4 6 8 10 9 7 5 3 1

Cover and book design by Pedro Marques.
Text set in Baskerville and Amasis,
titles set in Roman Engraved HPLHS
Printed in England by the T.J. Books

PS PUBLISHING LTD
Grosvenor House, 1 New Road
Hornsea, HU18 1PG, England

E-mail: editor@pspublishing.co.uk
Visit our website at www.pspublishing.co.uk

For Johnny Mains

WHITS

TABLE

HE COULDN'T FACE going outside. He couldn't face placing his bare feet into his cold, hard slippers. He couldn't face sitting up. He couldn't even face opening his eyes. To what? The day. Another day without Helen in it. Another day without the sun shining.For a moment or two before being fully awake he'd imagined himself married and happy, the luckiest man on earth, then pictured himself seeing her for the first time outside the stage door of the Theatre Royal, Drury Lane: she a shining star who said a platypus looked like "an animal hot water bottle"—he in his vagabond corduroys, battered suitcase, hands like a Dürer drawing, breath of cigarettes and lavender. Then as sleep receded like the waves outside his window, he felt that dreadful, dreaded knot in his stomach as the awareness of her no longer being there—her non-presence—the awful, sick emptiness, rose up again from the depths. The sun was gone. He might as well lie there with his eyes shut, because when his eyes opened, what was there but darkness?

Habitually he'd rise with the light, drink tea, take in the sea view from the balcony, listen to the wireless and sometimes go for a swim. He did none of these things. They seemed to him to be activities another person undertook in a different lifetime. *Life. Time.* He could no more picture doing them now than he could see himself walking on the moon. The simplest tasks, the very idea of them, seemed mountainous. Impossible.

Yet it was impossible, also, to lie there like a dead person, greatly as it appealed to do so. It was something of which he knew his darling would so disapprove, her reprimand virtually rang in his ears, and it was this that roused him to get up rather than any will of his own.

His will was only to…

But he didn't even have the strength for that.

She was his strength, and she was gone.

Helen. Oh, Helen…

Even as he sat hunched on the edge of the bed, the burden of his loss weighed on his skinny frame. He had no choice but to let the tears flow with the same cruel predictability as his dream. Afterwards, weaker still, he finally rose, wiping his eyes with now-damp knuckles, wrapping his dressing gown over baggy pyjamas and shambling like something lost and misbegotten towards the landing. A thin slat shone between the still-drawn curtains onto the bedroom wallpaper. He left the room with them unopened, not yet ready to let in the light.

A half-full milk bottle sat on the kitchen table and the smell hit him as soon as he entered. The sink was full to the brim, but he poured the rancid liquid in anyway, not caring that it coated a mound of dirty plates, cups, saucers and cutlery with a viscous white scum.

He opened the refrigerator, but it was empty. He hoped the milkman had left a pint on the doorstep: he hated his tea black. Then he remembered why he had no groceries. Joycie did it. Joyce, his secretary, did everything for 'Sir'. He recalled again the hurt in her voice when he'd told her on the telephone she would not be needed for the foreseeable future, that she needn't come to check that he was all right because he *was* all right. He'd said he needed to be alone. Knowing that the one thing he didn't want to be was alone, but that was not the way God planned it.

Nasty God.

Nasty, nasty God…

He shut the fridge. He didn't want food anyway. What was the point? Food only kept one alive and what was the point of that? Sitting, eating, alone, in silence? What was the point of that?

He put on the kettle. Tea was all he could stomach. The calendar hung facing the wall, the way he'd left it.

The letter box banged, startling him, shortly followed by a knock on the door. It was Julian the postman, he thought, probably wanting to give his condolences in person. He held his breath and had an impulse to hide. Instead he kept quite still. Julian was a sweet chap but he didn't want to see him. Much as he knew people's wishes were genuine, and appreciated them, his grief was his own, not public property. And he did not want to feel obliged to perform whenever he met someone from now on. The idea of that was utterly repellent. How he dealt with his inner chasm, his utter pain and helplessness, was his own affair and other people's pity or concern, however well-meaning, did not make one iota of difference to the devastation he felt inside.

He stood furtively by the doorway to the hall and watched as a package squeezed through and fell onto the welcome mat, and beyond the glass the silhouette of the postman departed.

It had the unmistakable shape of a script.

His heart dropped. He hoped it was not another one from Hammer. He'd told them categorically via his agent he was not reading anything. He knew Michael had newly found himself in the chair as Managing Director, and had a lot on his plate, but could he really be so thoughtless? Jimmy was a businessman, but he also counted him a friend. They all were. More than friends—family. Perhaps it was from another company, then? Amicus? No. Sweet Milton had his funny American ways, but would never be so callous. Other companies were venal, greedy, but not these. They were basically gentlemen. They all knew Helen. They'd enjoyed laughter together. Such laughter, amongst the gibbets and laboratories of make-believe. Now, he wondered if he had the strength in his heart to meet them ever again.

He picked up the package and, without opening it, put it on the pile of other unread manuscripts on the hall stand. Another bundle sat on the floor, a teetering stack of intrusion and inconvenience. He felt no curiosity about them whatsoever, only harboured a mild and uncharacteristic resentment. There was no small corner of his spirit for wonder. They were offers of work and they represented the future. A future he could not even begin to contemplate. Why could they not see that?

He sighed and looked into the mirror between the hat hooks and what he saw no longer shocked him.

Lord, the make-up job of a master. Though when he sat in the make-up chair of late he usually had his hairpiece to soften the blow. Never in public, of course: he abhorred that kind of vanity in life. Movies were different. Movies were an illusion. But—fifty-seven? He looked more like *sixty*-seven. What was that film, the part written for him but one of the few he turned down? *The Man Who Could Cheat Death*. But he couldn't cheat death at all, could he? The doctors couldn't, and neither could he. Far from it.

Dear Heavens…

The old swashbuckler was gone now. Fencing in *The Man in the Iron Mask*. The Sheriff of Nottingham. Captain Clegg of Romney Marsh…He looked more like a Belsen victim. Who was it said in a review he had cheekbones that could cut open letters? He did now. Cheeks sucked in like craters, blue eyes sunk back in deep hollows, scrawny neck, grey skin. He was positively cadaverous. Wishful thinking, he thought. A blessing and a curse, those gaunt looks had been his trademark all these years, playing cold villains and erudite psychopaths, monster-hunters and those who raised people from the dead. Yet now the only person he desperately craved to bring back from the grave he had no power to. It was the one role he couldn't play. Frankenstein had played God and he had played Frankenstein playing God. Perhaps God had had enough.

The kettle whistled and the telephone rang simultaneously, conspiring to pierce his brain. He knew it was Joycie. Dear Joycie, loyal indefatigable Joycie, who arrived between dry toast and correspondence every day, whose concern persisted against all odds, whose emotions he simply couldn't bear to heap on his own. He simply knew he could not speak to her, hear the anguish in her voice, hear the platitudes even if they weren't meant as platitudes (what words could *not* be platitudes?) and, God above, if he were to hear her sobs at the end of the line, he knew it would tip him over the edge.

Platitude:
An animal that looks like a hot water bottle.

Hearing Helen's laughter, he shut his eyes tightly until the phone stopped ringing, just as it had the day before. And the day before that.

Quiet loomed, welcome and unwelcome in the mausoleum of his house.

He stared at the inert typewriter in the study, the signed photographs and letter-headed notepaper stacked beside it, the avalanche of mail from fans and well-wishers spilling copiously, unattended, across the floor from the open bureau, littering the carpet. He pulled the door shut, unable to bear looking at it.

Hardly thinking what he was doing, he re-entered the kitchen and spooned two scoops of Ty-Phoo into the tea pot and was about to pour in boiling water when he froze.

The sudden idea that Joyce might pop round became horrifically possible, if not probable. She wasn't far away. No more than a short car journey, in fact, and she could be here and he would be trapped. Heavens, he could not face that. That would be unbearable. Instantly he realised he had to get out. Flee.

Unwillingly, sickeningly, he had no choice but to brave the day.

Upstairs he shook off his slippers, replacing them with a pair of bright yellow socks. Put on his grey flannel slacks, so terribly loose around the waist. Needing yet another hole in the belt. Shirt. Collar gaping several sizes too big now, too. Tie. No time for tie. Forget tie. Why was he forced to do this? Why was he forced to leave his home when he didn't want to? He realised he was scared. The scaremonger, scared. Of *this*. What if he saw somebody? What if they talked to him? Could he be impolite? Unthinkable. Could he tell them how he really felt? Impossible. What then?

He told himself he was an actor. He would *act*.

Back in the hall he pulled on his winter coat and black woollen hat, the kind fishermen wear, tugging it down over his ears, then looped his scarf round his neck like an over-eager schoolboy. February days could be bright, he told himself, and he found his sunglasses on the mantelpiece in the living room sitting next to a black and white photograph of his dead wife. At first he avoided looking at it, then kissed his trembling fingertips and pressed them gently to her cheek. His fingerprints remained on the glass for a second before fading away.

**

He walked away from 3 Seaway Cottages, its curtains still drawn, giving it the appearance of a house in slumber. As a married couple they'd bought it in the late fifties with money he'd earned from *The Hound of the Baskervilles*, because having a place by the sea—especially here, a town they'd been visiting for years—would be good for Helen's breathing. "You have two homes in life," she'd said, "the one you're born in and another you find," and this one they'd found, with its big, tall windows for painting under the heavens and enjoying the estuary views across Shell Ness, clapboard sides like something from a whaling port in New England. They were blissfully happy here, happier than either of them could have dreamed. Now it seemed the house itself was dreaming of that happiness.He paused and breathed in deeply, tasting brine at the back of his tongue.

Good, clean fresh air for her health.

The mist of his sighs drifted in short puffs as he trudged along the shingle, patchy with errant sprigs of grass, in the direction of the Neptune pub, the wind buffeting his fragile frame and kicking at the ends of his dark, long coat. Above him the sky hung Airfix blue, the sky over a cenotaph on Poppy Day, chill with brisk respect, and he was small under it.

Automatically he'd found himself taking the path he and Helen had taken—how many times?—arm in arm. Always arm in arm. His, muscular and taut, unerringly protective: hers light as a feather, a spirit in human form, even then. If he had grasped and held her, back then...stopped her from...*Stupid. Foolish thoughts.* But his thoughts at least kept her with him, if only in his heart. He was afraid to let those thoughts be blown away. As he placed one foot in front of the other he felt that stepping from that path would be some sort of blasphemy. That path was his path now, and his to tread alone.

His heart jumped as he noticed two huddled people coming towards him, chequered green and brown patterns, their scarves fluttering. A man and wife, arm in arm. He felt frightened again. He did not want to see their faces and fixed his eyes past them, on the middle distance, but in his peripheral vision could tell they had already seen him and saw them look at each other as they drew unavoidably closer. His chest tightened with dread.

"Mr Cushing?"

He had no alternative but to stop. He blinked like a lark, feigning surprise. Incomprehensibly, he found himself smiling.

"Sorry." The man had a local accent. "Er...Brian. Brian and Margaret? Nelson Road? We came to that talk you...I just wanted to say how...well, we're really sorry, both of us, to hear about your...your..."

He took Brian's hand in both of his and squeezed it warmly. He had no idea who Brian was, or Margaret for that matter.

"Bless you."

The man and woman went on their way in the direction of West Beach and Seasalter and he walked on towards the harbour, still smiling. Still wearing the mask.

He was an actor. He would act.

Act as if he were alive.

The sky had turned silver grey and the wind had begun whipping the surface of the water. After passing the hull of the *Favourite*, that familiar old oyster yawl beached like a whale between Island Wall and the sea, he sat in his usual spot near Keam's Yard facing the wooden groynes that divided the beach, where he was wont to paint his watercolours of the coast. But there was no paint box or easel with him today. No such activity could inspire, activate or relax him and he wondered if that affliction, that restless hopelessness, might pass. If it meant forgetting Helen, even for an instant, he hoped it would not.Usually the music of the boats, the flag-rustling and chiming of the rigging, was a comfort. Today it was not. How could it be? How could anything be? When there was nothing left in life but to endure it?

He took off his sunglasses and pulled a white cotton glove from his pocket onto the fingers of his right hand, momentarily resembling a magician, then lit a John Player unfiltered. It had become a habit during filming: he said, often, he didn't want to play some 'Nineteenth Century Professor of the Nicotine Stains'. As he smoked he looked down at his bare left hand which rested on his knee, lined with a route-map of pronounced blue veins. He traced them with his finger tips, not realising that he was enacting the gentle touch of another.

He closed his eyes, resting them from the sun, and took into his smoker's lungs the age-old aroma of the sea. Of all the senses, that of smell more than any other is the evoker of memories: and so it was. He remembered with uncanny clarity the last time he and Helen had watched children building 'grotters'—sand or mud sculptures embellished imaginatively with myriads of oyster shells— only to see the waves come in and destroy them at the end of a warm and joyful Saint James's Day.

Clutching his arm, Helen had said, "Such a shame for the sea to wash away something so beautiful."

He'd laughed. His laughter was so distant now. "Don't worry, my dear. They'll make more beautiful ones next year."

"But that one was special," she'd said, "I wanted that one to stay."

The fresh salt air smarted in his eyes.

"I know who you are," said a disembodied young voice.

Startled, he looked up and saw a boy about ten years old standing at an inquisitive distance, head tilted to one side with slats of cloud behind him and a book under his arm. He and Helen had no children of their own, or pets for that matter, but felt all the children and animals in the town were their friends. He remembered talking to the twins next door and asking what they wanted to be when they grew up—clergyman, sailor—and them innocently turning the question back at him, albeit that he was already in his fifties: *What do* you *want to be when you grow up?* Good question, for an actor. But this one, this boy, he didn't recognise at all.

"You're Doctor Van Helsing."

The man's pale blue eyes did not waver from the sea ahead of him.

"So I am."

The boy threw a quick glance over his shoulder, then took a tentative step nearer. He wore short trousers, had one grey sock held up by elastic and the other at half-mast. Perhaps the other piece of elastic had snapped, or was lost.

"I…I saw what you did," he stammered eagerly, tripping over his words, but they nevertheless came nineteen to the dozen, a fountain. "You…you were powerful. He escaped back to his castle and he… he leapt up the stairs four, five, six at a time with his big strides but you were right behind him. You were *determined*. And you couldn't find him, then you *could*. And he was about to go down the trapdoor but he saw you and threw something at you and it just missed and made a really big clang, and then he was on top of you squeezing the life out of your throat and it hurt a really lot…" The boy hastily put his book between his knees and mimed strangulation with fingers round his own neck. "He had you down on the floor by the fireplace and you couldn't breathe he was so strong and mighty and you went like this…" His eyes flickered and he slumped. "And he was coming right down at you with his pointed teeth and at the last minute you were awake…" The youngster straightened his back. "And you pushed him away and he stood there and you stood there too, rubbing your neck like this. And he was coming towards you and your eyes went like *this*—" He shot a glance to his left. "And you saw the red curtains and you jumped up and ran across the long, long table and tore them down and the sunlight poured in. And his back bent like this when it hit him and his shoe shrank and went all soggy and there was nothing in it. And he tried to crawl out of the sunlight and you wouldn't let him. You grabbed two candle sticks from the table and held them like *this*—" He crossed his forearms, eyes blazing, jaw locked grimly. "You forced him back and his hand crumbled to ashes and became like a skeleton's, and he covered his face with his hand like this, and all that turned grey and dusty too, and his clothes turned baggy because there was nothing inside them. And everything was saved and the sign of the cross faded on the girl's hand. And after you, you...*vanquished* him, you looked out of the coloured window at the sky and put your woolly gloves back on. And the dust blew away on the air."

Indeed.

The man remembered shooting that scene very well. The 'good old leap and a lunge' from the Errol Flynn days. Saying to dear old Terry Fisher, "Dear boy, I seem to be producing crucifixes from every conceivable pocket throughout this movie. Do you think we could possibly do something different here? I'm beginning to feel like a travelling salesman of crosses." He'd come up with the idea himself of improvising using two candle sticks. He remembered the props master had produced a duo at first too ornate to work visually, but the second pair were perfect.

"That was you, wasn't it?"

"I do believe it was," Peter Cushing said. "The candles were my idea."

"That was *brilliant*."

"Well, with all due modesty, I do believe it was, yes."

He did not look at the boy and did not encourage him further in conversation, but the youngster ventured closer as if approaching an unknown animal which he assumed to be friendly but of which he was nevertheless wary, and sat on the wall beside him squarely facing the sea.

The man was now patting his jacket pockets, outside and in.

"What are you looking for?" The boy was curious. "A cross? Only you don't need a cross. I'm not a vampire."

"I'm very glad to hear it. I was looking for a photograph. I usually have some on me...I really don't know where I've put them..."

"Photograph?"

"Yes. A signed one." No response. "Of yours truly." Still no response, puzzlingly. "Isn't that what you'd like?"

"No," the boy said, sounding supremely affronted, as if he was dealing with an idiot.

"Oh…"

"I want to ask you something much more important than that. *Much* more important."

"Oh. I see."

Cushing looked around in a vain attempt to spot any parents from whom this child might have strayed, but there were no obvious candidates in evidence. If the boy *had* got lost, he thought, then it might be best for him to keep him quietly here at his side until they found him, rather than let him wander off again on his own. He really didn't want this responsibility, and he certainly didn't want company of any sort, but it seemed he didn't have any choice in the matter.

"I said I'm not a vampire." The boy interrupted his thoughts. "But I know somebody who is. And if they get their own way I'll become one too, sooner or later. Because that's what they do. That's how they create other vampires." The child turned his head sharply and looked the man straight in the eyes. "You said so."

Quite right: he had done. It wasn't hard to recall rewriting on set countless scenes of turgid exposition on vampire lore so that they didn't sound quite so preposterous when the words came out of his mouth.

"Who is this person?" Cushing played along. "I probably need to take care of him, then."

"He's dangerous. But you don't mind danger. You're *heroic*."

Cushing twitched an amused shrug. "I do my best."

"Well it *has* to be your best," the boy said with the most serious sense of conviction "Or he'll kill you. I mean that."

"Then I'll be as careful as possible. Absolutely."

"Because if he finds out, he'll hurt you, and he'll hurt me." The words were coming in a rapid flow again. "And he'll hurt lots of other people as well, probably. Loads of them." The boy drew up his legs, wrapped his arms round them tightly and tucked his knees under his chin. His eyes fixed on the horizon without blinking.

"Good gracious," Cushing said. "You mustn't take movies too much to heart, young man."

"Movies? What's *movies* got to do with it?" The abruptness was
nothing short of accusatory. "I'm talking about *here* and *now* and
you're the vampire hunter and you need to *help* me!" The boy
realised his harsh tone of voice might be unproductive, so quickly
added, sheepishly: "Please." Then, more bluntly, with an intense
frown: "It's your *job*."

It's your job—Vampire Hunter.

You're heroic.

You're powerful.

Cushing swallowed, his mouth unaccountably dry.

"Where are your mother and father, young chap?"

"It doesn't matter about them. It matters about *him!*"

The boy stood up—and for a second Cushing thought he would
sprint off, but no: instead he walked to a signpost of the car park
and picked at the flaking paint with his fingernail, his back turned
and his head lowered, as he spoke.

"My mum's boyfriend. He visits me at night time. Every night
now. He takes my blood while I'm asleep. I know what he's doing.
He thinks I'm asleep but I'm not asleep. It feels like a dream and I
try to pretend it isn't happening, but afterwards I feel bad, like I'm
dead inside. He makes me feel like that. I know it. I can't move. I'm
heavy and I've got no life and I don't want to have life anymore."
He rubbed his nose. His nose was running. Bells tinkled on masts
out of view. "That's what it feels like, every time. And it keeps
happening, and if it keeps happening I know what'll happen, I'm
going to die and be buried and then I'll rise up out of my coffin and
be like him, forever and ever."

Something curdled deep in Cushing's stomach and made him
feel nauseous. He obliterated the pictures in his mind's eye—a bed,
a shadow sliding up that bed—and what remained was a bleak, dark
chasm he didn't want to contemplate. But he knew in his heart what
was make-believe and what was all too real and it sickened him and
he wanted, selfishly, to escape it and pretend it didn't exist and didn't
happen in a world his God created.

He felt a soft, warm hand slipping inside his. *Helen?* But no. It
belonged to the little boy.

"So will you?"

"Will I what?" In a breath.

"Will you turn him to dust? Grey dust that blows away, like you did with Dracula?"

"Is that what you want?"

The boy nodded.

Oh Lord...Oh God in Heaven...

"That's right. That's what you do. Pray."

Cushing stared down without blinking at the boy's hand in his, and the boy took his expression for some sort of disapproval and removed it, examining his palm as if for a splinter or to divine his own future. The man suddenly found the necessity to slap his bony knees and hoist himself to his feet.

"Gosh. You know what? I'm famished. What time is it?" His fob watch had Helen's wedding ring attached to its chain: a single gold band, bought from Portobello Road market when they were quite broke. The face read almost twenty past eleven. "There's a shellfish stall over there and I think I'm going to go over and get myself a nice bag of cockles." He straightened his back with the aid of his white-gloved hand. "I do like cockles. Do you like cockles?"

The boy, still sitting, did not answer.

"Would you like a bag of cockles? Have you ever tried them?" He took off the glove, finger by finger.

The boy shook his head.

"Do you want to try?"

The boy shook his head again.

"Well, I'm going to get some, and you can try one if you want, and if you don't, don't."

The boy observed the old man closely as he flicked away the tiny cover of the shell with the tip of the cocktail stick and jabbed the soft contents within."Stake through the heart. Thought you might approve."

"They're not vampires though. They're disgusting."

Cushing twirled it, pulled it out and offered the titbit, but the boy squirmed and recoiled.

"You know, long, long ago, people believed in superstitions instead of knowing how the world really worked." He popped the tiny mollusc into his mouth, chewing its rubbery texture before swallowing. "They didn't know why the sun rose and set and what made the weather change, so sometimes they thought witches did it. And because they thought witches might come back and haunt them after they were dead, they'd bury them face down in their graves. That way, when they tried to claw up to the surface they'd claw their way down to Hell instead. But, you know, mostly superstitions are there to hide what people are really afraid of, underneath."

"You know a lot. You're *knowledgeable*," the boy said, happy to have his presumptions entirely confirmed. "But you have to be. For your occupation."

"Vampire Hunter."

Cushing had had enough of the taste of the cockles. In fact, he hadn't really wanted them anyway. He wrapped the half-empty tub in its brown paper bag, screwed up the top and deposited it in the nearest rubbish bin a few feet away. Whilst doing so, he scanned the car park, again hoping to see the errant parents.

"All right. Do you see him in mirrors? Does he come out in daylight? Because that's how I discover whether someone is a vampire or just someone human that's *mistaken* for a vampire, you see."

"He does go out. In the day time, but…"

"Aha. What does that tell you?"

"Different ones have different rules. There are different sorts, like there are different cats and dogs, but you can put a stake through their heart. That *definitely* works, always. And that's what you're brilliant at."

Cushing sat back down next to the boy, put on his single white glove and lit another cigarette. He remembered something that had troubled him in his own childhood. He'd mistakenly thought the Lord's prayer began: *Our Father who* aren't *in Heaven*. But if God *wasn't* in Heaven, where was He? The question, which he dared not share even with his brother, had kept him awake night after night, alone. Where? He rubbed the back of his neck: a gesture not unfamiliar to fans of Van Helsing.

"I know what you're thinking," the boy said. "You're wondering how to trap him."

"No. I'm not."

"What are you thinking then?"

"Do you want me to tell you, truthfully? Very well. I believe if there's something troubling you at home, whatever it is and however bad it is, the best thing to do—the first thing to do—is to tell your mother."

The boy laughed. "She loves him. She won't believe me. Nobody will. That's why I need *you*."

"Perhaps your mother wants to be happy."

"Of *course* she does! But she doesn't want to be killed and have her blood sucked all out, does she?"

"This man might be a good man, trying his best. I don't know him, but why don't you give him time to prove himself to you, and I'm sure you'll accept him for what he is."

"I *know* what he is! He won't change. He *won't!* Vampires don't become nice people. They just stay what they are—evil. And they keep coming back and coming back till you stop them!"

"Listen. I'm being very serious…"

"I know. You're *always* serious—because it's a serious problem."

"Yes, well. These feelings you have about your mum's new boyfriend?"…Peter Cushing felt cowardly and despicable, and even as he was uttering the words disbelieved them almost entirely, but did not know what else to say. "They'll go away, in time. You'll see. They'll pass. Feelings do."

"*Do* they though? Bad feelings? Or do they just *stay* bad?"

Cushing found he could not answer that. Even with a lie.

"My mum wants to marry him. She loves him. He's deceived her because really he doesn't love her at all. He just wants to suck *her* blood, too."

"But you have to understand. I can't stop him."

"Why?"

Cushing stumbled for words. Fumbled for honesty. "I…
I don't know how. You have to talk to somebody else.
Somebody…"

"You *do!* The villagers are in peril, and *I'm* in peril, and you're
Doctor Van Helsing!"

A large seagull landed on the rubbish bin and began jabbing its
vile beak indiscriminately at the contents.

"I'm sorry. I'm—"

"You *can.* I know you can!"

The desperation in the boy's voice and the rolling eye and the
hideous ululating of the seagull was too much.

"I *can't!* Good grief. Why don't you please just *leave me alone!* I said
I can't."

He felt pathetic and cruel and lost and selfish and small—but he
wasn't responsible for this child. Why should he be ashamed? The
vast pain of his own grief was heavy enough to bear without the
weight of another's. Even a child's. Even a poor, helpless child's. He
was an actor, that was all. Van Helsing was a part, nothing more.
All he did was mouth the lines. All he did was be photographed and
get his angular face blown up onto a thirty-foot wide screen. Why
was the responsibility his? Who asked this of him, and why shouldn't
he say no?

Now a second gull, even bigger, had joined the first and added to
the cacophony. In a flurry of limbs they squawked and spiked at the
bag the cockles were in, then began snapping at each other in full
scale war with the yellow scissors of their horrid, relentless maws.

When their aggression showed no sign of abatement, Cushing
crushed out the remains of his cigarette on the stone, hurried over
and shooed them away with flailing arms from the debris they were
already scattering with their webbed feet and flapping wings. He
felt their putrid dead-fish breath poisoning his nostrils. They
coughed and gurgled defiantly and showed their pink gullet-holes
before begrudgingly ascending.

After stuffing the brown paper bag deeper into the bin he turned
back, and to his sudden alarm saw the boy walking briskly away.

"Wait. I'm sorry..."

But the boy did not wait.

Where were the parents? Where were the dashed parents and why were they not—?...But all Cushing's thoughts and recriminations hung in the air, incomplete and impotent. He had denied the boy the help he had craved—however fantastical, however heartfelt, however absurd—and now the lad was gone.

"Wait..."

Cushing sat back down, alone, and saw that the book from under the boy's arm was still sitting there.

Movie Monsters by Denis Gifford. He placed it with its cellophane-wrapped cover on the desk of the public library. They knew him well there. They knew him well everywhere, sadly, and he intuited as he approached that there was an unspoken choreography between the two female assistants, vying for who would serve him and who would be too busy. It was not callousness that made them do so, he knew—merely the all-too-British caution that a wrongly-placed word might cause unnecessary hurt. Did they realise their shared eye contact alone caused hurt anyway? He forced a benign smile.

"Good afternoon."

"Good afternoon, Mr Cushing." The younger one drew the short straw. He was still unshaven, had been for days, and he wondered if he looked rather tramp-like. Little he could do about it now.

"I'm terribly sorry to trouble you, my dear, but I wonder if you might help me? I found this library book near the beach today and I wonder if you'd be so kind as to tell me the name and address of the person who's taken it out? They must be dreadfully worried about losing it. I'd be most awfully grateful."

"By all means. Just a moment, sir..." She checked the date stamped inside the cover and turned to consult the chronologically-arranged index of book cards behind her. Her rather thick dark hair fell long and straight across her shoulder blades. She wore a tight green cardigan and high heels that made her calves look chunky from behind, and he pondered whether she was happily married and, if so, for how long. With how many years ahead of her? "That's fine, Mr Cushing. We'll make sure he knows his book has been returned."

"No, no, what I mean is, you see—bless you —it's no trouble for me to return it to him personally. I really am quite grateful for the distraction."

A flicker in her eyes. "Oh…I understand. Of course. In that case…" She coughed into her hand and looked at the details a second time. "The name is Carl Drinkwater." She read out in full an address in Rayham Road. "That's one of the new houses over on the other side of the Thanet Way, off South Street. Do you know it?"

"Not in the slightest."

"Let me see…Where have they—?"

She opened a drawer and produced a small map of the town, unfolded it and marked the street with a circle in red Biro as the black one was empty.

"Splendid. Thank you so much." He took her hand and kissed it, as was his habit ("immaculate manners; such a gentleman") before walking to the exit.

"Mr Cushing?" He turned. "Mrs Cushing, sir. I'm so very sorry. She was such a lovely woman. We'll all miss her terribly."

He nodded. "Thank you so much."

He was astonished to hear the four words come from his throat, because the fifth would have stuck there and choked him. He hoped the woman was married and happy, with children and more happiness ahead of her. He truly did.

He returned home to fetch his bicycle, the Jaguar of more joyful days secreted in the garage these many months: memories preserved in aspic, too painful to be given the light of day. He swapped his woollen fisherman's hat for a flat cap, grabbed a heavier scarf, and, with the library book in his pannier, rode via Belmont Road and Millstrood Road to the boy's house—what appeared to be a two-bedroom bungalow on the far side of the railway track. The February sun was low by now and the sky scrubbed with tinges of purple and ochre. He chained his cycle to a lamp post opposite and stayed in the protective shadow between an overgrown hedge and a parked white van ('*For All Your Building Needs*') as he scrutinised the place from afar.

The garage had a green up-and-over door with a dustbin in front of it on the drive. The lawn grass was thin and yellowing. He could see no garden ornaments and the flatness of the red brick frontage was broken only by a plastic wheel holding a hosepipe fastened to the wall. Two windows matched, a third didn't and the door, frosted glass and flimsy, was off-centre.

He looked at his watch—Helen's ring tinkled against the glass face—and placed it back in his pocket. He blew into his hands, preparing himself for a long wait, hoping he had enough cigarettes left in his packet and, no doubt because of the worry this engendered, lit one, no doubt the first of many. He might of course smoke the lot and find this turned out to be a fruitless enterprise. There was no guarantee the man went out on a Saturday night, though a lot of men normally did. He was not dealing with, perhaps, the most normal of men.

After fifteen minutes or so a dog-walker in a quilted 'shortie' jacket passed and Cushing pretended he was mending a puncture with his bicycle pump, never more conscious that his acting had to be as naturalistic as possible. Believability was all. The labrador sniffed his tyres but the dog-walker, who resembled the sports commentator Frank Bough, yanked the lead and progressed on his way with only the most cursory of nods.

Cushing fixed his bicycle pump back into place and looked over at the house.

Hello. The light was on in the hall now, beyond the frosted glass. Shapes were donning coats. The door opened. He ducked down behind the white van, craning round it to watch a man in a donkey jacket tossing his car keys from hand to hand, a few steps behind him a boy in a football strip following him to a parked Ford Zephyr. Reflections in the windscreen stopped him from getting a good look at the man's face.

Cushing quickly hid in case Carl, whose eyes were on the road ahead, saw him. He listened for the engine to start and waited for it to sufficiently fade away.

As soon as it had, he crossed the road and knocked on the front door. He could hear the television on inside, so rapped again slightly harder. "All right, all right, keep your hair on…" A woman approached the glass and he could already make out she wore a red and white striped top, a big buckle on a wide belt and bell-bottomed jeans.

The door opened to reveal someone who, he imagined, thought herself at-tractive and feminine but who seemed to have endeavoured to make herself anything but. Her hair was drastically pulled back from her forehead in a pony tail, her clothes did nothing to enhance her figure, and there was nothing graceful or pretty in her demeanour or stance. He thought of the quiet perfection of Helen by comparison and had to quickly dismiss it from his mind. He reminded himself of his abiding belief that all women should be respected and accorded good manners at all times.

He took off his flat cap. "Mrs Drinkwater?"

"Yeah."

"You don't know me…"

"Yeah, I do."

His eyebrows lifted. Was she a fan of Hammer films, then, like her son?

"Of course I do. I've seen you on the telly."

"Ah."

Fool. He'd been the BBC's Sherlock Holmes over a number of televised adventures alongside Nigel Stock as Dr Watson. Naturally she recognised him. His portrayal of the great detective, after all, had been widely acclaimed.

"Morecambe and Wise," the woman said.

Oh dear, he thought. How the mighty are fallen. Serve him right. The Greeks had a word for it: *hubris*. The sin of pride.

"You live round here," she said.

"That's quite correct. My name's Peter Cushing."

He extended a hand, which the woman saw fit to ignore.

"I know."

"May I come in, please? It's about your son, Carl."

"What about Carl? What's he done now? I'll kill him."

"Nothing. Absolutely nothing, Mrs Drinkwater. Nothing wrong." He showed her the copy of *Movie Monsters* which he'd tucked under his arm. "I found this library book of his and I'm returning it, you see."

She took the book off him and looked at it but didn't move or speak, even to say thank you.

He said again, equally politely: "May I...may I come in, please?"

More from being taken unawares than hospitality, the woman stepped back to allow him to enter. He cleaned his shoes on the mat while she walked back into the room with the television on, without asking him to follow her. Though his own manners were faultless, he refused to judge others on their inadequacy in that area. It was often down to their upbringing, he believed, and that could not be their own fault. We are all products of our pasts: none more so than he himself. Some said he was stuck in it. Another, unwanted, era. But he merely believed politeness and courtesy between human beings was a thing to be valued, in any era. Treasured, actually.

The ironing board was out and she was making her way through a pile of washing, which she resumed, clearly not about to interrupt her workload on his account. She did not offer him a cup of tea or coffee and did not turn down the TV, but simply carried on where she'd left off, halfway through a man's shirt, tan with a white collar, Cliff Richard's variety show the activity's accompaniment. The ceiling was textured with Artex swirls, the fireplace with its marble-effect surround boarded up with a sheet of unpainted hardboard, and a patio door led to a garden enclosed by fencing panels.

He saw a recent edition of the *Radio Times* lying on the arm of the sofa, its cover announcing the introduction of a new villain into the *Doctor Who* pantheon. Dear old Roger Delgado looking as if he'd stepped straight from a Hammer film with his widow's peak and black goatee. He thought of Jon Pertwee's dandyish Doctor compared to his own "mad professor" saving the Earth from the invading hordes of soulless Daleks. He thought how easy it was to save the world, and how hard, in life, to save...

"Why d'you want to talk to me about my son?"

"It was Carl who chose to talk to me, in fact. May I?" He noted she seemed confused by the question, so sat himself on the sofa anyway, his voice having to compete with Cliff Richard's. "It was curious, very curious indeed. You see, he approached me earlier today confidently believing I was *actually* Doctor Van Helsing, the character I played in the Dracula films for Hammer several years ago." He chuckled. "Many years ago, actually. How time flies..." He noticed a stack of books on the cushion next to him: *The Second Hammer Horror Films Omnibus* with Christopher Lee on its orange cover offering his bare chest to a victim; *The Fifth* and *Seventh Pan Books of Horror Stories*; the Arrow paperback editions of *Dracula* and *The Lair of the White Worm*. "I see he's a fan..."

"Monster mad. I wish he wasn't. Not healthy if you ask me. None of it."

He smiled. "Dear lady, that's my bread and butter you're talking about. For my sins."

She didn't match his smile and still didn't turn down the television.

He loosened his scarf. The gas-effect electric fire was cranked up and the skin on his neck was beginning to prickle.

"Carl loves you very much, Mrs Drinkwater." He chose his words carefully. "He cares an awful lot about what happens to you. The more he was talking to me, it was very clear he felt you were in danger. And he was in danger too. Very much so."

She grunted, straightening her back then slamming down the iron and running it back and forth up the shirt's sleeve. "He's got an active imagination. Always did, always will. Got his bloody father to thank for that. Telling the kid those stories of his—ghosts, ghouls, monsters—scaring him, keeping him awake. What do you expect?"

"I don't think stories hurt people, Mrs Drinkwater. Not really hurt."

"How do you know?" She set the iron on end with a thump. Rearranged the garment roughly. "Have you got children?"

"No. Sadly." He and Helen had not been blessed in that way.

"Then you haven't sat up with them crying and hugging you. Over stories. Or anything else for that matter, have you?"

"That's very true."

"So you don't know anything about it, do you?"

"No, I don't. You're quite right. But..." He gazed down at the carpet and noticed he was still, rather ridiculously, wearing his bicycle clips. He reached down and took them off, idly playing with them as he talked, as if they were a cat's cradle or a magic trick. "But what he said concerns me. I'm sorry. You must understand, surely? Children don't say things without reason."

"Don't they? Kids can be cruel. You lead a sheltered life, you do. Kids can get at you in ways you wouldn't even dream of. If they think you deserve it."

"Can they?"

"They know the buttons to press." The iron hissed. "You should hear what I get in the ear every single day. Dad this, Dad that."

"He idolises his father."

"Yeah—the father who sneaked him into the cinema to see that *Dracula* you're so proud of when he was eight years old. Oh, yeah. Bought one adult ticket, pushed the bar of the emergency exit, let him in. Like the teddy boys or mods do. To an 'X' film. His *son*. Don't tell me that helped any problems he had in school or anywhere else, because it didn't. He was scared to death of the world before that, and, you know what? It made him *more* scared. That's why he's playing silly beggars."

Cushing rubbed his eyes. Dare he ask the question? He was compelled to.

"Very well, I take your point, absolutely—but I'd never forgive myself if I didn't ask this...Because I cannot walk away from this house without doing so."

"What? What are you on about?"

This was difficult. He knew this would be difficult. "Has your boy-friend ever...ever raised his hand to Carl? Hurt him in any way?"

"No." The woman cut into his last word. "Les loves that boy."
Loves.

"How long have you known him?"

"Long enough." She stiffened. "Why?"

Les loves that boy.

"As I say…Carl seemed, well, I have to be honest, Mrs Drinkwater…troubled."

"Well there's nothing troubling him in *this* house, I tell you that for nothing. It's all in his bloody mind. Or yours." The shirt flicked to and fro, the iron hitting it repeatedly like a weapon. She turned her body to face him, hand on hip. "Why do you make those horrible films anyway? Eh? *Horror* films."

"To be truthful I hate the term 'horror film'. Car crashes and the concentration camps and what's happening in Northern Ireland, that's horror. I think of the fantasies I star in as fairy tales or medieval mystery plays for a new generation. If you take the 'O' from Good and add a 'D' to Evil, you get God and the Devil—two of the greatest antagonists in the whole of history. And Van Helsing is important because he shows us Good triumphs. After all, Shakespeare used horrific images in *Titus Andronicus*, and mankind's belief in the supernatural in *Macbeth*, and nobody belittles the fellow for that. I think the best so-called 'horror' shows us our worst fears in symbolic form and tries to tell us in dramatic terms how we can overcome them."

"Yeah, well…" Her face, turning back to the ironing board, betrayed an ill-concealed sneer. "I didn't pass enough exams to understand all that. We didn't have books in our house. My dad was too busy working."

He sighed. "Mrs Drinkwater, I'm quite sure you don't want this discussion, and neither do I. Please just put my mind at rest, that's all I ask. Truly. Just talk to Carl. Listen to him."

"You've listened to him. Do you believe him?"

"My dear, I'm just an actor. It's his mother he should talk to."

"Or a psychiatrist."

"If that's what you genuinely think."

"It's no business of yours what I think."

"You're quite right, of course." He stood up, putting his bicycle clips in his pocket. "Perhaps I shouldn't have come, but please believe me when I say I did so only out of concern for Carl. I apologise profusely if I've upset you. That wasn't my intention at all."

"You haven't upset me," she said.

"I'm sorry for disturbing you. I'll see myself out." He thought the conversation was over but he'd barely reached the door to the hall before she said behind his back:

"Why don't you make nice, *decent* films, eh?"

He turned back with sadness, both at the slight and his own ineffectiveness. He knew she felt accused and belittled by his very presence, undermined by his unwanted interference and presumptions and posh voice and good manners and wanted to attack it, all of it.

"Don't you think I've got enough problems with him, without this…? Without him talking to strangers…? Talking rubbish…?"

His blue eyes shone at her.

"I can't believe he's saying what he's saying, honest to God. He's got no business to." Her cheeks were flushed now, voice quavering on the edge of losing control. "I swear, Les is good as gold with that kid. Better than his real dad, by a mile. You want to know who *really* hurt him? If you want to know the truth, his *father* did. He did that by buggering off. And there isn't a day goes by I don't see that in my son's eyes, so don't come here accusing me or anybody else when the real person isn't here anymore." He could see she fought away demons, the worst kind—and tears.

Instinctively, he walked over and took her hands in his. "I beseech you, my dear. Talk to your son."

Appalled, she backed away from him.

"I don't need to talk to my son."

She reached the wall and couldn't back away any further. His face was close to hers and he looked deeply into her eyes, his own vision misty, almost unable to get out the words he must.

"My dear, dear girl. I've lost someone I loved. Please don't do the same."

She snatched away her hands as if the touch of him was infectious.

"How fucking *dare* you!" She shoved him in the chest. Then shoved him again. "Get out of here." He staggered backwards, feeling it inside the drum of his old, brittle ribs. "Get out of my fucking house! Get *out!*"

Gasping for breath and words, he stumbled to the front door as she berated him with her screams and obscenities and later remembered nothing of getting to his bicycle or getting from Rayham Road to Seaway Cottages except that he had to stop a number of times to wipe the tears from his eyes and by the time he got indoors a thin film of ice had formed, covering his cheeks.

A girl sat up in the tree and it didn't seem at all peculiar but it worried him. It was an oak tree, old and sturdy, with deeply wrinkled bark. The little girl didn't seem distressed but she did seem determined, a strong-willed little soul. She wore a frilled collar like a Victorian child and he thought she was clutching a toy or teddy bear but couldn't make it out clearly through the leaves and branches. "Come down," he called to her. He looked around but there was no-one else about. Only him. So it was down to him to do something. "Come down." But the girl wouldn't come down. She just looked down at him, frowning seriously. "Come down. Please," he begged. But still she didn't move. A man came along. A man he didn't know. The man said to him: "What are you doing?" He couldn't answer. He got confused, he didn't know why, but before he could answer anyway, the man stepped closer and went on: "You know exactly what you're doing don't you? Don't you?" Rage and aggression built up in the man's face and his tightly pursed mouth extended to became a vicious-looking yellow beak. And this beak and another beak were prodding and poking at a boy's short trousers, snatching and tearing out gouts of underwear. The underwear was made of paper. Newspaper. And somehow he was upset that what was written was important, the words were important.He woke to the sound of seagulls snagging and swooping above his roof.

At the best of times, he despaired at their racket. And these were not the best of times. Now the noise was no less than purgatory. As a child in Surrey he'd thought they were angels, but now he held no illusions about the species. The creatures were the very icon of an English seaside town, but they were relentless and without mercy. He'd once seen a large speckled gull going for a toddler's bag of chips, almost taking off its fingers, leaving it bawling and terrified in its mother's embrace. They were motivated only by selfish need and gratification, thought only of their own bellies and their own desires. It seemed almost symbolic that we never ate sea birds, knowing almost instinctively that their insides would be disgusting, inedible, rank, rancid, foul. It seemed to Cushing that their screeching was both a bombastic call to arms and a cry of pain.

He sat up, finding himself on the living room sofa.

He looked at the clock and saw it was four o'clock. Since it was sunny beyond the drapes, he deduced it must be four o'clock in the afternoon. He was still in his pyjamas and dressing gown and still too tired to care.

He'd hardly slept a wink all night. In fact, the short, shallow period of sleep broken by the dream had been by far the longest. Perhaps an hour. The rest, when he could, had been spent at most in a fitful doze, and that only occasionally, interspersed as it was with shambling wanders round the house or up and down stairs in the dead of night. That darkness inculcated fears was a truism, but such knowledge did nothing to abate it. Fears multiplied as he'd curled up wide-eyed, turning circuitous thoughts over in his mind, multiplying still more while he'd walked aimlessly from room to room, in a futile search for distraction, illumination, resolution or peace of mind. All evaded his grasp.

He had lain in his bed thinking of Carl Drinkwater lying in his. The boy's words, the whole encounter, replayed in his ears. What did he hear? Was he misguided? Did he take it all at face value when he shouldn't have? Was the mother right? All kinds of doubts set in. Most of all, that he was mentally accusing a man he'd never met of the most despicable act, the vilest *crime* imaginable—based upon what?

He had woken, walked round like a penitent, unable to sleep, as these questions went round and round in his head. Who was he to pronounce? Who was he to judge? Who was right? Who was wrong? Who was good? Who was evil? He wished he could talk to somebody, but who would listen to the silly gibbering of a recently bereaved man whose very job was spinning a preposterous yarn and making it seem true?

It was Sunday but he didn't want to go to church. Too many people. Too many eyes. In fact he hadn't been to church since Helen's funeral. Afterwards the young vicar at St Alphege's had told him: "If you ever want to come and talk, Peter, for any reason, you know where I am." He'd said: "My name's Godfrey. You can call me God." Then he had nudged Peter's arm with his elbow. "I'm joking." Peter didn't want to hear a joke and he didn't want to laugh. He didn't want to go back for a chat with 'God' either. 'God' could find other people to chat to. He'd rather have a good actor like Peter Sallis or Miles Malleson playing a vicar than that young fake who was acting the part anyway. As Olivier had said, "Be sincere, dear boy, always be sincere—and when you've faked that, you've cracked it."

But if you cannot do good, he thought now, where *is* God? Where?

Unable to turn without a painful reminder confronting him— the furniture was all Helen's choice from her favourite antiques dealer, and every piece of it held a story—he dragged his feet up to his studio, the 'playroom', at the top of the house. For five or ten minutes he sat and gazed up through the windows along one wall at the darkening sky above. The far table was strewn with art supplies, palettes rainbowed with dried paint and uncapped tubes of aquamarine and burnt sienna gone hard as concrete. The miniature theatre sets he'd made to the original Rex Whistler designs sat like frozen moments of time waiting patiently to be awakened. Model aeroplanes dangled on fishing line: Lancaster bomber; Spitfire; Messerschmitt; a veritable Battle of Britain suspended in the air. Frozen in time, like he was in so many ways. A child with his toys. A boy playing at being a man. What was a 'play' anyway but 'playing'? He thought of Captain Stanhope in *Journey's End*, the part he never got a chance to do. In glass-fronted cabinets the length of the room stood hundreds of model soldiers, the British Army through the ages: the Scots Greys at Waterloo; Desert Rats at El Alamein; Tommies at Normandy. In days gone by he'd get them out and solve international problems on his knees on the carpet. His men were clever, bold, indefatigable, strategic, victorious—always. But they were no use to him now. They'd fought all those battles, but what could they do to fight this one? Now they were as useless and impotent as he himself. He suddenly wanted to give the boy all those toy soldiers. He wanted to give him all the toys in the world.

Helen gazed out at him radiantly from a pastel drawing pinned to the wall.

He slid a record out of its sleeve, placed it on the gramophone and slumped in the threadbare rocking chair letting Symphony Number One by Sibelius wash over him. It always had the effect of reminding him of the wonder of human achievements, the humility with which we should revere, in awe, such pinnacles of artistic endeavour, but it struggled to do that now. He cast his mind back to being on set singing Giuseppe's song from *The Gondoliers* to Barbara Shelley, competing with Chris Lee to see who could sing the nightmare song from *Iolanthe* fastest without missing a word. He tried to think of singing and old friends laughing, whilst knowing a child somewhere wept into its pillow.

The door bell rang.

He opened his eyes. Rather than lift the needle and risk scratching the surface, he let the music play as he went downstairs to answer it.

A figure stood outside in the dark. He could make out the distinctive square shoulders and upturned collar of a donkey jacket. He could see no face, just a man's outline and the collar-length hair covering his ears backlit by the almost iridescent purple of the night sky. He had not replaced the light bulb in the conservatory, which had blown weeks ago, nor had he switched on the hall light in his haste to open the front door. Now he wished he had done both.

"Mr Cushing?" It was a light voice and one he didn't recognise, or have reason to fear, but some part of him tightened.

"Yes?"

Instinctively, Cushing shook the extended hand—calloused, dry as parchment from physical work, not the hand of a poet, an ugly hand—and gazed into the face of a man in his thirties with sand-blond, almost flesh-coloured hair and beard. *Thirty-three*, the older man thought, peculiarly, unbidden. The age Jesus was when he died: *Thirty-three.* The long hair and beard was 'hippie'-like, the style of California's so-called 'flower children', but now ubiquitous, of course. Under the donkey jacket Cushing saw a red polo-neck jumper and blue jeans, flared, faded in patches from wear—a working man, then. No. He corrected himself from making any such assumption: threadbare jeans were, inexplicably to him, the fashion of the day. Students at Oxford wore jeans. Jeans told him nothing.

"Hello, mate. My name's Les Gledhill…"

Les loves that boy.

"First of all, I've got to say—I've always been a massive fan of your films, sir. I know, I know, probably everyone says that. You probably get bored with hearing it. But I really, really mean it. Feel quite nervous talking to you, in point of fact…" Realising he had not released the actor's hand, the man now did so, laughing and holding his hands aloft, pulling faces at his own crassness and ineptitude.

Les loves that boy.

Cushing didn't ask himself how the long-haired man had found his address. Everyone in town knew where its most famous resident lived—though most conspired in respecting his privacy.

Les loves that boy.

"Sorry. Sorry. Am I disturbing you? Only, it's really important I have a word." The visitor rubbed his hands together vigorously in the night air, hopping from foot to foot. "I, ah, think there's been a misunderstanding. A really, really *big* misunderstanding, mate…"

he chuckled, "and I really, *really* want to clear it up before it goes any further." Still laughing, he pointed both index fingers to the sides of his head, twirling them in dumb-show semaphore for the craziness of the situation.

"I'm so sorry to be a bore…" Cushing's voice retained its usual mellifluous charm. "It's Sunday evening. This isn't a very good time, to be perfectly honest. In fact, I'm expecting guests any minute…" On tip-toes he craned over the other man's shoulder, pretending to be scanning the path beyond. Blast. The pyjamas and dressing gown were a giveaway that he was lying, and he had to think fast. "I'm, I'm just about to get changed. This really isn't convenient. If you'll excuse me…"

"This won't take long, honest to God. Just a minute of your time, mate. If that. Honestly."

"I have food in the oven. I'm most terribly…" He did an excellent job also of covering up the fact that his heart was pounding thunderously. *When you can fake that, dear boy…*

A hand slapped against the door. "Sorry, mate. Hold on. Hey. *Mate*…"

It stopped the door from closing but Gledhill, almost immediately embarrassed by his brisk action, quickly removed it and stuffed it in his jacket pocket, laughing again.

"Listen. Please. I really, *really* want to clear this up, sir. I swear— you have no idea what this is doing to me. You, a respected man in this—this community, I mean, *loved* in this town, let's face it. And you, of all people, Christ, thinking…" One cheek winced as if in momentary pain. "So when she…that's why I had to come over, see. I couldn't let…"

Cushing wondered why he still felt afraid. Much as he hated to admit it, the man seemed reasonable. Why did he *hate to admit* it? What had he *presumed* the chap would be like? Here he was. Not an ogre. Perplexed, certainly. Bewildered, genuinely. It seemed. And— unless a consummate actor himself—shaken. The voice didn't sound angry or vicious in the least, or beastly. Or *evil*—that was the remarkable thing. It sounded confused, and quite upset. No—*hurt*. Terribly hurt. Devastated, in fact.

"Of course, if you're busy, sir, I understand. Blimey, I have no right to just barge over here, knock on your door, expect you to… Okay." Running out of words, the man in the donkey jacket backed away, then turned to go. Then, as he reached the white-painted garden gate, turned back. "Look, the truth is…I'd hate you to think I'd done anything to hurt that boy. Or whatever you think. That's just…just *not* the case. Truly." He made one last, haltering plea. "I… I just wanted to explain to you that you've got the wrong end of the stick, that's all. That's what concerns me, more than anything. You're a decent man. A perfect gentleman. And you don't need this. It's not fair. If I can just…" The front door had not shut and, this being so, he took this for some kind of invitation and walked quickly back into the conservatory.

Peter Cushing's fingers did not move from the latch on the inside of the door. "I'd rather we discuss it here, if we must."

Gledhill stopped, suddenly bowed his shaggy head and plunged his ruddy, working man's hands deep in his jacket pockets, shuffling. "Yes, of course, mate. No problem."

Letting the front door yawn wider in a slight act of contrition, Cushing retraced his steps and switched on the hall light, then returned to stand on the welcome mat whilst the man in the donkey jacket hovered in silhouette at the mercy of the shrill wind cutting in from the sea. It buffeted the door, sending an icy breath though the house, room to room, riffling paperwork like a thief.

Picked out of the darkness by the paltry spill of light from the hall, Gledhill shook a solitary Embassy from its packet. "Listen." He rubbed one eye. "Carl is a good kid, a great kid. He's quirky, a laugh, in small doses, don't get me wrong. He's a character. But he has problems, that's what you don't realise." The lighter clicked and flashed, giving a splash of illumination from his cupped hand to his chin and upper lip. "He says things. Things that aren't true." A puff of smoke streamed from the corner of his mouth. "All the bloody time. Not just about me. About everybody. The school already has him down as a liar. And a bully. They have problems with him. He hurts other kids. That's what kind of child he is, Mr Cushing. His mother worries about him day and night. So do I. Day and bloody night."

Night.

Cushing remained tight-lipped. The face of a hundred movie stills. Immobile. "You're telling me I shouldn't believe a word that comes out of his mouth."

"Honest to God." The man's next exhale was directed at the moon. The whites of his eyes seemed flesh-coloured too, now. Perhaps it was the ambient yellow glow from within. He dawdled in its penumbra. "You think he's some kind of angel? You don't know him. You don't know any of us." He let that fact, and its obvious truth, bed down in Cushing's mind. "I didn't have to take on this woman with her boy, did I? Let's face it, lots of blokes would run for the hills the minute they knew there was a kid in tow. And I haven't, have I? Because I love her. I'm trying to piece this family together. God knows. I'm going to marry her, for Christ's sake. Put everything right for both of them. The boy, too. I'm not a bad person." He offered the palms of his hands.

"Then what do you have to fear from me?" Cushing spoke quietly and with precision.

"I don't know." Gledhill shrugged. "I don't know *what* you think."

And he laughed again. And the laugh had a *wrongness*. There was something in it, a grace note, deep down, disingenuous, that the older man detected and didn't like. If pressed, he couldn't have explained it any more than he could have explained why, on meeting his wife, he knew instantly they were meant to spend the rest of their lives together. It wasn't even love, it was that he'd met his *soul*. Similarly, the thing embedded in Les Gledhill's laugh was inexplicable, and, inexplicably, *enough*.

"I think you'd better leave now. Good night to you."

He shut the door but found something wedged into the jamb, preventing it from closing. The laughter had stopped. He didn't want to look down and didn't look down, because he knew what he would see there. A foot rammed in between the bottom of the door and the metal footplate.

O, Lord. O, Jesus Christ.

"Hey. I'm trying to be reasonable. I'm trying to..." Gledhill's teeth were clenched now, tobacco-stained, his face only inches from the other man's. "Why are you doing this?"

"I beg your pardon?"

"Why are you *doing* this?" The Kent accent had become more pro-nounced, transforming into a Cockney harshness. "I've done nothing to you. I'm a total stranger to you. Have you ever met me before? No. So why are you doing this to me? Going to my house, upsetting my girlfriend. I come home to find her in bits. How d'you think that makes me feel? Before I know it she's firing all kinds of questions at me. Stupid questions. *Ridiculous* questions—"

"Please..." The older man's voice was choked with fear. He couldn't disguise it any more. It took all his strength to hold the door in place. "I have nothing more to say."

Gledhill's face jutted closer still, his shoulder firm against the door, holding it fast, and Cushing could detect the strong sweet reek of—*what, blood, de-cay?*—no, alcohol on the man's breath. But something else too. *Something of death.* "What kind of person are you, eh?"

Cushing stood fast, half-shielded by the door, half-protected, half-vulnerable. "I was going to ask you exactly the same question. Except Carl answered that for me. In his own way."

"How? What did he say?"

"He said you're a vampire."

The laugh came again, this time a mere blow of air through nose and mouth accompanied by a shake of the head, then the bubbling cackle of a smoker's hack. It came unbidden but there was no enjoyment behind it or to be derived from hearing it.

"That kid cracks me up. He really does. Such a joker. You know what? That's hilarious." The turn of a word. "*You're* hilarious." Now Gledhill's expression was deadly serious. "You're being hilarious now."

"That doesn't mean I can't stop you."

"I'm innocent! I've done *nothing* wrong! Haven't you been listening to a bloody *word* I've said? You need to clean your ears out, mate. Get a hearing test, at your age. Pay attention to people. Not just listen to idiots."

"Carl isn't an idiot. I don't consider him an idiot."

"I know you don't." One elbow against a glass panel of the door, Gledhill jerked his other arm, tossing his spent cigarette into a flower bed without even looking where it fell. "Why do you believe him and not me, eh? What gives *you* the right to cast judgement on *me*, anyway? You, a stupid film star in stupid films for stupid people."

So much for being a lifelong fan. His true colours, at last. "I know evil when I see it."

"What? Dracula, Frankenstein, and the Wolf Man?"

"No. I'm talking about the true evil that human beings are capable of."

"And what's that, eh? Tell me. Tell me what's going on in your *sick* mind, because I have no bloody idea."

Cushing did not reply. Simply stared at him and with supreme effort refused to break his gaze. He saw for the first time that the monster's eyes were as colourless as the invisibly pale eyebrows that now made an arch of self-pity over them.

"You think I'd hurt him? I wouldn't hurt a hair of his head. Cross my heart and hope to die." With the thumb of one hand, Gledhill made the sign of the cross, horizontally across his chest, then from his chin to his belly.

"It's curious," Cushing said, one hollow cheek pressed to the side of the door. "In vampire mythology, evil has to be invited over the threshold. And she invited you in, didn't she? With open arms."

"Yeah, mate. It's called love."

"Love can be corrupted. I will not be witness to that and let it pass."

"How Biblical!" The glistening eyes did not suit the sneer that went with them.

"I have been a Christian all my life. It gives me strength."

"You Bible-thumpers see evil everywhere."

"No, we don't. But to God innocence is precious. It's to be valued above all things. It must be protected. Our children must be safe. It's our duty as human beings."

"Too right. They *do* need to be protected," the creature that was Gledhill said. "From old men talking to young boys on the beach. Boys all alone. What did you say to him, eh? That's what the police are going to ask, don't you think, if you go to them?" His voice fell to a fetid, yet almost romantic, whisper. "That's what people are going to ask. What were they talking about, this old man who lives all alone? This old man who makes horrible, sadistic films about cruelty and sex and torture, someone who's never had any children of his own, they tell me, someone who *adores* other peoples' children? This old man and this innocent little boy?"

His skin prickling with the most immense distaste, Cushing refused to be intimidated, even though the nauseous combination of beer and cigarette breath in the air was quite sickening enough. "I'm quite aware he is innocent, Mr Gledhill. And I'm quite aware what you might say against me."

"Good. And who do you think they'll believe, eh? Me or you?"

"They'll believe the truth."

"Then that's a pity. For you," the mouth said. It wasn't a face any more. Just an ugly, obscene mouth.

Cushing did nothing to back away. He knew that once he did that, physically and mentally, he was lost. But he was backing away in his mind like a frightened rabbit, and he feared that Gledhill could see it in the clear rock pools of his eyes. Frightened eyes.

"I should knock you into next week," Gledhill breathed. "Just the thought of what you were doing, or trying to do, makes me want to puke, d'you know that? But I'm not someone who takes the law into their own hands. I obey the law, me. I'm a law-abiding…"

Though he wanted to cry out, Cushing stood his ground. He was resolute, even if he didn't feel it. He felt crushed, battered, clawed, eviscerated. The truth was, he knew, if he gave into impulse and stepped away, then he was afraid that would mean *running* away. And what might follow that? His visitor was clearly big enough and strong enough to barge through a door held by a flimsy old man with no effort whatsoever. Yet he hadn't. Why, the old man dared not contemplate. Sheer *inability*, not bravery, glued him to the spot. But how much of that could the other eyes looking back at him see?

"You need to drop this, I'm telling you," Gledhill said. "For your own good, all right? I'm doing you a favour coming here. You don't get it, do you?"

"Oh, I do. I 'get it' entirely. Thank you for clarifying any doubt in my mind."

Cushing instantly wished he'd kept that thought to himself, but now there was no going back and he knew it.

With all his strength he shoved the door hard in the hope the latch would click and he'd turn the key in the Chubb to double-lock it before Gledhill got a chance to push from his side—but Gledhill had already pushed back, and harder. He was a builder, labourer, something—*heathen*, Cushing didn't know why that word sprang to mind, but he didn't want him in his house, he wasn't a reader he was a destroyer of books, and people. He fell back from the door, panting, a stick man, brittle. Then he did decide to run, the only thing he could do as it flew open, banging against the wall.

He dashed to where the telephone and address book sat on the hall table and snatched up the receiver and put it to his ear, swinging round to face the man in the doorway as his finger found the dial.

To his astonishment Gledhill stopped dead, his feet see-sawing on the threshold, his boots pivoted between toe and heel.

"Sorry! Sorry. Sorry. I'm really sorry, mate! I shouldn't have talked to you like that. Shit! That, that's the booze talking. I sank a couple of shorts. Dutch courage, to come here. Don't normally get like that. Don't normally say boo to a fucking goose, me." The swear word pierced Cushing like a blade, deep and hard and repellent. He knew people used it, increasingly, but he hated such foul language. But now he had the measure of the man, and the difference between them, and it gaped wide. In the full glare of the hall light, scarlet sweater radiant, a bloody breast swimming in the older man's vision, Gledhill wiped his long, shiny, slug-like lower lip. "Sorry. Sorry. But I don't like people making allegations against me, okay? When they're lies. Complete lies, all right? What normal man would?"

Les loves that boy.

The low burr on the telephone line changed to a single long tone and Cushing tapped the cradle to get a line.

"Please go. Immediately. Please. I don't want to continue this conversation."

"Mate, honestly…"

"I'm not your 'mate', Mr Gledhill, quite frankly. And you've invaded my privacy and I don't want it. You leave me not alternative but to call the…"

His heart thudding in his ears, Cushing dialled with a forefinger he prayed was steady. The wheel turned anticlockwise with the return mechanism, waiting for the second '9'.

The cold had infiltrated and he felt it on his blue-lined skin as he stared at the long-haired man framed in his front doorway against the February night and the other did the same in return. Neither man dared give his adversary the satisfaction of breaking eye contact first. Gledhill hung onto the door frame, meaty hands left and right. Passingly, Cushing thought of Christopher Lee in his big coat as the creature in *Curse*. But all that monstrousness on the outside, for all to see.

He dialled a second time, straight-backed, not wanting to show the stranger he was afraid, but he *was* afraid. Of course he was afraid. He wasn't a young, athletic man any more, sword-fencing beside Louis Hayward or leaping across tables. Far from it. If this man chose to, cocky, powerful and threatened, he could stride right in and beat him to a pulp, or worse. There was no guarantee that a man prone to other acts, *despicable* acts, would be pacified by a threat of recrimination at a later date. Or a mere *phone call*. Criminals did not think of consequences. That was one of the things that defined them as criminals. There was nothing, literally nothing, to stop his unwelcome guest killing him, if he decided to.

For the third time he placed his index finger in the hole next to the number '9' and took it round the circumference of the dial.

"All right," Gledhill said. "All right. I'm going. I'll say this, then I'm going. There's nothing going on here, okay? It's as simple as that. Nothing for you to be involved in. *Nothing*. Okay?"

Emergency. Which service do you require?

Cushing stared. Gledhill stared back.

Emergency. Hello?

Gledhill laughed with a combination of utter sadness and utter contempt. "Jesus Christ. You're as loopy as he is. You're losing your *fucking* marbles, old man."

Hello?

Then Gledhill left, slamming the door after him and the hall shook, or seemed to shake, like the walls of a rickety set at Bray, and Cushing did not blink and did not breathe until he was gone, and his after-image—the halo of redness—departed with him. Cut!

Hello?

"Yes, yes. I'm still here, yes. I'm most awfully sorry," he whispered into the receiver. "I thought I had an intruder. I can see now that's not the case." He tried to cover the tremor he knew was in his voice, and tried to make it light and chirpy. "No, no. That's quite all right. Really. I'm perfectly safe. Thank you."

Cushing hung up, re-knotted the cord of his dressing gown, hurried into the sitting room and parted the drawn curtains with his fingers, a few inches only, to see—nobody. Even the last fragment of light and colour had faded from the sky. It was now uniformly black and devoid of stars.

The dryness in Cushing's throat gave him the sudden compulsion to breathe, which he thought a very good idea indeed but strangely an effort. It was as if he had done a ten mile run, or heavy swim. Not only was his chest still thumping like a kettledrum, he could not get air into his lungs fast enough, and lurched, quite light-headedly, needing to prop himself on the arm of a chair in case he should fall. Sweat broke on his brow. He undid the buttons at his throat but they were already undone. He opened more, but his fingers were frozen and useless, fumbling and befuddled and half-dead.

This man who makes horrible, sadistic films about cruelty and sex and torture...

Someone who's never had any children of his own, they tell me...

Someone who adores other peoples' children...

This old man and this innocent little boy...

Liquid surging up his gullet, he gagged and stumbled from the room to the little lavatory under the stairs, pressing his handkerchief to his mouth, but gagging nonetheless.

*
**

After he had vomited on and off for half an hour he half-sat, half-lay in the dark, drained and pathetic, too weak to move. What was the point of moving? He was clean here. He was untouched, though his fingers tingled from the bleach he had thrown liberally down the pan and the acid of it almost made him retch all over again. At least here, huddled on the cold linoleum, he could imagine the Domestos coursing through his veins, ridding him of the foul accusation that had contaminated his home. Here he could bury himself away from vile possibilities, horrid dangers, unspeakable acts and, yes, responsibility to others. What did others *want* of him anyway? He despaired. What did his *conscience* want of him? To go to the police— with what? The fantasy of a backward child? A child with a vivid imagination, or psychiatric problems, or both? And what would that do but cause trouble, of the most horrifying nature, not least for himself? *An old man talking to a young boy*, he'd been accused of being by the boyfriend. The insinuation turned his stomach anew. What was wrong with that? How dare people misinterpret—but misinterpret they would: they *wanted* to misinterpret, that was the vile thing. Then again, what if he *himself* was misinterpreting? He could see it now, in a flash-forward, a dissolve: 'FAMOUS ACTOR UNHINGED BY GRIEF.' If he stepped forward and spoke up, *he'd* be just as likely the one arrested. Sent to prison. Shamed. *His* picture all over the newspapers. If he was pathetic now, how much *more* pathetic would he be behind bars, or even in the witness box? But what churned in his belly more than all of that was the terrible thought that his failure to act would suit the true offender down to the ground. The creature would be free to continue his cynical, sordid depredations to his heart's content. And that poor boy…
God…
He shut his eyes. He felt like the terrified Fordyce, the bank

manager he played in *Cash on Demand*. Mopping perspiration from his brow. Prissy, emasculated, threatened. Affronted by the taunts of his nemesis. Goaded. His psychological flaws exposed. But that didn't help. What could he *do*? He wanted, wanted so desperately for someone to tell him. But who was there?

Aching and chilled, he clawed himself to his feet, clambered to the kitchen, poured himself lukewarm water from the tap, and drank. He needed Helen, his bedrock. Now more than ever.

He realised he felt so weak and ineffectual, not just now, but always. He remembered the spectacle of breaking down in tears in front of Laurence Olivier, thinking then, as he thought now: Am I strong enough? Am I strong enough for this?

Yes you are, Helen had reassured him. *If you want to be. You're worth ten of them, Peter. You're strong enough for anything...*

Back then, she'd nursed him through a nervous breakdown that had lasted a good six months. Dear Heaven, is that something this odious man could use against him now? His doctor's records of psychological unbalance? He felt the terrifying possibility like another blow to his physical being. The awful likelihood of the dim past regurgitated, raked over in mere spite and venom. It would bring with it dark clouds, as it had done then.

Six months of misery it had been, for him and for Helen too, without a doubt. God only knew how she'd endured it, but she had. And he had endured it too, thanks to her, and her alone. How could it be, he'd wondered, that he, the husband, was supposed to protect her, and there she was, sacrificing everything completely selflessly so that he, this worthless actor, of all things, could pull through?

Then he could hear her voice again, even clearer this time:

Peter, you are completely unaware of your own value. I expect that's why I love you, and so do so many of your friends and colleagues. Can you not see? You must think more of yourself, darling, as we do. You do not need the backbiting and jealousy of the court of King Olivier. Your heart is not suited to it, and I know your enormous talent will out...You just need the right opportunity to come along, and it will...You must believe that too...

Once again he remembered her love and sweetness and once

again he felt devastated. He teetered to the living room and collapsed in a chair.

Through the doorway to the hall he could see the pile of unread scripts and it reminded him of the single day of shooting at Elstree, just over a month earlier, on *Blood from the Mummy's Tomb*, the eleventh of January, the day he'd had the phone call to tell him Helen had been rushed to Kent and Canterbury Hospital. His scenes had been hurriedly rescheduled but Helen had died of emphysema at home on the Thursday. There was no question of him returning to the production. The already-filmed scenes with Valerie Leon were scrapped and the role written for him, that of the Egyptologist Professor Fuchs, given to Andrew Keir. Quatermass replacing Van Helsing. The curse of an ancient civilisation; it seemed like ancient history now.

Yet clear as a bell was his memory of wandering out alone, all, all alone onto the deserted beach just after Helen had breathed her last from those accursed lungs of hers, the seagulls reeling and swooping and cackling, the gale force wind hard in his face, the waves that crashed on the shingle sounding to him like a ghastly knell, the thoughtless pulse of the planet. And he'd sung *Twinkle, Twinkle Little Star*. He thought he'd gone a little mad that night.

Up above the world so high
Like a diamond in the sky...

He'd then found himself, unaware of the passage of intervening time, back at 3 Seaway Cottages, running up and down the stairs repetitively, endlessly, far beyond the point of exhaustion. To an impartial observer this might have given the appearance of madness too, but was anything but. In those moments he'd known exactly what he was doing. He'd run up, run down, run up again and so on in the vain hope of inducing a heart attack so that he might be reunited with her. He may have cursed God too, a little, that night under the stars. God didn't approve of taking one's own life, but damn God. He'd wanted to be with Helen and that was all he cared about. Then, racing up and down, up and down, he stopped dead as he realised the cruelty of it all. That, if he did commit suicide, he might find himself in purgatory, or in limbo, and separated from Helen forever. The crushing realisation had hit him that *that* Hell would be even more unbearable than this, and he crumbled finally, spent.

Helpless, he'd found himself sitting on the stairs gasping for air, wheezing as she had wheezed, his lungs filling like bellows as he wept.

When the blazing sun is gone,
When there's nothing he shines upon,
Then you show your little light,
Twinkle, twinkle, through the night…

But God, as they say, moves in mysterious ways. And soon afterwards he had found the letter. Heard her voice as he'd read it:

"My Dear Beloved. My life has been the happiest one imagina-ble… Remember we will meet again when the time is right. Of that I have no doubt whatsoever. But promise me you will not pine…or, most of all, do not be hasty to leave this world…"

He had shivered then at the terrible thought that he might have, stupidly, done something so contrary to her wishes. Helen wanted him to go on, and he would go on. He would do what she wanted. He would do anything for her.

Do not be hasty to leave this world…

That's what she'd said to him. But the truth is, he thought, I didn't have the courage then, and I don't have it now.

Dear Peter, of course you do. Dying isn't hard. Living without the love of your life is hard. That's the hardest thing of all.

But now I am feeling more lost than ever…the child, the boy…

You care. That is your greatest strength. People feel it. They see it on the screen.

But this isn't the screen. This is life.

You will know what to do. You make the right choices, Peter. Just believe in yourself. As I do, my darling. Always…

He remembered, as if being in the audience watching a scene

on stage in a drawing-room play, his father telling him, without any note of malice or cruelty, as if it were a statement of fact like the earth revolving round the sun, that he, Peter, was forty and a failure.

Even the memory of the hurt made him take a quick, sharp breath. But he remembered also the way Helen had stood up to the old man and given him a piece of her mind. His father had never been talked to like that, and certainly not by a woman. The fellow hardly knew what had hit him. And afterwards, when the two of them were alone, what had she said to him?

You have to believe in yourself, Peter…Believe in yourself and your abilities and not be brought down by those lesser mortals who for some reason of their own want you not to succeed. God gave you an amazing gift, darling, and God wants it to soar, and so do I. Have faith in your talent. That's all you need, Peter…Faith, and love…

The stink of bleach burned in his nostrils. It clung to the air and he knew he would not be able to rid the house of it for days. Perversely, he inhaled it deeply, as an act of defiance, determined to breathe in his own house, undaunted.

Faith and love *were* all he needed. Faith in himself, and the love of Helen, which he knew was immortal. That would be enough to get him through. Even this turmoil. Even this pestilence. He suddenly knew it. He was not weak. He was not pathetic.

With her courage, he could soar.

The floor of the interview room was concrete under his feet, the walls whitewashed, the single window set with bars beyond the glass. An old window. A window with tales to tell. *If walls had ears*, the saying goes. Indeed so, he thought. He wondered if it had once been an actual cell and how often names, jibes, scrawls, remarks, obscenities had been eradicated with a new coat of paint. As possible lives had been eradicated, set on this path or that, turned, curtailed, saved, doomed, the guilty punished, the innocent punished come to that. There was nothing on the table in front of him but his hands, so he stood and paced with them clasped behind his back. They were still dry and cold from the walk. The sea, so often heralded as life-giving, ossified them. Made them into a mummy's hands. Leather-like.

Old man...

He closed his eyes. Inside his skull images of the scene from the night before ran though his brain. Multiplied. He saw them again and again. Take after take. Wait a minute, in that one he's quite aggressive. That one, more sympathetic. The clapperboard snapped, making his eyes flicker. Close-up. Take eleven. Man steps from the shadows, his lips open in a horizontal grin...No, take twelve, smiling evilly, the hands rubbing together...

He always wondered how editors remembered every nuance, every glance or inflection: now, only twenty-four hours later, he had difficulty doing the same. Now he had trouble remembering if the man had said anything to incriminate himself—anything actual, *tangible*—or whether his threat and bluster was born out of sheer panic, a bombastic act of frightened self-defence. What did he know for certain? Just that Gledhill had verbally attacked only the person who'd verbally attacked *him* first, in his absence. Was that inhuman, the behaviour of a cornered animal? Or the all-too-human reaction of an innocent man?

You're losing your fucking *marbles, old man...*

He flinched again at the obscenity scrawled on his memory like graffiti on the wall of a public lavatory. Then saw Gledhill's face again, at the gap in the door.

An old man and a little boy...

The insidious words' capacity to appal him was undiminished, sickening him to his core. He took a deep breath and dispelled any misgivings. The man was a liar, and had shown his cards. Hadn't he?

Aware of a slump he normally only affected when 'old man acting' was required, he pushed his shoulders back, stretched his spine, scratched his chin, the bristles rasping there. While there was nothing on the walls to see himself in, in the mirror at home before setting out he'd seen a salt-and-pepper beard emerging, starting to give him a look like 'Dr Terror' from Milton's portmanteau extravaganza, though he knew the particular nastiness in this tale he was living was nothing so comfortably *outré* as ancestral werewolf, voodoo jazz or malignant vine. He wished to goodness it was. He wished he could even be as pragmatic and unflappable as his Inspector Quennell in *The Blood Beast Terror* when luring a gigantic moth to its inevitable flame. But it was all too easy to face monsters with a screenplay in your hand. Even a bad one.

The previous night he had slept in erratic bursts, but not as sporadically as the night before, and did not dream as he had feared he might after his encounter. The framed photograph of Helen had rested on the pillow at his side and the influence of too many third-hand superstitions from bad scripts made him feel it had fended off evil. He'd allowed the thought to comfort him without analysing it too much. Still sorely sleep-deprived, he had awoken at dawn spiky and brittle but strangely purposeful, and had played Berlioz's *Royal Hunt* from *The Trojans* while he dressed, pausing only to turn it up louder. Twice.

The door opened, the turn of the handle surprisingly sibilant, and a thick-set man entered wearing a brown suit, beige shirt and mustard tie. The shirt had been acquired when he had less of a paunch, and consequently the buttons were under stress and had tugged the ends out above his belt. He ran his index fingers round the rim of his trousers to re-insert them before settling his rump in the chair at the table. His socks and some inches of bare, hairless leg were exposed above slip-ons.

"Peter."

"Derek, dear boy…"

"Did you get my card?" The man, in his thirties, had hair slicked back with Brylcreem, and his fluffy growth of incipient sideburns was both ginger and ill-advised.

"Yes." In fact, Cushing knew full well it was with all the other cards, in a pile on the bureau, unopened. He was an actor. He would act. "Thank you so much."

Inspector Derek Wake did not waste time.

"Right. How can I help you?"

His bluntness bordered on impatience. Whether the policeman was particularly busy or merely lacking in sensitivity, Cushing didn't want to consider. Perhaps neither man wanted to indulge in the ritual of feigned sympathy, feigned appreciation. Anyway it was unimportant. That was not why he was here.

"Well, I hope you can. You have done in the past, with regard to screenplays I'm having difficulty getting my teeth into."

"Teeth."

"Quite."

"In the research aspect?"

"Quite."

"In the police aspect?"

"Exactly."

He had been to the inspector several times before for advice when preparing for a part. Usually he was greeted with a measure of perky, hand-rubbing delight, doubtless providing as it did a welcome diversion from the normal, irksome jobs officers of the law are tasked to perform, many of them unpleasant, many downright dangerous. Advising on a screenplay was many things, however 'dangerous' was not one of them. But today Wake was taciturn. Perhaps he had too many things of greater importance on his plate. Cushing didn't imagine meeting a man recently bereaved would make a seasoned copper awkward or restless, given his profession, but perhaps it did. Perhaps this was how he showed it.

He'd brought a few pages of script from *Scream and Scream Again*, the Christopher Wicking draft. He was taking a gamble that Wake hadn't seen the film and didn't know it had already been made and released a year ago. He'd torn off the title page and said the film was called *Monster City* (not a bad title, he thought: he'd been in worse). His role had been Benedek, a Nazi-like cameo with only a couple of scenes, but he told Wake he was lined up to play the Alfred Marks part, Superintendent Bellaver, the Scotland Yard detective given the run around by a spate of vampiric serial murders.

"Fire away. I'll do my best. Your GP still offers you his wisdom regarding brain surgery and such like, I take it?"

"Oh yes. I think he looks forward to our little chats about severed limbs, gouged eyeballs and violent amputations. It's marvellous what you can get on the National Health these days."

For a full three-quarters of an hour he asked the policeman questions about playing Bellaver. How would he address his assistants? How would he talk to a murder suspect? Whether a line seemed plausible. Whether another was properly researched. And when Wake replied, he scribbled notes copiously in the margins, underlining or circling the text, *double-underlining* on occasion, when he received details of special, usable significance. This, he knew, would please Wake as a kind of flattery. These days, people's hearts were warmed by an affiliation to Hollywood in the way that past generations were by touching the hem of royalty. But, of course, it was all nonsense. He wasn't the slightest bit interested in the inspector's advice, and was hardly listening to his answers. The important ques-tions—the *vital* questions—were yet to come. He was treading water, if the man but knew it. He had a plan. And it was nothing to do with the neatly-formatted pages in front of him.

"Well, thank you. You've been most helpful. I shan't take any more of your time." Cushing rose from the chair. "I'm sure you have better things to do than talk to me." He shook hands in his sincere, country-parsonish way, buttoned up his coat and moved to the door. Whereupon he paused, his fingers fluttering next to his mouth— perhaps too theatrical a gesture?—before turning turned back to the seated detective.

"Yes?"

"Actually there's another script. Not a script, a story treatment I've been sent by a film company. Very intense. Very troubling. I'm not at all sure I shall accept the part, but…" He hesitated, tugged his lower lip, waved his hand as if dismissing the idea, criss-crossing his scarf on his chest, showing Wake his back then peeking back over his shoulder. "Again, it's all about authenticity, you see. I feel in my bones the writer hasn't really done his homework. In terms of the legal ramifications of the scenario."

"Run it by me. I'll be able to tell you if it rings true. From a police perspective, at least."

"Are you sure? I don't like to encroach on—"

"Rubbish. Livens up my tea break. Plus, having a big film star in. Something to tell the wife."

Wife. Cushing could see the man quickly regretted using the word.

"Very well." He sat back down and placed his fingertips together in a steeple. Very Sherlock Holmes. Too Sherlock Holmes? "This is an Anglo-Canadian co-production, actually. The lead is a Canadian actress who plays the mother. But the setting is this country. I think the screenwriter may be Canadian, hence..." He didn't like improvising, but in this instance an off-the-cuff quality was essential. The telling details were most important in a barefaced lie. "Anyway, I'd play a headmaster. I suppose it's essentially a version of *M.*" No flash of recognition. "The Fritz Lang film?" Still nothing. "Peter Lorre starred in it? Set in Germany?"

"Oh."

"Have you seen it?"

"Yes, of course..." Clearly he hadn't. "Remind me what it was about again."

"Lorre plays a disturbed man. A man who kidnaps and murders children. A child molester who becomes hunted down by society. A horrible character, paradoxically portrayed as sad and lonely and even strangely sympathetic."

"No, I've never seen it." The policeman stood up. "Why would anyone want to see a film about that?"

"These things happen in the world, I suppose."

"All the more reason not to put them in films. I go to the pictures to enjoy myself, I don't know about you." He stood, running his fingers round the rim of his belt yet again. "What did you want to ask me?"

"My, er...character has evidence against the, um, perpetrator." His confidence had wavered. He speeded up his delivery. "In the story, I mean. It's the crux of the plot. Incriminating evidence. Evidence against a family member, not the vagrant who has already been arrested. And I'm curious. What would be the correct police procedure in a case like this?"

Wake shrugged, and having arranged his shirt and trousers to his temporary satisfaction, adjusted the knot of his tie. "We'd have to investigate. Long process. Doctors' reports. Court. It's complex. You'd have to give me the exact details."

"Everyone would be interrogated."

"Questioned. Yes. Obviously."

"And the boy?"

Another shrug. "Taken into care, straight off, any sniff of evidence. Whoosh. Can't take the risk. Get him out of there." The lick of a lighter on a cigarette tip. Secreted back in the jacket pocket. Smoke directed at the ceiling. "Mum and Dad can squabble till the cows come home. Right little cheerful movie this is going to be. Not a comedy, I take it."

"No."

"No. Too right." With his hands on his hips now, the belly jutted unabashed. "Nobody does well out of these cases, I can tell you. Nobody goes home smiling, put it like that. Families get broken up, pieced together again. Except you can't piece them together again, can you? Worst of it is, unless you virtually catch the bloke red-handed, it's one person's word against another, and often as not even the kid won't speak up against their own parent, even if they half-kill them on a daily basis. And the mum sticks up for the feller like he's a bloody angel. So they get off scot free. Buggered up it is, really buggered up. To be honest, I hate it, more than anything." More smoke, through teeth this time. Breath of a quietly-seething dragon. "Sooner string them up and have done with it, ask me. Know the bloody liberals say, what if there's a miscarriage of justice? I say, tell you what. Cut their bloody balls off they won't do it again. I guarantee that."

Which was as much as Cushing needed to hear. He stood up and shook the man's hand generously in both of his.

"Thank you so much."

"My advice?" The detective flicked ash into a metallic waste paper bin. "Don't take the part. You don't want to be associated with that kind of rubbish."

"Very probably not." One side of his mouth twitched. "I'll more than likely politely decline. But that's been useful. Definitely. Thank you, Derek."

Out in the corridor with the sound of a clattering typewriter nearby and garrulous laughter slightly more distant and out of sight, the old man heard from behind him:

"Peter, do you mind if we have a quick word? On an unrelated matter?"

It felt like a cold hand on his shoulder, which was absurd. Two uniformed constables passed him, a man and a woman. They both smiled, as if they recognised him. He touched the rim of his hat.

Smiling, he turned to see Wake leaning against the jamb of the doorway to the interview room, not smiling at all. The policeman switched off the light, closed the door and walked past him up the corridor in the direction of the sergeant's desk, then turned into a glass-sided office and sat behind a desk with several bulging manila files on it which he arranged in piles of roughly equal height.

When Cushing had stepped reluctantly into his office he stood up again, flattened his tie against his shirt front with the palm of his hand, and crossed the room to shut the door after him. The conversation and clacking of the typewriter became substantially quieter. Wake returned to his swivel chair.

"A man came in this morning and made a complaint about you."

"Oh?" He told himself not to betray anything in his expression. Certainly not shock, though that was what he was feeling. Now the reason for Wake's mood was all too clear. "May I ask whom?"

"I'm not at liberty to say. I told him I'd prefer not to, but if he wanted to make it official, I'd make it official. But he was reluctant."

"I'll bet he was." Under his breath.

Had he heard? Wake's buttons really were straining across his midriff. "He was doing you a favour. He doesn't want to cause any trouble. So I'm having this quiet word. Off the record."

"What exactly did he say, Derek? Are you allowed to tell me that? Off the record?"

"He said you were talking to his little boy."

"That's absolutely correct. I was. I won't deny that. What's wrong with that, for heaven's sake?"

"Let's just say he doesn't want it." The way he lounged back in the chair was beginning to annoy Cushing. He found it louche, oikish and disrespectful. And the man's fly zip was distressingly taut.

"I chat to all the children. You know that. They chat to me. I'm like the Pied Piper. Helen and I..."

"I know. I know." Wake leant forward, elbows on the desk. Pushed the harshness of the angle-poise lamp away. "Listen, it puts me in a very awkward position, when someone comes in with a complaint like this. Especially when it's someone I know personally, like yourself."

"Oh, I'm sorry to be bothersome."

"I'm just saying I don't want it to go any further if I can help it."

"For my benefit?"

"For everyone's benefit."

Cushing could feel his lips tight and bloodless with rage and dared not speak for fear of what might come out. So, he's got his retaliation in first, he was thinking. Clever. Before I could make any accusations, he's made his.

Clever man.

Clever monster.

"Look, I know this bloke. He's a hell of a nice feller." Wake raked his hair with his fingers and offered his palms. "We went to school together. I've got drunk with him. He's not a troublemaker—not like some round here. He's got a decent job, down on the boats. My wife knows his family, has done for donkey's years. He visits his mum in the nursing home every Sunday. He helps out at Christmas, with the food and that."

"In other words, you believe him."

"I think things can be misinterpreted, that's all," Wake said. "And he has, probably. I don't mean 'probably'."

Cushing didn't think he could remember such anger building up inside him. It was white hot and it terrified him and he knew if it rose much more he wouldn't be able to control it, and that would be a disaster. He opened the door.

"Thank you so much. I think I'll go now, if you don't mind. Unless you have anything more to say to me."

Wake sighed and rubbed his eyes. When he looked up to reply, Cushing was gone. Wake sprang up, grabbed the closing door of his office, yanked it back wide and hurried to the sergeant's desk in pursuit of the long dark coat. Remarkably, the older man was out-striding him and he had to break into a run to catch up.

"Peter. Let me drive you home."

"No, Derek. Thank you all the same. I think I'd prefer some nice fresh sea air. Good day to you."

The detective followed him outside, caught up with him a second time and stood in front of him on the pavement, this time blocking his way.

"Look, all I'm suggesting to both of you is keep a wide berth from each other. You, and Gledhill and his family. Both parties. Either that, or sort out your differences without the police getting involved."

"I'm sure we shall," Cushing said, circumnavigating him.

The scenario had changed radically. The script had been rewritten, drastically. Now at least he knew with some certainty that he daren't rely on the police or the legal system. His adversary had prepared the ground, cleverly sown the seeds of doubt in a pre-emptive strike against him. If he made an accusation now it was too risky he would be disbelieved and, worse, far worse, the *boy* would be disbelieved—if the boy even spoke up at all. There was no guarantee he would do so, given his only way of dealing with the situation, it seemed, was through the prism of monsters and monster-hunters. Wasn't it Van Helsing who said "The Devil's best trick is that people don't believe he exists"? In Bram Stoker's novel, he thought, but certainly in the play and Universal film. He remembered the Van Helsing of the book—a little old man who literally talked double Dutch. He remembered asking Jimmy Carreras why he didn't cast a double-Dutchman in the part, and Jimmy saying: "We rather think you should play him as yourself." But the point was, how should he play *this* part, now? He had to stop this man. Alone, if need be. And he needed ammunition. In the words of Inspector Wake, he needed *evidence*.Without delay he resolved to visit the Fount of All Knowledge.

She was wrapping up a cucumber in newspaper for a customer with whom she was conversing breathlessly. Through a steady stream of clients like this one she gleaned her vital information. A round-faced woman with the general shape of the Willendorf Venus and the given name of Betty, she knew everything there was to know about everyone in town: even a good deal they didn't know about themselves, he suspected. When Helen and he came to buy fresh vegetables from her and her husband's shop, they invariably came away a little wiser about something of high import, locally. In the woman's opinion, anyway. Which is why Helen had coined her nickname: 'The Fount of All Knowledge', and it had stuck. A private joke between Peter and his wife. A private look between them as she twirled a bag of tomatoes at the corners whilst dispensing the latest gossip. A private raised eyebrow. A private hand concealing a wry smile. It seemed so long ago, and only yesterday.

"Lovely morning."

"Hello, Mr C. Yes it is." She wiped the dry earth from her hands to her apron. "The sun's done us proud. For February."

"I should like one of these, please."

The Fount of All Knowledge took the cabbage from his hands and popped it into a brown paper bag tugged from a butcher's hook. The tiny stigma in the corner torn.

"Good to see you out, sir." She looked down at her shuffling feet. "We know how it must be for you. Everyone's been saying."

"Bless you."

"Everybody knows how much you loved each other. I'm sure that's no comfort to you at all." Her cheeks reddened appreciably. "Still…"

He held out a handful of coins—the new decimal currency, still a struggle—and allowed her to take the required amount. "I am comforted—by the certainty that I will be united with her one day. Of that I have no doubt whatsoever." He smiled. The woman nodded to herself, then rang up the money in a till secluded in the shadows under the awning. "Tell me, my dear. You may be able to help me. Do you by any chance know a woman by the name of Mrs Drinkwater? She has a boy named Carl."

"Annie?"

"Possibly. She lives in a bungalow on Rayham Road."

"That's the one." She picked up a broom and started brushing between the stalls. "Her brother had a hole in the heart. You know, like that footballer."

Cushing nodded but had no idea what she was talking about.

"I was wondering if she still takes in ironing? I believe her circumstances may have changed recently. I don't want to cause offence by enquiring unnecessarily. Someone tells me she has a new young chap in her life."

The Fount of All Knowledge shook the box of potatoes. "For all the good it'll do her."

"Oh? You sound sceptical."

"I wonder why."

"I've heard nothing but good reports of him. Les, I think his name is. He's excellent with the boy, apparently. Perhaps I've heard wrongly."

"Not got a great track record, has he? Married before. Divorced."

"We don't condemn people for that, do we? Not these days."

"I don't condemn anybody for anything, me." She took a large handful of carrots from a new customer. "I don't repeat what's told to me in confidence. I just wouldn't trust him as far as I could throw that building over there."

This was exactly the kind of information he wanted. But he wanted more. "His first wife? Now, was that Valerie Rogers, the hairdresser from The Boutique, by any chance?"

"No. Nice girl from Tankerton. Sue something. Blezard, as was. That's it. Works in a tea shop in Canterbury. Pilgrims, I think it's called."

"Pilgrims. In Canterbury."

That was all he wanted to know, and the rest of the conversation consisted of a short discussion about who might take in his ironing. He weathered that particular storm until the Fount of All

Knowledge ran out of intellectual steam, for which he was abundantly grateful. He touched the rim of his hat. *Bless you. Goodbye.*

"Bless you, sir. You're one of a kind, you are. A real gentleman. Not many of those around any more. They broke the mould when they made you."

"I should certainly hope so."

Which is when *Mr* Fount of All Knowledge appeared from the back of the shop holding aloft a pleat of garlic in two hands, eager to share the joke as if it were the first time he'd thought of it—which it most surely wasn't.

"Garlic, Mr C?"

"Very droll, Mr H," Peter Cushing said, as he always did. "Very droll."

He ran for the bus fearing he'd miss it, and by the time he settled into a seat his lungs were on fire. The pain and breathlessness reminded him of Helen's lungs as the vehicle pulled away from the bus station.Sadly he realised that he had always kept working to provide for their future together. An old age together without financial worries that was not to be. It made him feel foolish, not that he could have known it would happen like this—never *like this*—but somehow feeling God, a force for good, unaccountably laughed at one's futile plans. Still, the income he had provided from films was able to give Helen a few luxuries, as well as the all-important medical care and attention when her cough got worse and her breathing painful and difficult. He remembered the arrival of the oxygen mask and canister necessary to assist her lungs. Meanwhile he, as Frankenstein, effortlessly transplanted brains and brought back the dead.

Frankenstein always failed because his morality was flawed, because his drive to help humanity was misguided. But in reality doctors failed for much more mundane reasons. When they went to Dr Galewski, the pulmonary specialist, he'd said: "You have left it too late. You should have come to me ten years ago." Frankenstein had never uttered a line so heartless.

He'd taken Helen to France, driving his spanking new blue Mark IX Jaguar to the thermal springs at Le Mont-Dore, spending hours on meditative walks in the hills while his wife rested. Encountering solitary goatherds as he grew a moustache for his next role. Telling her his silly adventures every evening. He remembered how, day by day, her laughter had grown stronger. How she was revitalised by the experience. The doctor from Poland had performed a minor miracle after all. Her cough had disappeared.

But the precious respite was to be hideously short-lived. Her throaty laughter cut short.

The Return of the Cybernauts in *The Avengers*; *Corruption*; *The Blood Beast Terror*…

All as her illness worsened.

They decided to sell Hillsleigh, their place in Kensington—Helen had said London "smelled of stale food and smoke"—and move permanently to their beloved holiday home by the sea. He remembered the pitiful sight of her sitting at the bottom of the stairs saying, "Can we go there, please?"

"Of course, my love. Of course."

He had kissed her and held her in his arms. He'd always joked in interviews that they'd married for money: he had £15 and she had seventeen and ten. That came back to him now.

He thought mostly of all the wasted time travelling back and forth to London when he could have been at her side. Fifteen televised hours of the horrid, un-der-rehearsed BBC *Sherlock Holmes*, an experience he loathed, distracted as he was by Helen's condition, barely able to remember his lines. He remembered the stair lift being installed in 3 Seaway Cottages whilst he was shooting *Frankenstein Must Be Destroyed*—"Hammer's Olivier, impeccably seedy in his spats and raspberry smoking jacket," the New York Times said of him in that one. He remembered her reading it aloud to him, delighting in the phrase as she repeated it. And Amicus's Jekyll and Hyde variation *I, Monster*, catching the milk train to filming because he couldn't bear to spend so much as a night away from her.

After a short, callous period when she'd seemed to recuperate, Helen's respiration had become laboured again. He'd employed dear Maisie Olive to help with the housework because his wife was unable to function any more as the wife she wanted to be. That cut him to the quick, when she'd said it with tears in her eyes. But he didn't want a wife. He wanted *her*.

Her spirits lifted slightly as she decided almost on a whim that breathing exercises were the answer. He'd been buoyed by her sudden optimism but just as quickly her hopes were dashed by a young locum who told her they were a waste of time. He had wanted to strangle the man there and then, just like one of his villains would have done. He'd done it endless times on screen: how difficult could it be in real life? Or take one of those hack-saws of Baron Frankenstein and cut round his skull like a boiled egg, as he did to poor Freddie Jones. Take out that thoughtless brain of his. But the truth was, nothing he could do or think or dream would make the slightest difference to Helen's future, as well he knew.

As it was, that slap in the face by the locum took the heart out of her. He saw it. At that point exactly her spirit crumbled. And he feared his would too, but he dare not let it. He dreaded that her seeing an inner agony written in his features would compound her own. He would act. Act. Act. Act.

He gazed out of the filthy window of the bus. The countryside lay under a gauze of grime and dead insects.

On December the sixteenth, he had his last job before Helen died. Recording *The Morecambe and Wise Special* for transmission on the coming Christmas Day. As scripted, he was required to appear unexpectedly beside Eric and Ernie to complain he hadn't been paid the five pounds for an earlier show. It was a running gag: quite a good one, he thought. People had enjoyed his 'corpsing' when he had guest-starred for the first time playing King Arthur, and it was gratifying that the team had asked him back. Helen had said, go on, it would do him good to play against type. To show there was a side of him that was warm and humorous and bright. The side she knew and loved.

Bring me sunshine…

He had thought he could get through it, and he had. Now, once again, he could hear the audience laughing through the grime and gauze of the world around him.

Bring me sunshine…

Even then, he had known deep down that, while the nation roared with laughter, his wife was at home, dying.

"Cream tea for two, please." He said it automatically, without thinking. "No, how stupid of me." He smiled. "I mean a pot of tea for one, and a single scone with jam and clotted cream. If you'd be so very kind." He placed the plastic menu back behind the tomato sauce bottle. "Thank you, my dear.""Ta." She finished scribbling on her little pad using a Biro with a feather Sellotaped to it in order to resemble a quill pen.

"Excuse me. I'm terribly sorry. Sue?"

"Yes?"

It hadn't been hard to find The Pilgrim Tea Room on Burgate after a short meander through Canterbury's narrow streets. It couldn't have looked more like a tea room if it had tried, with its dark timbers and white-painted plasterwork overhanging a bulging bow window. If not Elizabethan it had a distinctly Dickensian feel about it. He could imagine Scrooge walking by, muffled against the cold in a heavy snowfall, wishing everybody a Merry Christmas and carol singers holding lanterns on sticks. Not a bad role, Scrooge. He would have made a decent fist of it, he thought, had it ever been offered. Standing outside the restaurant, it struck him The Pilgrim was exactly the kind of emporium he and Helen would have gravitated to on one of their day trips. Exactly the kind of place Helen would have chosen. He had almost felt her arm tighten around his, guiding him in.

"Do you mind if I have a quick word? Whilst it's not too busy. I don't want to interrupt your work. It'll only take a moment, I promise."

The woman looked confused and a little frightened. As well she might be. He didn't blame her.

"We're about to close."

"It won't take long, I promise."

She hesitated. "I'll put this order in first, if you don't mind."

"No, of course, my dear. Please do."

He watched her glide to the far end of the shop, collecting empty plates and cups on the way. A Kentish Kim Novak dressed in a black ankle-length dress with a pinny over it, her hair pinned up under a frilly bonnet, the sort Victorian kitchen maids used to wear. It was an illusion dissipated somewhat by white plimsolls that had seen better days, and the lipstick. The overall effect was cheap and, combined with the ridiculously Heath Robinson quill, somewhat absurd. But the whole place was grubbily inauthentic, designed to milk the tourists for a quick bob or two. History was merely its gimmick. She returned with a damp cloth in her hand and wiped down the plastic table cloth. He lifted his elbows to give her room for her comprehensive sweeps and lunges.

"I've seen your films." She lifted the duo of sauce bottles out of the way one by one. "You're Christopher Lee aren't you?"

He corrected her with consummate politeness, tugging on his white cotton glove.

"No, I'm the other one."

"Vincent Price?"

He kept his smile to himself. "That's right."

He pulled the ash tray towards him and lit one of his cigarettes.

"I'd like to talk to you about Les Gledhill."

The sweeping actions of her arm were energetic but he detected the tremor of a pause which she quickly attempted to hide. The skin on her face seemed to tighten, betraying a tense irritation. Her former relaxed, if busy, manner was suddenly gone. It was as if he had flipped a switch in one of his Frankenstein laboratories and she suddenly looked ten years older.

"Well you might want to. I don't. I don't want anything to do with him. He's a nasty piece of work. A sick, nasty piece of work."

The swirling motions of the damp cloth on the table became violent, as well as repetitive.

"Did you know he's with another woman now?"

"I hope they'll be very happy together."

"That's rather why I'm here."

"What do you mean?"

"She has a boy."

The woman stopped wiping the table top within an inch of its life and stood up straight. He saw her hand tighten round the dish cloth which she had swapped from one hand to the other. Her knuckles whitened and a few drops of water exuded, hanging like tiny baubles from the joints of her fingers.

"Look, I don't know why you're interested in him, but I don't want to know. I don't even want to remember his name. But I have remembered it, thanks to you."

She turned away but he shifted quickly onto the nearer chair and caught her hand. The one with the damp rag. He felt its wetness seeping through her fingers to his.

"The boy is named Carl. I'm concerned about him, and I'm concerned about his mother." He was looking up into her face but her eyes were darting around the room now, afraid that the scene was drawing attention. "I don't want this man to ruin any more lives. I want to stop him. Is there anything you can tell me? Anything? Please."

She looked down into the blueness of his eyes. She pulled away her hand, abruptly, to her side, holding it there, then seemed to realise it was an unkindness that was unnecessary to an old man.

"I wish I knew then what I know now, that's all."

"Which is what?"

Her voice remained hard, terse with discomfort and something else swimming vast and unpleasant under the surface.

"Please."

"He…He fastens onto vulnerable women. He can spot them. He homes in. He uses them. To get what he wants."

He knew she'd already said too much and regretted it. Horribly so. Giving the table a last, cursory wipe, she turned on her heel and walked towards the kitchen with her shoulders back, eyes front. A teenage boy with his head haloed in the fur-trimmed hood of a parka sat at one of the other tables with his shoes, laces undone, planted on a chair. She flicked his shoulder with the back of her hand as she passed by, hardly looking at him.

"Feet. Off."

The youth shot her a fierce look from under a heavy fringe. His mane of dark hair shook as he did so. His nose was long and square with a slight line above the tip from rubbing it too much. His eyebrows had begun to join in the middle. Thick lips, succulent yet dry enough to crack. Slightly crooked teeth. A constellation of pimples on his cheeks, some livid red, others turning yellow with pus. The affliction of the young. Another of God's little cruelties.

"Mum…" he complained in a sing-songy way under his breath.

Cushing felt an intense chill and imagined someone had opened and closed the door, but they hadn't.

He looked over at the boy in the parka as the latter played with the sugar dispenser, pouring a measured spoonful onto the table then scooping it, plough-like, with the flat of one hand then the other, prodding it into a perfect square, then making a dot in the centre of the square with the top of his index finger. Then destroying the whole artistic arrangement and starting again. He appeared both to be completely absorbed in the activity and completely bored by it. There was a lazy insouciance in the lad's countenance, something about his very physicality which bordered on barely-contained rage.

What had Van Helsing said in *Brides?* That he was studying a sickness. A sickness *part physical, part spiritual…*

As if aware of being spied on, the youth looked up. Their eyes met and he knew the old man was staring at him. His features froze, but not with any degree of guilt or foreboding. Without any fraction of self-consciousness or embarrassment. Quite the reverse. He stared back at Cushing with chilling assuredness. Aggression, in fact. A hard gaze, a vicious gaze which would take almost nothing to provoke to violence, and the old man wondered if he had provoked it already, and it scared him to the core to think of what a young man with such a cold gaze might be capable.

"I've said all I'm going to say to you."

It was Sue Blezard's voice again as she placed his cream tea on a tray in front of him.

"I understand."

"No. You don't," she said.

But he feared he did. Very much so.

"Always the one to take the boy to bed…" She stood with her back to her son, blocking him out. "Read him a story. Their 'special time', he said…" It was as if she didn't even realise she'd said the words. Her anger had said them, spilled them, from some disembodied place, before she'd had a chance to rein them back. Then her back stiffened. That was all. No more. The muscle in her cheek flexed. "Pay at the till when you're ready."

She walked away.

"Thank you," Cushing said, knowing that she had revealed more than she could bear and no less than she was compelled. He respected that. In seeking to end pain, he had caused it, and hated himself for doing so. But it was necessary. So necessary.

The cup and saucer were Wedgwood. He thought it pathetic that he cared about such things.

Some of the pustules on the lad's skin had broken and there were small streaks of blood where they had been picked at. After some minutes his mother brought the youth a hot chocolate and Cushing continued to watch him as he drank it. There were cuts and bruises on his hands as well as nicotine stains, and his fingernails were chewed to the quick. His knee jiggled with the spastic tremor of an old and hopeless alcoholic. It spoke of an inexorable slide into a life Cushing did not want to contemplate. Where was this boy? Not in school, clearly. Then *where?*

He thought of hurt and anger…the road to dissolution, evil, decay.

Their special time…

The hurt that prowls.

The scar that infects.

The darkness that perpetuates itself.
He stirred his tea. When he drank it, it was cold.

Afterwards, for a stroll, he visited the Cathedral. It was only yards away and he had not set foot inside for years. He was surprised to find the interior so vast and daunting, more so than he ever remembered feeling before. A massive, overwhelming, empty space. A space in which you could fit several normal-sized cathedrals, certainly. He thought of it now, quite literally. Dozens and dozens of churches, stacked like Lego bricks. He wondered if there was any limit to how large the masons could build an edifice to proclaim their faith? How big does faith have to be to fill a space the size of this? How much love does God need? The last tourists of the day moved around the aisles, looking up in awe and wonder, but he was the only one who knelt in the pews and prayed.

With his eyes tightly closed, he heard a baby crying. The sound echoed dis-tinctly in the Cathedral's canyon of stone, but when he stood and looked all round, he could see nobody. No baby. No mother. Nothing. And all was absolutely quiet again. Except for the side door creaking gently as it closed to keep out the sun.

He did not know how long he had been sitting in the bath but the water was stone cold and the Imperial Leather had turned it milky and opaque. He felt pins and needles in his bony buttocks so he thought he'd been there a long while, but it worried him he didn't know how long and now his shoulders were shivering and he was sure that under the scummy water his penis had shrunk to nothing. He wanted to pull the towel off the rail but it was slightly out of reach. Then the door of the bathroom opened and Christopher Lee came in, dressed exactly as he had been in the first Hammer *Dracula*, in that formidable entrance descending the staircase. Immaculate hair. Virile. Vulpine. The top of his head almost touched the ceiling as he paced back and forth beside the claw-foot bath in his ankle-length black cloak. He looked terribly upset. "Where's my wife?" he was saying. "Where is she?" Cushing could do nothing. He felt frozen and invisible.

He woke feeling the millstone presence of death, its crushing inevitability, in a way that he hadn't been so frightened by, or made helpless by, since he was seven years old.

Staring at the ceiling, he thought of the youth in the Pilgrim Tea Rooms, but instead of the pimply, hunched teenager in the parka, the boy sitting there was Carl Drinkwater, his hands wedged between his thighs, staring down at the plastic table-top which his mother was wiping with a wet cloth. Carl looked up and stared, just as the other boy had done. He had tiny smears of blood on his cheeks like the squashed bodies of dead insects.

Like massing vultures they gathered in the sky over the concourse of carrion, an echo of the prehistoric and primal. As the soles of his wellington boots pressed into the shingle with a hushing musicality of their own, their beckoning grew louder, a virulent and unforgiving choir. An announcement, spiteful heralds of his coming. Had he been blind, he thought, he could have purely followed the direction of the cries of the seagulls and found his way to the harbour, where death was perpetually on the menu. He carried a shopping basket. Not exactly becoming for a gentleman, but he didn't care. It was his late wife's, and now it was his. He remembered the two *Harvesters* in the fifties, when he and Helen had first come here, often used as umpire boats during the regatta. The remains of the railway were still there, the lamp standards still in evidence though the tracks were gone. Two whelk boats still operated on East Quay, commercial ships came in carrying stone and timber, Danish stuff, he was told, and beyond West Quay he often saw grain boats unloading into lorries with a hopper.

Meanwhile fishing boats unloaded their silvery spoils and the gulls were there, hovering, fighting the wind, ready to clash and kill for the pickings they could get from what bloody morsels fell before the trucks loaded up and shipped it out. Old families tended to work the trawlers. Generations. Fathers, sons, grandfathers.

A sheen of blood and seawater striped the concrete. His wellingtons crossed the mirror of it in the direction of the ugly store shed on South Quay, corrugated asbestos on a breezeblock frame, both its barn doors open to the wide 'U' of the harbour, the air punctuated by the tinkling of pulley metal and puttering slaps of wet ropes and lapping water.

It wasn't hard to find out the time of the tides and discover when exactly the boats came in, and he wasn't the only one who gravitated to the harbour to get the pick of the 'stalker'—as they called the odds and sods, small fry not sorted with the prime fish already boxed up and ready on its way to London. If they were regulars, they'd know when a certain boat would berth and they'd be there waiting for the bargains when it returned on the flood tide.

He watched as fishermen in sou'westers and oilskins hurried up and down the ladder on and off the vessel. They weren't hanging around, even with a small crowd present. Business took precedence. A small truck waited, taking the stacked plastic boxes—the catch already sorted during the two-hour steam back from fishing off Margate in Queen's Channel—straight to market.

Les Gledhill was one of them, strands of long wet hair hanging from his hood, cheekbones shiny and doll-like over his damp beard. The stalker was bagged up and marked at the quayside beyond the parked cars, some of it wrapped in newspaper. No airs and graces. '5 DOVER SOLE'S £1.' The misappropriated apostrophe was almost obligatory. Others who'd arrived first were helping themselves, and Gledhill was taking their cash in a wet, outstretched palm, skin peeled pink from the scouring weather.

Seeing Cushing out of the corner of his eye, Gledhill at first attempted to ignore him. A transistor radio set on an empty oil drum was playing the recent Christmas hit, *Grandad* by Clive Dunn. Unable to avoid doing so any longer, Gledhill stared at him as he rinsed his hands under a cold water tap on the quayside and wiped them on a towel. The DJ on the radio switched to the current single at the top of the charts, George Harrison singing *My Sweet Lord.*

"What do you have today?" Cushing presented himself as bright-eyed and bushy tailed.

"Depends what you're after."

"Oh, I think I'm open to suggestions." Cushing smiled broadly.

"Well. Got a load of dabs," Gledhill said, forcing a retaliatory smile to match. "Sprats. Herrings. Good winter fish. Dover sole. Skate. Nice skate backbone, if you know what to do with it." His hands looked frozen and painful to the older man as he watched him turn to serve an elderly woman who had the right change. A great deal of nattering was going on between the other customers and the other fishermen—quite sprightly, good-natured banter—and to an onlooker, this conversation would seem no different.

Cushing adjusted his scarf, scratched the side of his chin and pointed at one of the packages lined up before him. "That one will do perfectly."

"Pound."

"Thank you." Cushing happily delved into his purse.

Gledhill picked up the fish in newspaper and handed it to him, and as he did so Cushing saw the blue blur of an old tattoo on the back of his wrist, together with blue dots on his finger joints.

"You know, I was reading the other day…" He placed a pound note in the other man's palm. "The fish is the old symbol of Christianity. Older even than the cross."

"Fascinating," Gledhill said.

"Yes, it is, rather. Some people say religion has lost its way, but we are all God's children, when all is said and done. Whether we choose to see that or not. Don't you think?"

"You've got a bargain there, squire. I'd go home very happy if I were you."

Turning his back, Gledhill went back to the tap of ice cold water and washed his red raw hands with the thoroughness of a surgeon. Cushing had researched surgeon's methods for the Frankenstein films and it was the kind of thing he watched and made a mental note of, habitually. He found it interesting, vital, that there were telltale rituals and practices that made a profession look authentic, or inauthentic if wrong. It was essential to make the audience believe in the part one was playing, however ludicrous the part may be on paper. That was one's job. That was why they called it 'make-believe'. Make. Believe.

Cushing waited.

Believe in yourself, Peter…

"Anything else you want, mate?" Gledhill turned his head and stared at the old man. "Apart from the Dover sole?"

Peter Cushing decided he would not be hurried. Why should he be?

"Let me see…"

He lingered. And the more he lingered the more he realised he was enjoying the discomfort his lingering engendered.

Les Gledhill did not do anything so obvious as a quick, shifty look towards his colleagues to reveal his unease. He would never have been that blatant. Nor did he become twitchy or self-conscious in any way. In fact his motions became slower and more considered. That, in itself, told a story—that the very presence of the old man in wellington boots made him uneasy. And he didn't like it. A person who got a certain thrill from the control of others seldom enjoyed the feeling that someone else had control of him.

"Here. Ever tasted oysters, sir?" Gledhill picked up one of the shelled creatures from a plastic bucket in front of him.

"I thought the ones round here had all succumbed to disease and pollution."

"Not if you know where to look. I think of it as a hobby. Go out on a Sunday. Maybe get a hundred. You haven't answered my question, sir." His intention was to intimidate, rather than *be* intimidated. That much was clear.

"My preference is towards plain food."

"Then you don't know what you're missing. Marvellous stuff." Gledhill took a knife from a leather satchel. It was a short, stubby one with a curve in the blade. "You break them open." Metal scraped against the shell. He turned the object in his hand and opened it as if it were hinged. "Dab of vinegar if you prefer. Or just as it comes." He ran the knife under the slimy-looking bivalve, cutting its sinewy attachment. It sat in its juices. "Then into the mouth they go." He slid it off the half-shell onto his tongue, savouring it for a second or two, no longer, then swallowed. "One bite. Two at the most. Then down like silk. Nectar. Nothing like it."

"Not for me, I'm afraid."

"Not for everybody, that's for sure. Some people find it repulsive. Some can't even bear the idea and run a mile. But to chefs and gourmets and whatnot—those who appreciate the good things in life—well…they're a little taste of Heaven." Gledhill's eye was steady again. Unblinking. "Acquired taste, of course…"

"If you say so."

"'Don't knock it 'til you try it.' As they say."

"Something eaten while it's still alive? Simply in order to derive pleasure? I find the idea rather…obscene."

"In a way. In another way, it's the peak of civilised behaviour. The stuff of banquets and kings. Of aristocracy and riches and palaces. The supreme indulgence. The Romans introduced them here two thousand years ago. Long ago as the time of Christ. Makes you think, doesn't it?"

"Perhaps."

"Lot of algae and low in salinity, the Thames Estuary. Knew a thing or two, those Romans." He tossed away the empty shell into a bucket half-full of them, shortly to add to the cultch bed upon which the 'spat' of the next generation would settle. "Besides. If we humans don't live for pleasure, what do we live for?"

Cushing thought for a moment.

"Love?" he suggested. But really it was nothing like a question, to his mind.

Gledhill gave a snort, as if it were a bad joke, and wiped his hands on the grubby towel.

"Anything else I can do for you, sir? Or will that be all?"

"Actually there is one thing." Cushing was careful to maintain a matter-of-fact air. "I'm going to a matinee at the Oxford Picture House this afternoon. I rather thought you might like to join me."

Gledhill did not look away. "I don't like going to the cinema as a rule. Not in the daytime."

"Don't tell me you're afraid of the dark?" Cushing's wit fell upon deaf ears. "I'm sure you can make an exception."

"Sorry. I'm busy."

"I think not. Your working day is evidently over by—what time is it?"

"I didn't say I was working, I said I was busy."

"Oh. That's a shame. It really is a shame." Cushing feigned disappointment. "Because I've been to see your ex-wife and son, you see. Yes. Sue and I had a most edifying chat, and I thought you might be interested in what she had to say. It was quite—what can I say? Quite—*special.* I'm being dreadfully presumptuous. I shall go alone."

"Hang on."

He placed the wrapped Dover sole deep in his shopping basket and walked away a few steps before turning back, as if the next thing he said was a mere afterthought. "I believe the main feature commences at half past two. I do so hate missing the start of a picture, don't you? You can't really enjoy a story unless you see it from the beginning, right through to the bitter end. Don't you find?"

Gledhill was still staring at him. A few foolishly courageous seagulls descended in a flurry on the 'stalker' in front of him and took stabs at it, one trying to skewer some fish offal in rolled-up newspaper. Gledhill stamped his feet and clapped his hands, yelling sharply and waving his arms to scare them off. "Go! *Go!* Bloody pests!" Behind him, another fisherman directed a high-powered hose to wash down the flag stones. The gulls took to the skies.

Cushing tapped his shopping basket before walking away.

"Thank you for this. I shall enjoy it."

*
**

Fetching coal to build the fire for that coming evening, he remembered entering the same way from the garden, closing the door with his foot, finding Helen hunched on the divan looking like a frightened child. "I thought you'd left me."

"I'm not going anywhere," he'd reassured her.

She'd closed her eyes. He'd wrapped a blanket round her and made a fire, as he did now on his knees before the grate. He screwed up sheets of old newspaper in makeshift balls and laid a criss-cross pattern of kindling on top of them.

Maisie Olive had brought tea and said, "She'll be all right, sir."

He'd been smoking a cigarette. "Thank you, yes. She'll be all right."

At nine o'clock the night nurse helped Helen to bed. The last thing she said, clutching his hand, was, "Goodnight, Peter. God bless you."

At three o'clock some instinct he could not explain woke him, and he found her skin cold and clammy to his touch. He switched on the light and the electric blanket and went down to make tea. Her pupils were small dots. He fluffed up pillows and prised them behind her. When he returned with the tea, the night nurse was there saying her breathing was painful and then what breathing there was, painful or not, stopped.

The nurse looked at him and shook her head.

He looked down at Helen and saw all pain and suffering gone from her face. She was serene and at peace. The nurse must have seen his stricken features because she extended her arms, then lowered them.

At that moment Cushing had felt nothing, just a supreme hollowness inside. He'd thought, most strangely of all, *if this was in a film I wouldn't be reacting like this at all. I'd be shouting and jumping around and wailing.*

"You'd better get dressed now, Mr C," the night nurse said. He was still sitting in the armchair with the tea tray on his lap and it was daylight.

When the undertakers came, they showed him an impressively shiny catalogue of head stones. Many of them reminded him of the ones made out of polystyrene in the property shop at Bray. He'd been in a few graveyards in his time. Most of them taken apart afterwards to be reconstituted as other sets: barn, ballroom, bedroom. If only life could be dismantled, he thought, remade and reconstructed the way sets were, with a fresh lick of paint, good enough for the camera to be fooled. After looking at the brochure, he'd given the undertaker only one absolute specification for the gravestone: that there be a space left beside Helen's name for his own.

In that last year her weight had diminished drastically to under six stone, while he himself lost three. It was as if, unconsciously, he'd been keeping pace with her decline, wanting to go with her every step of the way—and beyond, if necessary.

The previous summer he had dropped out of filming Hammer's *To Love a Vampire*, the follow-up in the Sheridan Le Fanu 'Karnstein' saga (even though the part of occultist schoolmaster Giles Barton had been written for him) because Helen had become gravely ill, yet again.

"No more milk train," he'd said.

When she'd been rushed to hospital that last time and he'd been telephoned by Joyce at the studios, he was shocked how tired she looked when he arrived at her bedside. It was immediately clear this was not just a case of a few check-ups, as he'd deluded himself into thinking. He'd held her hand tightly and said to her he wasn't on call the next day and he'd bring in a picnic lunch. She smiled and said that'd be lovely. But when he'd arrived with the wicker hamper, like some character from a drawing-room farce, the nurses had told him he was not to be admitted under any circumstances. The doctors said his wife had had a serious relapse and her heart and lungs were terribly weak. He heard very little after that.

He succeeded by sheer persistence in persuading the specialists to let her home. Nobody precisely said that these coming days were her last, but their acquiescence made it obvious. Cushing shook their hands and thanked them profusely. The Polish doctor long ago had said he feared there were no miracles, and this was clearly what he meant, he knew that now. And he knew his wife would need constant medical assistance for the short, precious time she had left.

He arranged day and night care, and rang his agent to cancel his role in the *Mummy* picture they'd started shooting. He was not irreplaceable. Other people in this life were.

Now he remembered the crew sending flowers to the funeral.

As families do, of course.

He remembered, too, sitting at her bedside, tears streaming down his face. "I've made mistakes. I've done things of which I have been entirely ashamed, foolish things...Yet through it all, you have been perfect. You forgave..."

"I told you so many times, my love," Helen had said. "I never wanted you to feel I possessed you. That was our bargain, remember? What I know doesn't hurt me, so why on earth should it hurt you? It's unimportant. Those things simply didn't happen. You hear?" She'd wiped his cheeks with a corner of the bed sheet. "Not a person in the world could have done for me what you have done...But I'm tired, my darling...I can't talk now..."

In the bedroom now, all alone, he took the crucifix Helen wore from the jewellery box in front of the vanity mirror where she would put on her make-up every morning.

He placed it deep in the hip pocket of the Edwardian tweed suit made for him by Hatchard's, the outfitter in the High Street. It was where he bought most of his traditional clothes: caps, cravats, gloves. They knew what he liked there and never let him down. People didn't let him down, that was the remarkable thing in life. He remembered wearing this, his own suit, when filming *I, Monster* with Chris Lee. Now he faced another Jekyll and Hyde, another beast hiding under the mask of normality. A clash with evil in which he could only, as ever, feign expertise. Fake it. But at least with the right tools. And in a costume that felt proper for the fight.

Downstairs, the scripts and letters he had trodden over to get in still lay on the mat inside the front door. He picked them up. Clutched them to his chest. They felt full and heavy. Full of words and ideas and powerful emotions, and his chest empty.

"What if I fail?"

She was as clear in his ear as she'd ever been in life.

You shall not fail, my darling... With faith, you cannot fail...

"What faith?"

He faced the closed door to the living room.

Your faith that Goodness is stronger than Evil. It's what you believe, isn't it? You always have.

"I know. But is that enough?"

You know it will be. It must be.

He turned the handle and pushed the door ajar.

The room was in darkness as he walked through it. He placed the scripts and cards on the bureau, adding to the pile. He looked at one envelope and held it between his thumb and forefinger. He recognised the handwriting. It was a friend.

"So many friends. And yet…I feel so alone."

Darling, never fear…You are the one good thing in a dark world…and I am with you…

"Helen…"

How could he be downhearted when countless individuals led their entire lives without finding a love even a fraction as powerful as the one he had found?

He picked up her photograph and pressed it to his lips.

Square and temple-like, it had gone the way of all flesh. Now mostly a bingo hall, The Oxford in Oxford Street was a piece of faded gentrification, a mere memory of past glory, a vision of empire slowly turning to decay, a senile relative barely cared for and shamefully unloved. All those things. He remembered being told, at some official council function or other, that the original cinema opened in 1912, long before talkies, even before he was born. Rebuilt in 1936 in Art Deco style by a local architect, the regenerated Oxford's first film show was Jack Hulbert in *Jack of All Trades*. Extraordinary to contemplate, looking at it now.He trod out a cigarette on the pavement.

Behind glass, Ingrid Pitt's fearsome, fanged countenance loomed over a tombstone. *Beautiful temptress or bloodthirsty monster? She's the new horror from Hammer!* He noticed his own name amongst the other co-stars, George Cole and Kate O'Mara. Inevitably it brought back the letters of condolence he'd received from both of them. And the strangers who had done so, too. He thought it peculiar, yet immensely touching, that those who'd never even met his wife or himself personally would feel moved to make such a gesture. The foibles of the human heart were infinite, it seemed, at times. But that notion did more to give him a chill of apprehension than stiffen his nerves.

Inside, the carpet tiles were disastrously faded and the disinterested girl at the ticket booth barely old enough to be out of school. He did not need to say 'upstairs' as he used to, because the seats in the stalls had been removed for bingo tables. Upstairs were the only seats left. With a clunk the ticket poked out and he took it.

"Excuse me for asking. Are you Peter Cushing's father?"

"No, my dear. I'm his grandfather."

In what used to be the circle the house lights were up and he had no difficulty finding his way to a middle seat, halfway back. As yet he was the only one there. He took off his scarf and whipped the dust off it before sitting. It was more threadbare than when he'd come last, but he couldn't blame the owners. Trade was dwindling. The goggle box in the corner was sucking audiences away from cinemas: not that he should complain—there was a time, at the height of his success in that medium, when people joked that a television set was nothing so much as 'Peter Cushing with knobs'. But now people were becoming inert and frighteningly passive, like the drones predicted in *Nineteen Eighty-Four*, which so horrified when he starred as Winston Smith in the BBC production in the fifties that it caused a storm of outrage. Questions were raised in Parliament, no less: the remarkable power of drama to jolt and shock from complacency. Some outrage was necessary, he also considered, when picture palaces like this, almost jokily resplendent in Egyptian Dynastic glamour, were becoming as decrepit as castle ruins.

He thought again of Orwell's masterpiece and wonderful Helen standing just off-camera, her radiant smile giving him a boost of confidence to overcome his chronic nerves. What had been the play's theme? Love. And what was the ghastly phrase of the dictatorship? *Love crime*. Two words that were anathema in juxtaposition. Except, perhaps, in a court of law. Indeed, he wondered if this was his own 'Room 101' in which he had to face the very thing he feared most: love, not as something sacred, but as something unspeakably profane.

His stomach curdled—as it often did of late—and he tried to shift his musings elsewhere. To Wally the projectionist, who once proudly showed him his domain, with its two 1930s projectors that used so much oil that, when it came out the other end, he'd use it in his car.

Cushing took his coat from the seat next to him and folded it over the one in front. He was hoping the vacant seat would be occupied. Eventually, if not sooner. For now he had best try to endure the sticky smell of popcorn and Kia-Ora embedded in the surroundings.

He put on his white cotton glove and lit a cigarette. Before he'd finished it Russ Conway's *Donkey Serenade* faded and the house lights went down.

Without the pre-amble of advertisements, often the case in a matinee, sickly green lettering was cast over the rippling curtains as they creaked begrudgingly open. Mis-timed as ever.

An American International/Hammer Films Production.

Ah yes...

Jimmy ringing him in a panic saying AIP were getting cold feet because they'd cast an unknown in the lead, and a Polish girl at that. They'd already had to defend their decision to the Ministry of Labour, for God's sake: now the Americans had said they'd feel more secure with a "traditional Hammer cast". And so he'd stepped into the breach at the last minute to save Hammer's bacon. He could hardly believe that only a year ago he was filming it all on Stage Two and at Moor Park golf course, with Helen waiting for him at home, alive, when they called it a wrap.

He squinted as colour flecked the dark air and dust motes as *lugubrious Douglas Wilmer's Baron von Hartog closes the book on his family history, watching from a high window in the ruined tower of Karnstein castle as an apparition floats around the fog-swathed graveyard below. A phantasm in billowing shroud-cloth, the Evil not yet in human form...*

The words of the actor in voice-over blended with the words Cushing re-called dimly from the script. *How the creature, driven by its wretched passion, takes a form by which to attract its victims…*

How, compelled by their lust, they court their prey…

"Driven by their inhuman thirst—for blood…"

Cushing shifted in his seat. Why were cinema seats so desperately uncomfortable?

The camera tracks in towards a drunk who has staggered out of a tavern and stands urinating against a wall. His stupid face opens in a lascivious grin. Back inside the tavern, his scream chills the air and everyone freezes in horror— the way Hammer does best. The serving wench runs to the door and opens it to find the drunk with twin punctures in his neck. Lifeless, he falls…

Cushing looked at his watch. Tricky to see in the dark. The merest glint of glass. Hopeless. Hearing the screech of a sword drawn from its scabbard, he lifted his eyes back to the screen.

Douglas Wilmer waits in the chapel for the apparition to return to its grave. As his eyes widen, the camera pans to a diaphanous shroud more like a sexy Carnaby Street nightgown than anything from the nineteenth century, and the naked, voluptuous figure beneath it. The camera rises to the face of a beautiful blonde. She steps closer and wraps her arms around the frightened, mesmerised Baron. When her cleavage presses against the crucifix hanging round his neck she recoils sharply, her lips pulled back in a feral snarl. Close up: bloody fangs bared in a lustrous, female mouth. With a single swipe of his sword he decapitates her. Moments later, her severed head lies bloody on the castle flag stones at his feet. The lush music of Harry Robinson, as romantic as it is eerie, wells up over the title sequence proper…

Still the seat beside Cushing remained empty. He lit a second cigarette. By now he was wondering if he would be sitting through the film alone. Perhaps his attempt to entice the creature hadn't been as clever as he'd thought.

The pastiche Strauss made him cringe every time. He'd never been impressed by the tatty ballroom scene at the General's house. The Hammers were always done cheaply—the ingenuity and commitment of cast and crew papering over inadequate budgets— but now they were starting to *look* cheap. It worried and saddened him. Like seeing a fond acquaintance down on their uppers. Byronic

Jon Finch looked heroic enough, he had to admit. He didn't look bad himself as a matter of fact, in that scarlet tunic and medals…

The General looks on, presiding over his party. He kisses the hand of the delightful Madeline Smith, bidding her and her father, George Cole, goodbye. Or rather: "Auf wiedersehn."

Until we meet again. Obviously. The audience knows he will appear later in the picture. He's one of the stars, after all.

He watched Dawn Addams as the Countess introduce her daughter Mircalla, played with languid hunger by Ingrid Pitt—plucked from her brief appearance in *Where Eagles Dare* after Shirley Eaton (from *Goldfinger*) was deemed too old, even though they were actually the same age. Perhaps Eaton, he thought, simply hadn't given Jimmy Carreras what he wanted, as Ingrid with her European eroticism undoubtedly had. Poor Ingrid, who'd spent time with her family in a concentration camp—("concentration camp: that's true horror")—and for whom he'd organised a cake and champagne on the anniversary of her father's birth: Helen had wheeled it onto the set and Ingrid had blown out the candles with tears in her eyes.

The General, himself, asks the Countess if she would like to join in the waltz. "Enchanted," comes her reply.

"The invitation to the dance." A voice in reality: one he recognised all too well.

Without turning his head, he saw the usherette's torch hovering at the end of his row of seats. A silhouette moved closer, given a flickering penumbra by the fidgeting and then departing beam. The donkey jacket seemed almost to be bristly on the shoulders, like the pelt of some large animal, especially with the long, flesh-coloured hair running over its collar.

Eyes fixed on the screen, Cushing felt the weight of Les Gledhill settle in the cinema seat beside him. He detected the strong whiff of carbolic soap and Brut aftershave, a multi-pronged attack to cover the daily tang of blood and gutted fish.

"You missed a good part. Evil first taking human form. You can't go wrong with a bit of dry ice, I always say."

"Cleavage and crucifixes," said Gledhill. "Not exactly the RSC, is it?"

"I was never exactly Hamlet."

"A see-through negligée and fangs. How original."

"A predator is invariably seductive. To me, that rings incredibly true."

Jon Finch is waltzing with the General's niece, Laura, now and In-grid—Mircalla—is looking over at them. Laura thinks she is eyeing up her boyfriend but he says no, it's her she's looking at. A sinister man enters the ballroom dressed in a black top hat and a red-lined cloak. His face is unnaturally pale. He whispers to the Countess, who makes her apologies to the General. She has to go. Someone has died.

The General tells her, "It's my pleasure to look after your daughter, if you so wish."

"Nice uniform," said Cushing. "You can forgive a lot when you take on a part if you get to wear a nice uniform."

"Tell me. Was your wife dead when you filmed this?" Sitting beside him in the auditorium, Gledhill's face was entirely in darkness, and completely immobile. He knew the effect his words would have, and they did. He didn't care. He only cared about himself. "Why are we here? What do you plan to do anyway? Tear down the curtains and let in the light?"

"I thought you didn't watch my films."

"They're okay for a cheap laugh, I suppose. All they're good for nowadays." *Peter Cushing says goodbye to the Countess and watches her depart in her coach. Ingrid stares out. The pale, cloaked man on horseback in the woods gives a malevolent grin, showing pointed fangs.* "Things have moved on, haven't you noticed? Blood and gore, all the rest of it. Nobody's scared of bats and castles and bolts through the neck."

"I think you'll find..." But it wasn't worth pointing out his mistake.

Mircalla fondly places a laurel on the General's niece's head. Puts a friendly arm round the young girl's bare shoulders.

"Nobody's afraid of you anymore."

"You'd be surprised. I still have a small but devoted following."

"Oh, yeah. We can hardly move for your adoring fans." They were, of course, the only people in the cinema.

"You've got to remember this film's already been released for five months. This is a small town. And it's a matinee. In fact you'll find it's been a box office hit. So much so that it's rejuvenated the company."

"You're living an illusion, mate. These old films are on their last legs. Everyone sees them as comedies now. You need to get a grip on reality, old feller—before you lose it completely. Choc ice?"

Cushing imagined it was not a serious inquiry.

"Please yourself. Hey, this is getting a bit racy, look. Two girls showing all they've got. Bit of French kissing. Bit like a porn film, this is..."

Peter Cushing's beautiful niece is sleeping now. Swooning in some kind of 'wet dream'—if that was the expression. He remembered that this was one of the many scenes that Trevelyan and Audrey Field, who had been campaigning against Hammer for decades, were unhappy about, even with an 'X' certificate. The censor had strongly urged the producers to keep the film "within reasonable grounds"— meaning the combination of blood and nudity, the very thing Carreras was gleeful about now they'd entered the seventies ("The gloves are off! We can show anything!"). *In monochrome a hideous creature crawls up the bed. Wolf-like eyes out of blackness become Ingrid Pitt's— Mircalla's.* To Cushing the girl looks as though she has a bearskin rug crawling over her. Nevertheless, the dream orgasm so worrisome to the BBFC is curtailed with her scream.

"Nice tits, mind. Nothing against nice tits."

Cushing cringed involuntarily. "Please. We both know why we're here."

"We do," Gledhill said in the gloom "We're here because you went and saw the bitch."

"Please. Dear God. Afford your wife a modicum of respect, even if—"

"Like you did with these actresses, baring their all? How much 'respect'—"

"I didn't come here to talk about me, or my films."

"No, I bet you didn't. What did she say, anyway? Bloody liar that the cow is."

"There seem to be an extraordinary number of liars in your life, Mr Gledhill."

Peter Cushing and an elderly housekeeper run in and calm Laura down. They say it was a nightmare, that's all. He kisses her forehead and they leave the room. They think of checking on Mircalla, but when they knock there is no answer. They presume she's sleeping. But the bedroom is empty. Ingrid Pitt is outside under moonlight looking up at the window...

"I thought she seemed perfectly charming," Cushing said, his eyes not straying from the screen. He pretended that it absorbed his attention. "Another woman with another boy who perhaps doesn't dream of vampires, like Carl, but of another kind of...creature of the night."

His companion remained silent. He found it uncommonly difficult to deliver the lines he'd prepared in his head.

"She told me you'd invariably take him off to bed, rather than her. That you'd spend time reading him stories, as a doting father should. Quite rightly. Your, ah, 'special time' you called it, I believe...I wonder what your son might call it?"

"Now you are starting to annoy me, old man."

"I'm rather glad about that."

The Doctor, played by reliable old Ferdy Mayne, tells Peter Cushing that his niece just needs some iron to improve her blood. Cut to Ingrid Pitt at the girl's bedside. Laura tells her she doesn't want her to leave. Ingrid lowers her head and touches her lips to the girl's breast...

"What are you planning? A parade of peasants with flaming torches, perhaps, to storm up to the Transylvanian castle, beating at the gates?"

Peter Cushing tells a visiting Jon Finch that his niece doesn't want to see anyone but Mircalla.

For a moment Cushing was taken aback by his own close-up. In spite of the make-up he looked tremendously ill. Of course he knew the reason. It was the toll of Helen's illness, even then. He could see the strain in his eyes. But it was a shock to see it now, thirty feet across, vast, on display for the entire public to see. He'd been oblivious to it at the time. He'd had other preoccupations. Now it hit him like a blow and it took a second for him to steady his nerve, as he knew he must.

"You think you're safe because you consider everyone to be as selfish and self-interested as yourself." Cushing did not look at the other man as he lit another cigarette. A scream rang out: the General's niece, after another nocturnal visitation. "You really are unable to contemplate that someone might act totally for the benefit of another human being, even though they themselves might suffer. And that's where you're misguided, and wrong. That's precisely your undoing, you see."

"Oh. You obviously know me better than I know myself."

"We shall see if I do."

"*Shall* we?" Mocking even his language now.

Peter Cushing's niece moans Mircalla's name in her delirium. He holds her hand. When Mircalla is discovered not in her room, he barks angrily at the maid to find her. Ingrid Pitt glides in, nonplussed, saying she couldn't sleep and went to the chapel to pray. She tells him bluntly—cruelly—that his niece is dead.

Cushing blew smoke and watched the horror ravaging his own face on celluloid, vividly reliving playing the scene, having to play it by imagining the devastating loss of one you love, and hating himself afterwards for doing so.

He cries out the name of "Laura! Laura!" Jon Finch rushes into the room with Ferdy Mayne, but no sooner has the stethoscope been pressed to her bare chest than the Doctor sees the tell-tale bite mark, accompanied by a glissando of violins…

"Consider this," Cushing said. "If I talk to the police, yes, they might think I'm a crazy old man, they might think I'm guilty—that is a matter of supreme indifference to me, I assure you. But because of my so-called fame as an actor, *your* name will be in the *News of the World*, too, whether you like it or not. Before long the disreputable hacks will be rooting round in *your* past, talking to *your* wife, *your* past girlfriends, *your* other—yes, I'll say it—victims. And if some of them, if only one of them speaks…Annie…Carl…Sue…Your son…And I think they will. I think they'll *need* to…irrespective of what happens to me, you'll be seen for what you are." *The General's keening cries echo plaintively through the house, the camera pans across the graveyard of the Karnsteins…* "And Carl's mother will know exactly what kind of man she is intending to marry."

A peasant girl walks through the woods. She hears a cry. It's only a bird, but it spooks her. She runs. The camera pursues her like a predator through the trees. She drops her basket of apples.

"And have you thought about what *I'm* going to be saying about *you?*" Gledhill said.

"You're not listening to me. I said I don't care."

The peasant girl trips, falls—rolls through bracken and thorns—screams, as a woman's body descends over her...

"Don't you? What about *your* name? Your good name: 'Peter Cushing'." If Gledhill smiled, the man next to him was happy not to see it. "Up there on a thousand posters. Like the one out in the foyer. Your name—'Peter Cushing'—rolling up at the end of hundreds of movies. 'Peter Cushing'—the name you fought for so long to *mean* something, to be *worth* something—turned into dirt. A name nobody'll say out loud any more, except with disgust."

"My name is unimportant." The old man did not tremble or take his eyes from the images projected by the beam of light passing over his head. He would not be wounded. He would not be harmed.

"Oh?" Gledhill turned his head to him. "Then what about your *wife's* name, dear boy? Because it's *her* name too, since you married her. 'Helen Cushing.' Are you going to be happy to see *her* name dragged through the filth? Because it will be. I'll make sure it will."

Cushing tried not to make his tension visible.

The gong sounds for dinner and Ingrid—Carmilla now—and Madeline Smith descend the staircase of George Cole's home in striking blue and red, Madeline looking coy and slightly embarrassed about what's just gone on in the bedroom.

"You can't hurt her, and you can't hurt me," he said. "It's impossible. You see, she knows I'm here, and she's with me, even now."

"Oh dear..." Gledhill laughed in the cinema dark. "I think you're going a little bit mad, Peter Cushing. I think all those horror films have done something to your mind. Made you see horror everywhere."

The monochrome dream comes again, and this time it is Madeline Smith doing the screaming. Kate O'Mara, the governess, comes in. Another dream of cats. Or a real cat? "The trouble with this part of the world is they have too many fairy tales."

"Horror isn't everywhere," Cushing said. "But horror is some-where, every day."

"*You* might believe that."

The man was trying to imply that there would be forces of doubt, powerful forces, to face in the battle ahead. Cushing knew full well there might be—but was undeterred.

"I do. Unmistakably. And you think you have power. You think you're all-powerful, but you have no power at all, because you have to feel powerful by attacking little mites who can't fight back. You take their souls for one reason and one reason alone—because you can. And now you're frightened. I can tell. Even in the gloom of this cinema. Good. Excellent." Cushing smiled. "It's my job to frighten people. You could say I've made a career of it."

A shadow hand creeps along a wall. The peasant-girl's mouth opens for a scream but no scream comes. Cut to the exterior of the hovel—then it does. The mother finds her daughter lolling from her bed with two red holes in her neck. Cut to Carmilla—Ingrid Pitt—floating through the graveyard, her voluptuousness under the Carnaby Street negligée…

"Do you want me to suck you off? Eh?" Gledhill said.

Cushing could sense his own breathing like a hot whirlwind. Could feel the creaking rise and fall of his chest and hear the beat of his heart, everything about his body telling him to scream, but his brain telling him to remain calm.

"Or a nice stiff cock up the arse? Uh? Come on. Actor. Cravat. All the rest of it. Well-mannered. Cultured. I know the type a mile off. It's written all over you."

But this actor found, to his great surprise, he could not be offended. The splenetic assault was as ludicrous as it was desperate, and, strangely, it had the opposite effect to the one intended. The very force of the invective meant his enemy was on the ropes, and it made him feel—empowered.

"Are you trying to disgust me?"

"I *know* I disgust you," Gledhill snarled.

"Well you're wrong. You sadden me. More than you can possibly know."

"You think you're a wise old *cunt*, don't you? But really you just want to *fuck* someone, or something, find the nearest convenient hole, just like the rest of the human race. You look down on me from on high, but you're in the swamp with the rest of us."

Cushing was astonished that the bad language didn't hurt him any more. He was quite impervious to it.

"I've never thought myself greater or lesser than any human being. And I've never judged you," he said. "My only concern is the boy."

He felt Gledhill's arm snake round his shoulders like that of an eager lover and curve round his neck to the side nearest him, then a coldness in the air and something icy and sharp pressed to his throat, right next to his jugular vein. He knew instantly it was the stubby blade of the oyster knife.

"What if this sad old actor, full of grief, decided to end it all, eh? What if he topped himself, all alone, in a cinema, after watching one of his own, sad, rubbish films? Sat there and slit his throat from ear to ear? Or is that too much blood? Even for an 'X'? Never get that past the *fucking* censor, would we, *dear boy?*"

The cold of the knife seemed to spread through Cushing's body. He felt it numbing him inch by inch but remained still and becalmed.

"You forget one important thing, though."

"Shut up."

"You made yourself known, didn't you?"

"Shut up!"

"To the police. I'm simply pointing out your mistake. You made it plain you had a grudge against me. You think they'll forget that conversation? Of course they won't. They'll—"

"You think I care? I don't care about anything."

"You care about your downfall, surely?"

"Shut…!"

Cushing's eyes were fixed on the screen. Unblinking.

"They embrace, and she dies. The young girl dies…When did you die?" Not even the slightest quaver in his voice, now. "In your heart, I mean?"

Madeline Smith and Ingrid Pitt are sitting in the shade because Ingrid finds the sunshine hurts her eyes. They watch the peasant-girl's funeral moving sedately through the woods, the priest intoning the Agnus Dei...

Agnus Dei, qui tollis peccata mundi, miserere nobis.

Agnus Dei, qui tollis peccata mundi, miserere nobis.

Agnus Dei, qui tollis peccata mundi, dona nobis pacem...

Full of rage and sadness, Ingrid hisses that she hates funerals. Madeline says the girl was so young. The village has had so much tragedy lately. Ingrid begs her to hold her. They embrace...

"She's only too happy to do what the older one asks," said Gledhill.

"She is not herself. She's infected." The knife tip dug into his skin, a slight rasp against the stubble, loud in his ear.

"What if she's like that, deep down in her nature, and the other one has just awakened her to what she really is? Set her free?"

"That's probably exactly what a vampire might argue. But no-one becomes a monster willingly." The knife against his jugular did not move, but he felt it tremble.

Both men's eyes were glued unwillingly to the screen.

That night Madeline begs Ingrid not to leave her room. She never feels tired at night any more, only excited, she says. But so wretched during the day. She hasn't told anyone. Not everything. She can't. How the cat comes onto her bed. How she tries to scream as it stretches across her, warm and heavy. How she feels its fur in her mouth...

Both men stared.

Madeline Smith says it's like the life running out of her, blood being drawn, then she wakes, screaming. Ingrid Pitt unties the girl's nightdress—poor Madeline told by the producer it was for the Japanese version, but there was no Japanese version—*and Ingrid pushes her back against the plump pillow. Her mouth is on the young girl's throat, then slides down to her young breasts. In close-up, Madeline's pretty eyes*—poor child, Cushing remembered, a virgin, didn't know what lesbians were—*roll wide in simulated rapture...*

"How were you bitten? Infected?"

Gledhill pressed the blade harder, making the old man's head shy away. "Life. Life made me like this."

Cushing could not be sure whether he detected glee, sarcasm or resignation. "Others need not be hurt. The very ones who—"

"You think *I* haven't been hurt?" Gledhill spat through locked teeth. "I've been hurt in ways you can't even *fucking* imagine."

"That's what made you what you are." Cushing tried not to think of the knife any more, or the threats, or the obscenities. "You know that. And you know deep down the boy must suffer, because you suffered."

"Jesus Christ."

"Who was it?"

"Jesus *fucking* Christ…"

Gledhill snatched the oyster knife away from the old man's throat, straightening his arm, then plunging it dagger-like into the soft upholstery of the seat under him, between his legs, sinking it in deep, then slicing it across. The dramatic surges of the soundtrack seemed to accompany his action, and when he was finished he hunched forward, the oyster knife gripped in both fists, his forehead resting on the seat in front of him.

"Who?"

"Leave me. Just go, will you?"

"I hate to disappoint you, but I'm not going anywhere."

"I hate to disappoint you, but you can *fuck off.*"

"I'm quite aware I can."

"Why the *fuck* don't you, then?"

Peter Cushing prised open the other man's fingers and gently took the knife from him.

"Who?"

The pale man from the General's party appears. The cadaverous man in the red-lined cape stands in silhouette in the woods as if bearing witness to Gledhill's words.

Gledhill's whole body was shaking.

"Someone who said he loved me. Someone who twisted me round his little finger." He sniffed. A mocking musicality came to his voice, lifting it, lightening it: a delusion. "I fell for his charms, you could say." He seemed fearful the bitterness in his words evoked no sympathy. "I have feelings too, see. Did have. Till he fucking ripped them out of me. Why the fuck am I telling you this?"

Madeline cries out. The house is in darkness. Kate O'Mara, the governess, runs in.

"Because confession is good for the soul," Cushing said.

A wettish snort, not even a snigger, in reply. "Bless me Father, for I have sinned. You'd make a good priest."

"I have done. Though he was a smuggler on the side. Captain Clegg. Doctor Syn. The Scarecrow."

"And did he get punished for his secret life?"

"The burden of secrecy is a punishment in itself. If you repent, as the Lord teaches, all is not lost."

Gledhill laughed, bitterly and hopelessly.

Outside the door the two women look at each other knowingly. Kate goes into Carmilla's bedroom and turns down the lamp. In darkness Ingrid slips out of her dress. The moonlight outlines her naked form. Kate moves closer.

"Tell the police. Surely nothing can be worse than the Hell you're enduring now. Do it. I beg you. For the sake of your immortal soul."

"Soul?" Now the sound through Gledhill's nose was more weary than dismissive.

"Which God holds precious, even if you don't."

"I can't. How can I?" Gledhill sat up straight again in the cinema seat and shook his head. "The boy…Carl…What would he think of me?"

"Dear God, man." Peter Cushing could not disguise his bewilderment. "What do you imagine he thinks of you *now?*"

The blurry vision of Carmilla enters Madeline's room. The vampire appears to be comforting her in her sickness. The young girl wonders if she'll live until her father comes home…

"He loves me," Gledhill said. "I know he does, because he shows it. I never have to force him. He never says no. What I want, he wants. He always has. He led the way. I followed. Don't you think I…?"

The Doctor arrives saying Mr Morton asked him to look in on his daughter. Kate O'Mara tells him Madeline has been ill, but it's nothing to concern him.

"God…You know what they do in prison to people like me?"

Garlic flowers. Their antiseptic scent. Village gossip. The Doctor puts a cross round Madeline's neck.

"Sometimes…" Gledhill struggled to complete the sentence he had in mind. "Sometimes I…" He failed a second time.

Ingrid returns to the daughter's room. She sees the garlic flowers and crucifix and backs out fearfully.

The two men sat in silence facing the screen.

The Doctor rides through the woods, against unconvincing back-projection. His horse suddenly shies and he is thrown. Carmilla comes round the edge of the lake towards him. In a flurry of autumn leaves she wrestles with him and sinks her fangs into his neck.

Neither Gledhill nor Cushing spoke. It was almost as though they had come to watch a horror film, and nothing more.

George Cole rides for the Doctor, but runs into a coach carrying not only Peter Cushing but also Douglas Wilmer—somewhat aged by make-up since the decapitation prologue—a man the General says he has travelled miles to find. To George Cole's horror the dead body of the Doctor is on the back of the vehicle. Peter Cushing says: "Now I can tell you, and leave us if you wish. Our destination is Karnstein castle."

"What can I do? What do you want me to do?" Gledhill said.

"Me?"

Gledhill nodded.

The great chords crash. The coach pulls up at their destination. Douglas Wilmer holds a lamp aloft.

"First and foremost, I don't want anything to hurt Carl further, in any way. Bringing in the police and the courts will most surely do that. Horribly. But rest assured, I shall do that if you leave me no alternative."

"Tell me what to do. Please," Gledhill repeated.

Cushing said what had been in his heart all along, and begged that some sliver of humanity inside the man still might grasp the simplicity of it:

"Do what is right and good, for once."

"Good?"

Said more in genuine puzzlement than disdain.

"Vampires are intelligent beings, General. They know when the forces of good are arrayed against them."

"Save yourself, in the only way you can. Disappear. Take a leaf out from Count Dracula's book in the final reel. Turn to dust."

Carmilla is dragging Madeline down the stairs. She needs to take her with her. Kate O'Mara pleads with Ingrid Pitt to take her too. Ingrid sinks her teeth in Kate's neck. Madeline screams. Jon Finch leaps off his horse and bursts in. Ingrid sweeps his sword out of his hand and grabs him but he grabs a dagger tucked in his boot and holds it up in the shape of a cross. Ingrid backs away from it. He throws the knife. It passes right through her. Double exposure. She fades and is gone.

In the Karnstein graveyard the vampire hunters see the figure of Carmilla entering the ruins. They follow, led by Douglas Wilmer's lantern. The long cobwebby table is a nod to the first Hammer Dracula, *perhaps. One of them finds a necklace on the floor. Peter Cushing looks up. They've found the vampire's resting place.*

They lift the stone slab from the floor. Peter Cushing and George Cole carry the coffin into the chapel. Wearing black gloves, Peter Cushing rolls back the shroud. "I will do it." He takes off the gloves. George Cole kneels at the altar and prays. Peter Cushing takes the stake. Raises it in both hands. Thrusts it down into and through her chest. Back at the house, her victim cries out. Ingrid Pitt's eyes flash open, then close, as blood pools on her chest. It is over. But not over.

Peter Cushing says, "There's no other way."

He draws his sword. With it firmly in one hand, he lifts Ingrid Pitt up by the hair in her coffin. Cuts off her head in one swipe.

As George Cole utters a heartfelt prayer that their country is rid of such devils, Peter Cushing's General lowers the severed head into the coffin. And Carmilla's portrait on the castle wall, young and beautiful as she was long ago—in life—turns slowly to that of a decomposed and rotting skull.

Cushing turned his head and found the seat next to him empty. As the cast list rolled up the screen, he stood and looked round an auditorium lit only by the spill from the projector beam. He shielded his eyes with the flat of his hand but it was clear nobody was present but himself.

He was still standing facing the small, square window of the projection room when the house lights faded up. He found himself even more clearly in a sea of empty seats. The smell of popcorn and Kia-Ora returned. This time he found it almost pleasant.

He walked into the sunlit foyer with one arm in his coat sleeve. A number of young couples were queuing for tickets for the next performance. One person noticed him and smiled. He raised a hand, not too ostentatiously, not wanting to draw attention to himself, then criss-crossed his scarf on his chest and dragged on the rest of his coat. Another few people arrived. Quite a healthy gathering for an early evening showing. He was pleased, in a subdued way, as if one of his children had done well at school, with little help from himself. The film *was* a hit, and as long as the public liked it, he wished it well.

He let the heavy door shut behind him. Even more than usually when he had seen a film in the afternoon, the sunlight came as a shock. It almost blinded him, but he was grateful for the warmth on his skin. He raised his chin and stood with his eyes closed for several minutes, and when he opened them, found it noticeably strange that there was not a single gull in the sky.

Ten minutes later he committed the oyster knife to the sea with a throw worthy of a fielder at the Oval.

When he arrived home at 3 Seaway Cottages he felt Helen's smile in the air immediately, like the most delicate and distinctive fragrance. "Look." He lifted his hand up in front of his face. "I'm still shaking."

You were wonderful.

"Nonsense."

You are *wonderful, Peter.*

He felt a strange fluttering at the back of his throat and looked at the door to the living room but didn't open it.

"So are you, my love."

Suddenly he found he was ravenously hungry for the first time since he didn't know when.

In the kitchen he took two slices of bread and cooked cheese on toast under the grill, served with a generous dollop of HP sauce. His appetite undiminished, he made two more rounds, slightly burned, just the way he liked it.

That night he slept soundly, and without dreams.

He was woken early the following morning by the telephone ringing as if on a distant shore. He sat up in bed, body lifted as if by a crane, not particularly hurrying to do so. Recent events still had not returned fully to his consciousness. Images drifted. Feelings coagulated, some real, some imagined, all vague and irrepressible. His head was too thick with slumber to sort fact from fiction and he wondered if he was waking up or acting waking up. He needed a minute to think about that, if you'd be so kind. The telephone, impolitely, was still ringing with a persistence normally reserved for insects and small children. He slumped back onto the pillow, hoping to return to the land of Nod. The telephone had other ideas. When it started to ring the third time he could ignore it no longer. He picked up the receiver, rubbing sleep from his eyes with his other hand. He recited the number, automatically.

"Peter?" A man's voice.

"Yes?"

"Did I wake you?" It was Derek Wake. Appropriately named, in this instance.

"No. Not at all." He was about to add that he'd answered because he thought it was perhaps Joyce ringing, but the inspector interrupted his thoughts.

"I'm sorry, Peter—but I thought I'd better ring before you hear this on the jungle telegraph. I thought you might want to know. Les

Gledhill died in a car accident last night, on the stretch of the M2 between Faversham and the junction with the A249 near Sittingbourne. There doesn't appear to have been any other vehicle involved, and there was no-one else in the car at the time." Having said this quickly without pausing, he suddenly stopped.

Cushing felt the silence looming and wished his head was clearer. An element of him wondered if he was still asleep. Meanwhile he heard the detective's voice fill the gap with more words:

"His car left the carriageway. It was a head-on collision. He hit the central reservation, the barrier, span across into the hard shoulder. Complete write-off. As I say, no other vehicle was involved...Peter?"

"Yes. I'm here."

He was awake now. Fully. But he did not know what to say.

He wondered if the policeman would ask him next why he was in conflict with Gledhill over some issue concerning his son, and probe more fully why exactly Gledhill had made accusations against him. If he might resurrect the questions he himself had asked during his visit to the station concerning a film story about child molestation. A film which, when examined more closely, would be seen to be a complete fabrication.

But Wake asked none of these things.

"He was dead on arrival at Canterbury Hospital. Died instantly. Appears to have been driving at very high speed, from the tyre marks. No witnesses. Whether he lost control for some reason, or did it on purpose, we don't know. These things happen. You don't often see them coming. Those close to the deceased, I mean..."

Disappear. Turn to dust...

What he'd meant was, go. Leave town. Go away. Not this. Then he remembered:

What do you want me to do?

Do what is right and good, for once.

Good?

Save yourself, in the only way you can.

Dear Lord...

Was Gledhill in his final moments thinking of his immortal soul?

Had he simply decided to do something good, for once, as he'd been bidden, for someone other than himself? Or was suicide just what it often was, as Peter Cushing knew all too well, the act of a coward? A weak man's only escape from an unbearable future?

"Peter?"

He rubbed his eyes again. The room wasn't focusing, so he kept them shut. He was aware that the other man could hear his breathing down the telephone and was waiting for him to reply, so he spoke in as steady a voice as he could muster.

"Derek, can I ask you something, please?" he said with his eyes still closed. "This is very important to me. I can't tell you why, but it is."

The hospital, the car park, the very sight of the building itself inevitably brought back memories of Helen, and he was ready for that. Mercifully, she hadn't passed away there, but during her long illness visits were all too frequent, and each time accompanied by a sense of immense dread, of what might be discovered, of what one, this time, might be told. He was surprised, then, that no such feelings asserted themselves. On the contrary, he felt calm, in fact unusually so. Plainly there was a world of difference between visiting the love of your life and—this.Naturally Wake had questioned why he wanted to do it, and Cushing wondered how many other questions the policeman kept to himself, and for how long he would continue to do so. But in reply to the man's enquiries—clearly worried at a widower seeing a dead body so recently after the death of his wife—he could only reply honestly that he felt nothing.

"Peter, are you sure you're up to this? These places are cold and clinical at the best of times. They breathe death."

"Death holds no fears for me. Quite the contrary."

"Even so, coming here, of all places…"

"I assure you, dear boy. I'm perfectly fine."

As they walked along the antiseptic-smelling corridor Wake

explained that the sister's expression 'Rose Cottage' was the euphemism often used by nursing staff when talking about the hospital mortuary. As they approached it Cushing thought of the roses he tended in his own garden, round his own front door. The roses Helen loved. He pictured himself snipping one off and handing it to her, as he did, on many an occasion. How she'd invariably reward him with a kiss on the cheek.

They'd done their best to take the curse off the viewing room, of course, but it was still a hospital room badly playing the part of a Chapel of Rest. They almost needn't have bothered. As the door opened it had the feel of a shrunken and poverty-stricken church hall. The floor was the same slightly-peeling linoleum as the corridor, the walls insalubrious teak, with cheap beading intended to simulate panelling, and curtains on one wall a deep navy blue, the only colour.

He'd had it explained to him that the post-mortem had been done and the body was now being stored there—presumably in one of those pull-out fridges—until the undertakers collected it. He removed his hat and stepped closer to the bed, bier, table, whatever it was called. He was all too aware that the actions he was going through were normally the province of the close family, even though Wake had told him Carl's mother had no desire to see the body of her boyfriend. Accordingly, in spite of all he knew about the dead man, he felt he should behave with respect.

At a nod from Wake, who remained at the door, the assistant moved forward and folded down the white sheet covering the face so that the head and shoulders were exposed. Cushing noticed the clean, fastidiously manicured hands before the man stood back.

In death, they say, we are all equal, he thought.

He looked down and saw that a white linen cravat was tucked round the corpse's neck. He reached over and touched its rim with his fingertips. The attendant took a step forward and was about to speak, but Wake raised his hand. The man stepped back.

Tugged down, the elastic of the linen cravat revealed a livid scar running round the circumference of Gledhill's neck, the twine stitches, heavy and harsh, still abundantly visible. Frankenstein stitches. Holes dug deep with thick needles like fish hooks into dead, unfeeling flesh.

"Impact would have killed him outright," Wake said. "The front of the car was like a concertina. Steering column went straight through his chest. He had no chance."

Cushing pictured himself as General Spielsdorf again, holding the stake over Carmilla's heart and shoving it down with every ounce of his strength. Blood pumping up, filling the cavity as her wild eyes stared in perplexed fury.

"Cigarette?"

Cushing shook his head. Wake lit one of his own and blew smoke. It drifted in front of Gledhill's cadaver like the mist in Karnstein castle graveyard.

"As if that wasn't enough, he was decapitated too. The force of the crash sent him right into the windscreen. They found his head thirty yards down the hard shoulder. Apparently it's not uncommon. Tell you what. I'd never be a motorway cop for all the tea in China."

Cushing saw himself lifting up the body of Ingrid Pitt by the hair. The silvery flash of his sword as it sliced through her throat.

"Done a decent job, mind."

He wasn't sure what the inspector meant.

"After a real old mess like that. I mean…he looks at peace."

"Yes," Cushing said, gazing back at the figure on the bed and readjusting the white cravat to its former position. "I think he does."

He didn't know if it was the effect of chemicals used by the pathologist or the fluorescent lighting, but the man seemed years younger, as if, absurdly, all the sins had been lifted off him. His skin unblemished, his hair neatly combed as if by an insistent mother. He wondered what was strange and then realised that, for some mysterious reason, his beard had been shaved off. He seemed, in fact, strangely like a child.

Cushing looked at the crucifix on the wall opposite—the room's only concession to decoration—and found himself, in an almost imperceptible gesture, making the sign of the cross over his own heart as he turned away.

As he reached the door he heard Wake's voice behind him.

"So…have you got what you want?"

"Mm?"

He turned back. The assistant was covering Gledhill's face with the sheet, and Wake was standing beside him, ash gathering on his cigarette as he sucked it.

"For your research? For the film you're making?"

"Yes." Cushing tweaked the front of his trilby between thumb and forefinger before placing it on his head. "Yes, I have."

*
**

On the way home many thoughts went through his mind, but the one he was left with as he opened the front door was that, earlier, that morning, as his hand had picked up the receiver, he had wanted it to be Joycie at the other end of the line. Much as he feared talking to her, it was a fear he had to face—no, *wanted* to face, and that evening after a supper of Heinz tomato soup he decided to take matters into his own hands, and ring her himself. He was absolutely sure it was what Helen would want him to do. No, what she would *expect* of him. Because it was right.No sooner had he said her name, "Joycie", than they both wept.

Without hesitation he asked her to come back. Equally without hesitation, she agreed.

"I'm so sorry if I've been rude or inconsiderate…"

"No, sir. You've never been that. Never." He could hear her blowing her nose in a tissue. Soon he found himself doing the same.

"What a pair we are," he said. "Dear oh dear. I shall have to get more Kleenex tomorrow, shan't I? I think I need to order a truck-load."

She laughed, but it was tinged with the same kind of enfeebled anguish as his own. He wondered, as he often did, if he would hear his own laughter, proper laughter, that is, ever again.

"You see, Joycie, everywhere I see reminders of her. I can't help it. This room. Every room. Every street I walk. Every person I meet. It's simply unbearable, you see…"

"I know, sir."

"Do you forgive me?" he said.

And, before she could form an answer, they wept again, till the tissues ran out.

*
**

Facing the sea he heard the tick-tick-tick of the wheels of a pushbike approaching. His was an old black Triumph from Herbert's Cycles tending towards rust, with a shopping basket at the front, tethered to a bollard like an old and recalcitrant mare. The other, soon leaning against it, was one of these Raleigh 'Chopper' things (not hard to deduce as the word was emblazoned loudly on the frame) in virulent orange, with handlebars that swept up and back and an L-shaped reclining saddle like something out of *Easy Rider*. The boy, sitting next to him and finishing a sherbet fountain through a glistening pipe of liquorice, said nothing for a while in the accompaniment of sea birds, then, when seemed remotely fitting, pronounced that the vehicle on display was a Mark 1 and had ten speeds. Cushing pointed with a crooked finger and said there was no attachment for a lamp, and the boy said he knew, and they were made like that. He said it was called a Chopper, which Cushing already knew but pretended he didn't and repeated the word, as if the emblazonment had been invisible. But the object was new and gleaming and admirable, and dispensing some wisdom since he could, he advised the boy to look after it. Possibly the boy looked at the scuffed, worn, weary Triumph and thought that was like an elephant telling a gazelle to lose weight. But he'd been brought up by his mother not to be cheeky to his elders, not that that worried him a great deal when it was called for, but on this occasion he chose to hold his tongue and nodded, meaning he would look after it. Of course he would. He wanted it to look new and gleaming forever.

When the sherbet was finished the boy walked to the rubbish bin and dropped it in. When he sat back down he chewed the remains of the liquorice the way a yokel might chew a straw, moving it from one side of his mouth to the other along slightly-blackened lips.

"You look younger."

Cushing had almost forgotten he'd shaved for the first time in weeks. He rubbed his chin. Dr Terror's salt and pepper was gone.

"I have a painting in the attic."

"What does that mean?"

"Never mind. You'll find out when you're a bit older."

The boy frowned. "I hate it when grown-ups say that."

"So do I. Very much so. I apologise. Unreservedly."

"That's okay."

He looked at the boy and beckoned him closer. He took out a handkerchief and rolled it round his index finger. "Spit on it." Without considering the consequence, the boy did, trustingly, and Cushing used it to rub the liquorice stains from his lips while the boy's face scrunched up, an echo, the old man thought, of the infant he once was.

"How's your mum?" He folded the handkerchief away.

The reply was a shrug. "She cried a bit. She cried a lot, actually. I didn't." A show of resilience, sometimes stronger in the young. The show of it, anyway.

"That's very brave of you."

"But I felt sorry for her. She's my mum."

"Naturally."

Cushing did not enquire further. Out at sea beyond the Isle of Sheppey, a cloud of gannets hovered halo-like over a fishing vessel.

"They say it was an accident," the boy said presently, with a secretive ex-citement in his voice. "But it wasn't an accident, was it? It was you."

"It doesn't matter. It happened. He's gone now. It's over."

"I know you can't say because it's secret, but it *was* you, wasn't it? Acting on my behalf—Van Helsing, the great Vampire Hunter? I knew you would, in my hour of need. I knew you wouldn't let me down."

Cushing tugged on his white cotton glove and pulled down each finger in turn, then lit a cigarette and smoked it, eyes slitting.

"How do you feel now? That's the important thing."

The boy wondered about that as if he hadn't wondered about it until that very moment.

"It's really weird. I feel a bit sad. I feel a bit like it's my fault, because I asked you. I know he was evil and that. I know that—and I know he deserved it and everything…"

"It wasn't your fault, Carl." Would he ever truly believe that? "Look at me, Carl. Please." The boy faced the old man's pale blue, unblinking eyes and the old man took his hand. "When they choose people as a victim, it's not the victim's fault. It's their fault. You've got to remember that." Peter Cushing knew that now more than ever he needed to keep a steady gaze. "I'm the world expert, remember?"

The boy nodded and took his hand back.

"No need to show off."

Cushing trembled a smile and looked back to sea.

Periodically flicking his ash to be taken by the breeze, he gazed down between the groynes and saw a man in his twenties wearing a cheesecloth shirt and canvas loons rolled up to just under the knee and curly hair bobbing as he ran in and out of the icy surf. A dollishly small girl with a bucket and spade was laughing at him and he chased her and scooped her up in his arms, turning her upside down.

"She doesn't like me saying it but I keep thinking about my real dad. My old dad," the boy said, prodding a discarded Wrigley's chewing gum wrapper with his shoe. "I keep thinking perhaps he'll get tired of his new woman in Margate and come back to us. One day, anyway. I know he said he didn't love my mum any more, but he must have loved her once, mustn't he? So he might love her again. You never know. How does love work, anyway?"

Cushing could hear no voices, but saw a woman join the man and the toddler on the shingle. The wind tossed the woman's blonde hair over her face and the man combed it back with his fingers and kissed her.

"It's very complicated, as you'll learn as you grow up, my friend. Very complicated—but in the end so terribly simple." He felt a tiny piece of grit in his eye and rubbed it with a finger. The taste of the tobacco had gone sour and he prodded the cigarette out on the sea wall.

"Do you have bad dreams any more? You see, I have to check the symptoms, just in case. Are you sleeping well?"

The boy nodded, staring at the ground.

"Good. Very good." The old man took off his glove, white finger by white finger. Carl was still staring at the concrete in front of him. "Remember if anything feels bad…if you are hurting…or worried… Anything you want to say—anything, you can say to your mother."

"She won't understand," the boy said without looking up, as a simple statement of fact. "She doesn't understand monsters."

The people on the beach were gone and the waves were coming in, filling their footsteps. Sometimes it seemed full of footprints, criss-crossing this way and that, people, dogs, all on their little journeys, but if you waited long enough or came back the next day the people were always gone and the only consistent thing was the slope and evenness of the shore.

When Cushing put his single white glove back in his overcoat pocket he discovered something he'd forgotten. Something he'd put there before going to the Oxford to meet Gledhill. He took it out and looked at it in the palm of his hand.

Helen's crucifix.

Opening the thin gold chain into a circle he put it round the boy's neck and tucked the cross behind his scarf and inside his open-topped shirt. The boy did not move as the man did it, and did not move afterwards, imagining some necessity for respect or obedience in the matter, or recognising some similarity to the procedure of his mum straightening his tie, in addition daunted perhaps by the peculiarity of the tiny coldness of the crucifix against the warmth of his hairless chest.

"I want you to remember what I'm going to say to you. The love of the Lord is quite, quite infinite. In your darkest despair, though you may not think it, He is still looking over you. Never, ever forget that."

The boy thought a moment.

"Is he looking over *you?*"

Cushing had not expected that question, and found himself answering, as something of a surprise:

"Yes. Yes, I believe he is."

Then the boy appeared to remember something, something important, and dug into the pocket of his anorak. He produced a rolled-up magazine, unfurled it and thrust it in front of the man, who had to recoil slightly in order to focus his increasingly ancient eyes on it.

Claude Rains in his masked role as *The Phantom of the Opera* stared back at him. Garish lettering further promised the riches within: films featuring black cats, Ghidrah the three-headed monster, and *Horror of Dracula*—the US title of the first Hammer in the series. What he held in his hands was a lurid American film magazine called, in case of any doubt whatsoever in its remit, *Famous Monsters of Filmland*.

The boy reached over and flicked through until he found a double-page spread of black-and-white stills. He flattened it open and jabbed with his finger.

"Look. It's you."

Indeed it was.

Christopher Lee as the predatory Count, descending upon Melissa Stribling's Mina. Baring his fangs in a mouth covered with blood. Van Hel-sing—himself—alongside it, dressed in a Homburg hat and fur-collared coat.

"I can't read very well," the boy said. "But I like the pictures. The pictures are great. Who's Peter Cushing?"

Cushing looked at the younger man in the image before him.

"He's a person I pretend to be sometimes." He thumbed through the pages, touched immeasurably by the gift. "Is this for me?"

"What? *No.* I want it back. But I want you to sign it, because you're famous."

"Ah. Silly me."

Cushing thought of the close-ups they'd filmed of him so many years before, reacting to the disintegration of the vampire whilst nothing was there in front of him. He thought of Phil Leakey and Syd Pearson, make-up and special effects, labouring away on the last day of shooting to achieve the purifying effect of the dawning sun. He thought of the sun, and of the perpetual darkness he had lived in since Helen had died.

He lay the *Famous Monsters* magazine on the sea wall between them, took out his fountain pen from his inside pocket, shook it, and wrote *Van Helsing* in large sweeping letters across the page, blowing on the blue ink till it was dry.

"Brilliant." The boy held it by his fingertips like a precious parchment and blew on it himself for good measure. "Now I'll be able to show people I met you. When I'm an old man with children of my own." He stood up and held out his hand.

Cushing shook it with a formality the boy clearly desired.

"Enjoy stories, Carl. Enjoy books and films. Enjoy your work. Enjoy life. Find someone to love. Cherish her…"

The boy nodded, but looked again at the signed picture in *Famous Monsters* as if he hadn't quite believed it the first time. The evidence con-firmed, he pressed it to his chest, zipped it up securely inside his anorak, pulled up the hood and unchained his bike.

"Carl?" Cushing said. "Sometimes you can hide the hurt and pain, but there'll be a day you can talk about it with someone and be free. Perhaps a day when you'll forget what it was you were frightened of, and then you'll have conquered it, forever."

The young face looked back, half-in, half-out of the anorak hood, and nodded. Then he took the antler-sized handlebars and walked his Chopper back in the direction of the road and shops, another imperative on his mind, another game, idea, story, journey, in that way of boys, and of life.

As he tapped another talismanic cigarette against the packet, thinking of his own journey and footsteps filling with water as the tide came in, Cushing heard the tick-tick-tick stop, as if the boy had stopped, and he had. And he heard the cawing of seagulls, his nasty neighbours—The Ubiquitous, he called them—and heard a voice, the boy's voice, for the last time, behind him.

"Will you keep fighting monsters?"

His eyes fixed far off, where the sea met the sky, Peter Cushing had no difficulty saying:

"Always."

*
**

He sat in the forest dressed in black buckled shoes, cross-legged, a wide-brimmed black hat resting in his lap and the white, starched collar of a Puritan a stark contrast to the abiding blackness of his cape. Over in the clearing the bonfire was being constructed for the burning of the witch. The stake was being erected by Cockney men with sizeable beer bellies wearing jeans and T-shirts. The focus puller ran his tape measure from the camera lens. Art directors scattered handfuls of ash from buckets to give the surroundings a monochrome, 'blasted heath' quality. And so they were all at work, all doing their jobs, a well-oiled machine, while he waited, contemplating the density of the trees and smelling the pine needles. It was March now, and soon shoots of new growth would show in the layer of mulch and dead leaves and the cycle of life would continue. Work was the only thing left now that made life pass in a faintly bearable fashion. As good old Sherlock Holmes said to Watson in *The Sign of Four*: "Work is the best antidote to sorrow", and the only antidote he himself saw to the devastation of losing Helen was to launch himself back into a gruelling schedule of films. It was the one thing he knew he *could* do, after all. As she kept reminding him. *It's your gift, my darling. Use it.* And the distraction of immersing oneself in other characters was an imperative, he now saw: a welcome refuge from reality.

The third assistant director brought a cup of tea, an apple and a plate of cheese from the catering truck to the chair with Peter Cushing's name on the back.

"Bless you."

Occasionally, very occasionally, that's what he did feel.

Blessed.

It was a blessing, mainly, to be back working with so many familiar faces. Yes, there were new ones, young and fresh, and of course that was good and healthy too. The young ones, who hadn't met him in person before, possibly didn't notice or remark that he had become sombre, withdrawn, fragile behind his unerring politeness and professionalism—it was the older ones who saw that, all too well. In the make-up mirror he had never looked so terribly gaunt and perhaps they imagined, charitably, it was part of his characterisation as the cold, zealous Puritan, Gustav Weil. But it was nothing to do with the dark tone of the film, everything to do with the dark pall cast over his life.

Those who knew him, really knew him, acknowledged that a part of him had died two months ago.

Yet the un-dead lived on.

Here he was at Pinewood and Black Park in the company of vampire twins and a young, dynamic Count Karnstein so seethingly bestial-looking in the shape of Damien Thomas he might well snatch the reins from Christopher Lee and become the *Dracula* for a new generation. The third in the trilogy, this excursion was being trumpeted loudly by the company as Peter Cushing's return to the Hammer fold. Once more written by Tudor Gates, heavily influenced by Vincent Price's *Witchfinder General*, it was the tale of a vampire-hunting posse with Peter Cushing at its head. And with top billing.

He remembered clearly the lunch a month earlier with his agent, John Redway, and the leather-jacketed young director John Hough at L'Aperitif restaurant in Brown's Hotel, Mayfair.

"You're returning to combat evil, Peter," the director had said. But he wanted a darker tone. He didn't want it to be a fairy tale like other Hammers. He wanted to reinvent the horror genre.

Cushing had said nothing as he listened, but thought the genre didn't need reinventing. The genre was doing very well as it was, thank you very much. He did think the idea was original, however, and the director had convinced him over three courses and wine of his intention to make it as a bleak morality play, manipulating the audience's expectation of good and evil by having them side with the vampires against the pious austerity of Gustav Weil, the twisted, God-fearing witch-hunter, uncle to the vampire twins, Frieda and Maria, played by the pretty Collinson sisters—Maltese girls whose claim to fame was being the first identical twin centrefold for *Playboy*, in the title role. *Twins of Evil*—or was it called *Twins of Dracula* now, the American distributor's illogical and factually incorrect alternative?

"You see, Peter, real evil is not so easy to spot in real life," the director had said. "In real life, evil people look like you and me. We pass them in the street."

"Really?"

"Yes. And that's what I want to capture with this film. The nature of true evil."

Whether it would be a success or not Cushing couldn't know. He would do his best. He always did. He had an inkling how this sort of film worked after all these years and that's what he would bring to the proceedings. That's what they were paying for. That and, of course, his name.

His name.

He remembered the conversation in the dark of the Oxford cinema.

According to the Fount of All Knowledge, Carl's mother moved to Salisbury shortly after Gledhill died, to live with her sister and set up a shop together. He hoped for once the gossip contained some semblance of accuracy. If she sought to rebuild her life afresh, that could only be a good thing. For her, and the boy.

For himself, there were other films on the horizon. He'd told John Redway to turn nothing down. He'd read the script of *Dracula: Chelsea* and it was rather good. He was looking forward to playing not only Lorrimer Van Helsing in the present day, but also his grandfather, in a startling opening flashback, fighting Christopher Lee on the back of a hurtling, out of control stagecoach before impaling him with a broken cartwheel. And if that was a success there were plans for other Draculas. Another treatment by Jimmy Sangster had been commissioned that he knew of, which boded well, and he hoped Michael Carreras would grasp the reins and take Hammer into a new era.

One of the more imminent offers was a role from Milton in his latest portmanteau movie *Tales from the Crypt*, but he didn't care for the part, a variation of *The Monkey's Paw*. Instead he'd asked if he could play the lonely, widowed old man, Grimsdyke, who returns from the grave to exact poetic justice on his persecutor. A crucial scene would require Grimsdyke to be talking to his beloved dead wife, and he planned to ask Milton if he'd mind if he used a photograph of Helen on the set. Then he could say, as he'd wished for many a long year, that they'd finally made a film together.

As it was, her photograph was never far away. He kept one above his writing desk at home, and another beside his mirror in his dressing room or make-up truck. At home he always set a place for her at the dinner table, and not a day went by when he didn't talk to her.

Hopefully there'd be other movies in the pipeline. They'd keep the wolf from the door and the dark thoughts at bay—ironic, given their subject matter. Not that he could see his grief becoming any less all-consuming with the passage of time. Time, as far as he could imagine, could do nothing to diminish the pain. The lines by Samuel Beckett often came to mind: "I can't go on, I must go on, I will go on," and he knew that the third AD would be back before too long, to say they were ready for him.

But for the next few minutes until that happened, he would rest and try to clear his mind as he always did before a take, and picked up his Boots cassette recorder from between his feet, put on the small earphones and closed his eyes. He pressed 'Play'. The beauty of Elgar's *Sospiri* gave way to Noël Coward singing *If Love were All*.

One of Helen's favourites, and his own.

He had lost the one thing that made living real and joyful, the person who was his whole life, and without her there was no meaning or point any more. But what had others lost? Yet, they survived.

He pictured the boy on his bicycle riding away, the rolled up magazine in his pocket.

Whilst he was living, he knew, time would move inexorably onward and the attending loneliness would be beyond description, but the one thing that would keep him going was the absolute knowledge that he would be united with Helen again one day.

The spokes of the bicycle wheel turned, gathering speed, blurring.

Life must go on, yes, but in the end—*after* the end—life was not important, just pictures on a screen, absorbing for as long as they lasted, causing us to weep and laugh, perhaps, but when the images are gone we step out blinking into the light.

Until then he was called upon to be the champion of the forces of good. He would spear reanimated mummies through the chest. He would stare into the eyes of the Abominable Snowman. He would seek out the Gorgon. Fire silver bullets at werewolves. He would burn evil at the stake. He would brand them with crucifixes. He would halt windmills from turning. He would bring down a hammer and force a stake through their hearts and watch them disintegrate. He would hold them up by the hair and decapitate them with a single swipe.

He would be a monster hunter.

He would be Van Helsing for all who needed him, and all who loved him.

LEYTO

STONE

Some people think a film should be a slice of life.
I think it should be a slice of cake.
—Alfred Hitchcock

"**D**ESIRÉE...Maxine..." Pigeons nod at crumbs on a pavement.

"Burly Rose...Royal Kidney..."

Water empties over the flagstones. The winged pests scatter with a grey fluttering.

"Kennebec...Avalanche..."

Dark legs stride in mirror-black shoes. A man scrubs the pavement with the stiffest of brooms.

"Belle de Fontenay...Pentland Javelin..."

Indoors, a small framed picture sits like a window on the Byzantine Lincrusta wallpaper. Francis of Assisi, eyes turned piously upwards, arms outstretched like Christ on the cross, birds perched along them, treating them like branches, and aloft, circling his head and halo.

"Sharp's Express...British Queen..."

In the greengrocer's at 517 The High Road it is evening, but this room behind the shop is dark even at noon. The fruit and veg are out front to catch the sun, but the spuds, like the family, are kept at the back, in the gloom for safe keeping.

"Northern Star..."

The boy sits with elbows up on a plain wooden table, frowning with deepest concentration, hands cupped round his eyes.

"Eightyfold..."

Fred is a chubby little dumpling with a cockscomb of hair on top.

Born 1899, last knockings of the old century, when Victoria was still on the throne, making him just under seven now.

"Evergood…"

A woman's hand removes the potato from the table-cloth in front of him, replacing it in a flourish with another.

"Up To Date…"

Another.

"King Edward…"

Another—the last, and it's done.

"Red Duke of York…"

She shows him her empty palms. The silent, regal mime of applause that accompanies a miniscule tilt of the head is praise enough to make his cheeks burn. Sometimes it takes a lot to make his mother smile, he knows, but when she does it's like getting a gold medal from the Queen. A VC for gallantry. And she *is* the Queen. In this house, anyway. Prim and proper and elegant—so much more elegant than any of his schoolmates' mothers. A different class entirely. And dresses—oh, *immaculately*. Never seen outside without her white cotton gloves. Spotless. What are the others? Loud-mouthed fishwives, most of them, with brown baggy stockings and bruises where they've been on their knees all day.

"Onions!" he cries. "Test me on the onions now! Please, Mother! I know them all!"

"Back home they say onions are a great cure for The Baldness," she singsongs in her Irish brogue. "Rub the scalp with a spoonful of onion sap, it'd put hair on a duck's egg!"

Fred chuckles, but at the sound of the latch the moment between them is lost, and so is the chortle in his throat.

His father comes in, taking off the flat cap which confers upon him a degree of status to those he employs, and hangs it on a peg. Unties the knot of his tan apron at the small of his back and dips his fingers in the font, quickly genuflecting to Our Lady before hanging up the apron on the hook behind the door.

"The sailor home from the sea," Fred's mother says, as if some joke is being shared between her and her son. Fred twitches a smile, but just as swiftly it is gone and he lowers his eyes.

His father washes the earth off his hands under the tap at the Belfast sink. Water runs black down the plug hole. The soap is an unforgiving brick. A disinfectant smell bites at the air. There is no mirror, but while his face is still wet he flattens his moustache and eyebrows with several strokes of a forefinger and thumb.

"Father, I've been learning how to——"

"Is he ready?"

The stiff tap turns off with a harsh twist leaving a stain of grime where the man's thumbs went. He dries his hands briskly on a tea towel. "Now, Bill," his wife says. "Just a little longer…"

"No." For once he gives her no quarter. He is adamant. "If it's to be done, let's have it done."

"Name o' God, let him have his tea first."

"Name o' God nothing." He returns the tea towel to its nail and rolls down his sleeves, folding over his cuffs and prodding in the links which he keeps next to his shaving paraphernalia on the shelf. "Fred, put your coat on, son."

Fred's mother rises and lifts the small tweed jacket from the back of Fred's chair and the child puts it on. It matches his shorts exactly. It's a suit like that of a grown man. She crouches in front of him, buttons it up, tucks his shirt tail in at the back, adjusts the knot of his little tie. Fred notices her smile is still there, yes——but it is not the same smile as was there before.

"Where are we going?"

"You're going with your father."

She wraps a woolly scarf around his neck. Knots it. *There.*

"Don't mollycoddle him, Em. Leave him."

His father takes a black jacket from its hanger, flicks off dust with his fingers and slips his arms into the sleeves. He takes a different hat——a black bowler this time——from the peg next to the flat cap.

"Come here," says Fred's mother to her child. She gives him a hug——a swift hug, but a tight one, then a kiss on the cheek so hard it almost hurts. She rubs the red stain from her lips off with a licked thumb. Then kisses him a second time, even harder. He tries not to wince. "I'm going to make a great big steak and kidney pie. That's your favourite——a nice big steak and kidney pie, isn't it?"

Fred nods enthusiastically then turns at the sound of a cough.

His father cocks his head for Fred to follow him. Which the boy does, smiling and obedient as ever and smiling because his mother is smiling, after all.

They walk through the shop, the boy behind the man, smelling the sweetness of carrots and parsnips and the cloying heaviness of soil and sacks and straw and the boy does not see his mother sit back at the table, her knees suddenly weak.

When she hears the front door open and close, the shop bell tinkle, she clutches her rosary beads, closes her eyes tightly and for several minutes thereafter silently prays into her white-knuckled hand to Mary, the mother of her God.

As they emerge from the dark interior, his father flexes his hand without looking down. Fred takes it. His own hand is warm and soft but his father's hard and ice-cold from the water. They walk away from the shop side by side. Sheaves of brown paper bags are strung up on butcher's hooks and so are pineapples. Nets full of golden-skinned baby onions sit beside wooden crates full of bananas. The trays of Granny Smiths are being carried inside at the tail-end of the working day. One of the assistants, one he likes, flashes Fred a grin and a wink while a different one with a waistcoat over his apron climbs up a ladder carrying the bucket with which he washed the pavement earlier. At the top of the ladder, whistling *After the Ball is Over* with jaunty vigour, he wipes a wet cloth over the mirrored sign above the windows. "Where are we going, Father? Are we going to the sweet shop? Are we?"

Pigeons flee in the path of the two pairs of feet. Fred's grey school socks. His father's hobnail boots. Walking near enough in step past a horse and cart. The animal, barely a pony, is shorn halfway up. It has an unattended beard, but it has a horizon. And the name on the cart is the same as the one above the shop.

"Can I have some toffee? A big bit? The sort you break with a hammer? The sort grown-ups get?"

"We'll see."

Fred looks up at his father eagerly. "Can I?"

"We'll see."

Fred is level with his father's watch chain when he pauses before crossing the road, a dangling 'U' between his waistcoat pocket and his button-hole. His father takes his timepiece out, flips it open and looks at the face then tucks it away again.

The sun is sinking and the pigeons go where pigeons go when darkness falls. Fred mentally ticks off the manufacturers' names of cars as they pass. Panhard-Levassor, Humberette. Napier. An omnibus creeps by and he memorises the number. Next stop, the ice rink. The bus behind it, Walthamstow. He knows the routes by heart. His father has said nothing for fifteen minutes, but then he's a man of few words. That's what his mother calls him sometimes: "Here he is…Man of Few Words." But the remark never made him more conversationally-inclined, possibly the reverse. They cross the road to a red-brick building. Fred trails the fingers of his free hand along iron railings. Fixed to the bars is a shallow glass box and in the box he sees posters with faces on them. One shows a "heathen"—his mother's word, used ubiquitously—with staring eyes and a beard so stringy it looks as if it was combed with a knife. The one beside it displays a thick-necked lout with a V-shaped scar across his cheek. Next to it a woman with broken teeth, both pathetic and frighteningly aggressive, stares out at him. All three gone in a flash, but he has time to register the word 'WANTED' above each of them.

He accompanies his father up a flight of stone steps in through a swing door under a blue lamp.

Inside, his father sits him on a plain wooden bench and Fred watches as he walks to a large desk behind which stands a policeman with a sergeant's triple chevrons on the sleeves of his black uniform. As if in competition, the policeman has an even bigger and darker moustache than his father's—"black as sin" his mother would say—and a razor-sharp centre parting that matches his ramrod-straight back and military bearing. It takes Fred a moment to pin it down, but he reminds him of illustrations in the *Pictorial* of Viscount Kitchener of Khartoum at the Rawalpindi Parade when the Prince and Princess of Wales visited India.

Fred watches as the two men's heads bend closer and they whisper to each other. He cannot hear what they say. He sees only the back of his father's head, the stubble the barber shaves with a razor up to the level of his ears. As he listens, the policeman looks over at Fred with glassy, unblinking eyes.Fred looks sharply down at his own dangling feet, and is reluctant to look up again. He sees a game of OXO written in ink on his knee during Arithmetic. He sucks his index finger and uses it to rub it off.

He is aware somebody is sitting on the bench directly opposite him because he can see shoes a bit like his mother wears sometimes, but scuffed and worn as if somebody has walked a lot in them. He can smell perfume too, or perhaps slightly stale talcum powder covering up another smell which might be beer. The woman's coat is long and he can see splits in the seams and a worn hem trailing on the floor. Her legs are crossed but they're lumpy and he can see the veins without even trying. She has a large nose for a woman and a cleft in her chin. Her head sways and her eyes struggle to stay open. Her face is white with pink blobs on her cheeks. As Fred stares—he can't help it—he can see the dots of whiskers sticking up through the white pan-stick. And the thick-knuckled hand that lifts a cheap cigarette to her lips has long black hairs on the back of it.

Fred looks down, then over at the desk.

Both his father and the policeman are looking at him, then his father beckons him with a single crooked finger.

Fred walks obediently over.

The policeman finishes what he is writing with a sharp dot.

"This is him, is it?"

He comes round the desk. The handcuffs on his belt with the snake-shaped buckle are level with Fred's face. He extends a big flat of the hand, thumb curled up like a hook. Thrusts it towards Fred.

Fred retreats a step and sways unsteadily, looking up at his father. His father nods.

Thus reassured, Fred takes the policeman's hand and shakes it, as he's been taught to do. He's been taught manners. He thinks the policeman is being friendly, and he thinks he is being friendly back. But the policeman doesn't let go. He just keeps shaking Fred's hand until Fred thinks it's time he let go of it, please. But the policeman doesn't.

Fred looks at his father but his father doesn't say anything. Perhaps he doesn't know anything is wrong. *Is* anything wrong?

The policeman walks away but to Fred's surprise he still hasn't let go of his hand yet. He is taking his hand with him. He is taking *Fred* with him.

Fred is confused. The policeman leads him towards a corridor of the police station.

Looking back over one shoulder then the other, Fred expects to see that his father is following them. But he isn't.

His father is just standing there. Arms hung straight at his sides. Bowler hat in one hand. Then he places it on his head.

Fred tries to use the soles of his shoes for brakes, to no avail, as he enters a corridor lined with heavy doors.

He tries to prise his fingers out of the policeman's big hand, but it's impossible. The man's grip is like iron—it has to be like iron, for handling criminals. That's obvious. But he isn't handling a criminal. He's handling a *boy*. A boy who is making little squeaky noises now. Who doesn't want to, but can't help it. Who starts to struggle and squirm but the policeman doesn't even look down at him.

Craning over his left shoulder then his right, Fred looks back down the corridor—which smells of wee—but there's no-one there any more, back standing by the big desk, and this draws out his voice, echoing from the tiles.

"Father? *Father?*"

He feels his ear twisted and pulled vertically, hoisting him onto tip-toes. It hurts like the fires of Hell and he has no choice but to follow it, yanked as it is into the dankness and dimness of a tiny room where the smell of wee attacks him like a dog. Just as suddenly his ear is emancipated and he nurses it, red and sore, whereupon almost immediately it is treated to a reverberating clang.

Sensing abandonment, he spins round to see that the heavy door has been shut, cutting out what baleful light the corridor afforded, and he is alone. He flattens himself against it. Disembodied keys rattle as they turn in the lock.

"Father! Father!"

The peep-hole shrieks open. The beady eye of the policeman peers in.

With a gasp of fright, the small boy backs away into the room of wee. Of wee-stained underpants. Of fear.

"Now then, now then. I thought you was supposed to be a Well Behaved Little Boy." The voice rasps just as the lock rasped.

Fred goes quiet.

The peep-hole scrapes shut.

He can hear the echoing of the policeman's squeaky boots, the shiny key ring chinking on the man's black hip. He backs up further, until he sits on the creaky bed with its nasty symphony of rusty springs.

He looks at the long black shadows of bars cast on the floor. The big, grim door facing him. The four filthy walls.

"Father! Father! Father! Father!"

Another door slams, more distant, but loud enough—startling him, and he starts to sob from the bottom of his little heart.

A soggy dusk has fully established itself as his father wends his way back to The High Road. His hands feel icy and he puts them in his pockets but doesn't look back. He wants to get home but he isn't sure he wants to get home. He reaches the shop. A glow of sorts radiates from an upstairs window, through net and drape. The lads have packed the boxes of produce neatly inside. He expects no less of them, but it gives him some measure of pride. "Night, Mr Hitchcock."

"'Night, George."

He goes inside. Locks the shop door as he always does on the dot of six. Turns the sign from 'OPEN' to 'CLOSED'. He looks at his fob watch. Hesitates. Then comes out again and locks the door from the outside.His local is the Ten Bells. They know him there, but he isn't a soak. Nor is he there for idle chatter. He never is.

He admires the pint of stout in front of him while it settles, black separating from white, and when he is ready but not a moment sooner he downs it in one, long, slow, sure swallow.

The barmaid, cleaning glasses, flesh dimpled on her arms, watches him in some kind of awe. She is blowsy and his wife would call her "common". Her bust is more ample than most, and not unpleasant for that, but what warms him more is how sure she is in her skin. His head tilts back as the last of the nectar drains. His neck muscles pulsate. His Adam's apple bobs as he drains the last mouthful. And when he has finished he places down the empty glass as indemonstrably as would seem possible.

The barmaid continues to look at him with a half-set, halfjoking smile, full of knowing and forbidden promise. Which is lost on him, or not, as the case may be.

Beyond the window a lamp-lighter whistles *My Dear Old Dutch*. Fred weeps quietly to himself as a glow from outside illuminates the cell with a dull triptych thrown onto the back of the door. He pulls up a moth-eaten blanket over his cold, bare knees. The blanket has a hole in it. It also smells of something vile. Fred sniffs it and his face is punched by the rank niff of stale urine. Piss. He thinks of the word they use in the playground. *Piss.*Echoing footsteps approach. He stiffens and sits up.

"Father…Father?"

He wipes his eyes, staring at the cell door.

"I'm not your father," says the policeman. "Do you want to speak to your father?"

"Yes, please."

"Well he's not here, is he?"

Fred's face creases up. He tries not to cry. Tries to be brave.

"Oi, oi! Stop that snivelling! Cor blimey! Take it on the chin.

Take it like a *man*, for Gawd's sake!"

"Sorry."

"Sorry what?"

"Sorry, sir."

"That's better." Fred hears a rasp. Out in the corridor, the policeman has gone to look through a different peep hole. Check on another prisoner. Fred hurries to the door, fearful he will be left alone again.

"Please, sir. Sir? When's he coming back?"

"Who says he's coming back?"

"He...he's got to come back. He's got to take me home. For tea."

"Oh, he has, has he?"

"Yes."

"Why's that?"

"I haven't done anything wrong."

"Haven't you?"

"No."

"What? Never done *anything* wrong? Not *ever*?"

"No."

"Little lamb whose fleece is white as snow, are we? That's what your mother calls you, isn't it?"

"How do you know that?"

"Isn't it?"

"Yes."

The policeman puts his face up close to the heavy door. "Well, how come you're in 'ere, then—eh?"

"I don't know! Tell me. Please! What did I do? What?"

"You thought nobody was watching, but they were. Everybody was watching. *Everybody*."

"No. It wasn't me. I didn't do anything. There's been a mistake!"

"That's what they all say."

"Who?"

"Criminals."

"I'm not a criminal! I'm a little boy!"

The policeman's hoarse, pipe-smoker's laughter rings out. It echoes horribly, like a voice from deep down in a sewer. It goes on and on as he finds it funnier and funnier while Fred slides to the floor and covers his ears.

Presently he hears the footsteps depart with the same regularity as they came. A metal grille slides and bangs into place and gets locked with another of the fan of keys on the policeman's vast key ring. In his blackness, shadow of shadows, his gaoler, the policeman, is gone. Footsteps, keys, more footsteps, fainter—then not even that.

His father sits at the dinner table with one point of a diamond-shaped napkin tucked in at his throat. A trio of dry lamb chops sit in front of him, daubed with mint sauce. His mother serves up sliced green beans fresh from the shop onto his plate. She then spoons out potatoes from a steaming bowl. One, two, three, four…"That's enough."

As if he hasn't spoken, though it was more than a whisper, she keeps spooning out more—five, six…

Only slightly raising his voice, he repeats:

"That's enough."

His wife stops, places the bowl down heavily in the centre of the table. She sits down tidily, arranging her skirts and serving herself a more than adequate portion. One chop, two potatoes. (Only eats so much as a bird—a *bird!*)

"Bless us, O Lord," she says, hands clasped as if anxious. "And these Thy gifts which we are about to receive from Thy bounty through Christ our Lord, Amen."

She passes the salt to her husband with a smile he cannot fail to notice, a need in her to indicate to him he should now eat and take pleasure in the activity. Because he would never know this of his own account.

"A mother was bathin' her baby one night
The youngest of ten, the poor little mite
The mother was fat and the baby was fin
T'was nawt but a skellington wrapped up in skin..."

Fred is sitting on his terrible bed (wee the bed, *piss* the bed) wiping away tears with the heel of his hand as the singing of the nameless drunk in a nearby cell drifts in like a lullaby.

"The mother turned round for the soap from the rack
She weren't gone a minute, but when she got back
Her baby had gone, and in anguish she cried:
'Oh, where is my baby?', and the angels replied..."

Turning his head a fraction as the voice lurches into the chorus, Fred sees five-bar-gate scratchmarks gouged into the wall. Not just one. Dozens of them. All over. *Hieroglyphics.* He knew that word. He knew all about the Ancient Egyptians...

"Your baby has gorn dahn the plug'ole!
Your baby has gorn dahn the drain!
Your baby has gorn dahn the plughole!
You'll nevah see baby ah-gain!"

Days...Days upon days. How many days do they keep people here? The unanswered question makes his lip quiver all the more as he sinks into a ball, pressing his small body into the corner, tucking his knees under his chin, and covering his ears.

"It wasn't me! It wasn't me!"

*
**

Out at his desk, the policeman stirs his cup of tea. He's trying to read his newspaper, which is spread flat on the desk in front of him.

"Your baby is perfick'ly happy

He won't need no bathin' no more
He's working his way through the sewers..."

"Oi!" yelled the policeman. "Stop that effin' racket!" At which the drunk almost immediately desists. "That's better. Can't 'ear myself ruddy think out 'ere."

Except Fred's endless sobbing does not desist. Far from it.

The policeman sighs, removes his half-moon glasses and folds his newspaper. He stands up in his shiny boots and walks to the door to the corridor leading off. His keys jangle once more, in irritation now. Unlocks the grille, slides it back and walks right up to the door to Fred's cell.

"Blimey. What have we got in here, eh? A girl? That's what it sounds like, from out there. A scared little girlie."

Fred is perched, shivering, on his smelly bed, staring through red-rimmed eyes, shoulders heaving gently.

"I'm hungry, sir. I'm starving..."

"You should've thought of that, matey, shouldn't you?...No snake and tiddly pie in 'ere. No plum duff, I can tell you..." The policeman's face is stony, gargoyle-like in semi-shadow. "No Spotted Dick with nice thick custard in 'ere, son. Just bread and water, if you're lucky. If the rats don't get it first, that is."

Fred quickly lifts his feet off the floor.

"No toys...No books...No mum to tuck you in..."

"Mother'll come. Mother'll come and get me. I know she will..."

"Bit of a mummy's boy, are we?"

"No."

"Stay at home with your mummy, instead of playing with the rough boys in the streets, do you?"

"No."

"What *do* you do, then?"

"Lots of things...Play."

"Play? Who with?"

"Friends."

"What 'friends'? A little bird tells me you haven't got any friends."

"I do. Lots."

"Oh. What do you get up to, then? With these 'friends'? Football? Cycling? Arthur-let-ics? Yer, I can see that. You. Very arthur-let-ic."

"I go. I *do* go. And, and…—watch."

Outside the cell, the policeman folds his arms, leans against the wall.

"And what do you do up in your room for hours on end, eh? All on your own?"

"Nothing. *Nothing.* Read books. Puzzles. Maps. That's all."

"Books? What sort of books?"

"All sorts. Stories…And train timetables. I like timetables better than stories, even. Facts, numbers, times." And suddenly—something he's proud of. Something that might impress. "I've travelled on every tram in London!"

"Ah!" The policeman sniggers. "A real trolley-jolly!"

Fred takes the laughter as genuine interest from a like mind, and spouts forth with the gusto of a true aficionado. "Trains, boats, everything! I love it. I've taken the river steamer to Gravesend, all on my own. I've made a chart that's up on my wall at home showing the positions of every British ship afloat. And, and—I chart their courses and check them every day in the newspapers…"

"Trains, boats…Yer…That kind of information would be very valuable if it fell into the wrong hands."

Fred is taken aback. "What? What hands?"

"You think I was born yesterday? You think I don't know what type of person charts shipping lines on his bedroom wall?"

"No." Fred is frightened now.

"…the type of person who watches people? Watches them and observes them all the time…?"

"No."

"I'll tell you what sort of person. A spy. That's what sort of person."

"I'm not a spy."

"Who would suspect? Clever. *Very* clever."

"I'm not a spy! I'm not *anything*!"

"Don't come the innocent with me, Sonny Jim."

"But I *am* innocent!"

"No you're not. You're as guilty as sin. It's written all over you."

"I'm not guilty. Ask Mother."

"Everybody's guilty of something. Even Adam and Eve were guilty of something, weren't they?"

Fred's eyes fall on a graffito of an erect penis and pendulous testicles scrawled on the cell wall. He jerks his face away from it.

"I don't know…"

"What?"

"I don't know."

"I can't hear you."

"I DON'T KNOW!"

In a quiet tone, feigning both surprise and disappointment, the policeman says, "You don't know very much, do you?"

Fred hears a woman's giggling outside. A passer-by. A lady will help. A lady will understand.

He runs towards the window and jumps up from the mattress to try and catch hold of the bars. He can, just about, but his head doesn't come up high enough to see out. It's impossible. He wishes he had the breath to call out for help. His feet dangle and his hands aren't strong to hold his weight because he is fat. He drops back, onto his knees, on the bed, panting. Facing the grim, blank wall as the woman walks away, staggering from pavement to gutter and back again.

"See, there's such a thing as crime and punishment," says the policeman's voice, soft yet booming, as if from inside a drum. "Even in the Garden of Eden. Crime. Punishment."

"Punishment for what?"

"For being bad. See, you commit a crime, you don't just let your mother and father down, who brought you into this world, you let God down. And you know what happens when you let God down?"

Fred is too scared to answer. The voice coils like a serpent, slippery and encircling the brickwork.

"You go down. Down, down, *down*…You know what I mean by 'down'?"

"Yes."

"That's where you are now. Down. Down in the dark. With the nasty people. The slugs and snails who don't wash behind their ears."

"I wash behind my ears. All the time. Sometimes Mother says you can grow potatoes there, but she's joking. It's a joke."

"Yer, well. There are no jokes in here, I can tell you. I don't hear anybody laughing, do you? Do you?"

"No."

A mischievous expression adorns the policeman's face. He opens the peep hole to Fred's cell and puts his hairy, puckered mouth to it. It has the anatomy of a wound or other aperture.

"You know who's in the next cell?" he intones with mountainous relish. "Jack the Ripper."

Fred stiffens, terrified. Curls up tight, knees under his chin.

"You know who Jack the Ripper is, I take it?…How many women did he top, eh? And just round the corner from 'ere? Whitechapel. How d'you get to Whitechapel from here on the tram? Eh?"

Fred is struck mute.

"Never caught him, did they? No. So you'd better pipe down, or he'll have your giblets for garters, like he did them tarts." The peep hole closes. Then it opens again, an afterthought. The pink mouth is back. The wet wound, growling. "You know what a tart is, Fred boy?"

"Yes."

"What?"

"It's a little piece of pastry with some jam in the middle."

The policeman laughs horribly—even more horribly than before, if that is possible.

"That's right. A little piece of pastry with some jam in the middle. That's what Jack says—don't you, Jack? Jack's having a little chuckle at that, old Jack is."

Sure enough, Fred can hear cackling—*mad* cackling—but he doesn't know if it's Jack like the policeman says or it's the drunk and he doesn't want to find out. He hugs his horrid piss-blanket to his chest.

"Maybe if you ask nicely he'll tuck you in at night, instead of your dear old mum. That's who we've got in 'ere, see. Murderers who cut you up in tiny pieces. Thieves who steal your money. Spies who watch you when they shouldn't ought to…"

Fred bites into the blanket, wanting to shut out the words, the ideas, the terrors—but he can't.

"People who have dirty thoughts. 'Cause dirty thoughts don't wash away with soap and water, do they, eh?"

Fred shakes his head, great lurching sobs breaking out of his chest now, his chubby cheeks shining from hours of tears.

"Because this is Hell, Fred. That's what it is. Prison is a little taster of Hell, for people who see too much or say too little, people who haven't got any friends, or whose eyes are too big for their bellies… that's what prison is."

And Fred wants it to stop now. He can't bear it any more. It's overwhelming him uncontrollably. Stifling him. Suffocating him. And all he can do is shudder and rock and mumble like a prayer:

"Mother'll come. Mother'll come and explain. Mother'll come and get me. I *know* she will…"

"Will she?"

"Yes. She loves me."

"Does she? Oh, I don't think so. Not any more. Not after this. Not after what her darling boy's gone and done this time."

"Don't. Don't tell her. *Please!*"

"Nothing can save you now…Not your dad, not your mum. Not God. Nobody."

"I want to go home. Please. *Please.* Please let me go home…"

"This *is* your 'ome. You'd better get used to it, Freddie boy. This is your 'ome now. For the rest of your born days."

By this point young Fred is beyond mere weeping. Every ounce of him is weaker than jelly. He feels drained through a sieve. Diminished. The rind scraped off him, the juice running out.

The policeman, having carried out his self-given duty with not a little pleasure, turns and walks away, shooting the cuffs of his dark uniform. Army boots polished to oblivion clinking against the flag stones as their music recedes.

Fred can hardly breathe. He thinks he might choke. His throat is swollen from weeping and the salty saliva builds in his mouth because swallowing is too painful now. But the emptiness and loneliness is more painful still. And worst of all, he doesn't understand. Everything—*everything*—is a mystery…

"Nighty-night!"

The policeman switches off the corridor light with the brisk click of a chain pull. The grille shuts heavily and finally, with a clang that reverberates though the small boy's skull.

Easing back onto his perch, the policeman shakes his newspaper to its full swan-wing breadth and returns to the sports results. His tin mug of tea is stone cold and so is the pot.

"By the way, tuck them toes in," he calls out with some measure of glee, as a footnote. "The rats get a bit peckish in the wee small hours."

His father habitually sleeps as soon as his head hits the pillow, but tonight, while his body is weary, his mind is active. Perhaps it was the stout. His bladder feels full, but he fights the need to empty it and tries again to drift off. His eyes open in the dark and he turns round in the bed from one shoulder to the other, noticing that the space beside him is empty. Propped on an elbow, he sees his wife, Emma Jane, wrapped in her dressing gown with a green cardigan loosely draped over her shoulders, sitting at her vanity mirror, face triplicate in the mirrors. She sniffs into a handkerchief as if she doesn't know he is watching. A porcelain martyr gazing at herself with the kind of self-examination bordering on punishment he abhors. He wonders how long she has sat there while he snored, clearly unable to sleep—or so she would have him think. What would she have him think? And to what lengths would she go to have him think it? She amazes him every day. And here, now, wringing the moment for every ounce of tragedy she could muster.

"My baby. My poor baby…"

He droops his head, rubs his eyes and sighs, wondering how long this night will be.

"How can you do that to him?" she asks, not meeting his eyes in the mirror. "How?"

His answer is to turn his back on her.

"Aren't you speaking to me? Why aren't you speaking to me?"

Her husband closes his tired eyes.

"You're a monster," she says with a tremor in her voice. Then it's no more than a breath. "A *monster*."

The boy hasn't slept a wink, and yet the dawn creeps up on him. He lies buried under the sticky blanket, where his sniffles can be muffled and he can hide from the accusing walls. His covering has remained cold through the night, and only when he peeks from under it, after hearing the traffic increase in the street outside, does he see the shadows of the bars cast sharply on the back of the door by the morning sunlight.He blinks and unwinds himself. The huddled shape of him quivers and his stomach rumbles, having missed both tea and supper. He is frozen and pulls up his socks to get warm. He itches, scratches and thinks of insects seen and unseen. Then buries himself back against the wall like a cocoon and tries to sleep—though by now the noise of guttural engines and piping car horns from the street is making it impossible. The sounds go through him and he wonders if being awake forever would be even more horrible than being asleep forever, than being dead. It is the kind of thing you read in the tales of Edgar Allan Poe. That not sleeping sends you mad, and he wonders how long it might be before *he* goes mad. He wants to cry again, but at the sound of footsteps he sits up, hair tousled, on the crummy bed with big, startled, sleepcraving eyes.

A key rattles in the lock.

Someone opens the door with one hand.

Fred holds his breath, hoping it isn't the same policeman, but it is. The creature's silhouette fills the doorway but he sees light beyond.

"All right, Jack the Ripper. Let's be having you."

He doesn't sound the same now, and Fred wonders if he was sleeping and dreaming after all.

After he blinks he sees the policeman is gone and the door is open, leaving the way clear for him to walk out into the corridor, which he does.

The battalion of keys jangling on his hip, the policeman is walking back to his desk. He stops and offers his hand, fingers splayed, without looking back. Fred doesn't take it. Just stops dead too, with a small gasp of fright, then, when the policeman starts moving again, walks four or five paces behind him, upping his pace to hasten through the metal grille before the policeman slides it shut and locks it.

Fred sees his father. Flat cap. Tweed suit. Waistcoat. Starched collar and tie. Sitting on the bench where he himself sat the evening previously.

"*Father?*"

The man is already in the process of getting to his feet, saying: "Behaved himself, I hope?"

The policeman sharpens his pencil, turning the lever with a whirr. Grinds the lead to a point. Blows off the shavings.

"I think he's learned his lesson."

His father walks to the desk and puts a box of fruit and veg in front of the policeman, who lifts it off onto the floor beside his stool. Taking an apple from the top, he rubs it over the heart of his black, buttoned uniform taking a single chunk into his mouth which bulges in one cheek as he chews.

The transaction complete, then—and only then—does his father look down at his offspring, still reluctant to meet the boy's bleary, red-rimmed eyes.

"Now you know what happens to naughty little boys," he says.

Fred blinks. Sniffles. Nods.

The man holds out his hand. Fred takes it. His father's grip is firm and tight. A little too tight. Fred rubs his nose with his other hand to stop it running. A silvery trail coats his finger. He doesn't know what to do with it.

"Come on."

Fred looks back over his shoulder at the policeman.

The policeman winks.

Tweaking the ends of his moustache into points, he watches the fat little boy and his father walk out into the morning sunlight. Envying them their humdrum day, he opens the large book under his elbows and writes the date atop of a blank, sullen page, ready for the woes of the populace.

*
**

Without letting go of his father's hand, Fred looks back over his shoulder at the police station. It shrinks in scale. Around them London is starting to wake. Draymen on a brewery vehicle idle past at the clip-clop pace of the cart-horse. A blind man begs. Coalmen deliver sacks. Their ignorance almost makes the boy feel the night before never happened. Perhaps it didn't. If it did, why is everything so normal? Why isn't the world different? Changed?He doesn't feel he wants to cry any more, or scream, or shout. He just feels nothing very much. Not even happy. Not even now that he's out and free and has his dad to protect him. He doesn't feel free at all. It's a funny feeling, and one he can't explain.

He walks—not runs, *never* runs indoors—through the crisscross of busy shop assistants towards Mother, who rises then drops to a crouch to hug him tightly to her bosom. Tight enough to break him.

"My brave, brave boy!"

His father follows, hanging up his cap and wrapping on his work apron.

"Look at the bags under your eyes." She combs her boy's hair with her fingers. "Up the wooden hill for you, young man." Sniffing tears—perhaps she has been chopping onions—she takes him by the hand to the bare wooden stairs leading to the rooms above.

"He's got school to go to," her husband says.

"Don't be ridiculous! Look at the colour of him."

He looks in the mirror, not at his son. "Go and get your uniform on."

The boy obeys, ascending the stairs on his own.

"He can't go to school without something warm inside him."
Defiant, she follows.

Below, a figure knots an apron behind his back and goes into the shop to work. Work is what he does best, and what he understands.

In the kitchen his mother snips flesh-coloured sausages from a string and drops two into a frying pan. As they sizzle and brown, filling the room with a fatty aroma, she saws a slice of bread into triangles, to fry those too. A rasher of streaky bacon, mushrooms and a bisected tomato (but no eggs, he hates eggs!) are cooked in the same greasy pan, feast enough for a Navvy presented in a mound before a tiny little boy now dressed in his immaculate school uniform. Black jacket, stiff Eton collar and tie, short trousers. Knife in one hand, fork in the other. Starving hungry. Getting stuck in as his mother watches, hands on her hips and happy, though still dabbing at the residue of what he knows were tears. It makes him feel bad, so he eats, because he knows that makes her happy. He even smiles, and for a moment thinks she might burst into tears. Has he done something wrong? He doesn't know, so he just keeps on eating.

"Please may I leave the table?"

His father comes in just as Fred finishes breakfast.

"You may."

Fred brings over his cutlery and crockery to her, like a good boy.

"That's what I like to see—a nice clean plate."

He pulls his satchel strap over one shoulder and puts the school cap emblazoned with the letters 'SI' on his head. His mother bends for a kiss on both her cheeks, after which ritual he leaves by the stairs leading down to the back of the shop.

The boy having gone, his father sits in the same chair waiting for a similar cooked breakfast to be put in front of him, if with less grace. Fred's mother immediately turns away and busies herself washing the other dishes.

"He's got to toughen up. Don't you see that? All I want to do is protect him." But the man is talking to his wife's back, and isn't surprised when she doesn't deign to answer.

He stares at the food, cutting and chewing without the delicacy or poise she'd like, as she leaves him to enjoy his meal in the room alone.

Has he done something wrong, after all? Was the policeman right? Fred can't help thinking about it as he trails a finger along the bars, the prison bars, no—the iron railings of Saint Ignatius Catholic School for Boys, Stamford Hill. He grips them and looks through at the sight of a flock of young Jesuit priests playing football, black robes tucked in or knotted in bunches between their legs. They attack the ball with intense vigour. Their faces masks of simian concentration, ears protruding from severe haircuts. Shoes fly. Shins crack. Cassocks wheel. Mouths twist. Fists bunch. Arms gesticulate. Perspiration shines. Shaven throats pull raw against white dog collars as veins bulge. Legs blur.

In the hermetic gloom of the chapel stands an elderly priest with the wrinkled, desiccated skin of a Yuletide date. At the lectern, Father Aloysius Mullins faces rows of schoolboys as petrified in the pews as the statues that surround them. His wits may be dimmed by age, but he has a faith as resolute as iron. And saddlebag jowls that quiver and flap as he orates to his unedified congregation of youths and saplings. "We live in a world replete with the temptations of evil. And the greatest of these temptations is *frivolity!*"

Sitting amongst his peers, Fred silently gazes past the speaker to focus on the large carved statue of a crucified Jesus beyond him. "By *frivolity* I mean all the things that distract us from our duty to God.

By *frivolity* I mean music halls! I mean gramophone recordings! I mean picture palaces! I mean skating rinks! I mean the petty mingling of males and females…"

Christ on the cross hangs frozen in agony from his torments—face distorted, wounds spilling beautifully rendered droplets of blood.

"Be warned! These places deceive you by claiming they are life. They are not life! They are death! The death of your precious moral being!"

Gliding black shadows, a number of seemingly identical younger priests—the football-players—walk the aisles with stiff canes slapping against their legs. Their crow-eyes scan the assembly, eager to pounce on the slightest infraction. The schoolboys, Fred included, sit straight-backed, rigid with fear, terrified of the punishment that could descend on any one of them at the least provocation—or no provocation at all.

The old priest's eyes skulk behind narrow slits shielded by lenses the thickness of ale bottle bottoms.

"If we succumb to them, we succumb to the putrid. We succumb to the beast. By even *contemplating* them, we are giving our names to Satan!"

Fred thinks about Father Mullins' words as the boys later file past the priests, as they always do, to receive the holy wafer. There is a predictability in Communion today that comforts Fred, even though he is afraid. He is always afraid. The fear never goes away at school because it is never *meant* to go away.

"This is the vast peril of your lives. The vast cost that will be paid for abusing the God-given privilege of having *souls!*"

After the *Ave Maria*, Father Malachi administers the goblet of wine. Father Mullins places a wafer on Fred's tongue and makes the sign of the cross. Fred feels something invisible on his tongue. It tastes of nothing and Fred wonders, as he does often, whether it should. Does everybody else taste something, and is it only he who does not?

*
**

He stands in the rain-wettened playground, alone. This is not unusual. He is often alone. He doesn't mind. He likes his own company. In fact, most of the time he prefers it. He watches the other children and he doesn't think he belongs with them. They aren't like him. That's what his mother says. And often he thinks they might hurt him, and often he is right. When he is on his own he sometimes likes to dream up stories about them. Just think of exciting things that might happen to them, or crimes. Crimes he could solve, cleverly, and be a hero. Or just exciting things like war or jungle stories or adventures with chases and motor cars and danger. Or being trapped. Or something horrible and scary happening. "Cocky!"

Fred turns. It's Parkhill, beckoning. It's actually a group of three individuals in uniforms identical to his own. The other two are Murphy, red-haired and so Irish-looking it saddens, and O'Connor, less so. Not posh but, like him, lower middle-class Cockney sparrows. If anything a bit threadbare. They go into a conspiratorial huddle, heads down. Fred hurries over to them and joins in.

"There's a hole in the wall of the lavvies, and you can see right through to the girls' next door." Parkhill's face is full of rattish glee. "When they drop their skirts and knickers you can see their fannies and *everything!*"

The boys look at each other with hungry eyes, barely, if at all, understanding why they should take an interest in such things, beyond the fact they are forbidden and if observed, the fires of Hell will rain down upon them for their misdeeds. But that is reason enough, for boys. For Catholic boys in particular. And they run off, and Fred runs with them.

The urinals are daubed with the sickly yellow of usage. White tiles echo with the scampering of small, eager shoes. The lads scuttle into one empty, filthy cubicle. The stink—but not the stink—makes Fred hang back with his neat socks and smart jacket. Murphy beckons him excitedly. Fred is thinking about wrongness, and what his mother says, and what the policeman said, but he is thinking also about doing what his friends want him to do.Parkhill extracts a bolus of newspaper which is plugging up the now-infamous hole. He holds it in the air, trophy-like.

Fred takes a single step closer. He sees the others crowding in, jamming their heads together to get an eye to the aperture. A toilet chain sounds on the far side of the wall and the boys giggle and titter into their hands, then cover their mouths secretively.

"What is it?" Fred asks.

The boys are busy whispering, blushing, poking each other.

"Let me see."

They move aside and Fred sees the peep-hole gouged out of the wall. It looks like a wound. Something vicious, made by a dagger or weapon. He hesitates, nervous now. Not sure at all if this is a good idea.

"Get an eyeful," says Parkhill, sibilant amongst the dirty tiles. "It'll put hairs on your chest." The other boys giggle.

Fred moves between them and kneels on the rim of the toilet seat. Palms against the sticky wall either side, he slowly presses his eye to the hole. Light shines dimly from the other side. His eye lashes flicker. He sees something indistinct.

The policeman's eye stares back at him.

He recoils with a sudden jerk, retreating away quickly, past his friends and outside the cubicle until his back hits the far wall.

His pals look shocked and glances shoot to and fro between them, their eyes then converging on him. The cigarette that Parkhill has in his mouth ready to light up droops.

Fred stares at the small, round hole stiff with horror, mouth wide open and eyelids pulled back, gasping in short little bursts. "Bloody hell," says Parkhill, snatching the crumpled Wood-bine from his lips. "It ain't *that* bad."

*
**

A hand bell tolls in the jerking motion of Father Boyle's fist as Fred crosses the playground at speed, head hunched over. The priest looks barely older than some of the boys he teaches. Eyes narrowing, he sees Fred shoot a quick look back at the lavatory building. Father Boyle looks over at Father Nolan-Keegan, wordlessly bringing it to his attention. The two priests turn in unison, walk over to where Fred emerged, and go inside. The bell is placed on the ground.Fred stops in his tracks and turns around. He stares at it. As soon as the two priests are inside he is in no doubt that something bad will result. He chews a thumb nail, then, remembering the reprimands he gets from his mother for doing so, stuffs his hand deep in his pocket. He continues staring at the doors with dread anticipation, red patches burning on his cheeks, islands in his otherwise cold skin. He is positive these are beacons already advertising his complicity in the boys' thoughts about the hole and what they might see but can't do anything to stop it except press his frozen palms to the sides of his face to make them go away.

Though he doesn't have to wait long. It's less than a minute before Father Boyle comes out holding Parkhill by the scruff of the neck and Father Nolan-Keegan follows clouting the other two with the back of his hand.

Fred turns sharply away. He doesn't want to be part of that gang. Not any more. Well, he'll *say* he wasn't, if they ask. He *wasn't*. Not really.

And if they walk past him and he isn't looking at them and they're not looking at him, perhaps the Holy Brothers won't see that he was with them at all. So he'll do that. He'll look the other way. He'll pretend.

Guilty as sin.

He thinks of the policeman's eye again and he thinks of hardboiled eggs. He loathes hard-boiled egg sandwiches, sliced with that little egg-slicer in the kitchen—the guillotine type thing he always thought could be the makings of a torture instrument in the wrong hands. In the hands of a murderer, or spy. He didn't like the eye staring at him though. From a hole. He didn't like that one bit. And a little drop of wee (piss) oozes out and wets his underpants. And just then he hears children laughing and he wonders if they know he has just…

He swings around.

A group are looking down at him through railings. Girls from the Convent School next door. Up at a higher level than the boys—both physically and spiritually—they look down on him and his kind like angels in judgement. (When their playtimes coincide, at least.)

Fred blinks, realising that they *don't* know—*can't* know—but are nevertheless giggling into their hands, twisting their knees this way and that under the heavy drapery of their ankle-length skirts, covering their blushing cheeks, turning their backs and exchanging frenetic whispers simply because he is that unknown, unfathomable, mythical creature: a boy. And as soon as he is *looking at them* they are off. Gone. Like a flock of frightened geese taking to the air.

Except for one. A girl with hair the colour of ripe bananas. Of lemons. Of sunlight. Taller than the rest. Slimmer. Straighter. No chest. No *bosom*. None at all. Not like Mother. They don't even look like the same species. She's more like a foal, a colt. And not timid like the others. Not afraid to remain behind for a few moments to have a good look at him. Perhaps as curious about him as he was about her, if that could be possible. What did she find curious or interesting about *him*, for a second, he wonders? Her head is at a tilt, like the picture of Saint Francis of Assisi on the wall at home or one of the Madonnas in the Leonardo da Vinci book in the library. Her face is heart-shaped. Her chin and lips small. Her powder blue school pullover too baggy. It comes down over her wrists and hands. Her fingers are long. Her neck is thin and dove white and unblemished and doesn't quite fit her school uniform collar. Her skin is scrubbed fresh-looking and her hair pulled back in a pale blue bow that matches her eyes. And as he wanders away he can't help asking himself—because they, his *friends*, put the thought there—...what is underneath that dark, voluminous skirt?

Outside Father Mullins' study he takes his school cap from a hook, screws it on, and walks down the corridor with his satchel clutched tightly to his chest. The door is on his right. Outside it on a long bench sits O'Connor, weeping and nursing a pulsating red hand. Beside him Parkhill, who has his arms wrapped tightly around his body and is rocking in mute anticipation of what awaits him.*Cocky… Cocky…*

Dreading they might speak to him, and terrified to meet their eyes, Fred carries on past, stiffly, but already beyond the door he can hear the *swish* and stinging *slap* of the ferule as the designated punishment is meted out, slowly but surely. *Swish-slap.* Substance upon flesh. *Swish-slap.* Upon young flesh. *Swish-slap.* Again, child. *Swish-slap.* Again, the punishment. *Swish-slap…* six times. Always six times. *Six of the best.* Best what? *Swish-slap…*

Trying to block it out, he carries on walking as the door clicks open and his third friend, Murphy, shambles out in a daze nursing a crippled hand against his stomach. The creature-shape of Father Mullins emerges behind him, strap of gutta-percha like a flat ruler hanging from his hand.

"Parkhill."

Without turning, Fred hears Parkhill enter and Father Mullins shut the door. He feels his stomach roll like a yacht in a stormy sea. Quite soon he is too far away to hear the ferule fall, but every few seconds he flinches. He almost considers it his duty to flinch, even though he feels no physical pain himself. It is the least he can do.

He arrives home to see his father sawing an ungainly doorstep sandwich on a breadboard. This is not a task to which the man is accustomed, or suited, let alone skilled at, and the boy knows he can only be attempting it of necessity. "Where's Mother?"

"Having a little lie down. She's had one of her 'turns'."

He knows what that means all too well. It's strange what can be encompassed in one little word. Especially the way he said it. He wonders whether his father feels sorry for her or cares about her because he doesn't show it, not very often. But then Fred knows how she wants so much, and a lot of the time it's difficult to tell what. One time Fred's father told him she could "change like the wind", and said it like he was tired, or sad, but not angry. Just wishing things could be different, that was all.

⁎⁎

The cup of tea in its saucer rattles slightly in his hands. The room is dimly lit, curtains drawn, but it is still daylight outside. Nowhere near night-time.Mother lies in state. Her death bed would be less dramatic. She's a perfectly arranged tableau of listless woe, ready for a painter to commit to oils.

"Oh, bless you, my sweet. Sure who needs sugar when I've got you in the house?" She takes the tea and allows Fred to plump the pillows behind her, then to kiss both her cheeks. "Don't raise your voice today. Your mother has a head on her. She's weak as a bird."

"We could leave it 'til tomorrow."

"You will not." Her limp hand waves him to the foot of her bed, where he stands, ramrod-straight. A ritual that won't be foregone. "Now then. First lesson."

"English."

"And where would you be without your own Mother Tongue?"

"We started Charles Dickens today. *Great Expectations*."

"Ah, Magwich!—Terrible man."

"I like him."

"And poor Miss Havisham…"

"We haven't got to her yet."

"In her bridal weeds…If she doesn't break your heart, well, you haven't *got* a heart, that's what I say." She sips her tea. "Next?"

"Geography. We learnt all about rainfall in The Pennines."

"Never a raindrop fell in England that didn't fall tenfold in Ireland. You tell your teacher that. He might learn something."

Fred's mouth tugs a smile.

"Then?"

"Then History. The French Revolution."

"Off with his head! Let them eat cake!"

The boy chuckles. "And in Scripture we did John the Baptist."

"More decapitation!"

Fred nods.

"Who won today? Romans or Carthaginians?"

"We did. Romans."

Fred's mother claps lightly, soundlessly. Fred beams. His cheeks seem to swell.

"And what did you *see* today?"

Fred hesitates. He can't mention the hole. He can't mention the eye. He can't mention Parkhill and his friends, beckoning him to look. He can't mention their punishment. The girls behind the railings tittering behind their hands. What *can* he mention?

"A blue tit and a thrush." He uses his imagination. His imagination is all he's got. "And…and a hearse with four horses, all with black feathers on their heads."

"*Plumes!*" his mother booms it like a theatrical declamation, puffing her chest, delighted to the point of exclamation by his daily report. Then suddenly remembering her phantom illness, her voice becoming weak and plaintive as that of an injured chaffinch. "To your homework, young man. Make your dear mother proud of you." As pleading and pitiful as if they were the last desperate words she uttered on this sorry earth.

A lamentable skin forming on the Bournville cocoa at his elbow, Fred sits at a small table with his homework open in front of him, staring at the curtain covering the window, lost in thought. Snapping out of it, he places blotting paper over the last thing he wrote in his copybook. Rubbing it dry, he puts it in his satchel together with his school text books, which are wrapped in brown paper for protection. He screws the top on a bottle of Blackwood ink and wipes the nib of his pen with an old handkerchief. He buckles the straps of his school bag and hangs it up in an 'A' behind the door, eager to get to more serious work undertakings…His knees land on the bed and he faces a large chart of ships pinned to the wall. He examines it with great intensity. Tugging a newspaper closer, he moves around pins with little flags attached, placing them according to the latest details of the locations of convoys he reads in the small print.

The gaslight breathes on the wall. His bedroom is barely bigger than the awful police cell—but not cold, and not dirty, not for *dirty* people. It's warm, and tidy. The way he likes it. A place for everything and everything in its place. Puzzles and games on the top shelf, books on the bottom. Picture books to the right, novels to the left. In alphabetical order, by author's surname. Just like they should be. Conan Doyle. Stevenson. Swift. And maps almost obscuring the floral wallpaper beneath—the London Underground, together with the Trans-Siberian Railway. He doesn't suppose he'd ever be lost in Siberia, but if he were, he'd know his way around, at least. Knowing maps means you know your way around everywhere. If you know your maps you'll never be afraid.

He takes a sheaf of magazines from a drawer and lies face down on his bed with them in front of him on the pillow.

The top one is an American magazine, *Life*—the cover of which is dominated by an image of the Statue of Liberty. Of course there are statues all over London, but not like this. Not in *colour*. Everything in London is so black and white. He leafs through it, savouring even the shininess of the pages. It feels like success, it feels like happiness, it says excitement, it says glamour. In a way he only flimsily understands, the smiling women in the advertisements say pleasure. Though what kind of pleasure is a mystery. A secret. The kind of secret spies pay money for. And grown-ups kill for. And he devours it. Every word.

Underneath this is *Kine and Lantern Weekly*, a cinematic trade magazine. He turns the pages, reading amongst the camera adverts taciturn reviews of the latest releases: *Dick Turpin's Last Ride to York*, *A Slippery Visitor*, and *A Pair of Swindlers*...

He unwraps a mint humbug from his pocket and sucks it as he reads.

And as he reads, the pictures play in his head. He can see them happening. The horse's hooves blurring. The flintlock firing. The masked face of the highwayman...Chased by the law for a crime he didn't commit...

He turns onto his back.

The next magazine is *Motor Stories*—described in brazen lettering as *Thrilling Adventure Fiction!* Featuring on its cover a squarejawed driver in a frenetic chase—a lariat thrown from a moving car to catch a man on a bicycle...*Motor Matt: The King of the Wheel!*

The boy's eyes shine. The pursuit. The arrest. The criminal locked up securely behind bars. He looks at the man on the bike. He looks at the square-jawed hero. He looks at the wooden slats of the headboard of his bed. He doesn't like the things that are coming back into his head, but he can't stop them.

He sits up and looks at the back of his hand, and touches it to feel if there are any hairs growing on it. He can feel his heart beating. He bends down to the chest of drawers where his magazine collection is kept. He rummages and digs out one from the bottom of the pile. The one he is looking for. He sits back on the bed, cross-legged, and opens it across his thighs.

It is an edition of *The Illustrated Police News*, its headlines proclaiming THE BERNER ST VICTIM and TWO MORE WHITECHAPEL HORRORS: WHEN WILL THE MURDERER BE CAPTURED? In the central oval a policeman is sounding his whistle. In another box a man is finding FIFTH VICTIM OF WHITECHAPEL FIEND. Next to it a caped policeman's bull's-eye lamp illuminates the MUTILATED BODY IN MITRE SQUARE. He thinks of the woman who wasn't a woman. He feels a prickling sensation on the back of his neck and feels he is being watched. He darts a glance over his shoulder. And he *is* being watched.

On the wall is a painting of Jesus on the coast of Galilee, hands offered, chin upturned, in beatific mode, the blood-red 'Sacred Heart' bursting from his chest with golden rods of light. So well painted, his mother says, that "the eyes follow you round the room". And they do. He knows that because he's tried going into every corner, but wherever he does, Jesus is watching.

"Hail Mary, full of grace
The Lord is with thee

Blessed art thou among women
And blessed is the Fruit of your womb, Jesus
Holy Mary, Mother of God
Pray for us sinners
Now and at the hour of our death."

In pyjamas, Fred kneels on one side of the bed. His mother kneels on the other. Both have their hands clenched in prayer, and their eyes closed. Then it is time for her not to speak and for Fred to voice an additional bedtime prayer on his own:

"There are four corners on my bed,
There are four angels overhead,
Saint Matthew, Mark, Luke, and John,
God Bless the bed that I lie on."

He opens his eyes and unclasps his hands, but his mother's expression makes it clear he has not quite finished.

"And if I die before I wake," he says,
"I pray to God my soul to take,
And if any evil comes to me,
Blessed Lady waken me."

And they finish, as they always do, by saying in unison... *"Amen."*
"Good boy."

He climbs into the chill, freshly laundered sheets, and she pulls the heavy, stiff blankets up under his chin. Circling the bed, she tucks in the edges tautly under the mattress and comes upon the book at his bedside.

"How is it?"

Treasure Island.

"Scary. Exciting, but scary."

"You and your stories."

His mother leans over and kisses him on the forehead. It's slightly sticky as her lips pull away. He doesn't know whether he likes her doing it or hates it. He doesn't hate *her*—but he doesn't know if it's right for him to like it or if it's babyish. But men like kissing, don't they?

She stands up and turns the hiss of the gas light off. A faint warmish aura spills in from the landing through the half-open door behind her. And he has to ask the question before she's gone.

"Mother?"

"Yes?"

"Is Jack the Ripper still alive?"

Standing at the bedroom door, she laughs lightly at his silliness, poor thing. But it doesn't put his mind to rest.

"Did he dress as a woman? Is that why they never caught him?"

She moves back to the bed and crouches in her gathered skirts. "He ended up in a lunatic asylum. In a room no bigger than this one. For the rest of his days. Don't worry your head about him, now." She strokes his hair three times, then stands and glides back to the door.

"Can I have the light on please?"

She sighs. Walks back and re-lights the gas lamp. Turns it down slightly. Returns to the door. "There."

"Can you please leave the door open? Just a little? Please?" He has the blankets up to his chin, but he lifts his head and shoulders to watch that she does as he asks.

The door slowly closes…but stops, slightly ajar.

He swallows, his throat moistened by relief.

He sinks back into his big pillow. Into his tightly-wrapped blankets and sheets, as the gas lamp flickers above him. He thinks of the gas poisoning people. Killing them. Murderers using it to put people to sleep. To knock out women. To do what they like to them. And though he wants to sleep, he can't. It's the gas. The gas makes bad things happen. Like the gas lamp outside the police cell window. Every time his eyelids get heavy the sound of the gas makes them snap open again. He doesn't want to sleep because the thing about sleep is, you might not wake up. But if you stay awake and your parents find out you get punished for that, too.

He hears his father's boots ascend the stairs laboriously. The leather squeals and the boards groan.

He holds his breath. He hears his father sit on his bed next door, undo his laces and take off his boots. They fall to the floor. Slam. *Clunk*. He pictures his mother delicately removing the string of pearls from her neck. The bedsprings creak as she gets in beside her husband in the dark.

He hears his father coughing long and hard and a *plop* as he spits into the chamber pot. A few moments of silence later weights shift with the gentle easing of the springs and all is still.

Fred lies motionless. Almost too afraid to breathe. He's not sure why. He doesn't want to be detected. He doesn't want to be found. He is on the run—but he's not sure what he's on the run from, or why.

He turns onto his side. Eyes tightly shut.

The shadows in his room lie replete on the tiny flags on the shipping chart...on his satchel...on the cover of Robert Louis Stevenson's *Treasure Island*...

He pulls up the bed sheets to cover his face, but finds the action has exposed his bare feet at the bottom of the bed. He sits up and hastens to cover them, then lies back quickly and does his best to huddle up, foetus-like under the covers.

He determines to shut his eyes and, much as part of him fights it, lock out everything that is disturbing him, thinking only of sheep, counting sheep, that's it—or telling himself the hot cocoa is calming him like it's supposed to, and his chest isn't turbulent any more.

Little lamb whose fleece is white as snow...

What did he say? Don't think about it. Sleep. Sleep...

And he *tries* to sleep. Just as he did in that cell. That cell that seems a million miles away. That smelly, disgusting cell like one in a dungeon in some story in some fairy tale with an ogre. But he isn't there now. He's safe. He's warm. There is no ogre. No lock and key. He has his mother and father on the other side of the wall. He can even hear them breathing they are so close. He's not locked in. He's not imprisoned. He's not in any danger. He has nothing to worry about at all.

"Wakey wakey!"

His eyes refuse to open.

"Been dreaming, have you?"

The policeman's voice—from the corridor outside.

"Dreaming you were home, safe and sound, I bet…"

Fred's eyes widen as the policeman's laughter echoes like it's coming from that drain, that sewer. From the worst place in the world.

"Well you're not!"

His little tummy churns as he realises first of all that he is not nestled on his nice white mother-puffed pillow: instead his head is resting on his own crooked arm. And the mattress under him is not a mattress but hard wood. And the blankets over him are not his nice thick eiderdown and clean, newly-laundered sheets but the stiff grey, piss-infected blanket of the police station cell.

Which is what he sees around him, now, as his chest caves in. The filthy, scrawled walls. The tiny, iron-barred window with the moonlight beyond.

"You're here. I've got you, matey. I've got you forever!"

The eye.

The eye at the hole, looking in.

Fred sits up—jerks up, gulping air. Gulping enough of it into his lungs to scream—except the scream isn't necessary any more.

The dark, stinking cell is gone.

The room around him is his own bedroom in 517 The High Street—not the police station at all. He can hardly believe it. That the voice was only in his head. That his imagination—his *fear*—had put it there. And as his body tells him to breathe again, he tries to shake off the reality that was the dream, and the heavy dread that came with it. The knowledge it was a concoction doesn't free him of it. The terror in his bones doesn't listen to reason. Doesn't want to. Can't. Why can't it? Please!

His bare feet hit the icy floor. No time for slippers. He dives to the door, knocking it shut by accident. His small hands wrestle to pull it open and fling it wide.

He rushes into his parents' bedroom, sucking and panting breath as if he has run for miles.

"Can I sleep in here tonight? Can I? Can I? Please! CAN I?"

"*Jee-sus* Mary and Joseph!" His father emerges in curses and groans. "I have to be over to Covent Garden at a sparrow's fart!"

"Oh, let him be. Let him be!" His mother, wakened by the bang of the door, is already sitting up, if not fully awake. Her arms are outstretched, fingers twiddling, an instinct even be consciousness, and she hugs her son to her night-gowned body.

Simultaneously his father gets out of bed, pulling on his dressing gown from the chair, swirling the tasselled cord and yanking the knot. The man says no more, knowing of old what he has to do and not choosing to make a conversation of it. Not a fan of conversation at the best of times.

He pulls the door shut after him, knowing that his son will be taken into his wife's bed and embrace, not for the first time, and too tired to protest about it, the arguments all being well-aired and futile. He cricks his spine, wondering what's the blessed time in the name of God, walking in his darned grey bed-socks to the smaller bedroom down the landing, passing a small, framed photograph of a policeman in full uniform hanging on a nail in the wall.He shuts the door of Fred's bedroom and hangs up his dressing gown on the hook on the back of it, a large one draped over the smaller one. He sits on the bed, punching the pillow a few times. Gets in. Gets out again and turns off the gas lamp, which gives a low *phut* of annoyance as it extinguishes.

He rolls back on the bed, too small for him by far, tucking his knees up and lying on his side with his back to the door, with no intention of moving a muscle until he has to. And no intention of letting his thoughts—and, Lord knows, there are many—keep him awake. He loses too much sleep over his son as it is.

Fred's three friends never mention their punishment and neither does he. He doesn't know if shame compels them to keep it to themselves, or they harbour a resentment that he escaped unscathed. He never asks them if it hurt, though he wants to know, and they don't tell him he's not their friend any more, which he expects. They just behave as though nothing has happened. Which worries him far more than if they did, because he supposes he deserves it. He deserves something. The end of another school day, and he is walking home with them. Parkhill has something in his cupped hands that Murphy and O'Connor are peeking at. Parkhill looks over at four schoolgirls walking parallel with them on the other side of the road. Fred sees that one of them is the long, lemon-haired girl who stared at him through the Convent School railings.

Her hair is not fastened and falls in a curtain over half her face. Her tie is pulled loose, the way the boys tug open their own the minute they exit the school gates.

"Watch this."

With a jerk of the head, Parkhill leads the other boys across the street to the girls. With a confidence that Fred envies, he stands in front of them, hands in pockets, walking backwards in pace with them.

"Hello, ladies."

"What does SI stand for?" One reads the emblem on their school caps.

"Silly idiots," explains the Girl With Yellow Hair.

Her minions titter and snort into their hands. Fred removes his cap as if it is tainted. The fair-haired girl, who seems superior to the others because she is the tallest, parts a way through the boys with her hand like an ice breaker.

"Oi," Parkhill says. "That's not very nice, when we've come all the way over here with a present for you."

The girls stop and turn coldly, almost with pity, and look at them. Curious, but wary. As with everything concerning boys.

"Where is it?" The Girl With Yellow Hair says, affecting only the mildest of interest.

Parkhill shows her the palms of his hands.

"In my jacket pocket. If you want it, you have to take it."

"I don't want it."

"Are you sure about that?"

Parkhill tugs said pocket open with finger and thumb, peering inside tantalisingly.

Fred watches as one of the other girls steps forward but the Girl With Yellow Hair steps in front of her.

"He's talking to me."

"No he isn't," the other girl protests. "Anyway, you said you didn't want it."

"I changed my mind."

The other, dumpy and easily affronted, slumps off in a sulk. "Maria!"

Her friend, black hair in pigtails, flounces off with her. "Silly idiots!"

"I don't want it anyway," the dumpy girl hurls back at them. "Whatever it is."

"Well?" Parkhill says. Two left. "Who's it going to be?"

The skinny, freckle-faced girl is keen, but looks nervous, tugging at her lower lip. The Girl With Yellow Hair waits for her to make a move for it, but when she doesn't, The Girl With Yellow Hair does so herself.

She reaches out to put her hand in Parkhill's pocket—then pauses, staring Parkhill squarely in the eyes. Hoping something might be revealed there, but Parkhill's grin gives nothing away. It's a gamble she will have to take.

Fred watches. Waits.

She looks at her freckle-faced friend, then back at her other two, who are waiting at a considerable distance now. Then, unexpectedly abandoning the last vestige of caution, she plunges her hand deep into Parkhill's pocket. A hesitation, then—

She retracts it with a piercing *SHRIEK.*

Fred jumps in fright, just hearing it.

The Girl With Yellow Hair backs away quickly, mouth wide open in an 'O', her chest rising and falling rapidly.

"You horrid, *horrid*—!"

Grinning, Parkhill takes the 'present' out of his pocket. A

mouse—a wild one caught in the bushes near the playground, tiny and brown—which is now running over one of his hands then the other with its miniscule pink paws and black pearl eyes. Murphy and O'Connor laugh loudly in an almost hostile manner, almost jeering at their victory. Fred doesn't. He is too busy looking at The Girl With Yellow Hair, who is gulping her breath, near to tears, wiping her hand—the hand that touched the mouse—on the thick material of her skirt as she backs rapidly away.

"You think you're funny? Well you're not. You're just—you're just...*horrible!*"

And because he is frightened and because he is upset, Fred starts laughing too—realising most of all, even though it might hurt the girl, that his laughter bonds him with the other boys, and that is far more important than what any *girl* might think. Isn't it?

Ignoring the taunts and poked tongues, Murphy dangles the mouse by the tail and drops it back into Parkhill's open pocket. They have achieved some victory. They have scared a girl, and it was fun.

Fred watches the females, long skirts, long hair, uniforms, stride away but only the one in pigtails looks back, briefly. He blinks. A frown is etched on her forehead. He wants to smile. He wants not to be nasty. It was a joke. He realises he *is* smiling, and he wonders why. He feels excited, too—and he wishes it could last longer. Much longer. Forever, in fact...

Then he realises Murphy and O'Connor are following Parkhill in the other direction, and he follows, upping his speed to catch up with them before they disappear round the corner.

"What happens to the mouse?" Fred asks.

"We kill it," Parkhill says, as if the remark hardly needed saying at all.

They emerge from a path beside some allotments and cross a stile into a field dotted with dandelions and tall weeds. O'Connor breaks a branch from a low-hanging tree and swishes it against the long grass. Fred snaps off another, briefly 'sword-fencing' with him before

O'Connor stabs him in the tummy. It hurts, but he doesn't say so. O'Connor holds his weapon above his head triumphantly, then slides it into a belt-loop of his shorts. Fred tiptoes around nettles. Hacks at a leaf with a ladybird on it. The stone gateposts of an old house. One that has been derelict for years and has fallen into ruin. The windows are smashed or non-existent. There are no actual gates. In the overgrown garden, Fred and his mates kneel in a circle. Parkhill holds the mouse in his cupped hands. Each of the boys holds a house brick aloft.

Parkhill lets the mouse free on the ground between them and the boys madly attempt to clobber it—but the animal is too fast for them. It gets away. It's gone. They jump to their feet and rush around trying to find it, stamping, prodding with mossy sticks and dropping stones, lifting rolls of old carpet and heaving aside a rusty tin bath full of orange rainwater.

Fred just stands there. He thinks the mouse got away fair and square. He isn't keen to catch it any more and he isn't sure he wanted to see it squashed and bloody in the first place. It didn't do anything wrong. It was just a mouse.

Instead he turns and stares at the old house behind them.

His friends aren't watching. They're hunting.

Fred walks inside. He's a little bit scared. Just a little bit. But in another way it is really quiet and peaceful. He feels he is exploring like Dr Livingstone or Stanley and he feels he is being brave in a way that will make his friends like him and make his father proud of him. If there is fear in this house—this *haunted- looking* house— he wants to face it and prove to himself he *can* face it, because he is tired of trying to imagine what fear is like all the time, what it is like to be terrified out of your skin, and die of terror, of something so frightening your heart just stops. If it's going to happen, he'd rather get it over with.

In his polished black shoes he treads across the assorted debris, the broken plaster work and strips of wood layered in stone dust.

He looks up above him. Through the large holes where floorboards have caved in he can see into the shabby, abandoned rooms above.

He looks around him at the cracks in the walls, the wattle and daub exposed. The peeling paint of the door frames and fire surrounds. Outside he can hear Parkhill calling.

"Cocky! Cock! Where are you, mate?"

Fred doesn't answer.

He is looking at a filthy door with chipped paint. A plain door with a sliding bolt on it. He steps closer to it, touches the bolt. It's rusty, but with a bit of what his father calls "elbow grease" he pulls it back and yanks the door open.

He stares inside.

*
**

Lying in bed that night, eyes open and sparkling in his doughy complexion, he blinks away his thoughts of the house and the door as he hears footsteps and a voice outside his window. A woman's nervous laughter. A woman like his mother but not like his mother at all."No. No." Playful—then insistent. "No. *No…*"

He gets out of bed and goes to the window, clambering up onto his homework desk, pulling back the curtain and cautiously looking out, his breath clouding the cold glass of the pane. He rubs it away with his fingers.

Through the clear oval the street and night look cold and grey. It's black and white out there, like a film. A man and a woman, both in raincoats and hats, linger under the down-light of a street lamp. The man has his arms around the woman's waist. His head is nuzzling into her throat and cheek, a dog with a bone. She is pushing him away—but half-heartedly. In earnest one minute, then giggling the next.

"No! I said—*No!*"

The man embraces her more tightly—more *roughly*, forcing her body against his—and plants a long, unrelenting kiss on her lips. After it she separates from him, getting her breath back, then turns her back on him and walks away, a sway in her hips and her handbag dangling from her hand. He looks up unexpectedly, and sees Fred looking down at him.

Fred's spine stiffens. He hops back a few inches.

But the man grins. His chin bluish and unshaven. Still looking up at Fred, he makes his left hand into a fist and inserts his right index finger repeatedly into the hole he has created.

Fred swallows.

Grinning enough to show his teeth, the man pulls down his hat brim and lopes away after the woman, who has slowed down, clearly expecting him to follow her. Dawdling. So what she was protesting about Fred is at a loss to know. Was it a game? What sort of game? The sort of game he played in the playground with his friends? Do grown-ups play those games? What for? Fun? What kind of fun? And why did she say no when she meant yes? And why, after pushing him away, is she now hooking her arm around the man's?

Fred remains motionless, kneeling on his homework desk, trying to make sense of the gesture the man gave, the tight expressive movement of it, the vulpine glee in the night-eyes that went with it. Something upsets him about it and he doesn't know what. It was like stabbing. It was like hurting. It was like a wound. It was like Jack the Ripper.

He lets the curtain fall back, but before he can shrink away back to bed he hears whistling. Again from outside. Ululating from the brickwork. Some human nightingale. And a song that he knows intimately. Though it diverts from the melody quite a lot, pausing then trilling, the words can't help but go through his mind—he can't stop them…

A mother was bathin' her baby one night
The youngest of ten, the poor little mite
The mother was fat and the baby was fin
T'was nawt but a skellington wrapped up in skin…

Afraid what he might behold, but compelled to look just the same, he lifts the corner of the curtain again and peers out. The pane has started to mist up again but what he sees through it is all too clear…

The *policeman*—the very same sergeant of his incarceration no less—walks into the cone of light of the street lamp. Buttons glinting like stars against the night-black of him.

Fred hops back off his desk, landing on his feet, shuffling back quickly from the window until the bed hits the back of his knees, forcing him to sit on it. He presses his hands under his behind but he can't keep still. The invisibility of the policeman is somehow worse than the seeing of him, and he can't bear it. Because if he isn't out there—where is he? Inside the house? Outside the bedroom door? Why can't he hear the jaunty yet sinister whistling any more?

He jumps up again and scrambles back onto his desk on all fours. Not wanting to look but *having* to look, he plucks up sufficient courage—where from, he hasn't a clue, he isn't a hero, he isn't even a *man*—and bends his head round the curtain, pulling it taut with his hands, a shield...

The policeman pauses on his beat, hands behind his back, rocking back and forth on the balls of his feet, bending his knees in a slight squat. His truncheon dangles from his leather belt with its 'snake' clasp. His eyes are buried in extreme shadow—grim, dark orbits of a skull on the Jolly Roger of a pirate ship. The strap of his helmet sits on the jut of his chin. The Brunswick Star on his midnight helmet glimmers. He blows into his cupped hands and rubs them together for warmth, but they remain white as chalk. As bone. Just up the High Street the bells of Saint John the Baptist (C of E) chime the hour—dull, solemn, funereal.

Fred jumps back, right onto the bed this time, with his knees in the air. He scuttles against the headboard and holds his breath, covering his mouth with his hand, convinced for a horrible minute that the policeman is coming to fetch him. That he is about to knock the door. That he is out there, looking up at the window the way the man with the stabbing finger looked up...

But why—why would he come at night-time? Why would he come *at all?* Was it a 'surprise raid'? Is that what they did with spies or suspected murderers? Did the sergeant have more evidence against him? Had somebody out there blabbed? Told lies about him? Perhaps his friends had. Parkhill. O'Connor. His socalled friends, that he trusted. And now…

But wait—can he be sure? The policeman hasn't knocked the door—*yet*. What is he waiting for? Is he waiting for Fred to give himself up? Come out with his hands up? Confess everything? Is *that* why he's here?

The little boy creeps back to the curtain. Hooks his fingers around the edge of it. Moves it gently, so gently, aside. Holding his breath…

The downward-pointing cone of lamplight is empty but for a duo of moths doing tiny figures of eight.

The policeman has evaporated, like the holy wafer on his tongue, into nothingness.

Not much but a crack of light gets in, even on a sunny day, and on a dull one it's like pitch. They know no-one looks here during school hours, and the priests *never* look here. They'd never get their hands dirty. They leave that to the caretaker. So this is where the gang go to be alone. The coal hole is their place. Their domain. Their den. It smells of soot and they have to blow their noses before they go home because their nostrils are full of black dust. It's dirty and Fred knows Father Mullins—old scrotum-face, as they call him—would say that's why it suits them, because *they're* dirty too. Nothing but *dirty, dirty* boys. O'Connor and Murphy have a pack of cards and are playing Strip Jack Naked. Parkhill sits smoking a pipe. It's his grandfather's. There's no tobacco in it but it smells of rough Navy shag. Parkhill likes sucking it, believing it confers on him a wisdom beyond his years, and does so with great gravity, cross-legged, as he considers what Fred is reporting.

"He went like this." Fred repeats the obscene gesture of the man under the street light.

Inscrutable until now, Parkhill gives a grin from ear to ear.

"You know what that is?"

"What?"

"That's what your father does to your mother," Parkhill says, eyes narrowing with enjoyment, leaning forward for emphasis. "Puts his winkle in her whatsit…" Hushed now. "*Regina.*"

Fred is sceptical. "Don't be stupid!"

"I'm not being stupid. It's true."

"My father wouldn't do that."

"He would. They all do. They have to. They enjoy it!"

"Who?"

"Your father. *And* your mother."

"My mother wouldn't enjoy *that*!"

"Yer, she does." Parkhill's pipe jabs Fred's shoulder. "*And* they do it all the time. Not just when they want to make babies, either."

This is a serious revelation for Fred, and he disputes its veracity almost entirely.

"*I've* never seen them do it."

"'Course you haven't, you berk. They do it in secret, don't they? In bed. In private. It starts with kissing and that, usually."

Fred is confused, as well as appalled. "But you wee with it. That's what it's for. How can it be for—what you say?"

"It's why women and men are different. So they can fit inside each other." The end of the pipe is back clenched in Parkhill's teeth, springing erect as he pokes his right index finger into his left fist with the same jabbing rhythm of the man the night before.

Fred looks away. "You mean that's why God made them like that?"

"Well he did, didn't he?"

"But that's a sin. Isn't it?"

Parkhill shrugs.

Fred asks, "Will we have to do it too?"

"If you want to have children you will."

"I don't."

"If you want a girl to love you, you do."

"No, I don't."

Fred stands up, wipes the coal dust off the rump of his shorts, to go back to lines before the bell rings. Parkhill shrugs that he can please himself but Fred doesn't care. He's heard enough nonsense and Parkhill is being stupid. O'Connor and Murphy look up, as if only just aware of the conversation, mainly because he is standing on their cards. They slap his legs. It doesn't hurt but Fred feels tears in his eyes a little bit and doesn't want them to see them because he's angry at them too. He's not sure why.

"You ask Father Mullins where babies come from," Parkhill pronounces as Fred lifts the latch on the door. "He'll tell you. They come from the hole between your mother's legs where your dad put his dickie in."

O'Connor and Murphy giggle.

"I know that." Fred looks back at him sternly. "*Everybody* knows that."

He pulls the coal house door shut after him.

In the lavatory cubicle, Fred unbuttons his shorts, standing at the toilet bowl.He stares at the peep-hole in the wall. It has now been plastered over. Instead of weeing he buttons up his shorts and reaches over and touches the rough texture of the plaster with his fingertips. He turns round and sits on the toilet. Elbows on knees. Thinking.

Small, unevenly cut-up pieces of old newspapers hang up on a nail. He tugs one off but the nail falls out. He picks it up.

He places it in the palm of his left hand, a daring action occurring to him and instantly filling him with fear and trepidation. But also a compulsion that makes him feel quite excited at the prospect. The prospect of doing something he shouldn't.

He starts to cut into the wall of the stall with the point of the nail, using it like a tiny pencil, drawing a swift image in large, definite sweeps.

Of a large, spouting penis and balls—the same crude graffito that he saw on the stinking wall of the horrid police cell.

He looks at it with some satisfaction. His mother often brags that he is "a good drawer" and here is the evidence—not that she will ever see it. He has reproduced the ferocious genitals exactly. It is quite an achievement. He realises his heart is beating hard in his chest and he swallows. He can hardly believe that he did it. He is proud of himself, but terrified. He thinks of the priests and the slap of the dreaded ferule. He thinks of his mother. He thinks of the policeman under the street lamp. He thinks of the squelchy, nasty gesture made by Parkhill and the man in the hat— even though he doesn't know why it worries him and makes him feel odd. He doesn't even know why he wanted to do it, but it's too late for that—he has.

He prods the nail back through the hole in the sheets of newspaper and presses it back into the wall, but it falls out onto the floor. He tries again but the nail falls out again, tinkling. This time he leaves it there. He stands up, pulls the chain of the cistern to flush it and leaves.

And the thing is this, he finds.

Once he is in the playground, nobody knows he has done an awful thing. The crime might be discovered, yes, but anybody might have committed it. There is no way for anybody to tell it was *him*. It is exciting in a way he didn't expect. It makes him feel like he knows what it is like to get away with murder.

The Yellow-Haired Girl who had been frightened by the mouse is walking along, a pair of ice skates slung over one shoulder. "Leave me alone."

"I'm not doing anything," Fred says.

"Yes you are. You're bothering me."

"No I'm not."

"Yes you are." She turns to face him. "Go away."

He stands his ground. His inner terror is blatantly obvious, though he imagines it does not show. He is shorter than her and plumper than her. In every regard imaginable, it is an uneven match.

"This isn't the way you go home," she says.

"Sometimes it is."

"Where are your friends?"

"They're not my friends. Not really."

He has his hands in his pockets.

"What have you got in your pocket?"

"Something."

"A mouse?"

Fred opens one pocket slightly and looks in.

"It might be…Go on."

He's asking her to reach inside. She huffs. He must be joking if she'll fall for that a second time. Is he really that stupid?

"I see," he says. "You're scared."

"No I'm not."

"It might be something nice."

Of course, it might be. But…

She steps closer.

Her shoulders are square and she shows a certain bravado, but Fred can see she is tense inside. Untrusting. And why should she trust him? She shouldn't. But she doesn't know for *certain* there's something bad in there, either—and that's why he has her. The element of doubt. The element of doubt that one boy might not be as nasty as the last one. She's nobody's fool, and he likes that. She isn't pretending to be weak and watery and she isn't acting being scared so that somebody will look after her. She will look after herself. She's almost a boy like that. But she isn't *completely* a boy. She isn't *completely* safe. She isn't shy and she isn't mouthy and she isn't silly and she doesn't run away, but he enjoys the look of fear on her face. The look that wants to trust him but doesn't. Can't…

He nods.

Go on. It'll be all right. You'll see…

But will it? Will it be all right?

His stomach tightens as she forces herself to take another step closer to him in her ankle-length school skirt and lace-up boots. He senses her incipient bosom under the immaculately-ironed shirt.

She runs her tongue over her lips. Her eyes flicker. She swallows.

Go on…

She reaches into his pocket and retracts her hand quickly.

Though, wait. Nothing awful happened—her hand is still

attached to her arm with no visible sign of attack. So she slides it inside, more confidently a second time. Wondering what is supposed to be there. Fingers spidering. Feeling around for it…

He watches her expression change. The fear dissipate. She looks at her palm.

"Empty. What was the point of that?"

Fred smiles.

"The point was, you did it."

She wrinkles her nose. "Very funny."

"Oh, sorry…It's in *this* pocket…" He rummages. Takes out a box of England's Glory matches. Holds it out to her. "Look inside."

"You must be joking."

"Open it. Please."

She carefully slides off the outer sleeve. And jumps with a SQUEAL—then almost immediately emits a honeyed, tremulous laugh that has the same effect on him as his mother's tickle.

In the matchbox is a child's thumb. A severed child's thumb, in cotton wool, with dabs of blood around it.

Fred extracts his own thumb from the hole in the box. Shows her how the trick was achieved.

"Why did you do that?"

"It's funny."

"No it's not, it's frightening."

"I thought it was funny. It made you laugh, didn't it?"

The Girl With Yellow Hair backs away, tilts her foot, swivels her ankle, walks away. Fred follows a few paces behind. She lets him, now.

"You know, you could kill people with those."

He means the ice skates.

"Why would I do that?"

"I don't know. No one would suspect the murder weapon. You'd get away with it. That would make a good twist."

"Twist?"

"That's a thing in a crime story you don't expect. Like the person who did it seems really nice, but they're not."

"I don't like to think about people not being nice."

Fred's mouth tugs down at the ends.

"I do."

They go up the steps to cross the railway line via an iron bridge over the tracks.

"Finsbury Park. Gillespie Road. Holloway Road. Caledonian Road. York Road. King's Cross. Russell Square. Holborn." He wonders why she laughs at him, but it isn't a nasty laugh, it's a nice one. "I know all the underground lines," he says. "And the bus routes."

"What's your name?"

He tells her.

The girl sniggers. She can't help it. "Itch. Cock. Itchy cock." She sees his intense embarrassment, and blushes. Just like he is doing already. "Sorry."

"I hate my name. What's yours?"

"Olga Butterworth."

"That's nice."

"No it isn't." She watches him pondering. "I'm not foreign. I'm English. My dad is from Lancashire and my mother's a Suffragette."

"Is she?"

Before she can answer, Fred hears a train chugging into the station below. Automatically, he takes out his note book and pencil to catch its number. Then double-takes and looks at Olga, who is smiling slightly. He fumbles to put it back in his pocket without writing anything inside.

As the train pulls into the platform underneath them, the billowing smoke rises from it like a great fog. It envelops them almost supernaturally, like a theatrical effect. Olga laughs. Unafraid of the supernatural, or of theatrical effects, and strangely, makes him feel unafraid too. But when the billowing clouds disperse, Fred sees that she has vanished, as if in a magic trick—just like his. He goes to the railing. Relieved to see her descending the steps on the far side.

He keeps watching as she walks from the railway bridge to the back door of a terraced house beside the railway track, leading into a small back yard. She shuts the door and a dog starts barking.

His eyes go up from the ground floor, where she enters, to the next floor up, where a bird cage hangs outside a half-shuttered window…to the next floor, where he sees Olga walk in and hang up her ice skates. In the little room her mother and father greet her. Olga laughs and demonstrates a little pirouette.

On the railway bridge, Fred looks down at something clutched in his little hand. It is the England's Glory matchbox. He takes out the inner tray and holds the hole up to his eye.

*
**

His mother swishes the blade of a carving knife and a sharpening iron back and forth vigorously. Her body jiggles. Her breasts and hips shudder under her clothing.Fred sits at the kitchen table, a book in front of him. He turns to look at his father, who is seated by the fireplace in an armchair, one hand in a boot which he is blacking to a rare shine, dabbing the brush periodically in a one penny tin of Cherry Blossom.

His mother glides to the mantelpiece and winds the clock. One of her many onerous tasks. Fred watches her bottom, the taut lines from the waist of her skirt and the way they change as she moves. His father stops brushing and looks at the boy.

Fred puts his nose back in the book. Coughs. Then closes it.

"I've done my homework. May I go out and get some train numbers?"

His mother adds, "Please."

"Please."

Fred takes the silence for a yes. He heads to his room.

"Don't be late for bed."

The door closes. Her voice follows him.

Unseen by his parents, Fred kneels beside his bed. Pulls a case out from under it. *Up to no good*, someone might say. The policeman might say. But he doesn't know whether it's good or not good, he just has to do it. And takes out a pair of binoculars and puts them in his satchel.

"Early to bed and early to rise makes a boy healthy, wealthy, and wise."

Fred's father looks at his wife who has spoken as the boy passes between them. A quiet man, who seldom finds that quality valued by many. Who sometimes thinks himself a freak of nature in the calamitous racket and rush of the new century.

*
**

Steam rises. He stands on the railway bridge. A train lingers on the platform below. But Fred's gaze—and the binoculars—are set on the back of the terraced house that Olga Butterworth calls her home. The bird cage is being attended by an age-dappled old woman who is sprinkling bird feed through the bars.

He tilts the binoculars up.

Above, in a sitting room, Olga's father is wearing a fancydress black beard—a comical, ridiculous disguise.

In the room above that, Olga leans out of the window to peg out a pair of socks to dry. White socks. School socks. She pulls the curtains, then a gas light brightens, casting her silhouette on the hanging wall of cloth as she walks back and forth within.

He watches.

He is *there* to watch…

It's his job.

He wishes he could hear her voice.

He wishes he were closer.

The binocular lenses are fogged-up from the steam.

He cleans them diligently with a handkerchief wrapped round his first two fingers.

When he raises the object back to his eyes, there are other shapes cast on the curtain now—hand-shadows in the shape of a duck, then a rabbit…

Then the light dies like a vast disappointment.

*
**

Eyes fixed on the pavement ahead, he walks home past a large poster on a wall advertising the local skating rink, with a smiling woman sporting ice skates. He doesn't look up. It's later than he intended and he doesn't want to get a row. As he crosses the road he hears a hubbub of noise from the nearby pub. It becomes considerably louder when the doors open and two people are briefly regurgitated. A drunk woman in a second-hand fur coat is swaying, hardly able to keep upright, or even find her own mouth with her cigarette. She stops dead when she sees Fred staring over at her."Got a good eyeful, have you, love?"

Fred can almost feel her rancid alcoholic breath in his face at twenty yards. There's laughter and Fred turns his head to see the equally drunk man in a bowler hat swaying on his heels, pissing at full flood in the doorway of a church. The flow of his urination, now trickling down the steps between his legs, would be the envy of a stallion.

Fred ducks his head down and walks away, his walk very quickly breaking into a run.

He reaches the doors of his father's grocer's shop, out of breath. The sign on the inside of the door says 'CLOSED'. Shooting desperate glances over his shoulder, he fumbles for his key. In his urgency to get inside he drops it.It hits the ground and bounces, tinkling, towards a drain.

He falls to one knee, sprawls, snatching it up from the very edge of the gutter. Saved. Just before it was lost to the sewers.

He jumps to his feet, inserts it, turns it quickly in the lock, hurries inside, locking the door behind him.

He brushes the dirt off his knee and runs through the dark of the shop but forgets he has his satchel on and the satchel catches the edge of a box of apples which cascade onto the floor. Fred tries to stop them but it's too late. They are tumbling all around him.

"Who is it?"

Mother's voice, from above.

"Only me!"

Fred takes off his satchel and starts packing the apples back into the box on the trestle table. He collects them by the armful. Arranges them neatly one by one. He doesn't want his father giving him a look the next day with his beady eye. When he has done so to his satisfaction, he stands back to finally assess his work.

Hello?

He sees that a corner of the matting on the floor is turned up and there is something under it. Something—but *what?*

Curious, he kneels down and peels the mat back further.

Under it is a brown envelope.

He takes it out, thinks a moment, looks around—stupidly—to see if anybody is watching (how could they be?) then hides it up his jumper.

He smoothes down the matting and presses it flat with his toe before venturing up the stairs. Dipping his fingers in the font as he passes, and genuflecting before Our Lady, but almost forgetting to.

"Where's Father?" He closes the door.She sits reading a slim volume by gaslight. The Saint Francis picture flickers on the wall in its sepia glow. The birds seem to flutter.

"Gone to the pub." She closes her book—the Romantic poets—and pats the settee beside her. "Just the two of us. Just the way I like it."

"Mother, I'm tired. All those trains…And it's school tomorrow."

She pulls a sad face. Then makes a smile. But it's a sad one. It has to be.

He knows how this works and he has to ignore her or she'll get her own way. He has to be 'not nice'. He has to be like a man. He walks in the direction of his bedroom. His hand reaches for the door handle.

"Ah-ah!"

He turns around.

She points to her cheek.

He is duty-bound to come back and kiss it. It smells of Parma violets. He presses the flat of his hand to his tummy to hold the envelope there, in case she notices it.

"You don't have tummy ache, do you?"

"Me? No."

He backs away a few steps, smoothes his pullover flat, puts his hands behind his back. Turns. Goes.

"Don't forget your prayers, now."

Bare boards, hard seats, cheap beer. In the Public Bar of the Ten Bells, an assortment of drinkers laugh raucously at the spectacle before them. In the light of a crackling fire the policeman who locked up young Fred is carousing—that's the word, *carousing*— with the drunk woman. Her fur coat is on the floor and some loutish working men are standing on it with their big, filthy boots as they swig back the thin, brown liquid from their pint glasses. The policeman occupies a stool by the grate and she is sitting, swivelling on his knee. He has the drunk woman's shoe in his hand and is holding it high over his head, out of her reach. She is trying to reach up and snatch it off him. She can't, but by doing so she is rubbing her body against his tunic. As she jumps in short, sharp jerks, her fingers stretching, her breasts are in his face. Her breasts jiggle.

Fred's father stands at the bar watching this.

Pairs of trousers surround her as she sways. The spectators ogle the entertainment like dogs on heat. Half a jug more and their tongues would be waggling. It's not often they get a show like this, that's for sure. A knees-up or a singsong round the Joanna and that's it. Where's the harm in it, eh? It's only a game. *Only a bit of fun, innit? Cor blimey…*

Fred's father finishes his beer and knocks back a chaser of whisky.

"That'll put hairs on your chest," says the barmaid.

He pushes the shot glass towards her, succumbs to a nod, meaning he'd like a top-up.

The barmaid shows him her back as she upturns the whisky

bottle into the copper measure. He turns his head as he sees someone reflected in the etched bar mirror behind the array of bottles. He looks along the counter. The boy Parkhill is sitting on a tall stool behind the bar with a kitten on his knees, stroking it and drinking ginger beer from a bottle with a straw in it.

Parkhill sees him, and knows him, but doesn't smile.

Having emptied the second glass down his throat, Fred's father looks back at the policeman, who is having a great time. Red-faced in his uniform. Looking as if his collar might burst. Laughing and puffing on a fat, thick cigar that is wrapping both figures and audience in great gouts of smoke. The copper's tunic pulls at shiny buttons as he leans back on two legs of the stool. His belly, thrust out against the woman, threatens to pop them. And other buttons threaten to pop too. She doesn't find him even slightly odious. She runs her hands over his body, her white skin baby-soft against the black. The policeman's yellow teeth are exposed as he laughs and coughs cigar detritus. His tongue is layered and slug-like, eyes lost under puffy lids.

Fred's father imagines that a kiss is imminent, and turns back to the bar.

The policeman is repulsive, yet the woman hangs herself around him as if he is the most handsome man in London. He reminds Fred's father of some Roman Emperor at an orgy. A Nero being peeled a grape. Being pleasured by his concubine. He realises Nero is the only Roman Emperor he knows by name. His son no doubt knows the lot of them. His son could give him a list. With dates, probably. His son is good like that.

A cheer goes up as the woman closes her teeth around one of the brass buttons, threatening to bite.

*

He opens the brown envelope in bed. His heart starts beating faster. Inside he finds a small selection of saucy photographs. He knows the word *saucy* because O'Connor told him it once. Because he recognises a few foreign words he knows these are the kind made in a French photographic studio with nude models showing *all they've got*. The women, buxom, curvaceous, are striking exotic, theatrical poses. Chubby, rounded hips. Breasts cupped and offered in their hands. Peacock feathers in their hats—which is all they have on. Nipples like the suckers of the arrows he fires with his bow in the back yard. Ladies bent over with a coy finger to their chins, showing the camera the crack of their behinds. Curly hair falling loosely to shoulders, and other hair on display, dark and plentifully, below…

The policeman puts the drunk woman's shoe to his eye. He peers through a hole in it, eyeballing the other drinkers like a pirate through a telescope. The other male drinkers laugh uproariously. Framed by the hole, the sergeant's iris is gigantic. His pupil dilated, engorged. His laugh rumbles from the cave of his chest and fills the pub with his presence, his dictatorship. Not that you could call it a laugh. Nothing of pleasure. The sound of a gravedigger's spade sinking into soil and bones.

He thinks of The Girl With Yellow Hair in her long skirt and lace-up boots. He covers the face of one of the nudes with the flat of his hand.He catches his breath as he hears the gramophone in the other room start to play: a thin, high-pitched recording as an orchestra strikes up a spritely popular tune. Who is it? Who's there? Has somebody broken into the house? A thief? Have they come to get him? He's going to be caught red-handed! His bedroom door starts to open.

In a blur he hides the risqué photographs under his pillow.

The door swings open, slowly—wider…

From behind the half-open door a female leg graced with the diamond pattern of a fishnet stocking kicks in and out in time with the music.

For a bizarre moment he wonders, is it the policeman? In disguise? Is it the woman from the police station with the hairs on the back of her hand? Is it Jack the Ripper?

But no…

His mother saunters into the room trailing an umbrella as if on a Sunday stroll, the fingers of one hand a platform under her chin. She wears her petticoat over a short-sleeved frock and a huge bonnet with a big ribbon is perched jauntily on her crowning glory.

> *"I'm a young girl, and have just come over,*
> *Over from the country where they do things BIG*
> *And amongst the boys I've got a lover*
> *And since I've got a lover, why I don't care a FIG…"*

She sings with gusto, accompanying the trill voice on the recording like the proper music hall *artiste* she imagines herself, in another life, to be. Nailing every giddy double entendre despite her son's evident lack of comprehension.

> *"The boy I love is up in the gallery,*
> *The boy I love is looking now at me*
> *There he is, can't you see, waving his handkerchief*
> *As merry as a robin that sings on a tree…"*

Fred grins with instant relief, but she thinks it is because he is adoring it. Adoring *her*. But he is grinning because he has to. He knows. He's her (captive) audience, of one—and it's not for the first time. Though never at this time of night. Though never *wakened* for a performance, 'til now…

> *"The boy that I love, they call him a cobbler*
> *But he's not a cobbler, allow me to state*
> *For Johnny is a tradesman and he works in the Boro'*
> *Where they sole and heel them, whilst you wait…"*

Fred beams, feigning his enjoyment—no, feeling it, a little—as she plays up the innuendo with saucy winks and big, pantomime gestures, as she always does. What a turn! What a star!

> *"The boy I love is up in the gallery*
> *The boy I love is looking now at me*
> *There he is, can't you see, waving his handkerchief*
> *As merry as a robin that sings on a TREE!"*

As expected, she ends on a big finish, arms flung wide. Face upturned to the Gods as the music ends and the trail of the gramophone needle renders a scratchy liturgy on the air.

"*Bravo!*" Fred applauds madly, kneeling up in his striped pyjamas.

In the glow of imaginary limelight his mother curtseys like a little girl. Exits stage left. (To take the record off the turntable.) Returning daintily for her all-important curtain-call. Soaking up the adulation. Every single grocer's weighing scale ounce of it.

"*Encore!*" Fred cries out till he's hoarse. "*Encore!*"

His mother sits on the end of the bed, getting her breath back. A modest hand resting lightly on her breast bone. Her chest rising and falling. He keeps on clapping furiously. Doesn't know when to stop. Daren't stop. Sometimes it seems no amount of applause is enough for his dear old mum.

Her hand doesn't move. Her eyes are on the floor. Her face darkens. Her mood slowly changes. He sees a mysterious pain cross her doll-white features.

"Stop. *Stop* it," she says curtly. Almost like a spit. Then catches his hands to immobilise them, as if the very applause she craves is now anathema to her, and unbearable.

Immediately she realises she was harsh, and is horrified—it was unforgivable, and she pats his little fists. She sits at the side of the bed. Takes his hand in hers and kisses them, full of remorse and utter self-doubt. Making amends for something Fred doesn't even begin to understand, but feels like a dreadful and inexplicable ache.

Eyes shining in the semi-dark, she tucks aside a stray curl from his forehead. Looks into his face, sadly but lovingly. Desperate to ask something but afraid of the answer that might come.

"Do you think your mother's as pretty as an actress?"

"Yes. Of course," Fred says.

"Really and truly?"

"Yes, definitely. You're better than Marie Lloyd."

She laughs lightly. A half-caught breath. "And Florrie Ford?"

"*And* Florrie Ford!"

"Oh, you terrible boy!" First of all she sounds delighted, then she sounds bereft—full of heartache. "You terrible boy…"

She is thoughtful for a moment. She sniffs. Seems to be wiping away a tear. Then gets up quickly, turns the gas light down and walks to the door. A different person turns back.

"Your father'll want his bed tonight. You understand, don't you? It's time to be a big boy."

Fred nods.

His mother leaves the room, closing the door after her.

A few seconds later it eases open a few inches. She leaves it like that. The way he likes it.

And he lies back in his bed, head sinking into the pillow, staring at the ceiling. Thinking of the applause he gave. Thinking he would like it too, one day, for himself.

* * *

She wears earrings at the breakfast table. "I've been thinking." His father dips a corner of bread in the yolk of his egg. "He should come on the cart today. Time he started learning his trade."

"There's no need for that." His mother eats her triangles of toast carefully with her finger tips. "He's destined for bigger things than being a *greengrocer*…" That last word a sing-song of derision, insensitive to her own insensitivity.

"He won't go far wrong in life if he knows how to get his hands dirty."

They talk as if he isn't sitting between them. He looks from one to the other as they speak. But there is no more to say.

* * *

He follows his father through the shop. When he is sure nobody can see, he drops to his knees and swiftly takes the envelope of naughty photographs from under his jumper, slipping them back beneath the matting, where they belong.

*
**

His father holds the reins of the cart as the horse pulls it along at a steady pace. He wears a muffler round his neck tied in an untidy knot of which his wife would not approve. Fred sits next to him, hands neatly resting in his lap, mainly because he doesn't know what else to do with them. He feels like it's riding on a stagecoach in the cowboy stories he reads. Riding shotgun for Wells Fargo, protecting the US Mail from marauding apaches with paint over their bodies and feathers in their hair who might catch them and scalp them. Or bury them up to their necks in the sand and wait for the poison ants to bite and give them a slow and agonising demise.His father makes a click-clicking sound with his tongue. Flicks the reins and guides the horse over to the pavement. A Thomas Flyer beeps and overtakes him, its engine growling.

He hands Fred the reins.

Fred grips them tightly.

His father gets down from the cart and lifts a stack of vegetable boxes from the back.

Fred watches as he walks to a grocer's shop. The woman who owns it stands outside with her legs apart. She looks like she owns it, anyway, because she doesn't call out her husband. Perhaps her husband is dead. Perhaps she poisoned him. Put him in a barrel. A tin bath. A bag of potatoes…

She is big-busted and thin-waisted, with her hands on her hips and sleeves rolled up from tiny wrists. They exchange words chattily which Fred cannot hear as another car passes, rattling and tooting.

His father puts down the vegetable boxes, laughing easily with her which Fred thinks is not right. He doesn't laugh with his mother. He watches him strike a muscle man pose and the woman feels his bicep. She strikes a similar pose. He tickles her under-arm and she laughs not at all coquettishly. No play-acting. Earthy. As earthy as a man. Perhaps she *is* a man.

The horse snorts and shakes its mane.

Fred snaps out of his thoughts. Grips the reins for grim death. Locked in position. Hasn't moved an inch.

His father returns to the cart to lift off a sack of spuds which he carries to the shop.

Awaiting his return, Fred hears children's laughter and sees a couple of young lads, his own age but less well turned out than himself, running off at a clip that implies some nefarious deed. He turns to see what nefarious deed it might be.

The answer is instantaneous. One of the terraced houses has a front window with broken eggs running down it, the whites and the yolk combining into a rancid slime. Obviously the young guttersnipes responsible are now 'legging it'. The door of the terraced house opens and a woman rushes out into the street, looking right and left. But it is not a woman at all. It is the man dressed as a woman he saw in the police station. What shocks him more is that he or she is not well-off. He or she doesn't have a hat or furs. He or she is impoverished-looking, ill-clothed in a shabby dress and apron and garish face powder, making the stubble on his or her chin no less obvious, and ludicrously grotesque.

Fred ducks down slightly. Not wanting to be seen. Not wanting to be *remembered*.

Clearly upset, the man or woman cuts a gaudy, exotic and tragic figure as he or she disappears inside and returns with a wet cloth, mop and bucket to apply to the mess. Which is when he or she is aware of Fred, staring.

The boy looks sharply away, feeling the weight of the seat lurch as his father gets back up on the cart and takes the reins from him.

"Hup."

The cart moves off again and Fred fixes his eyes on the road ahead.

Behind him, the man or woman scrubs the pavement, presses the wet cloth in soapy circles to the window panes. Why was he or she in police custody, he can't help asking himself? What had he or she *done?*

But he doesn't look back—though he stiffens abruptly on the hard platform when he sees what is up ahead of him at the next street corner.

Because the policeman in the black moustache—the same one, the *very same one* who locked him up—has one of the young tearaways by the scruff of the neck, and is whacking him hard round the back of the head. The ragamuffin squirms, flinches, struggles, baby face contorting in distress, but the sergeant doesn't let go of him, literally lifting him from the ground, filthy bare feet dangling. A sprat held aloft by a fisherman proud of his catch.

The horse and cart trundles past the scene. Not quickly enough for Fred's liking.

Something of the sense of impending violence caught in a single moment reminds him of the posed figures at Madame Tussaud's Chamber of Horrors, with the policeman as the murderer and the child as his victim. He could have a carving knife in that hand he's not showing behind his back, ready to cut the urchin's throat. Ready to *dispose of him...*

The scruffy kid wriggling in his iron grip, the copper finds himself distracted momentarily as he recognises Fred's father. He straightens his back, almost forgetting the dangling perpetrator of the ghastly crime while the impoverished whippersnapper dangles like a hanged man from a noose. Like Charlie Peace.

"That boy of yours behaving himself, Mr H?"

Fred's father does not look at him directly.

"Oh yes."

"He'd better be!" the policeman says. "Or I'll have a bone to pick with you!"

And as Fred's father drives the cart on past the Keeper of the Law drain-laughs, belly taut behind his belt, like it is the most wonderful joke imaginable. And keeps on laughing. Like it is the best joke ever told in the history of the world.

*
**

The organ drones the *Agnus Dei* (God's little lamb) in the chapel of Saint Ignatius as Fred performs his duties as an altar boy. Preparing the Holy Communion, lighting candles, opening the book of prayer, holding it so the priest can read from it with the minimum of personal effort. The priest in question being the formidable and fearsome Father Mullins.Old bollock-features.

The elderly man mouths his words with his usual salivaspraying zeal, but today Fred doesn't hear a single one of them. He has more important things on his mind.

*
**

"Now then, Hitchcock. I hear you have some questions you want to ask."

"Yes, Father."

Mullins sits behind his desk in a study armoured by books. He gives a gracious wave of the hand as if to say "Proceed".

"Father...How do you know if you've got bad thoughts or not?"

Father Mullins has a hard-boiled egg on a plate. He cracks it and starts peeling the shell off it.

"Well, ask yourself what God would think. Ask God."

"How do I do that?" Fred says. "Where is He?"

"Everywhere."

"Isn't He a person then?"

"No, of course He's not a *person*. He's Maker of Heaven and Earth. Father, Son and Holy Ghost."

"That's three people," Fred observes.

"No, that's one. One Trinity. That's what that is. He's all around us, as I say, in different forms."

"I can't see Him."

"Ah. That depends how hard you're looking. If you look, thou shalt find. Look for instance in your own heart. Look there. That's a decent place to start." The Jesuit bites one end off the hard-boiled egg and masticates.

"What if He's not there?"

"If He's not there, you're in trouble." Father Mullins pours salt in a little triangular mound on the side of his plate.

"What kind of trouble?"

"I don't know. Do *you* know?"

Fred shakes his head. Sighs.

"I'm confused, Father."

"Well, don't be. Don't be at all, in the slightest. All you have to remember is, He died for our sins."

"But didn't He commit a sin in the first place?"

"How d'you mean?"

"Well, Mary had a boy child—God's son, Jesus. That was a sin."

"How d'you make out that? How was it sinful? It was within wedlock. She was married. To Joseph."

"But Joseph wasn't the father, was he? So Mary sinned. With God."

Father Mullins shifts in his seat, uncomfortable. His hand waggles in the air in front of him.

"Look, this is not the kind of thing you need to worry about at your age. Believe me. It isn't."

"But Jesus was crucified as a criminal. For a crime he didn't commit. What was the crime they thought he committed?"

Father Mullins emits a long, quiet, mewling sound.

"It's...*complicated*."

"And why did God allow Him to be punished and hurt like that if He was His father and loved Him?"

The old priest coughs. His throat is unaccountably dry, all of a sudden. Possibly the egg. "It's—it's extremely—*complex*..."

"Why didn't His father help Him?"

"Well, there you have it." The chair soughs under the old feller's weight as he rocks back. "That's the eternal mystery. Of our inability to understand Christ. And—and, and, and God. Because— because we are merely, you see, *human beings*." His eyes swim limpidly in his bollock face. "Does that answer your question?"

Fred doesn't think it does. Not at all. Not really.

"I just..."

"Look, all you need to know is He died for our sins, all right?"

"Why?"

"You don't need to know *why*. For Heaven's…"

The Holy Father has had enough. The hard-boiled egg, yellow and white, rests on the plate, half-eaten on its china Golgotha.

Fred looks no less troubled than he did before the discussion began.

"Will I find out if I become a priest?"

"Will you what? Do you *want* to become a priest?"

"Yes, Father," Fred says. "Yes, I think I do."

"Why's that, in the name of God?"

Fred thinks for a moment, staring at the desk, the fountain pen, the blotter, the hard, claw-like hands riven with the blue cables of veins.

"Because if you're a priest, you're innocent," the boy says.

"Lars Porsena of Clusium
By the Nine Gods he swore
That the great house of Tarquin
Should suffer wrong no more…"

He sits at his small wooden desk, idly playing with his nib pen, pressing his fingertip to it to see how sharp it is. His friend, the willowy reed O'Connor, is standing in front of the class reading Macaulay's *Horatius* from a poetry book in a drone absent of both conviction and understanding.

"By the Nine Gods he swore it,
And named a trysting day,
And bade his messengers ride forth,
East and west and south and north,
To summon his array…"

The dullness of the words lulling him to the point of hibernation, he presses the nib of the pen into the palm of his hand. For no substantial reason except to feel something—anything—he tests it with idle curiosity against the soft flesh.

Ouch! It hurts!

He puts the pen down in the ridge next to the inkwell and folds his arms tightly, praying no child or master has seen the action of such a nitwit.

*
**

Their grey duffel coats billow behind them like cloaks, sleeves knotted round their necks. Parkhill, considered the leader especially by himself, turns and mimes fencing with Murphy, who is easily defeated by the most dangerous swordsman in the whole of France. *Voilà, pig dog!* He sees Fred joining in, corkscrewing his own rapier, free hand aloft and limp."Oi. What do you think you're doing?"

"*En garde!*" Fred stops, arms hanging, matching the other boy's pose. "What? What have I done wrong?" He always assumes he has done wrong, and he is usually right.

"I said we were playing *The Three Musketeers.*" Pulling a sour face, Parkhill points at the other two, then himself. "One. Two. Three."

"Yes, but there were four musketeers in the book." Fred states his case. "There was D'Artagnan, too."

"Don't be stupid! It's called *The Three Musketeers*, idiot."

Murphy and O'Connor snigger.

"Yes, I know. But I'm right. There was Athos, Aramis, Porthos and…"

"*Four* Musketeers? *Twerp!*"

The minions snigger some more. Fred knows they will not listen to reason. They will listen to Parkhill. They have never read the book, and neither has he: Fred wants to tell them that. That they're stupid. He wants to tell them he is smarter than them, but he can't. He can't because even though they're wrong if he persists he thinks they will stop liking him. So instead he stands there mutely as they laugh at him, cheeks flushing red with rage and hurt—but mostly hurt.

"Come on, you lot." Parkhill swivels on his heel to Fred and jabs a finger at his face. "Not *you!*—Buzz off!"

Fred watches them scamper across the road, exuberantly

swishing at each other with sweeps and thrusts of imaginary swords, letting off a round from an invisible flintlock pistol, clutching a flesh wound that then, miraculously, disappears.

He tells himself he didn't want to play their stupid game, if their idea of accuracy is so lax. You know where you are with books. Books are the same every time you open them. Every time. But people aren't. Boys aren't. And he hates that. Hates them. Because he wanted to be brave and courageous just like they did, and now what is he, his chest rising and falling as he holds back stupid, girlish tears? The kind of tears that would get him thrown out of the Musketeers, that's for certain. In his mind he thrusts his rapier through their hearts, one by one. *One, two, three.* Sees the rose of blood opening as the blade comes out. The look of bewilderment coming over their features before they crumple to the ground.

"Hello."

Fred turns. "Hello." He should put his weapon in its scabbard, he thinks.

It's Olga Butterworth. Milady. The mysterious. The fair.

"Are you crying?"

"No."

"Come here."

She sounds soft. Nice. Like a friend. A better kind of friend. He walks over to her, not sure why. His chest—the feeling inside his chest—is still funny. Crushing but fluttering. Funny. Not funny ha-ha, funny strange.

She takes out a handkerchief. At the sight of it he backs away, recoiling from a possible blow.

"Please yourself." She sounds hard again.

She turns and walks away. He desperately un-knots his duffel coat sleeves from his neck, ties it quickly around his waist, and catches up with her.

They sit on a bench halfway along a path beside a hedge. They are facing allotments. Beetroot patches. Bean poles. Paltry scarecrows in old, torn shirts. One has an army cap on its head, tilted at a jaunty angle. Fred takes a comic from his school satchel and hands it to her."You fill in the spaces and they add together to make a story. It's great fun."

She gazes at the cover. "*Plotto.*"

She's as little enamoured with the title as she is with the concept, he can tell. He watches her leafing through it, feigning interest to spare his feelings. At least she thinks of his feelings. Which is something. Isn't it?

"Do you want to go to the pictures?" he asks.

"Don't you need to go home?"

He shakes his head.

"Won't you get into trouble?"

Fred shakes his head.

"I can stay out as long as I like," he says. "I do it all the time."

"What? All night?"

"If I like."

"You won't get a hiding when you get in?"

Fred shrugs. "I don't care."

"What if your mum and dad complain to my mum and dad?"

"They won't."

"They might."

"They won't."

Olga hands him back the *Plotto* comic.

"Did you see *Scenes of the World*? I've seen it nine times," he says. "It shows scenes of The Black Hills of Dakota, and Monument Valley, with those whopping big rocks in it. That was great, but my favourite was *Ride on a Runaway Train*. The camera was mounted on the front of the engine car as it whizzed around the mountains… you'd never believe it! When it took a bend it made you go like this!" He leans over to one side. "Then like *this!*" He leans over even further in the other direction. "And it was under-cranked so it made it look even faster…plunging into a tunnel—and *you* plunging with it!"

Olga grins. The boy's enthusiasm is infectious.

He grins too. "The owner of the picture hall puts sheets of newspaper down because they get so many wet seats!"

She laughs. Fred likes the sound of it very much.

"The Theatre Royal on Salways Road is showing a new animation," he says.

"I haven't got sixpence."

"I've got a shilling. I can get us both in."

She is still smiling and he takes comfort in that, but it makes him feel guilty too, because he knows what he is thinking deep down and she doesn't. That is the whole point—*she doesn't*. His heart is beating faster as she stands up and begins walking back the way they came, lifting the hem of her skirt from being soiled by the mud of the path.

"No. This way," he says, keeping his smile in place. "It's quicker."

Ahead of him, her hands push back a branch and a curl of brambles, right and left. She walks past the stone gate posts with the derelict house beyond. It is all going exactly according to the plan. Exactly according to the plot. Just like *Plotto*. If he was a thief or a spy he couldn't have planned it better. Or if he was a murderer. He drops to one knee to do up his shoe lace. Not that it needs doing up. But it makes her stop and turn back to look at him, as he knows it will. And when her eyes are on him, he walks through the space where the gates used to be, into the overgrown garden beyond.

"What are you doing?" she says. "Come back."

"Do you know who lived in this place?"

"I don't know anything. I just want to go."

Fred looks back at her, puts down his duffel coat and satchel, then walks into the building.

"Get out of there! Somebody said there's a tramp living inside!"

"That's just a story."

The room is as it was the first time he stepped into it. Run to ruin. The discarded corpse of a room. A murder mystery waiting to be solved. It is slatted with shadows, a place that reeks of night even though the sun shines outside. An English sun, so that's not saying much. But he's not afraid of the dark. Not any more. Edgar Allan Poe and Robert Louis Stevenson have shown him there are worse things to worry about. They've educated him with apple barrels and Ben Gunn and eyes under floorboards and the police rapping at your door. He is safe because he is in charge here, away from the sun. He will make sure he is.

Full of trepidation, Olga follows him in. Fair maid. Damsel in distress. Not yet she isn't.

"This is mad, this is. I'm going. I'm going to leave you here."

"Don't," says Fred. "Stay."

"Why should I?"

"There's something I have to do. I have to do it to prove I'm not scared…"

"What are you talking about?"

"You'll see."

"'I'll see?' What will I see?"

Fred approaches the door he approached before. He loosens the rusty bolt with some effort and yanks it back.

Olga covers her ears—the groan and screech is loud.

Fred creaks open the door and looks inside. He recoils with a sharp intake of breath and takes a few steps backwards.

Olga rushes over and cuts in front of him, so that she can see what he saw. She stiffens, prepared for some kind of shock. But all she does is frown.

In front of her is nothing but a broom cupboard, with nothing in it—not even a broom. All she can see is skirting board and chipped paint and a few hooks on the wall. She releases her fear in the gasp of a laugh.

In the same moment she feels a weight against her from behind and finds herself shoved forward, neck cricking back and legs buckling. Her head hits the far wall as she flounders, grasps, bewildered, the rest of her sprawling against it.

Fred slams the door shut and swiftly closes the rusty bolt.

Plunged into immediate darkness, Olga scrambles quickly to her feet and starts pushing against the door from the inside.

Fred backs away from it, arms hanging vertical at his side. His smile has vanished. The mask of it has gone and he feels bad at the deception. But a clever spy, thief, murderer—where are they without deception? Without a smile that isn't a smile?

He jolts as the door shudders at the force of Olga's fists on the other side of it. He blinks furiously. The rusty bolt rattles and vibrates but does not give.

He bunches his little fists as he hears her get her breath back. He swallows, his feet fidgeting in little wee steps to and fro. Stop it, stop it—but too late now to stop anything.

"What are you doing? Fred?"

"Nothing." He's backing away further from his deed, stiffened with panic.

"Can you let me out, please?"

"I will."

"Do it then."

"No. I can't." And he knows, literally, that is true.

"Fred…"

"I don't want to. Not yet. Don't ask me to."

"Fred, why are you doing this?"

"Because. I don't know. I just have to."

"Why?"

"Because you committed a crime. You know you did."

She laughs. Mystified. "What?"

"You might not think you have, but you have. I know you have. I know everything."

"You've lost your marbles, you have. Now, let me out of here before you're in trouble!"

"*I'm* not in trouble. *You're* the one in trouble, Sonny Jim!" Fred's voice is shriller than he would like. "You're the one *going to Hell* if you're not careful!" The words are the best he can muster for the purpose. He wants her to be terrified. He wants her to feel awful. He wants her to sob her blinking heart out—but to his alarm she emits a different sound entirely. "Stop. Stop it! What are you laughing at? You won't be *laughing* down there, I can tell you! Not down there in Hell with your knickers burning. With your knickers burning *right off* showing all you've got—you won't be *laughing* then, will you?" He wants to be evil. He *is* evil. He knows he is.

As he holds his breath, the wetness of spittle on his lips, Olga goes quiet. Good. He's seething. Good!

"Don't be a bugger, Fred! Listen to me. Don't be a bloody bugger!"

"I will! I *will* be a bloody bugger! You'll see!"

And he's frightened—*he* is frightened, *and* enjoying it, too. And thinks of his mother seeing him like this, not her dear little lamb with its fleece white as snow, oh no, not that any more, a man—a nasty creature, a creature getting pleasure from tears and distress and feeling good about it. Yes! Feeling *good* about it. Feeling strong. Feeling the strongest person in the world, who will never get pushed around ever again. That's what he feels like. And the more the girl suffers, he thinks, and perhaps knows, even then, the more he will like it.

He turns and runs. Out of the room. Out of the house. Feeling the warmth of the sun again—English sun, no sun at all, the warmth being the blood pumping under his skin—and hears her squawking from within.

"Fred! Fred! Let me out! Let me out!"

But no. He doesn't. Can't. He picks up his duffel coat— scratchy, hairy, grey—from where he left it in the Dead Garden of broken tiles and twisted plants, and walking between the mildewed gate posts he cannot hear her any more. She is not Olga Butterworth. She is The Girl With Yellow Hair. She has to be, because he invented her. She is inaudible. Invisible. As if shut away in the pages of a closed book. A story only he knows, because he wanted to tell it. Tell it his way, this time.

His.

*
**

He slows down to avoid attracting attention but risks a smile. Straightens his back to look less furtive. Flattens his cow's-lick with fingers wetted by his tongue. A shop assistant (name of Kidney) ratchets in the awning above the windows with a hooked pole.Inside he is safe. Inside he is a little boy again.

*
**

A kettle whistles on the stove. His father fills a hot water bottle with boiling water, careful to press it against his chest to expel excess air as he does so. Accidents can happen. The hidden dangers of household chores are numerous. It's a job a husband does not leave to his wife. That's the way they apportion their lives— in tasks. He feels the heat against his chest. Feels the hot breath coming up against his face from the open rubber mouth. His nostrils quiver. Jesus Christ peers out from the Sacred Heart, as real as a scene from the Roxy, the flickering of the gaslight giving a sense of a hidden projector or magic lantern. The anticipation of a story to be told or a parable to be learned. Fred lies flat as a corpse in his bed, arms ramrod straight outside the covers. Eyes open wide, his breathing uneasy—wishing neither of them were the case. What terrifies him he cannot say. No one can know. No one can see.

The door opens and he flinches. Twists his head. He doesn't know who he expected—Jesus? Jack? Ripper? Redeemer?—but his father steps into the room. He hands Fred the hot water bottle, which Fred tucks down into the bed, manipulating it right down to his icy feet.

"Not reading?"

Fred shakes his head.

"Wonders will never cease." The greengrocer does not rest on his son's eyes. He hardly ever does, and neither of them knows why. "I'm taking your mother out for a nightcap. Will you be all right on your own for an hour?"

Fred nods. He knows he will have to be.

The man drifts to the bedroom door.

"Father? What's a spy?"

"A person who keeps secrets. Somebody who says he's one thing but he's really another. Why?"

"I just wanted to know."

His father moves silently out of the room, sliding the door shut after him.

In the broom cupboard her face is barely picked out in a string of moonlight. She tries to poke through at the bolt and move it using the pin of her hair clip—tortoise shell with rams' heads, influenced by the excavation at Nineveh by Sir Henry Layard. The pin head scratches ineffectively. Uselessly. It's frustrating and she expels a sound of that frustration. A snarl.After a breath she tries yet again. The pin snaps off.

This sends her insane in a short, sharp burst—banging her fists at each of the three walls, tearing at the door with her fingertips and kicking at it hysterically.

This also does No Good Whatsoever.

She now knows her physical efforts are useless. She has been at it for hours. She crouches down then sits, with her arms around her legs. All school skirt and socks both like sacking, dirt and a cut on her face where she hit the wall, hair tousled and messy without the hair grip. She gives in to a cascade of sobs.

"Help! Help me! Help me! Mum! MUM!"

Loud enough for insubstantial lungs, but quite futile.

Nobody can hear her. Nobody is listening. Nobody cares.

The ruined house is dark. Outside it, not a sound sails on the night air except for a distant train rattling melodiously on its tracks, oblivious to the petty anguish of a child.

The two worlds are separate. Standing at the bar of the pub, waiting to order drinks, Fred's father can see into the other half—the Public Bar—noisier and far more barbarian than the Saloon Bar he is in himself. The Saloon Bar is the place a businessman frequents. A place a man can safely take his 'lady wife' without there being any fear of her feminine sensibilities being affronted. The Public Bar is a sawdust-strewn den of beer breath, unshaven chins and language that would make a costermonger die of shame. He'd perhaps have gone there tonight, or any night, on his own. He doesn't mind mixing with working men—even though she says he ought not to. But tonight is different. Tonight she is in charge. It makes him tense, but he has to endure it as best he can. Though he will be happy when it's over. He sees another moustache opposite, for a moment like his own reflection emerging from the miasma of the uncouth. His 'friend' the policeman—if he *is* a friend—is getting a pint. The black uniform falls like the shadow of a tree. The sergeant sees Fred's father and brightens markedly, heading round to the sidedoor to meet him. Fred's father isn't terribly pleased about that.

The copper enters from the Public Bar, a Goth invading Rome. He is used to owning a room and swivelling heads, in his professional capacity, of course. Relishes it, in fact. He isn't cowed by the cushions and furnishings absent from where he came from, or by the presence of solicitors and shop-owners with their straight backs and sherries. He is as good as them, if not better. King or commoner, none of them is above the Law, and he *is* the Law. And knows it.

And wait. Fred's mother, done up to the nines, white cotton gloves, the lot.

"Well, well. *Enchan-tay*, as they say in gay Paree!" He takes her hand and kisses it. Fred's mother bends away from him, acting coy but flattered by the attention. His grin slobbers over every inch of her. "Good to see you taking in London's good air, Mrs H. Eel pie air that it is. Some people round here thought you didn't want to be seen down here with us *low types*."

"Perish the thought," she says. "We are all equal in God's eyes, Stanley."

"Well, here's to God, and all who sail in him!" He pulls up a stool. Closer than she would like. Or perhaps not. Fred's father returns to the table with a drink for himself and his better half.

She pulls the drink towards her. "The time has long gone when it was considered a scandal for a respectable woman to drink in a public house."

"Are you a respectable woman then, Mrs H?" The policeman would wink if he needed to.

"As my husband is a notable figure in the community," she says, "I like to show my face."

He points to her drink. "Few more of those, duck, and that's not all you'll be showing."

She blushes with shock, but enjoys the frisson of the innuendo. Fred's father pretends to, but his smile is a tired one.

"You are a one. He's a one, isn't he, William?"

"He's a one, all right."

"In the words of the prophet Isaiah: 'A little of what you fancy does you good.'" The dark sergeant sluices back his beer. Fred's mother hides her canary titter behind her hand. Fred's father empties his glass in the same long, slow swig as the other man.

Still grinning, the shadow with buttons rises and sidles to the bar to order more, not asking if anybody wants more. Just doing it, whether they want it or not.

**

Mice crisscross the floorboards. From behind the door of the broom cupboard in the mausoleum dark, a weak, irregular knocking emanates.*Mum. Mum. Mum. Mum…*

**

Deep in the comfort of his pillow, Fred turns to lie on his side, staring hard at the Sacred Heart on the wall. He wonders if Jesus is just a policeman in the end, a policeman of Right and Wrong. He wonders if He can see into his soul and what He can see there, because Fred doesn't know what is there himself. He really doesn't.Really he wants to cry inside, but he can't.

What *is* he inside? In *his* heart? Is he what the policeman said he was? Don't adults always know best? *Do* they, though?

The hot water bottle has lost its warmth and with it has gone his panic and the sense of dread of being found out. But he thinks of how cold the girl's feet are. He thinks of being there, touching them, warming them. He thinks of her allowing him. And closes his eyes.

He wishes he could turn the clock back. He doesn't like being a criminal. He didn't find it easy and it doesn't come naturally. There are too many feelings and he'd prefer to lock those feelings out. He was better off without them. He wishes he could understand feelings like he understands bus timetables and tram routes, but feelings don't stick to planned routes, before you know it they are zooming off in all sorts of directions. But for the first time, also, he thinks he knows why a murderer does what he does—because he really, *really* likes it, that's why, because it makes him feel superior: to the police, to the mothers and fathers, to the priests, to everybody. Even to God.

He stares at the Sacred Heart again, thinking of what Christ went through and wondering why He can smile like that. He thinks of The Girl With Yellow Hair and her suffering too—the girl who was kind to him and let him into her (sacred) heart. And the strangest thing is that he thinks he should feel something, and he tries to, but he feels nothing at all.

In the Saloon Bar more alcohol has been downed. The policeman has sunk quite a few and now stares at the floor, eyes glazed, with ale-froth icing the tips of the hairs of his grand moustache. Coarse laughter washes in from the Public Bar and Fred's mother cringes as if it's agony to her delicate ears. "My father was a bobby on the beat," she says in her brogue, laid on thick for his benefit. "West Ham. PC Whelan. Fine figure of a man."

"I'm sure he was," the policeman says, eye rolling over her corset-bound curves.

"You know, over there they have no respect for the law. No respect at all. Spat at in the street, he was—every day of his life. Had to turn the other cheek."

The policeman empties the bitter brown liquid from his glass down his gullet. "Spit? Bit of *spit* he had to put up with, did he?" Wiping his lips with his cuff and sucking his teeth. Face hard and sour, as if tasting something putrid off them. Smile gone and heaviness now upon his eyelids. "Face bullets, did he? Face *spears*, did he?"

Fred's mother frowns at the strangeness of the question, and the cold change that comes over the Life and Soul of the Party.

"That's what I've had to face," the pitch moustache says. "Flying column from Wadi Halfa. Heroes of the hour. Oh, yer. 'Cept the bleedin' Mahdi already had Gordon's head on a spike, didn't he? Dervishes to the right of them. Dervishes to the left of them…The hordes of Hell, I've had to face. The black hordes of Hell." In the yellow splutter of a match he strikes, his face looks as monstrous as something that belches water from the gutters of a church roof. Something carved to ward off bad spirits. Or a bad spirit itself, in human form. Every ounce of humour miraculously shed.

"That boy of yours." His head lolls. "Wait for him to kill somebody. That'll make him grow up. That'll make him grow up all right."

Fred's mother isn't amused by her attentive admirer any more. She's upset, and perhaps that's as he wanted it all along— she doesn't know and doesn't care, but doesn't like to be made a fool of. She looks to her husband in desperation, who sees the signs right enough. The noise, everything, too, too much. His wife is no longer happy and gay—that was too vain a hope. Not for the whole evening. She looks frightened. A doe that intuits the arrow of the hunter. Alert yet bewildered, as if she might faint.

"Come on." Fred's father has her. No fear. "Let's take you home."

She stands unsteadily. Neck tall and proud, like a swan. Her husband tucks her arm under his and they leave. And if they leave the policeman yawning and licking his dry mouth, murmuring laughter to himself at their expense, they pretend not to see him, or care.

*
**

Concentric circles ripple in the tiny font. The back room of the shop is in darkness and the guffaws and sing-song on the night air long vanished, but the piano, that torture instrument, still hammers on her nerves. Her husband takes her coat and hangs it up, before his own.She sinks at the table. Takes out her rosary beads and turns them over in her hands as he pours and hands her a glass of water.

"Leave me be."

Her dogged husband waits.

"Leave me be."

He turns and trudges to the wooden stairs. Weary in more ways than he can begin to tell. She unexpectedly speaks again, as if this thing could not be said to his face, only to his back, and even then in shadow.

"Am I a good person, Bill?...*Am* I?"

He stops.

She closes her eyes tightly, clasping her hands together in prayer and sobbing quietly as she prays. The scripture pours out of her in a rush. It can't come fast enough.

Her Bill, William, sits down across the table from her and takes her hands, separates them, kisses them each, one by one. She cannot understand his affection. It is the greatest mystery to her. He wishes it wasn't.

They look into each other's eyes. Too many questions ever to ask. She through tears, and trembling.

* *
*

"They fought the dogs, and killed the cats
And bit the babies in the cradles
And ate the cheeses out of the vats
And licked the soup from the cook's own ladles..."

As he reads, book open to Browning, Fred notices Father Mullins—old bollock-features—enter like a ghost and whisper into the ear of the young priest facing the class. He wonders why. He wonders what...

"Split open the kegs of salted sprats..."

The young priest nods. The soutane of Father Mullins, mummified skeleton inside, yaws from the room like the black sails of a funeral barge.

> *"Made nests inside men's Sunday hats*
> *And even spoiled the women's chats..."*

No sooner does the door close than it re-opens and he returns with a police officer at his side—not just *any* police officer, but with awful inevitability the dread figure of Fred's incarceration. Helmet tucked under one arm. Giant in a realm designed for boys. Black standing beside black. A dark duo. And Fred feels the air sucked out of him but dares not stop breathing or reading aloud however much he wants to.

> *"By drowning their speaking*
> *With shrieking and squeaking*
> *In fifty different sharps and flats..."*

The young priest waves his hands, gesturing Fred to stop and sit. Fred does so. Happily. If not happily, obediently. Obedience being second-best to invisibility—which is what he wants now more than anything. Murmurs of apprehension and excitement circulate around him. Rising in volume.

"Silence. *Silence!*"

Silence is thereby imposed in an instant.

"Boys." Father Mullins addresses them with no glimmer of warmth, the turkey-scrag of his neck rubbing the dog collar as he scans every face. "Sergeant Sykes is going to address you on a very serious concern. And I expect—nay, I *demand* you give him your *complete* attention—is that clear?"

In unison: "Yes, Father."

Mouthing the words, Fred can hear his heart drumming so ferociously he thinks they all must hear it too. His tell-tale heart. The one under the floorboards. The one inside his ribs. Wanting to be let out.

The policeman places his helmet on the desk beside him, badge gleaming, blinding like the Sacred Heart, and stands in front of it. The blackboard squeals in protest as it is wiped. Hands behind his back, he rocks back and forth on his heels and the schoolboys can hear the squeak of his polished boots as he does so. The crease in his trousers is sharp enough to slice a Sunday roast. His chin juts out like a prow.

"Now then." The growl. "Any of you lads know a girl named Olga Butterworth?"

A solitary (tell-tale) bead of sweat trickles down the nape of Fred's neck.

The boys look at one another. The former musketeers— Parkhill, O'Connor and Murphy—look at one another, then at Fred. Fred dare not look back at them.

"She goes to the Convent School next door."

"These boys do not consort with Convent School girls, Sergeant." Father Mullins says emphatically. "We're very strenuous on the matter. *Very* strenuous."

"If you say so," the policeman says. Taking nothing as gospel, he scans the boys at their desks.

Fred does not want to look into those steely eyes. Doesn't want them cutting into his soul. And that's what *he* wants, isn't it? To cut them open and see what's inside. What's going on in their minds. To know what they've been up to. What they've been dreaming, the butter-wouldn't-melt little tykes…

Fred being one of them. With more to hide than most.

A lot more.

He stares at the floor. Tightening his little fat fists to stop from shaking. To stop from shouting out loud: *It's me! It's me!*

"She went missing last night," declares the policeman with a commanding authority beyond even that of the Holy Brothers. "Her parents were expecting her home at tea time. If any of you know of her whereabouts, or saw anything at all suspicious, I'd ask you to report it immediately to either me or Father Mullins."

"You hear that?" the aging Jesuit repeats. "Immediately!"

But for now nothing is forthcoming. Not a movement. Not a whimper.

What *could* be forthcoming, Fred thinks, since the only person with anything forthcoming is himself?

"Don't worry about getting into trouble," the sergeant adds. "Or getting anyone else into trouble. You won't. You'll be doing good." His eyes fall on Fred and he doesn't recognise him instantly, but after a second he does. *(Bill Hitchcock's lad. Yer. The one I locked up for the night. Little fatty who cried for his ma...)* Fred feels a damp coldness cover his skin, but thankfully the policeman's beady eyes do not linger on him and his withering gaze passes onto other boys in the room. "All I'm concerned about is finding this little girl whose mother and father are worried sick."

From the tone of his voice now, Fred almost thinks the policeman seems compassionate. Even human. But he knows that can't be true. What's true is he is out to get the criminal. And the criminal is him.

Job done, the copper puts his helmet back under his arm, stands to attention, looks over at Father Mullins and nods his thanks. Father Mullins backs away and opens the classroom door for his guest. As the policeman walks to it with the innate swagger of a drum major, the boys all stand, the loud rasp of their chair legs against the floor surprising him no less than a sudden barrage of enemy gunfire. He pauses, startled.

"Thank you, Sergeant Sykes."

"Thank you, Father."

The boys feel the policeman's eyes on them long after he is gone. What Catholicism breeds in them is that they are guilty— but not, as yet, sure what they are guilty of. But there is plenty of time for that. Possibly the rest of their lives.

The bell rings. The lesson changes. The young priest leaves and a noisy hiatus ensues before the next teacher arrives. In the clatter of desk lids and the thump of textbooks Fred shuffles to the window and looks down. He watches the policeman striding to the school gates. Shiny boots, measured step, arms swinging as if crossing a parade ground. The figure stops and turns, pulling the huge gates closed after him, momentarily the other side of its iron bars. Pausing...

Fred backs sharply away from the glass, fearing the brute might suddenly look up and detect him.

He doesn't look back out again. But for a good few minutes, perhaps longer, wonders if the sergeant is down there, looking up at him, knowing he did it. Just wanting proof. Just wanting to catch him, red-handed. Get a confession. Beat it out of him. Standing there all day, if he has to.

He sits on the filthy floorboards in the abandoned house feeling abandoned himself, knees under chin, arms wrapped round his legs, one sock up and one at half-mast, school satchel dumped beside him. He has sat in silence for so long now he forgets, looking at the door of the broom cupboard. No sound has come from inside since he got there, and that frightens him. He thinks of calling out her name but doesn't. He has a good mind to go home and forget about her. Then how would she like it? Is she playing silly beggars or is she...Perhaps she's...

He walks to the door and makes scratching noises on it with the fingernails of one hand. He can hear her moving about inside now. Panting, agitated, bleating.

"Do you like mice?" he says. "It's full of mice in there." He gets the desired result. She shrieks loudly as well as panting hard in between times. But it very quickly gets on his nerves. "Shut up! Shut your racket! You sound like a girl."

"I *am* a girl!"

"Well stop *sounding* like one!"

He doesn't know if she is obeying him but she goes quiet, completely quiet, like before. Then he can hear her sobbing, piti-fully.

He doesn't like it. It sounds too much like he sounds. He's got better things to do than to listen to that. That's no fun at all. He backs away from the door and hauls up his satchel onto his shoulder.

"My brothers will get you," her voice says.

"You haven't got any brothers."

"I have. Two of them. And they're big. Bigger than you. They're grown-ups. They'll kill you."

"I don't believe you."

"One's a tanner and a prize fighter and one runs a factory and lives in Greenwich." She pronounces it as it is spelled: *Green Witch*.

"You don't even say it like that. You pronounce it 'Grennidge'."

"I don't care."

"You do care because you're lying. It's 'Grennidge', and you'd know that if your brother lived there."

"Oh, you're so clever."

"I am! I *am* clever. And you're stupid."

"And I thought you were nice."

Did she? Did she really?

"That's your fault. I didn't say I was nice. I'm not nice. I'm bad. Everybody tells me I'm bad, and I am. Bad as Judas!"

He notices his voice has become like Parkhill's and he wants to go on and tell her she is bad things, but he can't, because she isn't. She isn't those things, same as he wasn't.

What is she then? Like him? Hurt? Sorry? Innocent?

His victim has gone quiet, allowing him his musings. Then the voice returns, small, plaintive. Like another person's. Like a trapped angel. Like a butterfly in a jam jar…

"Will you let me out, please?"

"No."

"I didn't do anything wrong. What did I do?"

"You had nasty thoughts. Evil thoughts. Thoughts about boys." He presses his face to the broom cupboard door. "That you liked them and wanted them to kiss you. You wanted to touch them. And, and—and—let *them* touch *you!*" He lets her think about that. Yes. Consider her misdeeds, yes—consider them well. All night if she has to. In the dark. Like *he* had to.

"Is that what *you* want?"

"What?"

"To be touched?" The whisper comes through the wood. "To be kissed?"

"No."

How close are her lips? Inches? He pulls back again. Afraid.

But of what?

"Because I will if you want to." Her words seep with allure.

He cannot see her, but he can. In his mind's eye. In his camera mind she's as clear as Cleopatra on the big screen. In his big screen mind she's a star. She's voluptuous, whatever 'voluptuous' means. *"I'll let you if you want to,"* she says, the lost treasure of a promise. "Are you there? Fred? Fred? *Fred?*"

"Yes."

"Don't go," she says. *"Because I'm doing it now."*

He's puzzled. He's scared. He's excited. It's a mystery. The biggest, best mystery going. But the suspense is killing him.

"What? What are you doing?"

He thinks of old scrotum-face, and sin. Of the man under the street light.

"Just open the door and see."

He laughs. "That's the oldest trick in the book. I'm not falling for that one." Then he swallows. "See what?"

He stares at the door with its scratched and peeling paint. Picturing what may be behind it. Asking himself if the reality can ever, ever be as good as the pictures. Stepping slowly closer…

"I'm lifting my skirt," says the angel, butterfly, sunlight. *"I'm showing you."*

"Showing me what?"

"Showing you…All…I've…Got…"

Chubby fingers trembling, Fred reaches towards the rusty bolt. Knowing it will open the door to Salvation or Paradise or the confessional, or terror, or Hell, or the pit of endless prison, or the thrilling swirl of the Zoetrope. The organ ascends, its bass notes throbbing in his small chest with ghastly but blissful anticipation.

"Just open the door and you can see. See everything."

But his fingers never touch the cold of the metal.

She waits, but in the silence she knows. The footsteps, echoing, diminishing, confirm it.

"Fred? *Fred!* I mean it! *Come back!*"

But it is no good. The small boy is already gone.

He sees Union Jack bunting draped across the street from side to side, as if to welcome him home. Men with brown aprons and rolled-up sleeves are up ladders hanging it, cigarettes clasped between their lips as they add much-needed colour to the scene. The old red, white and blue. He's forgotten Empire Day is imminent. Walking under ladders is bad luck. He crosses the street. He wishes he hadn't. Under resplendent flags hanging from upstairs windows, a duo of uniformed constables wearing capes and gloves are knocking on doors.Fred knows what they're asking even though he can't hear. They're asking local residents if they can "help with their enquiries". He slows down to a walk as he passes them, trying to act normal and nonchalantly. Trying to be like an actor. Trying not to be himself. Because as himself he might give the game away. He keeps his head down, eyes on the pavement ahead. Not on them.

They don't even pause in their conversation with a barrel of a woman with a scarf knotted round her head who repeats that she don't know nuffink. He is past them and standing on the kerb to cross the road.

"Oi! Oi, you—little man!"

Fred stops, swaying slightly, but doesn't turn. Hopes it isn't him being addressed, but knows it is. It *bloody* is. He hears the crunch of the hobnail boots behind him as one of them approaches.

He turns. Too young for a moustache, this one. Chin-strap puckering his face, bisecting fat, crab-apple cheeks.

"Your shoe lace is undone."

Not that I'm a master criminal then? Not that you want to arrest me? Not that I'm guilty as charged?

Fred crouches to do them up. The young bobby puts his hands on his hips.

"You want to watch that. You'll come a cropper."

Fred stands up and, without looking the nice constable in the eyes, carries on his way, only seeing him on the periphery of his vision, shaking his head and returning to his colleague and his task.

*
**

Evening now, and he is kneeling on the carpet, playing with his Bing '1' gauge clockwork tin-plate model train set as his parents talk, thinking he is too absorbed in his play to be listening. "They're searching the canal," says his father. "If they find her, he'll swing for it, whoever he is."

"Shsh! Love of God. Don't talk like that in front of him. You know he's got a vivid imagination."

Fred carries on pushing his toy locomotive round the track with the accompaniment of suitable noises, pretending he isn't paying attention. But he is. Of course he is.

"What those poor parents are going through..." says his mother, lapsing into her own general opinion on the matter. "Children are a burden, such a burden and an agony..." Fred feels his father looking down at him, perhaps not so sure the lad isn't taking it all in, and wishing he wasn't, but not about to tell his wife to curb her tongue. "Sometimes I think it's better not to grow up at all, with all the pains of existence ahead of you. Sure, happiness is an illusion—like an actor on the silver screen."

"Best say a prayer for her, then," her husband murmurs through his teeth.

"I shall," she replies, sensing a veiled slight against her character. "Oh, I shall."

"Had a feeling you would."

He stands up, folds his newspaper, and heads for the living room. "Where are you going?" she asks.

Fred's father stops, holding back a sigh.

"You get out there and help them search, Bill Hitchcock." She is firm, as sometimes she can be. Nothing if not unpredictable. "I want you out there, where everyone can see you. And I want you to be the last one who comes home, d'you hear me?"

*
**

The black surface of the water barely ripples, periodically lit by the scan of policemen's bull's-eye lamps. A search party is out. Their footsteps echo in the brick drum of the tunnel, but they exchange not a word—their ponderous and unenviable work too serious, the possible outcome too solemn, to be leavened by chit-chat. They are skirting the realm of ghosts, and in dread expectation of the unspeakable. Methodically, their time-honoured art, they look all over, in corners, bushes, inlets, behind discarded crates and rubbish, dirt behind ears, secrets in pockets, bending over half-broken fences, shining the beams up at the curved underside of the canal bridge.Sergeant Sykes with his Kitchener moustache is one of their number. He moves along the tow path with a long bargee's pole delving into the water, looking for anything that might be lodged, submerged…Anything, or anyone…With what may be misconstrued as some kind of macabre relish he moves his pole in a regular motion as he walks, like a ferryman with an oar.

Further along the tow path Fred's father, Bill, walks into view from a pathway leading to the lock gates, two men at his side—the thin-necked assistants from the shop. Grocery boys, out of their overalls. Should be in the pub. Will be, at the end of this. Whatever the outcome. Quick snifter. Brass monkeys, what it is. Still, got to be done…

The policeman watches Bill as Bill speaks to them, sending them off in two different directions, to the sluices and the sewerpipe. Without given instruction, Fred's father has a broom handle and starts using it to prod at the canal-side foliage, hooking aside the spiky remains of a bicycle wheel.

Taking a breather, he notices the policeman still looking at him. He looks back at the man. Does not hesitate in doing so. Does not shift in any way or even blink.

The policeman stares also, in no hurry to desist from this, but the stare demands nothing—no answer, no acknowledgement. It is confident and knowing and empty, but will not back down. But of what does it constitute? Surliness? Pity? Threat?

Fred's father notices that one of his own shirtsleeves has rolled down to his wrist. He wipes his hand on his waistcoat and rolls it back up. His bare arms are dirty and there are smudges on his face. He wears no collar. He has no stud.

The policeman cricks his neck over his shoulder and whispers to the officer next to him. They exchange a small, unpleasant laugh.

Fred's father knows the remark was about him in some way and whatever its contents, he doesn't like it. He wants to get away. He wants to go home. But he can't go home. He has to be here.

The policeman lowers to a crouch, leaning on his pole which is in the water.

As he stares into it his face, lit by the bulldog lamp at his feet, is reflected upside-down in the murky water beneath him.

The bony grin of a skull and crossbones flag peers out from the cover of *Treasure Island*, lying as it does in the shadows at the foot of Fred's bed.He tries to get to sleep, listening to his mother gently weeping in her perpetual anguish in the next room. He wishes he could go to her but he can't. He wishes he could solve the mystery but he can't. He wishes he could stop her fear, but he can't. He can't even stop his own.

But then he gets an idea how it has to end. He is good at endings. The ending is the most important part, but the most difficult. But he knows what he has to do.

The kitchen drawer next to the sink slides open. A brass band is playing outside. Shooting a furtive glance to the door, he takes out a carving knife and puts it in his school satchel, quickly buckling it up.He trots down the wooden stairs with his satchel over his shoulder. The dingy back room is empty. He walks through the darkness of the shop to the front door. His father is at the cash register serving a customer. For Empire Day he is dressed in the khaki twill service dress uniform of the British army, with puttees and a wide-brimmed tropical hat pinned up on one side. Fred doesn't know whether his father fought in the war in South Africa or if he killed people. The idea of it is strange. If he ever did he has kept silent on the matter—as he is on every matter. He does not explain his costume and Fred does not ask.

While upstairs, his mother enters the kitchen and picks up her knitting. She sees that the cutlery drawer is open, and walks over and shuts it.

*
**

The brass band music is jolly, but distant. Bird song replaces it. Not unpleasant. He passes the spot where he and the other boys tried to squash the mouse with their bricks. He goes to the dark inside. Straight to the door to the broom cupboard.He can hear nothing within. He puts his ear to it.

Still nothing. He wonders if she is dead. Already. He wonders if he is too late.

He kneels down and unbuckles his satchel. He takes out the carving knife. He delves back inside and takes out something wrapped in a handkerchief.

It is a piece of his mother's fruit cake.

He places it down on the floorboards. He cuts it in two with the carving knife.

He wraps one slice in the handkerchief.

He pushes it through the gap under the door. It barely fits. He prods it. It disappears into the gloom.

He crabs away a few yards, leaving a trail in the thick snow of dust.

The carving knife still gripped tightly, he eats the other piece of fruit cake with his free hand. Licking his fingers one by one when they get too sticky.

"Cherries," a voice says. "I don't like cherries."

"Pick them out then."

"I won't pick them out. I'll spit them out."

Fred watches the darkness in the gap under the door as the girl moves around inside.

"Are you still crying?" he asks.

"Why do you care?"

"Do you like the cake?"

"No."

Fred finishes his own portion regardless.

"You won't really tell them, will you? Your brothers?" No answer was the stern reply. "It was just a game. We were just playing." No answer, a second time. "Don't say it was me. Say it was an accident. Say it was a tramp." Still no answer. Fred stands up. His legs feel wobbly. "I'll let you out, but you've got to promise you won't say it was me. Not to anybody." The girl still hasn't said a word. "…Hello?"

"Hello."

"Well?"

"Well what?"

"Will you do what I say if I set you free?"

"Yes."

"Do you promise?"

"Yes…Yes."

"On your mother and father's lives? Cross your heart and hope to die?"

"Yes."

Fred takes a step forward, gives the bolt a good wiggle and pulls it back. He retreats quickly, nervously—pulling the door open at the same time. A pigeon, trapped and now free, flies into his face, hooting. He paws away its fluttering wings, shutter-like, and button eyes.

Behind it she skitters, The Girl With Yellow Hair, semi-huddled in what used to be the dark. But what strikes him first is that her hair isn't yellow any more. It is lank with grime and cobwebs and pigeon white, no longer brushed and neat and glowing—nothing about her *glows*. She is not dignified or smart or clean but dishevelled, damp, her ankle-length skirt pulled up and torn and stained with droppings. This isn't the pretty girl he met in the street. This one is *dirty*. ("Needs a good bar of carbolic," as his mother might say.) This one looks *poor*. Worst of all she has a cut over one eye, swollen like a boxer's, with lines of dried blood down her cheek. What kind of girl looks like a boy after a fight? Is a girl with blood on her face and fear in her eyes easier or harder to fall in love with? And is it easier or harder for her to fall in love with you?

The girl gets stumblingly to her feet and emerges quickly. So quickly he has to side step to get out of her way. But she loses her balance and has to prop herself against a crusted, peeling wall.

Her transformation shocks him. Did he do this? No…This isn't what was supposed to happen. This wasn't the plan…

She stands with her back to him, chest heaving.

"I didn't mean anything," he says, near tears. "I thought it was a joke."

She doesn't turn.

She gasps. Chokes. Splutters. Sobs catching in her throat.

"Now you know what it's like," he says, almost sobbing too.

"What *what's* like?"

He says: "Being afraid."

Without turning, his girl hurries stiffly out into sunshine, breaking into an inelegant, lolloping run as she gets to the garden.

To his own surprise, Fred stays inside the derelict room, not moving from the spot, the carving knife held flat across his chest. He hears the pigeons, more of them, upstairs. Filling the room. Fluttering and scratching. Fighting something. Attacking. He doesn't like to imagine what's happening up there because it sounds like there are millions, and they are getting louder and louder in his head.

They are looking straight at us, frozen in time. William Hitchcock, still in the khaki uniform, standing in an upright pose holding the bridle of his horse, Fred sitting in the saddle dressed in a child's version of the same. We can see nothing of the little boy's fears or dreams as he sits gazing into the lens. The shop window is the backdrop, all its wares on display, onion strings and hares hung up by their feet—an advertising opportunity never to be passed up, as Mrs Hitchcock tells him. Father and son hold their poses as the photographer exposes the plate, then packs up his tripod and moves on, doffing his cap. Bill knows that in the dark of the window behind him, his wife Em sits, far away from the celebrations of the common people. Leaving life for her husband and son to report in despatches from the front.

The children have a day off for it. Rule Britannia and whatnot. But then it's back to normal. No strawberry jelly or trifle, or pigeon pie and mash like mountains making trestle tables groan. Now it is Fred dressed in a sports vest and baggy shorts at the boundary as his school friends play cricket. He has lost interest in the game as he always does. Mind in a far-off land. In crime and punishment. The breathless chase. The runaway train. The police in relentless pursuit. The pitiless rogue and his victim, the woman in peril, a hair's breadth from violent death…She screams, in his mind—but what he hears is his name, and snaps out of his daydream.

A black flapping shape like a tumbling crow stands at the crease, a gangly young priest having called the match to a halt. A ball bounces, caught by the wicket-keeper at the stumps. The rest of the players stand inert, and curious, all eyes on Fred. He is beckoned furiously.

Fred points at himself—*me?*

The spindly rake of a priest beckons harder, grim-faced. Fiercely impatient now. *Yes, you, boy! You!*

Oh no. Oh damn. Oh Hell.

Fred has no choice but to hurry to him briskly or face a box round the ears, but a box round the ears might be the least of his worries. What if…what if they—*know?*

The crow-shaped man leads him away from the cricket pitch, one hand gripping his shoulder so tight it hurts, but Fred dare not blubber or he knows he will get something that hurts much more. If he travels any faster his feet will leave the ground and he doesn't like it. And he doesn't like not knowing what is coming either. But he *does* know. He *does* know for certain—but he's praying, praying inside more desperately than he's ever done in his short life, that he's wrong.

They reach the school building without a word. He's escorted towards a familiar door, the huge hand still firmly attached to his shoulder, cutting off the blood, making him lean to one side, almost buckling under it.

The door looms. The crow priest knocks.

Fred wonders what it must feel like to walk to the scaffold. To feel the weight of manacles on your wrists. To hear the judge at the Old Bailey with that little black cap on his head say that you will be *taken from this place and be hung by the neck until you are dead*. He wonders if you feel this kind of hand on your shoulder, if you've cut up your missus, if you've robbed a bank, if you've plotted to overthrow the King, if you've kissed—

"Enter."

The door yawns. Fred steps inside. The young priest doesn't follow.

Father Mullins sits behind his desk, fingertips forming a steeple. To one side of him stands Sister Maureen Quinn, a nun with a face that would pickle an egg. But worse than that—*much* worse than that—is that in front of the desk with her back to Fred stands the girl, Olga Butterworth, her hands obediently behind her back and her head slightly bowed.

God! Oh God!

Fred wants to run. Or at least beat on the door to be let out.

Please! Please!

But that would be giving the game away, he knows that. And the one thing he can't do is Give The Game Away...

"And you've said none of this to the sergeant?"

Olga shakes her head. She glances over her shoulder at Fred, detecting in the old man's eyes that someone has entered. Fred blinks hard. That the nasty cut on her eye now has a bandage over it.

She's blind. Blind!

His stomach turns over.

"Hitchcock," continues Father Mullins. "Come in and stand next to this young lady. I have some questions I want to ask you."

His innards protesting, Fred steps forward and halts slightly behind but alongside the girl. He takes care that she can't easily look sideways at him. He doesn't want her to. He stares at his shoelaces.

"Look up."

For the first time, he sees a stuffed bird in a display case in the corner of the room. He thinks it is a cormorant. It has a fish in its mouth. He wonders where the taxidermists get the eyes because a real eye would decay. It can't be a real eye.

"Look at *me*, boy. Do you know the empty house behind the allotments?"

Fred snaps his neck erect. "Yes, Father."

"Have you ever been there?"

The slightest hesitation. "Yes, Father. Sometimes I play there with my friends."

"What friends, exactly?"

"Parkhill. Murphy. O'Connor, Father."

"Did you take Olga there?"

"No, Father."

"Are you sure about that?"

"Yes, Father."

The chair creaks. So does the man. "Then why do you think she said you did?"

Fred begs all that is holy that his cheeks aren't flushing. He hates his cheeks. "I—I don't know, sir. She, she must have been mistaken."

"Mistaken? How?"

"It must've been someone else who took her there."

"You mean she got it wrong?"

Fred nods.

"You mean it was a case of mistaken identity?"

"Yes, Father."

"Somebody of your height, weight, build…?"

Realising the ridiculousness of that idea, Fred accurately senses the scepticism behind the priest's words. And sees that sideways glance to the nun.

"No, Father."

"Who, then?"

He tries not to stumble. "Somebody…someone not like me at all, sir. Probably."

Mullins leans forward, easing his dark weight onto his elbows, flattened hands under his chin, eyes shining and cold, like those of the cormorant in the display case.

"Then why would she say it was you, pray?"

The boy's mind grasps at feathers in the air. "Because she wants to get me into trouble, Father."

"Why would she do that?"

His thoughts tumble. "Because she doesn't like me."

"Why doesn't she like you?"

The words cascade before he can even think about them or snatch them back. "I…I don't know, sir. Because I'm fat. Because I frightened her once. In the street. She called me a big fat baby."

The air in the room shifts as Olga flinches at the lie. He sees this and hears an intake of breath. He thinks she will speak up and denounce him, but she doesn't. Father Mullins sees her reaction, though, he's sure.

"So let me get this straight." Mullins drags his rheumy eyes to the face of the girl in front of him, then back to the boy at her side. "You didn't see her on the day she disappeared. You didn't talk about going to the pictures…"

"Yes I did, sir. But we didn't go because she didn't want to. So I went home and she…" He doesn't want his lies to become so elaborate that he becomes unstuck. That's the last thing he wants. "…she went somewhere else."

"You didn't go to the house together?"

"No, sir. Father."

"So she's a liar?"

Softly. "Yes, Father."

"Speak up."

"Yes, Father."

Mullins removes his glasses and rubs his eyes. The folds of wrinkled skin bulge and line round his fingertips. The impassive nun's hands are hidden in her voluminous sleeves. Fred halfexpects that she has a whip up there in case of emergencies. Or a meat cleaver. He wonders if she has ears under the wimple that encloses her vinegary visage at all, or if they've been sliced off, accounting for her acid demeanour.

Then he has an idea. An idea better than any story idea he dreams up at night time, or any idea for motion pictures he wants to see in the local flea-pit. This is a humdinger and he is keen to fill the silence with it:

"And I did see her with a man once. A grown-up. And it wasn't her father because I know what her father looks like."

"That's not—!"

"Silence, child!" Galvanised, Sister Maureen launches from behind the desk and is standing over Olga, teeth bared, a tree shaken by a storm, branches near to snapping. Olga recoils, jutting towards Fred, raising a protective arm—fearing the fierce blow of a hand, or worse.

"Miss Butterworth!" The voice of Father Mullins freezes them both. "You've had your say. This is Master Hitchcock's chance to defend himself against these—these *vile* allegations."

Allegations?

Fred no longer knows what to think. Is he accused or is he not accused?

Allegations?

He expected an assumption of guilt. He thinks of the policeman peering through the peep hole and gets the rank whiff of urine in his nostrils.

Guilty, Sonny Jim!

All the evidence is stacked against him, and the girl broke her promise not to tell. She betrayed him. Yer. He was silly to trust her. He hears the policeman telling him that. He was stupid to think she was nice. She was nasty. Horrid. She was destined for Hell. Didn't he tell her that, just as he was told it when *he* was imprisoned? So she *deserves* to get the blame. It's her fault, after all. All of it. He wouldn't even *be here* if not for *her*, would he?

He realises old Mullins is staring through him. In his tool box of stares, it is the one he uses most frequently, and to greatest effect. Fred chooses to stare back at him, trying to match the coldness he sees. Unblinking. Unfeeling. Intimidating. Powerful. Truthful. Right. Is this the way things are done? Is this the way you get your way? Is this how grown-ups get away with things, he wonders? *The one who blinks first, loses.* He will have to remember that, long after the playground. *Stare, and never look away. Never show you are afraid. Ever. Ever. Ever.* Never show what you are thinking. Not *really* thinking. Or feeling.

"All right." The elderly priest's patience is finite. "Let's get to the bottom of this before Sergeant Sykes arrives." Fred shivers and sees the peep-hole rasp shut. Hears the footsteps echo in the wet chill of the cell. Feels his willy go cold as ice. "Is that the sum total of why she doesn't like you?"

Fred thinks on his feet. "N-no, sir." He is not sure he has them yet. He has the hook in their mouths but he doesn't know yet if he can reel them in. It will be down to how he tells it. The story. It is all in the telling.

"I don't like to say in front of…"

"Say it."

The sharpness of the syllables, like a blade, frightens him. The old Jesuit's exasperation is palpable.

"Come along. Come along. Your academic future is at stake here, boy. Not to mention the reputation of this school."

Fred gulps and looks furtively at the nun, who looks no less artificial than the painted statues at the altar in the chapel, then looks away from them both. Making the most of the flush that has come to his face now. Wanting it to come because it will convince them he is embarrassed. And convincing him is all he wants.

"She…she wanted to show me her——" He swallows. "…private parts, sir, Father. And, and I said I didn't want to see them. And…"

"Horrid creature," says Sister Maureen.

"Wait a minute, wait a minute..." Father Mullins closes his eyes, holds up a hand. "Alfred, listen to me very carefully. This is extremely serious. You are absolutely sure you had nothing to do with Olga going missing? Not in the slightest? Even by accident? You didn't do anything bad?"

"Bad?" Bafflement. He'd learnt from the best actors of the silver screen. "What could I do bad, sir? I'm only a little boy."

Mullins leans back in his large chair, seeming in some degree of pain and anguish as he does so. He picks up a pencil and taps it on his desk nervously, one end then the other—peering at Olga as he does so. Tongue pressing into his cheek.

"She has lied before, Father," says Sister Maureen. "Several times."

"Has she indeed?"

"And stolen from other girls. Oh yes."

This is news to Fred. But welcome news, he has to admit. He risks darting his eyes sideways, the merest flicker.

Olga's expression is one of sullen defiance.

"Well," says the priest, arranging his papers. "We don't want to waste time with fantasies of an imaginative little girl and her foolish pranks, designed to get diligent, hard working schoolboys blamed for things they didn't do." The writing implement jabs the air repeatedly. "You will not repeat this balderdash, young lady. Not to Sergeant Sykes, and not to your mother and father, do you hear me?"

Fred cannot breathe. Dare not.

The pencil drops to the blotter, rolls. A sudden thought. "*Have* you said this to your mother and father?"

"Answer!" Sister Maureen yelps shrilly, clipping Olga Butterworth on the back on the head. Fred almost feels it himself, and jerks. He averts his gaze, looking at the floor. He sees Olga's scuffed boots. Grubby hem.

"No, Father."

"What *have* you said?"

"I told them I didn't remember, Father," she says.

"Another lie," Sister Maureen decrees.

Olga looks no less sullen. No less defiant. Fred expects her to look cowed and scared, but she isn't. Not a bit. Not even a tiny bit.

"You reserved your concoction for us," says Father Mullins. "Well…"

Olga says nothing.

"I suggest that you tell your parents the truth." The paperwork on his desk cannot bear any more rearranging. "That you went exploring in that empty house like the silly girl you are, to look for toys and whatnot. You clambered inside that cupboard and inadvertently the door closed and locked itself behind you. That's what happened, isn't it?"

The nun raises her hand in preparation for another blow.

"Yes, Father," says the girl, without recoiling this time.

"Good." Mullins gives Fred a long look, then directs it at Olga with a deep and abiding superiority in every way conceivable: physical, verbal, legal, moral, spiritual. Especially spiritual. "You should know that only when you confess your sins can you be truly forgiven. In order to be free, you must first acknowledge your guilt. Do you acknowledge your guilt?"

Without pause Olga says, "Yes, Father." As if in automatic reply to the most innocuous of questions in the classroom. As if it didn't even matter any more what she said. And perhaps it didn't.

"Good. Do you have anything more to tell us?"

"No, Father."

Mullins looks at the nun and nods. Sister Maureen shakes her capacious sleeves and escorts Olga to the door.

"You'll be punished for this, you little madam!" Fred hears the woman say (if nuns counted themselves as women: he wasn't sure about that). "Showing us all up like this! Who do you think you are? Never speak of it again—not a word, do you hear me? Not a _word!_"

"Sister Maureen?" The priest rubbed the plough-lines of his forehead. "Will you tell Sergeant Sykes that we've explained the mystery, or shall I?"

"I will, Father."

He nods. "Very well."

The door closes. The nun and the schoolgirl have gone.

Fred stands there, eager to be dismissed himself. But bollock-features stares at him for a little while, perhaps hoping that the boy's inexpressive gaze will break into an emotion of some kind. It doesn't. Peculiar lad. Bright enough. But something...Fred shuffles his feet. For a few moments Mullins considers the significance of this: the significance of everything. Good. Evil. The machinations of a small child's mind, and soul. The perplexity of it. Where it begins and ends. Then decides to leave God to be the knower of such things, and us to master only the errors of the flesh. He turns to a mundane pile of essays that require marking, and gives a dismissive if theatrical wave of the hand.

"Alfred?"

Fred stops and turns, with one hand on the door handle.

"Father?"

He hasn't seen this look in the old man's eyes before. "Find kindness in your life."

*
**

Fred shuts the study door after him. He looks down the corridor and sees Sister Maureen Quinn and Olga walking past the cloakroom towards the dull light of the playground. The girl, though tall, has her shoulders hunched, head down. Her woolly sleeves cover her hands. The nun dwarfs her. *Who is on their way to the scaffold now?* He smiles. Almost.

He wonders what punishment she is in for. How many Hail Marys or worse. Not that he can do anything about it—why should he? She didn't care about him, did she? Why should *he* care about *her*?

He imagines a title-card on a movie screen: 'THE END'. 'A so-and-so production.' But a shadow steps into view, blocking out the struggling rays of the sun filtered through the glazing of the creaky swing doors. A figure that makes his pulse race and his head pound. The policeman stands at the far end of the corridor and Sister Maureen stops and talks to him, the girl's small wrist harshly in her talon grip. She talks a lot, and Sergeant Sykes listens, occasionally nodding. He takes out his small notebook and licks the tip of his pencil.

Fred wishes he could see his face, but is also thankful he can't. He knows what the man is being told, of course, but sees nothing in his posture to tell him whether he takes it at face value or not. Whether the case is closed or he has his suspicions. Suspicions about what? Whom? He'd swear the copper is deliberately giving nothing away—just standing there with his snake-clip belt tight across his stomach with his legs planted firmly apart.

Chin on her chest, Olga Butterworth stands there without speaking or moving.

The policeman turns his head. Catches sight of Fred, watching.

The hand bell is still ringing. Schoolboys pour out of a nearby classroom, filling the corridor in a gushing torrent, and Fred is gratefully lost in the stream.

Polished black boots step over discarded bricks, ferns, foliage, cracks in the paving. The leather of them squeaks. The policeman, Sergeant Stanley Sykes of this parish, chin-strap tight, walks into the debris-strewn room, his weight crunching nuggets of plaster, snapping strips of lath. Birds coo and flutter in the attic, the broken roof giving them access, open as it is to the heavens. Mating and meandering.Scratching the match-board of his cheek, he walks over to the broom cupboard in question. Footsteps left in the white dust.

The door is almost shut, but not quite. He pulls it open and closed—as if trying out how this 'door' thing works. A simian new to civilisation and its fancy trickery.

He bangs it, shuts the rusty bolt, then tugs it open again horizontally. Orange flakes pepper his hands. He claps them off, brushes his trouser legs.

He looks at the small space inside—grubby, chipped paint,

pigeon droppings. Smelling of human excrement too. Piss. Shit. Little wonder. Poor bloody thing. How long? Not the least of his questions…

He sees something on the floor. He plucks at his knees and crouches down. His boots sigh. Well, well. He puts on black gloves before picking it up. As he pokes the valleys between his leather fingers, he smiles. The smile couldn't grow wider if he'd found a treasure trove. Which, now he thinks about it, he has.

***

The halo of a paraffin lamp descends the wooden stairs, filling the back room with a ruddy, imperfect glow. Fred's father holds it at chest height. If he was undressed he has dressed swiftly—shirt unbuttoned, slippers on, pulling the elastic of his braces onto his shoulders. The knuckle-knock sounds a second time, well-practised and formal in its musicality. Three raps followed by two.He walks through his shop to the front door accompanied by the tunnel of light. Getting closer he can see the distinctive silhouette of a policeman through the rain-dotted glass. He draws the bolt top and bottom and unlocks the Chubb. The lamp illuminates the waxy pallor of his friend from the police station. If he can call him a friend. He doubts whether he can any more.

"You'd better come with me."

There's a smugness and satisfaction about the man's expression that Fred's father wants to defy. But he will not defy the law. His wife would never forgive it. He has to behave. That's what she always wants, for her husband to behave. His lips tighten to a line.

The policeman is not waiting for a discussion on the matter.

"Bill?"

Fred's father looks over his shoulder. Fred's mother has descended in the dark to the back room. Even without seeing her face he can tell from the rise and fall of her shoulders and the tension in her body she is anxious.

"Your wife too, please," says the policeman.

Fred's father back-walks to his wife, her hand being extended for him to take, else she might float away or collapse—any manner of horrors.

"Shall I shout up to the boy?"

The woman shakes her head. "The boy's asleep."

Her husband fetches her hat, her white cotton gloves, her fox fur stole. Helps her don it, like protection. Then puts on his own hat and scarf. He asks no questions, as he can tell the policeman will tell them what he wants, when he wants, and not before.

An unholy hubbub exudes from the Public Bar. The policeman sits with Bill and Em at one of the small round tables in the Saloon. More civilised there. Less *unrestrained*. For the lady. He has a pint in front of him but the others have no glasses in front of them. No wish to drink. To socialise. Only to listen.Licking the ale froth from his upper lip and moustache, the policeman takes out something from his pocket and places it on the table between them.

He carefully unwraps it.

It is a slice of fruit cake in a grubby handkerchief.

They look at it. Then they look at him.

The policeman says nothing as he raises his glass and tilts back his head. Savouring the moment no less than he savours the hops.

Husband and wife stare down at the evidence. Evidence of what? What is he trying to say? Why isn't he saying anything?

But the policeman is in no hurry for them to grasp all it implies. He has all the time in the world. He is enjoying this. Enjoying it immensely. It's an unparalleled pleasure to him and he wants to extend its life indefinitely.

He downs the rest of the pint slowly but in one draft, placing the empty glass back down on the table. A random pattern of white foam slides slowly down the sides of it, pooling at the bottom.

They recognise the fruit cake.

They recognise the handkerchief.

Of course they do.

Fred's mother looks drained. Helpless. Made of glass. Her smallness, her delicacy, her fragility, make her attractive. She is snappable, breakable, so easily. Some men are attracted to that. Some men think they can mend women. Make it better. Then there are *other* men…

The policeman knows what he wants. It is obvious what he wants. He doesn't need to put it in words. He likes the idea that they find the words all on their own. That's much more to his liking, that is. He is looking directly at the petite woman, trying to engage her eye as he runs his index finger round the rim of his pint glass, then strokes the froth off it onto his tongue.

He takes out a packet of Will's Gold Flake. Opens it. Slides one out halfway and offers it to her.

She doesn't respond. Doesn't even look. If he'd shown her part of his anatomy she couldn't be more rigid, or feel more abused.

With indifference to her reaction, he takes the cigarette out of the pack and puts one end to her lips. She refuses to part them. He inserts it just the same. Her eyes flicker and her dry lips open as he pushes the cigarette between them.

She doesn't move as he holds it there a little too long. Daring the man of the household to react—if he *is* a man. And if he *does* react, what? Only a bit of fun, mate! Only a bit of harmless fun. What's wrong wi' you?

Smiling as if to put her at ease, but not that at all, the policeman slides his fingers down the length of it. He strikes a Lucifer briskly against the sandpaper of a matchbox and lights the tip, still grinning. He could light it on the fire burning inside Fred's father and he knows it, but he's not hugely bothered. He loves that fact. Loves seeing people squirm. Loves them not being able to act, for fear of his badge and position. Why wouldn't he, eh? One of the perks of the job, innit…Like the moral instruction of minors, in exchange for a turnip or two. I scratch your back, you scratch mine, cock. That's the East End, my son. That's proper London, that is.

I scratch your back. You scratch mine.

Taking another Gold Flake from the packet with his own lips, he lights that from the same match, puffing smoke into the air from the corner of his mouth before blowing it out. He drops the blackened, curled stick of wood into the ash tray.

Bill Hitchcock is not stupid. He knows what is going on here. The wordless bargain that is being made while the animal breath laughs and the tankards clink next door, and the beer fug seeps through, stale as a workman's sweat in the air. He is sickened by the thought of it. Sickened to his soul. But he's damned if he knows a way out of it. He doesn't. He fails. He is a failure, which is perhaps what he was always destined to be.

He stares at the slice of fruit cake.

The policeman shrugs, mainly with his eyebrows—as if to say, with the merest effort: *Up to you, mate.*

Before her husband can do anything, and he wants to, Emma Jane is standing and her husband is startled to see her glide round the table to stand beside the policeman's chair. She grips her handbag in tight fingers. Chin set. Eyes fixed. Shoulders back. It's clear from her expression she wants to leave now, but not with her husband—with *him.*

Fred's father sits aghast, the fight gone out of him before any fight was begun. Already the day, this scene, is etching itself into him. Carving into him until it draws blood. And he is grey and defeated, still keeping his emotions in check for her sake. For *her* sake? It's madness and he wants to scream it, but will it even move the air if he does, will it stop the wheel that turns?

She pretends she cannot see the furnace of his anger under the surface and gently shakes her head. He's not to think of her. This is her decision. It's the only way, and they both know it.

Jaw clenched, Bill stands up sharply.

He glares at the policeman, the look on his face telling him he knows what the man is doing and will never forgive him for it. But he has no choice.

Fred's mother picks up the piece of fruit cake, the tiny pressure releasing its smell and taking her back to the kitchen on the day she made it. Her nostrils quiver. She folds the handkerchief neatly over it and places it in her husband's hand, closing his fingers around it. He can do nothing, but he can leave, and he does.

Left alone, she fights back tears, but is beguiled and enamoured of the inner voice that tells her she is strong. She wishes that voice had spoken up before now. She would like to have heard it more often.

The policeman drills out his cigarette in the ashtray and stands, straightening his tunic. He crooks his elbow like a bridegroom, asking her to take his arm. Even now, knowing the hid- eousness which is to come, she takes it as the respectable gesture it is. It serves her not to believe it a sham.

He pats the gloved hand on his forearm and escorts her to the door to the smoke and stench of the Public Bar. To the swamp. To the mire. To Hell. It takes her, and she's greeted with laughter and applause, no better or worse than a woman of the night, and the door swings shut after her. Through the semi-opaque glass their shapes merge with the crowd—fangs and pitchforks; the martyr and the Philistines; bears, hyenas, gazelles; the predators and the prey.

Fred's father wonders if she is calling out for him. He prefers to believe she is not. But he wants to call her. Her name. Just say it. Just shout it. Instead he stares into the water, hearing nothing on the night air but trains. He thinks of his son's obsession—timetables, bus routes, the picture house. Fred. Son…Dear God in Heaven… He looks into his hand which holds the handkerchief and its contents.

He pulls back his arm and throws it with a pugilist's welt into the canal. It almost takes him off his feet, and every ounce of breath out of him in a grunt.

When he looks he sees only the moon reflected in rippling slivers. Nothing in the centre of the widening rings. Nothing at all.

Footsteps echo. Shoe leather squeals. The policeman has the big ring of keys in his hand. He unlocks the cell door.Fred's mother enters.

The policeman comes in behind her. He doesn't shut the door heavily, but even closing it gently results in the inevitable clang. The sound bounces off the brickwork. Echoes through the cor- ridors. Pierces her. Chills her marrow. The smell is inconceivable. The surfaces hard. She sees no softness, no frills. Nothing she would call homely, or feminine. No vestige of human comfort. Nothing of *her* home, *her* life.

What did she expect? Not tenderness. Not that. But...

She hears the pop, pop, pop as he unbuttons his police tunic.

Without turning, she uncoils her fur wrap and places it down on the bench, crouching slightly with her knees together. On top of it she carefully places her hat and her earrings. They gleam. She wants to remember how they gleam.

He takes her hand and unbuttons the wrist of her white cotton glove, slipping it off finger by finger, tugging the last as it comes away. He performs the same ritual on the other.

He slips his thumbs under his braces and lifts them off one shoulder then the other. He unfastens and unbuttons his trousers.

She thinks of the butchery in her husband's shop and wants to vomit. The redness and flesh. The dead eyes. The hanging limbs of bird and beast. The tufts of grey-speckled fur. The tightened skin over muscle. The taut shine of liver before it is seared in the pan.

Soon she is naked.

Soon it begins.

Her white palms and knees rub into the filth of the walls and floor. Fingernails claw at her back, the rancid blanket stuffing her mouth, teeth and beer breath gnawing her cheek, a spike breaking into her.

Soon it begins, and never ends.

*
**

She faces the wall, eyes open. She can hear customers downstairs in the shop. They trill happily, exchanging the time of day and chuckling with the staff, but it cannot warm her skin. Mrs Bates with her bosom, Mr Jarvis with his gammy leg. She hears the cash register ting. She can even see the sunlight trying to get through the drawn curtains, seeping round the edges. Urging her, but she doesn't want to be urged.She is curled up under the sheets with both hands squeezed between her thighs. She cannot separate them.

Her husband—a good man, and rare—enters with a tray. He places down a cup of tea on the bedside table and sits on the bed beside her.

They hear the door bang, and before they can speak—if they wanted to speak—their son bursts in excitedly, dressed in his school uniform. The sombre spell of the room vanishes instantly, as if a ray of light has broken through the clouds. Her ray of light. Her clouds.

Fred is surprised—but not completely surprised—to see his mother in bed. He wonders if he should go.

Not a bit of it. She struggles to sit up. The old ritual. His father puffs up the pillow behind her. She valiantly puts on a smile.

"What happened in school today?"

"Not much."

He's teasing her.

He removes a rubber band and unfurls a painting he has made on grey cartridge paper. He hands it to her.

Her smile widens as she sees what is in the corner.

"A gold star for Art! Will you look at this!"

She shows it to William fleetingly, then takes it back, shaking her head in proud astonishment. Tears welling up in her eyes—for reasons the boy thinks he comprehends, but does not. *Can* not. And will not. Because he will never know. Of that much his parents are certain.

"'An exceptional piece of work by a born artist.'" She reads the teacher's comment aloud. "'Excellent.' Oh my word…'Excellent.' Come here." He goes to her as he is bidden. She envelops him with hugs and showers him with a flotilla of kisses. He doesn't like it but he does, even though he wonders what a girl feels like rather than his mother. He smells perfume, or aniseed balls, but he smells something else under it he doesn't like. Something like the smell of a wet dog or the canal, or the bleach used to mop the floor. He doesn't know what.

His father digs into his waistcoat pocket and hands him a bright, shiny shilling.

"Well done, son."

Son.

Fred glows. It means everything to him.

Everything.

He'd like to see Parkhill and the others now. He'd like to see Father Mullins. He'd like to see the policeman, even, in his stupid moustache and polished shoes. He'd give them all what for. He'd tell them all what he thought of them. Because nothing can hurt him now. Nothing can scare him. Not now. Not today.

And he thinks of it now in the dimness of his recall, that moment when he showed his mother the little gold star. Of the little man he was becoming. Maturing like a wine. The grape informed by the soil, the hillsides, the rain.

When the boy has left the room, his father and mother look at each other. Afraid even their eyes might harm the other. She finds her hand taken in his, so lightly, as he did on her wedding day.

There are many days of education ahead for their child. Many a day of the altar boy trudging off to Saint Ignatius High School for Boys in his uniform and cap, heavy satchel over his shoulder. To work. To learn. To be praised. To be cowed. To be made. On this morning, wrapped in his thoughts as ever, he chances to look up and see Olga Butterworth walking along on the pavement opposite, parallel to him, to the Convent School adjacent to his. He hasn't seen her for days. Not since he was in Father Mullins' study. He'd supposed she was being kept at home, or had moved away, or was ill. He thought himself a detective, but there you are: he wasn't a very good one.

Olga stops, and turns. She watches him, but he does not break his stride. He has seen her expression. She has no expression. Just a scar on her cheek bone and her eye is still swollen and bloodshot. She is not blind. She can see. She can look, and she is looking at him.

He pretends he hasn't noticed.

He walks.

As he nears the school gates he hears the sound of his friends in the playground, arguing, joshing, joking, punching.

He trails his hand along the wrought iron railings.

Looks through the bars at them, gripping two either side of his face. The applause rises until it becomes deafening. A roar.

Ladies and gentlemen…He has thrilled us. He has scared us. He has given us excitement, tension, romance and terror like no other director who shouted "Action!"…Please welcome the beneficiary of the American Film Institute's Life Achievement Award. The "Master of Suspense"…

The whole room rises to their feet at the mention of his name. The swell of it washes over him. He is drowned in it, and touched by it and overpowered by it—all the time, simultaneously pondering what it means. What is he doing here? The ballroom of the Beverly Hilton Hotel—March 7th, 1979. Basking in the never-ending applause from dozens of tables populated by the Hollywood great and good, dressed to the nines. Furs his late mother could only ever dream of. Tuxedos a million miles—and literally thousands of miles—from the East End of his upbringing.

The glitz, the glamour his family would have found showy. Brash. So un-English. So...*American*. And that's what he's grown to love about them, for all their crassness, their loudness, their unerring lack of tact, and style—that they were never afraid to demonstrate what was in their hearts. Even if what was in their hearts was silly, sentimental. And undeserved. And embarrassing. And—perhaps— overdue.

Surely, surely, it will end now?

But no...The standing ovation continues. The wealthy and the well-to-do of Los Angeles.

The angels, indeed, have descended from Heaven tonight.

There are cheers. Cat calls.

Laughter. Something tells me they like you, Fred, lad!

He blinks. His eyes are completely dry. He thinks of those who aren't there to clap. The boys who worked in his father's shop, who climbed the ladders, who scrubbed the floor and knotted their aprons in the small of their backs. Who never had less than a good joke for him or a friendly wink. He'd just moved up to a bigger shop, that's all. A shop that sells dreams and nightmares, and advertises its wares with frocks and jewels and perfectly-coiffured women and immaculately-groomed men. The men we want to be, and the women we want to make love to. Or hurt. Because hurt them we always will, whether we want to or not. Weren't they made perfect for that reason? So that our sins could ruin them? And isn't it *our* sin we get a thrill out of that?

He stares out at them. The woman whose scream accompanied the mummified face as it turned in the chair. The woman whose blood ran black in the shower. The man with the pronounced Adam's apple—nervous of girls, but devoted to his dear old mother. The beefcake who fended off flocks of sparrows with a pillow. Others still that he hadn't worked with—the Jewish girl who sang ballads and starred in comedies, the Cockney who played a bespectacled spy—the other spy, whom he'd cast to rape the kleptomaniac, whose running and escaping in movie after movie was like a child re-enacting his own Mount Rushmore scene, or the villain's back-projected fall from the Eiffel Tower. Producers, dress designers—ah, gowns by the immortal!…casting agents he'd done battle with or seduced with a naughty pun. Names? So many names…So many lives…So many scenes…

All to pay tribute.

All with tears in their eyes.

Too late.

He is seventy-nine, and feels it.

He would rise from the chair if he could.

As it is, he remains seated at the Table of Honour. A vast Buddha as recognisable as any of the actors whose name he put up in lights. Even in silhouette, or rendered in a few strokes of an artist's pen, he is unmistakable. A household name. A brand name for terror.

His diminutive wife is seated on his right, and an actress synonymous with Saint Joan on his left. He is an old man now, suffering from arthritis and fitted with a pacemaker, but whatever is wrong with his heart it is no effort to think both these people beautiful. He does not understand how either of them tolerated his grotesque presence in their lives. How they can show their appreciation, any of them, when he is a mountainous pig. They must be lying. He must be the butt of an enormous joke. His vision swims, from the red wine and champagne. He is obese and almost immobile, long sustained by booze and pills. And, if he sometimes knows little else of what goes on around him, he knows he is dying.

Death. Oh, yes…

That, my dear…is *suspense*.

The applause falls quiet and the illustrious guests sit down at their tables. The CBS cameras are looking at him with their big black lenses.

He speaks with his distinctive, lugubrious aplomb in spite of difficulty with the 'idiot' cards held up by a floor manager in the penumbra of his vision.

"I thank the AFI for this…" Pause. "'Life *Amusement* Award'…"

Laughter. A Beautiful Blonde in sparkling earrings and immaculate lipstick giggles as she lolls. A passing waiter tops up her glass with bubbly, then moves on.

"I believe a man needs three things from sustenance in life," says

Fred—now called Fred no longer. "Encouragement, love, and delicious food. All of which have been provided tonight in abundance." A ripple of general thanksgiving. "I also wish to thank my wife for sticking with me through thick and thin. Well, *thick* anyway."

Guffaws and giggles. An actor, Californian teeth, laughs too, leaning over to light the Beautiful Blonde's cigarette.

Her red lips part slightly.

She blows smoke which hangs and drifts.

"And so many of my friends and colleagues…" The old man gazes at the assembled. "…What have I done to deserve this?"

They like that.

Another smattering of applause. Faces enraptured. Full of merriment with a dash of the maudlin. A sense of loss, not for what is gone but for something that will not last forever.

"You know, you may think because I make terrifying movies I don't fear very much. But I do. I fear *everything*.

" Eyes and jewels glisten. Silk gowns and black bow ties in the dark.

"For instance, I have a lifelong fear of policemen."

They treat it as a joke—and perhaps it is one. Or has become one, through repetition. In the shadows are empty plates, halffull glasses, but no talk. He has their rapt attention. He commands the set.

"When I was a child…I think I was six or seven. Or was it nine or ten?…My father took me to the local police station, and got the sergeant to lock me in a cell for a few hours. I was terrified. When he came back he said: 'Now you know what happens to naughty little boys.'"

Laughter cracks open the reverential silence.

"Now I *do* know what happens to naughty little boys," he says. *This.*

Obediently reacting to their cue, once more the audience rise to their feet as he is handed his award by the esteemed director of the AFI, no mean film-maker himself.

Saint Joan embraces him, smooth bare arms stretching around

his giant frame. So do his wife and daughter. The warmth of their affection punishes him and makes him feel even more alone, more of a fake. Everyone in the room is genuine, he knows. He is the only actor. The tall man who ran through the crop field attacked by a glider wraps him in a hug. A *real* man. He holds him to his heart. But nobody has come close to his heart. Not really. And it does not even make him sad any more. He would have liked to be tender, but it was never in his make-up. He could be a fool. He could tell a joke, preferably a bad one. Above all he could terrify. He was good at it.

He was a father, he was a husband. But terrifying people was what he did best.

At times, he thought, he'd terrified the whole world.

Now, flash bulbs are popping.

The old man looks out over his audience of movie-making alumni with no sign of obvious happiness, or any emotion at all— perhaps only half-seeing, half-knowing, half-believing the adulation. The approval.

Still half-waiting for the policeman to arrive.

RWOOD

"Netherwood"
The Ridge
Hastings.
23rd October, 1947.

Care Frater Scriptor

Do what thou wilt shall be the whole of
the Law.

I beg of you, come immediately. I need a
good man, with a strong heart.

A life is at stake-and not my own.
(Telephone number on reverse.)

Love is the law, love under will.

Oliver Haddo
A∴A∴

'Tis magic, magic that hath ravished me
—Doctor Faustus

T HE VIEW BEYOND the window was monochrome. A blighted land. Not green and pleasant, but ashen, a charcoal sketch. A thick layer of dirt separated him from the world, inhibiting his gaze as if ashamed of what lay beyond. Home and hearth despoiled. The very coach he was riding in, filthy, tired, dispossessed. Too weary, like the many millions of souls shivering by their firesides, to be a disgrace.He remembered the poster he'd stood next to on the platform at Southampton. 'SHABBY? YES! IT WILL TAKE TIME TO REPAIR OUR 800 SOUTHERN RAILWAY STATIONS— BUT IT WILL BE DONE AS SOON AS WE GET THE MATERIALS!' A war-devastated company slow to recover after it had ended, like so many. The line had suffered all the more because of its closeness to the Channel ports—vital to the war effort—its routes commandeered for troops and military supplies, not least for Normandy, and Overlord, resulting in its malachite green carriages and sunshine yellow livery running the gauntlet along the south coast and getting a real pasting.

He tried to create a clean oval with his fingertip, and failed. The grime was on the outside. Nevertheless he could see enough of what he didn't want to. Fields pitted by bomb craters. The landscape ravaged. Recovering, perhaps, like a crippled Tommy, but unbowed? Or was that a brave face it was putting on, still wracked with pain from its visible and invisible wounds? He felt it in deep his own body, too, as clearly as he felt the jostling of the track underneath him.

The Blighted Land.

A potential title? He took out his notebook and jotted it down, immediately capping his fountain pen self-consciously.

A young couple occupied the same compartment. Sweethearts, he guessed, from their whispered endearments, and the fact that they clasped hands so tightly. The man's uniform that of a lance corporal, the three feathers in his cap badge indicating the Royal Regiment of Wales. Clean shaven. Not that there was much to shave. Forehead wide, chin small, he reminded him of Chad, the graffito character chalked on every wall for the last several years with variations of the same *cri de coeur*: 'Wot, no sausages?' 'Wot, no girls?'—or, in this case, possibly: 'Wot, no war?'

Not wanting his lack of conversation construed as sullenness, he spoke.

"Glad to see you got through unscathed."

"Not exactly," the young man said. "Lost one of my balls at Zeeuws-Vlaanderen."

Dennis raised one eyebrow.

"You and Hitler both, then. If the song is to be believed."

The lad laughed, heartily.

Dennis reached out his right hand to shake the other chap's. The lance corporal reached out his left. Dennis quickly swapped to his left and clutched it vigorously.

"Right-handed before I left." The soldier still laughed. "Now I have to learn all sorts with my left hand. Quite fun doing so, to be fair."

The girl blushed and nudged him in the ribs with her elbow. He pretended it hurt more than it did, then snatched a mischievous kiss on her cheek. The grin did not leave his face, and peculiarly that made Dennis sadder instead of happier, though he didn't let it show.

He liked their playful banter, their intimate chatter, their sentimental need to touch. If there could only be that, he thought, they would be happy—and good luck to them. They probably read no newspapers, had no interest in world affairs. They'd probably had enough of 'world affairs' for a lifetime. He couldn't say they'd be wrong, either. We'd all had a big party, but there was still rationing. The war was over, but nothing had changed. There were no planes droning overhead, but there were still bombed and demolished buildings. After the blackouts, it was odd to see all the shops with their lights on, but things hadn't got better. Not in the way we'd all been led to expect. By a long chalk.

Was he the only person who felt the ubiquitous cheerfulness had a desperate, hollow ring to it? Under the surface, to him, there lay a mild sense of anarchy waiting to escape. He wondered how foreigners saw the British now? Could they perceive all too clearly we had a deeply false vision of ourselves? The jollity but a tiresome artifice? He for one still had the stink of the Blitz in his nostrils. A sense that he'd walked out of a burning building without so much as a scratch. He'd come out of Hatchett's, a new basement restaurant, one night to see Burton's the tailors ablaze, and Piccadilly lit up like a funfair. The Café de Paris, yards away, had suffered a direct hit, and he'd seen looters scrabbling amongst the dead and dying for valuables. One woman was bent over, cutting off fingers. He still had that feeling in his stomach now that he had back then, almost every day.

Best of all, he liked that the young couple didn't recognise him. He was hardly a public figure or a matinee idol. He suffered no illusion about that. But some did, from the dust jackets. For now, though, he could enjoy the welcome anonymity.

A lover and his lass. He shut his eyes and drifted back to The Savoy, 1940. The band playing *It was a Lover and his Lass* by Ken 'Snakehips' Johnson and his West Indian Orchestra. The usual, painfully predictable litany of questions that always came once he'd made the schoolboy error of saying he was a novelist.

Oh! What have you written that I've read?

He'd have to grit his teeth.

—I don't know. What have you read?

His darling wife, in her element. Ferociously well connected. Joan Gwendoline Vanden-Bempe-Johnstone, as was. Daughter of the

Hon what-what. Ex-wife of Sir what-what, Second Baronet whatwhat. And so it went back. Back to the dawn of time, it seemed.

So, old chap, do you make an actual living *from this 'scribing' lark?*

—Touch wood.

You know, I've an absolute corker of an idea. If I could only find the time to write the dashed thing.

—It does help.

Thing is, I know it would sell like absolute hot cakes! I say. Here's a thought. We could collaborate. I'd have all the ideas, you wouldn't have to worry on that score, but you can get it down on paper, you see? And you have the contacts. We could go 50-50. How's that? Make a fortune!

—Rescue me.

These were Joan's people, not his.

—Enjoy the claret, she'd invariably reply, from the corner of her mouth.

—About all I am enjoying.

The penguin suits were a far cry from the khaki sitting opposite. And he knew which he respected the more.

"D-Day?" he said to the lance corporal.

"Nothing so grand."

"I don't care if you spent all your time spud-bashing. You did us proud."

He meant it.

The young man looked embarrassed, and coloured slightly, examining his boots, which made Dennis admire him all the more. They were all heroes to him, and the sight of a uniform did peculiar things in his chest. He couldn't help it. He'd cursed the fact that he'd been forty-two, over the age at which ex-officers could be re-commissioned. Additionally galling as two of his stepsons and his wife were all either in the forces or employed by the government. The thought of enduring the war as a dreary civilian was anathema. He'd tried everything to get a posting, by hook or by crook—applying to the Ministry of Information three times, without getting as much as a reply—finally, rather ignominiously, settling for becoming a fire warden. He bitterly regretted not serving in the thick of it as he had in the Great War. But he did do his bit, as it turned out, thanks to an extraordinary stroke of luck. The kind of luck that had been his boon companion all his life.

Joan had put her motor car at the disposal of the War Office, acting as a driver for MI5. She'd always liked mucking about with engines and, doling out fuel rations, came into her own, known, rather amusingly, as 'The Petrol Queen'. One day she'd overheard an officer in the back seat saying it seemed horribly clear Germany would invade, but they had little idea how or when. "Why don't you ask my husband?" she piped up. "He uses his imagination for a living."

This was the welcome catalyst for him writing *Resistance to Invasion*. His avalanche of ideas went down well, and immediately. Greig and Darvall liked what they read and gave him his next assignment, to imagine himself as a member of the Nazi High Command. Not only a tough exercise, but a vitally important one, and he'd taken to it like the proverbial duck to water. In forty-eight hours solid, sustained by three magnums of plonk and tearing through hundreds of cigarettes, he'd churned out the 15,000-word *Invasion and Conquest of Britain*, putting himself in the shoes (or jackboots, rather) of a calculating and heartless enemy who'd think nothing of employing poison gas or bacteriological warfare, with no humanitarian considerations whatsoever. What followed, when his writing had gone to the Chiefs of Staff, and copied to the King himself, was a swift request for more reports—hundreds of thousands of words, delivered to 'Mr Rance's Room at the Office of Works': the cover name for the Cabinet War Rooms in Churchill's bunker under Whitehall.

Dennis was inordinately proud of his war work, and grateful for it. It taught him about the lives of real people and true bravery and danger that would help no end in making his own tales plausible and authentic. More than that, it made him desperately conscious of the things he held precious, and the things he feared. His mind had spun. His fingers had developed calluses where his pencil rubbed. His hands got cramp. Yet his fears urged him on. The narratives he was dreaming up dare not stop. If they stopped, he would feel like a coward on the battlefield turning his back and running away. His fiction could wait. Sleep could wait.

And yet, the question plagued him, constantly, even now...

Was it enough? His million words, for a readership of four?

Could anything *ever* be enough?

"We are champions of Light facing the creeping Darkness," he remembered writing, in those clearer, more terrified, more united days. But is the Darkness ever truly defeated?

The braying voices at the Savoy came back to him.

I couldn't sleep for weeks after those dreadful scenes of devil worship in the Home Counties.

—Quite right too.

And the appalling Mr Mocata!

Where do you get your ideas?

—Little shop off the Marylebone Road. Terribly useful.

—He writes about what scares him, said Joan, her hands on his shoulders. Don't you, darling?

Emboldened from his natural shyness by her kiss on his cheek, he'd happily sign with a flourish the next dozen, or two dozen, copies of the novel with his name on the cover. OVER THREE MILLION COPIES OF THIS AUTHOR'S NOVELS SOLD, it read. THRILLING BLACK MAGIC STORY, it promised. 'THE BEST TALE OF ITS KIND SINCE *DRACULA*'—JAMES HILTON, it heralded. In the bottom corner, a gigantic scarlet goat stood on its hind legs exuding flames from its nostrils, while around it danced naked figures, one in a pointed hat hunched over a broomstick. Dominating all, the face of a bald-headed man bathed in emerald green light, with searing, malevolent eyes, his hands twisted in conjuring gestures, thrown as claw-like shadows behind the author's surname.

That brought him back to the letter.

Its writer, behind the all-too-obvious pseudonym, not difficult to discern.

'Oliver Haddo'...the odious scoundrel in Somerset Maugham's novel *The Magician,* described as having a head like a pea balanced on an egg, who inflicted his awful poetry on unsuspecting guests.

Quite obviously an extremely thinly-veiled portrait of Aleister Crowley. In fact, when the subsequent film was released, Dennis seemed to recall, Crowley tried to sue for compensation, but there was, of course, no hope of damages. His reputation was deemed so black by then it essentially couldn't be made blacker.

But he had known the identity of the sender before he'd read as far as the signature.

The envelope had been sealed with the cartouche of Ankh-f-nKhonsu in blue-grey wax, made with the same seal ring Crowley had worn when they'd met, the significance of which he had gone to pains to elucidate. If further confirmation were needed, the letterhead was the telltale vesica enclosing Crowley's 'Magister Templi' lamen, which consisted of a crown bisected by a sword, scales on its tip balancing the Greek letters alpha and omega, surrounded by five Vs, indicating Crowley's motto of initiation: "Vi Veri Vniversum Vivus Vici"—again, imparted to Dennis by the man himself: "By the power of truth I have conquered the Universe".

Either an extraordinary statement of fact or quite remarkable wishful thinking.

He had met Crowley only the once, whilst researching *The Devil Rides Out*. He invited him to his favourite restaurant, the Hungaria, in Regent Street, owned by Joseph Vecchi of Splendide Hotel fame. Dennis had dined there frequently since, with Peter and Ian Fleming, or Roland Vintras and Dicky Dickson, 'eating for victory' as they called it, when they were involved in military deceptions such as Operation Bodyguard. Back in 1934, a couple of thrillers under his belt, he was pretty well read in mysticism and religions of the world, but, in embarking on a new novel about black magic, wanted to make sure he was up to the minute regarding occult circles in present day England. Tom Driberg, who lived a stone's throw away in Queen's Gate, had suggested he talk to Crowley. A rather dubious leftie with foul manners towards waiters and a strange predilection for public lavatories, Driberg considered democracy to be in its death throes and Crowley's credo that the 'secret few' shall rule the world doubtless appealed to him. He'd signed up for Thelema on the dotted line, and AC, down on his luck, was on the lookout for a protégé, or sycophant, or both. However, Dennis was never quite sure if Driberg's interest in Crowley was genuine, or whether he was working for their mutual friend Maxwell Knight, getting his hands dirty infiltrating secret societies for the professional nosey parkers at MI5.

In any case, back in '34, The Great Beast's reputation preceded him. Salacious rumours, half-truths, hearsay and downright lies abounded, though by then he was on the cusp of becoming a pathetic figure that people feared more for his blatant ploys for financial bail-outs than the possibility he might compromise their morals.

And so the magician succumbed to temptation, arriving in green plus fours and a tartan bow tie, saying grace in his "Do what thou wilt" fashion, and answering Dennis's questions with civility and aplomb. They ate and drank prodigiously, with incredibly good humour, though he smelt, Dennis thought, of an old operating theatre recently fumigated. Tittle-tattle had it that he started each day with a pint of ether, so that might well have explained it.

Some of what Dennis learned had absorbed him. Some of it had disturbed him. All of it had interested him, one way or another. The common-law wives and wanton hussies, the foolish philistines encountered along the way. Indignation. Repudiation. A mischievous, semi-winking pride under the surface. The 'prophet in his own land' scenario, though told without an ounce of self-pity. They'd talked about Swedenborg, Blavatsky, KrafftEbing and AE Waites. The "science of the old sanctuaries". Conversation taking by-roads and untrammelled tracks into the sublime Zohar and Knorr von Rosenroth's *Kabbala Denudata*, though Crowley violently dismissed MacGregor Mathers' "monstrous" translation.

If he'd wanted, or expected, to meet a grand master of supernatural evil, he'd been sorely disappointed. Crowley had struck him above all as an exceptionally good talker. Boaster, evidently.

Liar, most probably. But amusing, definitely—and never boring. At least the man stood out in a world populated by grey people with grey, excruciatingly dull lives. And he had certainly *done* things—such as climbing in the Himalayas—which put him above most people. Yet there was a cold detachment about him, a plain incuriosity about you, the listener, which made one feel very much a lesser mortal, but somehow made one crave his attention, as if being in his thrall was all that was important.

On the most banal level, he had wanted to sell some erotic MSS to realise some ready cash, and Dennis recommended the book dealer Percy Muir. This, like much of the encounter, seemed absurd yet vaguely sinister. All in all, Crowley came across like an old time music hall comedian down on his uppers. So emphatically *bald* that Dennis feared the top of his head might at any moment open like the lid of a Jack-in-the-Box and something truly demonic jump out.

Yes, it was a good lunch.

Three triple absinthes, a good Burgundy and several brandies saw to that.

He wondered what the lance corporal and his girl would think of him if they knew whom he was thinking about. Perhaps they'd immediately consider him the worst sort of deviant by association. Perhaps part of him did the same. He kept going over what the Sunday rags had told their readers. How Crowley had picked up the dregs of Bohemian London and spirited them off to Italy, satiating their lusts with heroin and cocaine and turning them into moral degenerates. Far from his lure of a commune of scholars and freedom, it was, they said, a hotbed of profligacy and vice, fuelled by blasphemy, filth, nonsense, and cakes made with goat's blood. The story circulated widely ("with typical insanity," according to Crowley) that he had forced a woman to have ritual intercourse with a he-goat—though the source of the rumour was clearly someone with a very blunt axe to grind. Then there was the mysterious death of Raoul Loveday. Catnip to the jackals of Fleet Street. Crowley told Dennis the truth was simply that Loveday had drunk the local water when warned not to. "Cause of death, paralysis of the heart. Due to acute intestinal distress" 'Satanic murder' made for much better headlines, and the man's widow was there to give all the fodder the press needed. Her husband had drunk blood from a chalice, she said. Crowley made him do it, she said. It was all Crowley's fault, she said. They'd sharpened their knives for the Beast, and now they stuck them in.

There the hate campaign began. "New sinister revelations" followed. "Abominations and unimaginable horrors: Turn to page seven" He planned to sue, but what was the point? Everyone was on the bandwagon. He was The Wickedest Man in the World. King of Depravity. He'd left a trail of abandoned lovers and rejected acolytes of both sexes along the path in his search for personal development through 'Magick'. True or false? Was he a learned academic with a serious interest in mysticism and philosophy, or just someone with incredible power over people, and more than anything a towering self-belief? Dennis's ultimate conclusion was that he was either a sexually liberated genius or a spoilt, indulgent dilettante of the most overbearing and selfcentred kind. One who lived his life theatrically, and to whom satanic splendour only added immeasurably to a personal façade of his own misguided creation.

One thing was certain, on the evidence. The man appeared to lay waste to every life he came into contact with. And yet Tom Driberg had laughed: "Crowley would never so much as hurt a rabbit!"

Is that what he needed to find out? Which of two mutually exclusive options was the truth? Is that why he phoned the number scrawled on the back of the letter? Is that why he had boarded the train?

More than anything, though, he needed to know why Aleister Crowley, The Great Beast, 666—prophet of the New Aeon— thirteen years after they'd broken bread with each other in London, was desperately seeking his help.

***

Netherwood, he discovered, was a large Victorian house on The Ridge, a road running across the haunch of the hill behind Hastings, two miles from the coast. The taxi, a Humber Snipe, brought him directly from the station at mid-afternoon, but he seemed to arrive in shade, the edifice sombre, hidden from road by trees, its narrow driveway hemmed in by bushes semi-overgrown even with the annual thinning of autumn. Getting out of the vehicle, giving the driver a good tip as he always did, he detected cordite in the air and had seen regular gaps where buildings— perhaps grand ones—used to be, neighbouring villas of the same or similar era, he supposed."Mr Wheatley, I presume?" Immediately on entering the porch he was greeted by a short, dapper, bouncy man in his late forties, with longish hair swept back from his temples and a widow's peak, reminding him instantly of Claude Rains. "Vernon Symonds" The man shook Dennis's hand vigorously. "Not *Simmonds*. My name is pronounced with a sigh, quite literally" He laughed. Dennis felt this witticism had been repeated many times, never quite to the same degree of amusement the teller himself enjoyed. More artistic than urbane, the man wore a cravat tucked into a V-neck pullover, making Dennis rather stupidly self-conscious of his Savile Row suit from Scholte, shirt from Beale & Inman, and shoes from Lobb.

A woman glided past, carrying an empty tray.

"*La Cuisinière*," explained Vernon. "My better half. Kathleen. But everyone calls her Johnny."

"*Bonjour*" 'Johnny' greeted Dennis with a swirl and bobbed hair. Automatically, he lifted her hand to kiss it, but she snatched it away, frowning and giggling as if to cover some dreadful faux pas, which took him aback somewhat. Good grief, he thought: Are these the type of people to whom good manners were a sort of affront?

She disappeared behind a frosted glass screen, presumably to the kitchen. A woman neither plain nor pretty, but occupying that same strange non-sexual hinterland as Vera Lynn. He could easily imagine her, sans apron, skirt rotating, like a prim dervish, at the mating ritual of the local tea dance.

"She rules the kitchen with a rod of steel. My realm is the bar"

Vernon tapped the side of his nose. Dennis easily deciphered the gesture.

"Well. I'm glad you had a spare room."

"Oh, we can always find a room for interesting individuals to add to our merry clan" Vernon lifted his suitcase and took it to the stairs. "Please make yourself at home. Someone will be around in a moment to take your tea order, if you want. Do relax and make the most of the facilities."

"Mr Crowley…"

"Is, ah…" Vernon turned back at the half-landing. "…indisposed at the moment."

When he had gone, Dennis took a few steps towards the dining room. The tables were laid with starched white linen but none of them were occupied. Beyond a pair of sliding doors he could make out a paunchy man in a vast armchair snoring contentedly, an incongruous contrast to the sound of children's laughter from outside. Lit cigarette in hand, he decided to explore.

Rounding the attractive battlement tower on the north east corner, he could get a better assessment now of the exterior. While the interior was nothing to write home about, clearly the setting, he perceived, was Netherwood's attraction, not only quiet and isolated, but with a large, impressive garden facing southward. The house from this side was largely ivy-clad, with two large chimneys, and two skylights sat between large gables, the building's most notable feature. These mirrored the design of the porch, with ecclesiastical spikes at their apices, their decorative woodwork a contrast to the plain, almost brutal style of the architecture.

Down the slightly sloping lawn, to his bemusement, he saw a thin man wearing a turban, face blackened with boot polish, entertaining a semicircle of children, cross-legged and wholly attentive before him. On a small table to one side Dennis could see three cups and a ball. Basically the same old sleight-of-hand trick he'd seen done by ne'er-do-wells with cards on Oxford Street. He'd been stung by it too. Once. Lost the most foolish twenty pounds he'd ever parted with in his life.

"Boys andgirls. Girls andboys. Mustaphas and Mustaphaven'ts.

Uncles and barnacles. Allez-oop!" The dangling rope in the magician's fist shot upwards, as stiff and erect as a guardsman's sabre. "Oopy-al!" Just as abruptly, it gave in to a terrible case of brewer's droop. Dennis half-smiled. The children laughed uproariously in their Stetson hats, Sitting Bull headdresses and war paint, even more loudly still as the trick was repeated—up, down, up, down— whereupon the mystical performer wound the rope into a tight ball and held it between his flattened palms.

"What's the magic word? Ready?"

"Abrahadabra!" cried the spectators as one.

Not the usual time-honoured 'Abracadabra', Dennis noted, but *Abrahadabra*. Only a true magician would get the word correct like that, surely?

The palms opened and the rope was gone.

The small audience declared their appreciation.

Dennis himself clapped too, lightly, realising as he did so that the blacked-up scarecrow in front of him must be, astonishingly, Crowley himself, dressed in his much-photographed 'costume de pacha' of jewel-encrusted turban, jade green robe with sash, bejewelled dagger, twig fingers ornamented by rings laden with huge turquoise stones. Almost unrecognisable—and not only due to the ink-black make-up—he sported a thin, white goatee beard.

The satanic old goat. Anti-Christ of the Apocalypse. Reduced to...what? But certainly reduced. The Crowley he'd last seen was rotund and, some might say, handsome, if debauched-looking: an imposing figure as he roamed Fitzrovia in top hat and astrakhan coat, bumming drinks, broke, declaiming the words of gods past and future, hovering between cheap lodgings. Now the Logos of the Aeon had shrunk inside his clothes. Itself a conjuring act.

The voice, too, was transformed. Feeble, tremulous, nasal.

"And now it is that time of day when all good magicians hibernate. So I say unto you all, goodbye, toodle-oo, pip-pip, *auf Wiedersehen, adios, adieu*, until next we..." The children protested noisily. He cupped a hand to one pink island of an ear. "I'm sorry. I can't hear you" They shouted even more madly. It was all part of the act, of course. "Oh, I was forgetting. I'm so sorry. I had an open mind once. Trouble was, my brains fell out" Crowley moved to a large flower pot covered with a black silk cloth. "Do you remember, children, right at the beginning, we put a carrot in here, just to see what would happen? Well, let's see what's in here now" He delved in with both hands and extracted a white rabbit, nursing it gently as its nose and whiskers twitched and the children came closer, petting and stroking it. "Now, careful, it's his bed-time too. That's the end of my show for today. Clive? Bridget? Jelly and blancmange in the Dance Hall. And don't forget that Latin homework of yours, young man."

Dennis stepped closer as the children hopped and skipped away, leaving him alone on the lawn facing the old man, though the latter did not seem to notice his presence as he tidied away his accoutrements.

"Simple pleasures," Dennis said.

Crowley blinked, like a blind man made suddenly aware of someone in the room, and turned his head jerkily. His eyes were glazed and Dennis wondered if he'd been recognised or not. They stood in silence, until Dennis saw droplets of rain create dark spots on the shoulders of the oriental costume. Crowley blinked again, looked up at the sky, and, as the drizzle became heavier, held out the palm of his hand.

"A little demonstration I arranged for your benefit."

If he smiled, it was the most minimal one imaginable.

Dennis wedged his cigarette between his lips and turned up his collar. He grabbed a stars and crescents-decorated cloak he saw draped over a nearby chair and wrapped it around the bent and shivering Crowley. As they made their way indoors, the Cherry Blossom began to run, and by the time they reached the lobby Dennis saw pink rivulets striping the old man's pan stick dark cheeks.

It was evident by then from his wheezing and laboured breathing that Crowley was exhausted. He hung onto the newel post of the staircase as Dennis divested him of the cape, shook the excess water from it, and hung it on a peg. Outside, the heavens opened. It was a downpour. By the time Dennis turned back, Crowley was struggling upstairs. At the mezzanine he paused, with a pained, inexplicably puzzled look on his features.

"We'll see him after dinner" Vernon appeared behind Dennis, eager and chirpy as ever. They both watched as Crowley disappeared to his room. "Don't worry. He often flags by the afternoon."

As Vernon turned away, Dennis reminded him politely he hadn't been given his room key.

"Oh, there are no room keys here" Vernon gave a laugh that Dennis was sure wasn't meant to be condescending, adding the essential information only as an afterthought. "You're in number nine. Top of the stairs, turn right" He smiled again, like someone who had a requisite number of smiles to use up on any given day, and had just remembered to implement one.

Hot and cold water. A radiator, warm to his hand. A bathtub, even. The room wasn't unpleasant, but it wasn't the Ritz. It wasn't even as grubbily cosy as some of those hotels he'd been billeted at in Amiens. He lifted his suitcase onto the bed and unpacked.Next to the bedside lamp sat a copy of Crowley's notorious *Forbidden Lecture*—his speech to the Oxford union on the controversial subject of Satanist and child-murderer Gilles de Rais, which he had been banned from delivering, and so published privately, cocking a magnificent snook at the university authorities. Somebody was rather pointedly suggesting his bed-time reading.

He took out the book he was halfway through, Gerald Kersh's *Neither Man Nor Dog*. 'An Undistinguished Boy' was masterful, while another story, 'The Woman in the Fire', he'd tried to read on the train, but found himself unable to concentrate. Whether it was the all-too-accurate description of the London bombings or for other reasons, he wasn't sure. But he *was* sure he didn't want to read Crowley's opus, and placed the Kersh on top of it.

Good God, he thought, after swishing his face with water at the sink. *What am I doing here?*

He lay on the bed and tried to get forty winks, but his mind was over-active.

He'd been shocked by seeing the corpulent, vigorous figure of memory reduced in every dimension to a wizened, shrunken relic. Even the distinctive sound of Crowley's voice was diminished. Once it had been fruity, orotund, weighed with a Churchillian sense of self-importance. Which reminded him of that lunch again. "As I conveyed to the BBC, and they conveyed to Winston…The swastika represents Isis in mourning, so the V-sign must be used, since it symbolises Typhon-Apophis, the Destroyer. It's a magical counter-attack, as Typhon slays Osiris, causing Isis to mourn. What I didn't tell them is that the V also represents the downward-pointing triangle of Horus, the Crowned and Conquering Child of the New Aeon, evoking Ra-Hoor-Khuit and Thelema, V for victory indeed!" Another of his fables. If they *were* fables, all of them.

Dennis must have nodded off because he opened his eyes and the clock said half past six. It was dark. He put on a fresh shirt and tie, combed his hair in the mirror, and descended.

Classical music wafted from a gramophone somewhere. He had no idea what. He preferred popular music like Noël Coward's *I'll See You Again*. Even the Rachmaninoff in *Brief Encounter*, which everyone found romantic, he found dreary and depressing. He liked something you could do the foxtrot to, or a slow dance. The Inkspots' *If I Didn't Care* or Buddy Clark's new hit, *Peg O' my Heart*.

Two types resembling Naunton Wayne and Basil Radford, the double act from *The Lady Vanishes*, hogged the open fire and showed no sign of budging. The library was reasonably stocked with books, magazines, pamphlets. For ramblers, walks to the delights of Ecclesbourne Glen and Firehills, a distance away. A bus excursion to Battle. Two women, one angular and stork-like, the other as svelte as a suet dumpling, ogled over maps.

He decided to retire to the bar.

Not a great fan of beer, unless it was Bismarck's favourite, Black Velvet—champagne and stout—he fancied a whisky. Vernon's emporium was surprisingly well stocked and he chose a glass of

Glen Mhor from Hedges and Butler in Regent Street, near his old stomping ground. His own family business had been in South Audley Street. He knew them there, and the taste of it brought back memories, welcome and unwelcome, of those days in the office, at the desk, wrestling with the books. Choosing his three courses from a menu typed daily, he fancied a Bordeaux, and ordered a bottle of Château D'Issan, the best on their list. He wondered exactly what the 'mock' in the mock turtle soup was, but thought it best not to ask.

The food proved surprisingly good. It wasn't the Café Royal or Quaglino's, but neither were the vegetables stewed to a pulp, or a wafer-thin strand of horsemeat eked out to feed the five thousand. Vernon told him proudly that the eggs, poultry and veg were all home grown, their aim being, ultimately, to become a self-supporting community. The phrase rang alarm bells to Dennis, but he let it pass. "Our priority is to guarantee impeccable cuisine."

It wasn't far off, and the lack of formality refreshing. No gong for dinner. The waitresses didn't wear pinafores but ordinary, almost slovenly, dress; cardigans over blouses. The girl serving at their table was flat-chested, unaffectedly pretty, with a long, graceful neck, though that was where her gracefulness ended. He actually found her gaucheness charming, but had to prod away the ungentlemanly thought that those incipient breasts had never been touched. He couldn't help detecting the endearing shyness girls had before becoming sexually active, indistinguishable from a vague aura of shame. He gave her a smile, more of encouragement than pity, or so he hoped.

It didn't take long to have Vernon down as a sociable, arty soul, who wasted no time in telling him their mutual acquaintance had arrived two years previously, heralded by a mysterious telegram: "Expect a delivery of frozen meat at such-and-such a date and time. Well, someone at the post office handed a copy to the Food Ministry, who came down on us like a ton of bricks" Vernon protested they hadn't ordered any. The day arrived, with two food inspectors ready to pounce. The ambulance doors swung open, and Aleister Crowley announced his arrival, together with forty or fifty bundles of books.

"He was the 'frozen meat' in question!" His appearance that day had been alarming, though, even then. Pale and wan, in ridiculously wide knickerbockers and buckled shoes, he'd struck both Vernon and Johnny as frail and vulnerable rather than menacing. "We saw him as a poor old boy who needed looking after." He'd opted for Room 13. No great surprise. South-facing, overlooking the garden and grounds.

"What exactly brought him here? Apart from the ambulance?"

"Apparently, reduced to a nervous wreck by the pounding the Luftwaffe was giving the West End, he'd decamped to Buckinghamshire, which proved a very bad idea." Crowley knew no-one out in the sticks and, starved of intellectual or physical stimulation, his health had deteriorated. Life proved bothersome; he was depressed, and suffered, as was so often the case, from 'sporadic income shortfall'. A worried friend, Louis Wilkinson, had heard about Netherwood from Oliver Marlow, who acted and stagemanaged with Vernon in local theatre group, the Hastings Court Players. Did they have space for the old reprobate? Vernon nervously asked his wife if she minded Aleister Crowley coming to stay. "Who's he?" she'd replied. "Clever chap, but they call him The Wickedest Man in the World." "Oh I don't care about *that*, as long as he's interesting!" They seemed positively eager to have such a character take residence, in spite of his colourful past.

"Brave," said Dennis.

"I never believe what I read in the *Sunday Express*."

Dennis found his dinner companion surprisingly swift to expound upon his lofty utopian ideas. To Vernon, in short, the British elite stank to high heaven. They valued nothing except money. To them, art for art's sake could go hang. Having worked in a bookshop in Paris, he'd decided to retire and return to acting and plays, his first love. "That's what the word 'amateur' means, of course—doing something purely for love." He and his wife had taken on Netherwood when it was near-derelict. "Had a vision, I suppose." It had been hard during the war—turned into a canteen for soldiers and ATS girls from the Grange School half a mile away, which was commandeered as a camp for prisoners of war. "Poor Johnny worked herself to a frazzle, what with catering for the staff at Ore Place as well. We just about survived, pulling ourselves up by the bootstraps, so to speak" Business picked up in the latter half of '45, but Dennis wondered if, in the dying glow of the war, idealism as a currency had become tarnished. Not to Vernon. "As long as I'm here, this will be what we always dreamt of. Not a guest house in the conventional sense, with silly regulations like dressing for dinner and boring pursuits like playing poker—if people want that, they can go elsewhere. Netherwood is about fine food, culture, arts. Conversation, interaction, mixing. Good cuisine in a relaxed atmosphere" He made it sound as though making a profit was secondary to stimulating good debate, be it with nature cure advocates or flat earth theorists.

Their clientele was certainly that varied. Political voices, stage stars, BBC broadcasters—Dennis was sure he recognised the small man in round, black spectacles at the far table—art critics, scientists, liberal thinkers, atheists, members of the Fabian Society, the odd Theosophist. "The head of philosophy at Birkbeck College gave an interesting talk about sexual desire. Though Mr Crowley said he was intensely bored by his lecture on birth control" Vernon could not disguise his excitement at the notion of the world being on the edge of great change. "I think any right-thinking individual believes the same. With the so-called democracies of the West proving duplicitous and corrupt, socialism is the only answer. If only it were properly explained to the general public, I'm convinced they'd embrace it."

Dabbing the corners of his mouth with his napkin, Dennis didn't really want to discuss the matter.

"Does he mix with the others much?"

Vernon shook his head. "Spends most of time in his bedroom. Likes his own company. Just as well, since he doesn't get many visitors" He stroked his fork with his thumb. "Makes no secret at times of the fact he's lonely. All his friends seem to have deserted him."

Or has he driven them away, thought Dennis? Had they been used and discarded? He'd too often heard tales of Crowley extracting money from people, then claiming they'd let him down. Such behaviour had consequences.

"Those who do come, he gets bored with, or irritated by. Chap was installed in the cottage, doted on him. Some acolyte. He treated him outrageously, like an errand boy."

"Who is paying for this, if you don't mind me asking? I heard he was broke."

"The OTO—Ordo Templi Orientis—offshoot of his society in California. They send sugar, soap, cigars, boxes of chocolates, silk handkerchiefs, caviar. And they pay, reliably, on time. From member donations."

Dennis heard himself grunt.

"How long have you been his friend?"

"I'm not his friend at all" Dennis reached for his glass of wine.

"Well. We try to keep him happy and amused as best we can. He's a creature of habit, though. Breakfast taken up by Miss Clarke at nine. Boiled egg. Not had a regular cooked meal for months. We sit with him when we have time, Johnny or I. Not too much to ask, is it? To listen to his tales of Cairo with Rose. His travels. India. Tibet. The Gobi desert. The mountain treks. Becoming a holy man."

Is that what he is, then? A holy man? thought Dennis. *Good Lord above.*

"Last winter was appalling, as you know. We had six inches of snow down here in January, and it didn't thaw till March. He had a hell of a bad time of it, what with the blizzards, the phone lines down, and the buses not running. I think it must have felt like a prison. And he was awfully ill this summer. Pneumonia. Colitis. You name it. Asthma attacks. Waking on the brink of suffocation. Dreadful. The staff thought he was at death's door. Some of them prayed for the end to come sooner rather than later."

"I wonder if our Christian God would listen to such prayers?"

"I very much hope he would. Yes" Vernon stared down, dewy-eyed, fidgeting with his cutlery, then looked up, a smile reinstalled. "In any event, under Dr Magowan, he rallied. That and the barley sugar. Something energised him. No idea what. Gave him a reason not to die. Albeit temporary, perhaps."

Dennis placed his knife and fork side by side at four o'clock on his plate. "By the way, I meant to ask, would a cheque be all right, or would you prefer cash?" He was met by a blank stare. "For the room?"

"Oh, we wouldn't dream of it. We ask only for payment in kind from our more distinguished visitors. A lecture, or talk. On novel writing, perhaps? The other guests would be most fascinated, I'm sure. Tips for those who wish to…"

His eyes shifted, and Dennis felt a weight pressing onto his shoulder.

Vernon rose.

It was Crowley, dressed in a scarlet blazer, striped pyjama bottoms and purple slippers, with a bottle of Martell's forty-year-old cognac dangling from his other hand.

"Do what thou wilt shall be the whole of the Law" His standard greeting.

Dennis had calculated he was seventy-one, but, frighteningly, in this light, he looked a good twenty years older. Minus the make-up of earlier, his face bore the pallor of grey mud. Devoid of colour, if anything. Mandarin beard so thin the slightest breeze might take it. Hardly a hair on his scalp, the merest cottony wisps above the ears only adding to the illusion of a skull.

Vernon departed, taking his napkin and plate with him. Reversing, Dennis observed, as if in the presence of royalty. Crowley replaced him in the chair opposite, and Dennis got a hint of it. The smell from all those years ago: strong, musky, thick, cloying, chemical, unnatural.

"Given we are still in the grip of rationing, she does weave an extraordinary spell" The eyes were brighter than before. The pupils small, but with an uncommon gleam. The kind of glittering eye with which Coleridge's mariner held his wedding guest. "Has Vernon given you a copy of his play yet? *The Legend of Abdel-Krim.* Dreadful rot, honestly. He was a halfway decent Colonel Pickering in *Pygmalion* at the De La Warr Pavilion, but that's his limit. You know he's talking about expanding into a beauty parlour? The man is mad."

"Certainly a dreamer. If that's a bad thing" Dennis found himself masking the fact that he felt on edge.

It was a flattish, yellow face under this illumination. Not wrinkled, but seemed to be eerily disintegrated and surrounded an aura of physical corruption. More intangibly repulsive than he'd expected. Perhaps the ill health transmitted itself. But the voice was the ugliest thing. Brittle, fretful, scratchy—but still supercilious, and still pretentious to a fault.

"I prefer far spicier food myself. A curry that'll burn the roof of your mouth off, that's the ticket. I once cooked a gastronomic feast for Charles Cammell, the poet. I asked him how he liked it. 'Oh, rather mild, please.' So I gave him my most infernal concoction. He washed it down with copious vodka and we were firm friends ever since. What is the point of life if one does not live it to extremes?"

Dennis noted he didn't seem to harbour any sense of irony, or indeed bathos, at being in such insalubrious surroundings. Secreted in the attic of a Hastings guest house. Wasn't black magic supposed to confer on the practitioner untold wealth and success? Dennis thought that was the whole point of it. And look at him. Here. How the mighty are fallen. But he didn't seem resentful of the fact in the slightest.

"Rudolf Hess complained of my spicy curries when I was questioning him at Midget Place near Aldershot."

"I heard there was a plan by Ian Fleming at Naval Intelligence to use you to get Hess out of Germany," said Dennis. "But it never came to fruition because Hess jumped on a plane to Scotland."

"Don't believe all you read in the official reports."

"Not even in MI5?"

"Especially not MI5" Crowley drained the last quarter-inch of Vernon's red. "Hess was at the upper echelon of the Third Reich and a confirmed occultist; who else would they call in to interrogate him about the Führer's plans for the magical future of the Aryan race?"

"I thought you might be clapping your hands with glee at the idea of wiping away the old order."

"Who could have blamed me? I owe this country no favours, the way I was treated after the first punch-up against the Kaiser. Working under cover, infiltrating German secret societies in America, making them look frightful asses, and getting branded as a traitor back home for my trouble? That's rich, as they say across the Atlantic."

"Who did you report to? I've quite a few pals there, still."

"Captain Guy Gaunt of British Intelligence."

"I'll look him up."

"Do. But I daresay his mindless devotion to official secrecy prevents him alluding to the truth. Which is that I almost singlehandedly brought America into the Great War. But don't let the facts get in the way of your innate conviction that I'm a wrong 'un."

Dennis flushed a little. "Not true."

"Any rate, I had no time for Hitler once he started locking up astrologers and mystics. Some of my best friends ended up in concentration camps" Crowley plucked Dennis's smouldering cigarette from the ash tray, sucked on it deeply, and exhaled. "*Seig Heil*, old boy" He gave a rolling cough and banged his fist against his chest. "Avoid cheap cigarettes like the plague. Pipe is the only real tobacco. But if you must, I recommend Weinsberg Specials from Burlington Arcade."

"I fear, too aromatic for my palate."

"Then I must initiate you to the joys of sun-cured Syrian Latakia, or Perique from Louisiana."

Dennis wondered what poisons he was being threatened with, and whether his throat could survive them. In any case, he was too much of a gentleman to point out that his cigarettes were a Turkish mixture made by Sullivan's. In Burlington Arcade.

"You've *leapt* from success to success since last we met" Crowley put undue emphasis on the word, as if for comic effect, for some reason. "I hear you're Hutchinson's top author. How many is it now?"

"A few."

To reel off the seventeen or so titles would have been unbearably arrogant, but Dennis felt annoyed that typically English modesty prevented him naming even one or two, just to convey he wasn't a one trick wonder. *They Found Atlantis* for instance— sheer action romance. *Contraband*, with his modern hero Gregory Sallust, a ruthless, promiscuous secret agent, pitted against a power-mad dwarf. Both entirely different. *Uncharted Seas*, very much in the Verne or Rider Haggard vein, with Sargasso weed, a monster octopus and a lost society marooned since 1680. Then there was *Strange Conflict*— his second black magic book—a meaty stew of Voodoo and astral projection, with the Duke de Richleau discovering how the Nazis were predicting the routes of the Atlantic convoys, battling the Panama-hatted Doctor Saturday after witnessing a sacrifice to Dambala.

"All best sellers. I've been extraordinarily lucky. Translated into fourteen languages. And every one of them still in print. My first book, *The Forbidden Territory*, was reprinted seven times in seven weeks" Oh dear, it sounded terribly like boasting after all. Dennis brought his glass to his lips. The wine business seemed a long, long way away now, and good riddance.

"Truly the self-made man" Crowley made it sound like a ghastly slur. Surely a self-made man, thought Dennis, is more to be admired than someone who acquires wealth by accident of inheritance? Clearly Crowley didn't see it like that, having got where he was almost entirely due to other people's money. A creative profession was to be disparaged, while the gentry, the upper classes, could follow their intellectual pursuits with impunity, unpolluted by the ghastly and rather common need to earn a living.

"The *Manchester Guardian* admired my *Jezebel* poems for their 'intense spirituality'," Crowley said, gazing around the room absently. "But financial success was never a goal of mine. I always found it rather vulgar."

Dennis smiled and didn't rise to the very obvious bait. He knew full well that Crowley's writing was impenetrable to all but his most committed initiates and completely unintelligible to the man in the street. At his most charitable he could say they were, at best, the insane ravings of an opium fiend.

"I never sought popularity with my literary works," said Crowley.

"When you arrive at the gates of heaven, nobody asks how many copies you sold."

"No," said Dennis. "I daresay they have more important questions to ask."

Did he see a smile? Almost.

"Touché."

Crowley clinked the rim of his glass against his.

Their elegant Francophile chef was circulating, gliding from the compliments of one table to the next. Dennis answered with a smile that he had enjoyed his meal, and, equally wordlessly, she glided on. Crowley watched her at his leisure, making Dennis uncomfortable, which was possibly the intention.

"Your letter...intrigued."

"Not here," said Crowley. "I would hate to startle the horses."

"I thought you made a career of it."

"You're thinking of your career, dear boy. Not mine. Despoiled virgins draped across sacrificial altars?"

"I wonder where I got that idea."

Crowley rose and made his way to the stairs, brandy bottle hanging by the neck from his fingers.

"I'd have preferred a Château d'Yquem 1870," said Dennis.

Crowley didn't turn round, but as he passed a chess board, moved one of the pieces. Dennis followed.

In an umbrella stand he saw a forked walking stick with the head of a child's doll wedged into the cleft of it. Near the first step, an octogenarian bulldog slobbered in its basket, semi-asleep, deigning to open one pink-rimmed eye with an air of supreme indifference.

"They had a cat," said Crowley, still not turning. "I crucified it."

Dennis heard Johnny's laughter and saw her hovering next to the kitchen partition with an 'oh, such a wag' expression. Who on earth did she think Crowley was? Tommy Handley from *ITMA*? Or, from that coy flutter of the eyelashes, Clark Gable? Did it hint of sexual coquettishness, a simmering abandon held in check under the surface of her husband's hot-blooded revolutionary fervour? Dennis heard a groan.

The stairs had defeated Crowley halfway up. His trembling hand clung to the banister rail. Dennis couldn't help but be saddened that the man who'd once been an accomplished mountaineer—he'd climbed Kanchenjunga, for goodness' sake—now couldn't climb this. He went to him, and took his elbow. The old man's weight soughed like a heavy branch in the wind, allowing him to virtually lift him, step to step. Dennis was horribly conscious of the lack of substance of the hand that gripped his tightly, almost fearfully. It felt not just cold, and bony, but mummified.

Perhaps he entertained the expectation of entering some satanic temple from one of his own novels—windows covered with silk damask to keep out the light, altar with a golden crucible flanked by black candles. In fact, he stepped over a tray with an egg cup on it, Crowley's untouched lunch, into a shabby room the mirror of his own, with a scruffy bed, cracked wash-basin, and shelves hanging crookedly from discoloured walls enlivened with disturbing pictures in wild, clashing colours—grimacing visages; a woman rendered feral and delirious; mountain peaks in rainbow hues. The only thing that gave the least hint of the alchemist's laboratory was a chemistry flask with a Bunsen burner under it. He felt almost disappointed to see a jar of Nescafé next to it.Crowley moved an OTO publication from one of two rickety chairs to allow his guest to sit. Dennis read aloud the title on its cover.

"*Olla.*"

"A receptacle or vase, a thing you put another thing into. I'm sure you get the symbolism, even if you don't know Catullus' particularly juicy epigram."

In fact, Dennis did. A characteristic joke by Crowley, for Crowley. Calling a book a vagina. How very clever. He was still writing, then. If there were ears to hear his pontificating. But wasn't it ever thus? Nobody in the world at large seemed quite as interested in his theories as he was himself.

Crowley opened a box of American Coronas. Dennis took one

and lit it while his host poured cognac into two tea cups. "Ten pounds on the black market. Scandalous."

Thankfully, the smell of ether in the air was masked by the reek of what seemed like tobacco smoke made with molasses. He could also detect body odours and strong perfume, making him think of the boudoir of a brothel, or a room where somebody had recently died.

"Your fellow guests seem to be friends of Attlee to a man."

"That nobody with a grocer's moustache? They can have him." Crowley ran his hand over the polished head of a jet-black statuette of the Minotaur the way a Catholic would dip their hand in holy water and genuflect. "A rum mob, wouldn't you say? A queer, a prude and a Darwinian" Dennis, in fact, already had it down as some Shangri-La of lost eccentrics. "The rock and the tree. Did you see them? Sisters of Sappho, of course. Arthur Askey has appeared on *The Brains Trust*. You wouldn't think so to look at him."

Dennis smiled. "A refuge for Bolsheviks, intellectuals and cranks."

"Quite. I fit in spiffingly, on two counts at least" Crowley lowered himself onto a divan, propped up by copious pillows. A little table sat beside him, on it a pile of books, an empty tin as an ash tray, a pipe, several bottles of medicine—Dennis noticed a tube of Liminal tablets, which he knew to be Phenobarbital for insomnia—and a small, mysterious cardboard box. "You pay penance by way of lectures to the inmates, has he told you? I had a fiery discussion on Thelema a few months ago with some erudite jews and a preposterously well-endowed female. Moll Flanders, Mephistopheles, and We Three Kings."

As Crowley filled his pipe, Dennis assessed the bookshelves. It was an automatic reaction, and he was doing it before he could stop himself. He guessed he might find Boccaccio, the Russians, Burton, Ovid. In fact he got *Nuttall's Dictionary*, Browning, two volumes of Rabelais, and WS Gilbert's *Bab Ballads*. He tilted his head horizontally to read the spines of those stacked on the mantelpiece. Baudelaire's *Petits Poèmes en Prose*, Arthur Machen's *The Secret Glory* and *Discourse on the Worship of Priapus* by Richard Payne Knight.

"There are some who would burn these books," said Crowley. "Are you one of them?"

"You know I'm not. But some books amount to playing with fire."

"But if one man long ago didn't risk being burnt, we'd never have discovered fire in the first place."

Crowley thought for a moment and smiled to himself.

"What?"

"Dennis Wheatley. Of all the people I dreamt of inviting to my bedroom, I never thought it would be you." He passed him limply one of the smaller, cheaper books. Dennis read the cover: *My Life in a Love Cult: a Warning to All Young Girls* by Marion Dockerill. "You might find this rubbish enlightening. I tupped her sister, incessantly. My magical *shakti* for a while. She was the more rational one."

Dennis pocketed the volume with no intention of reading it, if he was even meant to. A gift from Crowley, he thought, was always probably more than just a gift.

"Thank you."

He leaned back and discovered a bunch of dry, brittle poppy seed heads tied by string to the back of his chair, and almost crushed them before gently moving them aside.

"*Papaver somniferum*," said Crowley. "Isn't it remarkable that at the time of Christ the Arabs identified opium and used it for magical research, as a symbol of abundance and fertility. The divinities of the Greek underworld were often portrayed wreathed in poppies, you know. The Sumerians and Mesopotamians called it *hul gil*—the plant of joy."

"Fancy." Dennis sniffed his index finger and thumb and was pleased to find no abiding scent had rubbed off.

He couldn't help looking at the plethora of crude artworks, pastels on paper or oil on board, breaking up the monotony of the walls—each one, to Dennis's eyes, of unparalleled hideousness and lack of even rudimentary skill. Totem pole on a pier. Woman with bird. And lo, Frater Perdurabo himself, depicted with a huge head, all brain, and slitty, cunning eyes.

"The art gallery. All my own work. That one's a self-portrait."

"Not very flattering."

"Vanity, O Vanitas…"

"Even so…"

Inwardly, Dennis almost shuddered at the coarse landscape of three hills in purple, yellow and vermillion, so primitive as to be hard on the eyes. Below it hung an old engraving of Baphomet which Dennis recognised as taken from the book by Éliphas Lévi (that particular author being one of Crowley's 'past lives', he remembered—along with Cagliostro, Edward Kelly, Ko Hsuen, and the Egyptian high priest Ankh-f-n-Khonsu). Dennis knew the cross-legged Sabbatic Goat all too well, even rather fondly, since it had popped up in some of the most memorable scenes in his most famous novel. Poor thing—not only goat/human but male/female—originally representing 'the total sum of the universe' but used by Christian zealots to destroy the Knights Templars, Baphomet becoming Satan, Lucifer made bestial, uber-phallic god of the witches, the Devil with horns and cloven hooves rewarded with a posterior kiss.

The room was actually replete with visual distractions. Next to a rotting toothbrush, a ram's skull with a symbol painted on its forehead. Over the fireplace, a rusty horseshoe, probably dug up from the garden. A Hitler pin cushion. Reflective witch ball. Pestle and mortar. Mandrake root, as dried and desiccated as its owner. Wooden mask of the Balinese witch Rangda—all popping eyes, ragged hair and huge fangs.

"My former wife," said Crowley. "Now in Colney Hatch asylum."

"Your particular brand of enlightenment didn't have the desired effect, then."

"Perhaps it *was* desired. She would get sadistic, then savage, then suicidal. I'd say I'm well shot of her" He leaned back on his pillows, like a lizard on a rock. "Friends come, go, take what they want of me. I used to have thousands of books, a stately home in Scotland, a family of devoted followers. Now what do I have? Reporters lurking in the bushes, waiting for me to die. I'll be damned if I'll give them the satisfaction."

"You'll be damned anyway, according to them."

"Print the legend."

"Better to be a legend than not, I suppose."

"Even if it obscures the truth?" said Crowley.

"What's the truth? I didn't think we'd descend into a philosophical discussion quite so quickly."

"What other conversation is there? Ration books and amateur dramatics?"

Crowley tugged a tartan blanket around his shoulders. The black magician in repose. Inscrutable guru, end of the pier show-man, surrounded by medicine bottles, a cloth pouch and pen knife, smoking some toxic substance from a long Chinese pipe.

"The quack says I must give it up and save my eyesight. He's right of course. But what enjoyment ever came of doing right, I say."

"I'm sure you do," said Dennis.

A smile flickered on the thin lips between Crowley's sunken cheeks, all the more like craters as he sucked smoke down into his lungs. Perhaps, after all, he did recognise the tragedy of his final retreat, a boarding house full of all the mundane English comforts he had deplored, even railed against, his entire life.

"I have observed your success from afar. My contribution to it of course made all the difference."

"It was a pleasant lunch," said Dennis, wryly.

"And informative."

"Do you remember Vecchi told us how he'd served Rasputin at the Grand Hotel, St Petersburg? Lechery on a grand scale with twenty women of court, hidden away in a private dining room. And his fingernails, he said, were absolutely filthy."

"Filth is seldom far from godliness, in my experience. The mad monk must have seen abasement and sin as the only true route to salvation. Imagine."

Dennis felt awkward now.

He remembered the note Crowley had sent him soon after *The Devil Rides Out* was published. '*Dear DW, did you elope with the adorable Tanith? Or did the witches get you on Halloween?*' He had already received a customised copy of *Magick in Theory and Practice*, the title page personalised with doodles by 'Master Therion (AC)' with an added passport-sized photo glued in, 'The Beast' written above it and '6' written on the other three sides. Inscribed to DW: "In memory of that sublime Hungarian banquet" On the inside cover: "Recommendations to the Intelligent Reader humbly proffered" which included "Read Hymn to Pan aloud at midnight when alone with intention to get him" Dennis never had any intention of doing so. Or of sending a reply.

"I wrote to you saying I'd love another chat, especially about Magick, but we never did. You kept making excuses, I recall. I must have been a dull companion."

"Not at all," said Dennis, trying not to make his nervousness apparent. "I was simply busy. You know how it is."

He was lying. He *had* made excuses, and he hadn't been keen to resume contact. Read the Hymn to Pan aloud at Midnight? The very thought appalled him, and, yes, frightened him. He didn't want to step into the penumbra of such things. Far from it—did Crowley think he did? That was what had frightened him more than anything, being lured into a trap that others had so conspicuously fallen into.

"The Prince of Thriller Writers. Household name. Sax Rohmer stuff. Plucky English hero saving damsel from rapacious villains with their hypnotic eyes and foreign ways" For a moment The Beast's deliberately theatrical stare reminded Dennis of his father—humourless, frightening, frighteningly unread.

"What can you do, when you grow up on adventures in *Chums*?"

"Flag-waving gorillas versus dirty savages. The majority of English fiction being endless variations of the same."

"Conan Doyle? *The Prisoner of Zenda?* John Buchan?"

"Exactly. It's all quite vacuous. St George, to me, was never as interesting as the dragon. White knights are always so solid and dependable as to be tedious in the extreme. Still, I'm told you're a good plotter, even if your prose is like that of a bank manager."

Dennis laughed. "I'd have thought the subject matter might interest you, at least. Sex and Satanism."

"Satan and I fell out long ago. A clash of egos, inevitably."

The remark was pure Oscar Wilde, but for all his airs and enunciation, Crowley was no more a toff than he was. He'd come from a family of brewers in the Midlands—Crowley's Ales—and Dennis only lost his South London accent thanks to his father paying for elocution lessons. They were both fakes, when it came down to it. Things came back to Dennis then, as they had a habit of doing, things from the past, as if pouring from a ripped sandbag. The only certainty he ever had, of inadequacy. Of his undeserved wealth, of his shallowness of talent, of his own pretentions to culture which everyone on the upper echelons could see through in an instant. Something of which he knew he would never be free, and which angered him, even as he enjoyed the fruits of his labour, and the labour itself. What was wrong with him? And that brought him back to the words of the letter that had brought him there.

He stared at his hands, not at Crowley.

"Why do you think I am a good man?"

It was some seconds before he heard an answer.

"Do you not say your prayers at night? And go to church on Sunday?"

"So do the majority of men in England" Dennis looked up at him and repeated his question. "Why do you think I am a good man?"

After a pause, Crowley leaned forward, but the effort to do so must have shaken something about inside, because he jerked to and fro with his tongue poking out, then lapsed into an enormous coughing fit, retching pitifully. Dennis quickly stood up to come to his aid and placed a hand on his back, but Crowley just gurgled and gasped, waving a limp, claw-like hand in the direction of the sink. The crowing hack reminded Dennis brutally of his own bouts of bronchitis in the army, his own weakened lungs sending him home to recover instead of going with his battalion to the Somme. The helplessness of lack of breath had been terrifying.

By the time Dennis returned with a glass of water, Crowley had brought phlegm up into a handkerchief, now dropped to the floor, and lapsed to a rumbling, wheezing croak as the rush of air to his lungs became calmer, less spasmodic. His chest rose and fell regularly now, the tendons in his neck becoming stringy as he jutted out his mouth upwards to sip from the glass. Dennis watched him swallow, once, twice, a third time, then slowly, carefully eased him back into his pillows.

"Are you all right?"

Crowley craned forward for another desperate sip. Dennis held the back of his scrawny neck before allowing him to sink back again, eyes closed as he waved Dennis back to his chair, taking a few shuddering breaths before feeling able to talk.

"Our conversation made it plain…you'd had a deep and abiding interest…in the occult for a good twenty years…before you put pen to paper, albeit in the most lurid fashion" His eyelids slowly opened. "I hear you've given talks on black magic. One to the Eton Literary Society. You even mentioned me."

"How could I not?" said Dennis, honestly.

"I am convinced all this makes you…uniquely qualified to see the measure…the *reality*…of what we are up against. And to have the heart and resolve to take action, when this old man's heart is too fragile to do the task alone."

Dennis went cold.

"What…*task?*"

Crowley did not move for what amounted to a minute or so. His head was bent over, and he examined his hands as if they were curious things that belonged to a different person."Feel my hands," he whispered, eyes like golf balls semi-visible in their holes. "I can't get them warm for the life of me. Feel…"

Dennis reached out to touch them, but before he could, Crowley absently drew them back under his shawl-like tartan blanket, wrapping them up tightly in the fabric. His voice was almost normal now, less declamatory, with only a slight, musty whistle at the back of the trachea.

"I suppose you encounter fans of your work?"

Dennis shrugged. "Book signings. Frequently. Autograph hunters. Not so long ago, a friend told me he'd been drinking port with someone who said he was an '*enormous* admirer' of my work" He made a face. "Chap who'd been in the SOE. Ian Fleming's cousin. Budding actor, name of Christopher Lee. 'Seems to know your entire life history,' my friend said. Worrying."

Crowley sucked his pipe. "Not as worrying as receiving a sheet of paper written in Max Factor blood, disputing my ancestry, telling me I'll die of cancer in excruciating pain. Generic malignancy from the *Common Book of Nasty Spells*."

"What did you do?"

"I took it to the crossroads and burnt it with salt, rosemary and rue. Then there are the others, from women who want to accommodate my sperm at the earliest convenience. Or from Wormwood Scrubs, asking me for details of how to perform a black mass on Midsummer's Eve."

"I've had one from Broadmoor, signed Jesus Christ" Dennis was on the verge of a chuckle, more to change his mood than reflect it, but the sound refused to materialise. The expression on the face opposite him killed it before it was born.

Frater Perdurabo, 666, seemed lost in his thoughts for a few moments, then took a nip of cognac before he spoke.

Coming here, I thought I'd died and gone to heaven. It was everything I could wish for. Sea air, hill air—I've always found rough seas and high winds exhilarating—and Hastings has the best chess club in the world, to boot. However, with my numerous infirmities, it's not a good idea to risk going out in weather that's threatening to turn. At the best of times I can be confined to my room for weeks with this blasted chest. On such days my pen is my lifeline to the outside world. Or I dictate letters through a fog of sputum. But sometimes it's air in my lungs I crave, and a glimpse of sunlight through the clouds after that interminable winter that turned into a grey and miserable spring. I'd always stroll on my own. I'd call them my meditation walks. Netherwood is ten minutes from the seafront by a bus you can catch outside the front gates, but it was my habit to walk along The Ridge, either to Mr Watson at the Ridge Stores for my little packages from Heppel's, or past Riposo, where they offer hydrotherapy, heliotherapy, all sorts of other 'therapies'. It astonishes me that people pay for nature's treatments when simply walking in fresh air, with the morning dew on the leaves, is wondrous for the constitution without the help of any faddish embellishments. Heading past Ripon Lodge, the Hall and Sandhurst Gardens, I'd have to be careful not to trip over a mud flap or inner tube of a bicycle, the latter like a dead black mamba, and I'd often see boys with grazed knees playing on vast piles of bricks like beached whales, unaware of the ghosts they circled as they fired cap guns at each other. *Take that, Fritz!* Seeing who died best.

It was Easter Monday last, and I reached the upper station of the East Hill Cliff Funicular, leading down to Rock-a-Nore Road. I defy anyone not to extract a childish thrill from the whirr of oily machinery. There is also something eerily dramatic about being locked in the car with its large, exposed windows, though the views of the tar-coloured net stores of The Stade from on high are wonderfully impressive.

I took him for a queer at first. The man standing at the corner of the empty compartment. We were the only two passengers. He was looking at me peculiarly, with the furtive, shifty alertness of a bookie's runner. He wore a raincoat and was, I estimated, in his mid-thirties, with heavy eyebrows that met sketchily in the middle. His hair was jet black, in a short back and sides, the top thick and long, slicked back in a tall wave, almost a pompadour. Though handsome in a faintly loutish way, he had pockmarked skin and the mien of a pickpocket or murderer.

"It's funny to look down on so many tiny souls," he said, as if passing the time of day. "You feel you could take them between your fingers and crush them" Illustrating this, he extended his arm, aiming it with one eye shut, and pinched his index finger and thumb together as if squashing a grape.

I wasn't hugely amused, and this seemed to hurt his feelings immensely. He declared immediately that he knew who I was, and was a reader and devotee of my work. He told me I was a great mind, a brilliant thinker. I wasn't about to disagree, obviously. I'd not heard that in a good while, and it's nice to be reminded, occasionally.

To my astonishment he carried one of my books with him—*Magick*, and I agreed to sign it, asking his name. It was Donald—Donald Lamont—which contradicted his Welsh accent. He explained he was from the Valleys, but of Scottish parentage. Mystery solved. He thanked me with a sense of awe, as if I'd given him the crown jewels, and to my surprise called me 'Ipsissimus'— the highest level of accomplishment in the various stages of magical enlightenment. He asked nervously if I had time for a cup of tea, or something stronger? I said I was sorry, no.

The funicular jerked to a sudden stop and we disembarked and went our separate ways. The black monoliths of the fishermen's huts stood in front of me like huge clapboard sentinels. The smell of bladderwrack and whelks filled my nostrils. Ice hit the shingle and sparkled like gems. Thinking of coins pressed into red, permanently frozen hands, I pulled on my gloves. Then I saw that he hadn't moved away at all, but stood with a drab, plain-looking woman aged about twenty-five or thirty: platinum blonde hair of the Jean Harlow variety, the colour of raw silk, soft waves in an 'updo' as the fair sex call it, with curls on top. Her white skin looked frozen, and her lipstick seemed to be applied in order for her to remember that her mouth existed.

He shuffled away, hands deep in pockets. She followed like a dog.

"Something stronger," I said.

Consequently he led us to The Crown in All Saints Street, ordering a gin and lemon for her, a Haig's for himself, and honey and sugar in hot water for me. I couldn't tell if they were poor, but they weren't well off. He had frayed cuffs, but nevertheless insisted he paid, counting out coins with nicotine stained fingers, smoking fags—Senior Service—to the dog ends like a beggar at Charing Cross. He introduced the woman as Gisela, but called her Blondi. Her parents got out of Germany when Hitler came to power, he said. She was twelve (so my guess at her age was about right). Her father owned a sweet shop in Pontypridd, which Lamont had to explain to me, in my ignorance, was a town halfway between

Cardiff and Merthyr. "He had a brick through his shop window during the war, but it must've been boys from outside, because everyone in Ponty knew the Raabs weren't Nazis."

Her surname amused me. I said that pre-Islamic Arabs believed there were multifarious gods—the *aalihah*—but only Allah was the *Rabb*, Sustainer of Earth and the heavens, Lord, Cherisher, Creator. She gave no reaction, hardly meeting my eyes during the entire conversation.

"She doesn't say much because of her German accent. Gets her in trouble. People don't like it. I like it, don't I, Blondi?" He kissed her cheek then poked her rather hard on the side of the chin. "Wake up."

He offered to get another drink. "I've got nothing to rush home for, do you? We've lots to talk about" I placed my hand over my glass but he got another Haig's for himself. She'd hardly touched hers. "When I discovered your books it was a revelation. Your quest for self-discovery changed my life. Materialism as a dead end. The need for a total obliteration of old ideas. You were a voice in the wilderness. But I could hear. I was listening. Nobody else did. Your parents didn't understand…"

"Perhaps my mother did," I said. "Once, horrified by some act of childhood rebellion, she called me the Anti-Christ, Beast of the Apocalypse, whose number is 666, according to Revelation. But then, religious people are easy to horrify. One only has to kiss the Devil's arse to realise that."

Lamont laughed. "The Golden Dawn didn't understand, though. They held you back with their petty infighting. You had to forge ahead, all alone. You were the figurehead they needed, but you were decried, rejected, ridiculed."

Music to my ears.

"What you were saying was our civilisation was at a dead end, taking us further and further away from our true nature as magical beings. It was so clear!" He talked, with his sing-song lilt and hopping, guttural syllables, of having a rough time at school, beaten, absconding, running up the hills near his home, the black Merthyr slag heaps, head pounding as if something inside wanted to be let out, like some beast. "And I'd scream my lungs out and still nothing would come, but I knew it was in there, I just didn't know what. Destiny, I suppose."

"Everyone has destiny," I said. "Some are grand, some not so grand. It's a feat of humility to accept it."

"But *you* didn't accept it, did you? You didn't accept mediocrity and restraint and what small, insignificant minds told you to think and do."

He was right, of course.

"I had the Bible read to me every morning of my childhood," I said. "My father believed fervently that life and pleasure were incompatible. It turned me against indoctrination for life."

"Exactly! I knew praying to a Christian God was the equivalent of putting yourself in a permanent bloody strait jacket. I started writing my own prayers in my exercise books. The Elastic Ecclesiastica, I called it. For glory and celebration of doubt" He grinned. "I invented the opiscipi vaginas, the dirty-minded bishops, and the 'Jumping Jews', whose martyrdoms became more and more elaborate. Better fun than any lessons school could dole out."

I laughed. A man after my own heart.

"That's what I wanted," he said. "My own prayers and my own church, but how? I got the answer one day when my father went for a pint in The Merlin, a pub in Maesycoed. I had to stay outside, and I stood there for hours, looking up at this big statue over the door. A massive figure like a saint with blue and white robes and a long, thick beard and two curls of hair almost like horns. Enormous. And when I looked into Merlin's eyes I realised there could be other saints, other beliefs. Druids. Hindu, Kabbalah, Gnostics, Zoroastrians. I read books. Books that promised more. *Your* books."

I may have blushed very slightly.

"And suddenly it all made sense," he said. "The Gods of Egypt. What you were trying to do. Combine western and eastern traditions into one over-arching system of absolute knowledge. Astrology combined with the Goetia" He knitted the fingers of one hand with those of his other. "Ein-Sof, The Unending One, god of the Jewish Kabbalah—more mysterious and powerful than anything in the Old or New Testaments—joined with Hermetic occult iconography. The magic of Abra-Melin. The Gnostic tradition. The purpose of new life. Conversion to godhead. You…you discovered the key to revealing that humans are far more powerful than they realise. That we can achieve amazing things if only we open our eyes and consciousness. More powerful. More creative. More *magical*."

It was a long time since I'd heard such an explosion of excitement for my cause. I was reeling, but his words and ideas came thick and fast, as hard to catch, even for me, as a salmon in a fast running stream:

"But I knew, as Aiwass talked to you, I needed to hear my own spirit voice. Merlin presided over me, a force of knowledge of history, I knew that, so I subjugated myself to him, made offerings to him and prayed to him until finally he spoke to me. Clearer than any voice around me. Clearer than my own thoughts. But he said he wasn't Merlin. He was Enoch. I was conversing with angels, in their own tongue. And Enoch became my Holy Guardian Angel, as Aiwass became yours."

I could hardly believe what I was hearing. If these were the words of a madman, they were deliciously so. I felt like clapping my hands till they bled.

"Show him," he said to the woman. Gisela opened her shopping bag, which was filled with reams of paper tied up in parcels. He pulled the string off one and, licking his thumb, turned the pages. "My life work was clear. My every waking moment mapped out. The first objective being to find you—and for you to grant me access to the next phase of my spiritual development."

I looked down at a page full of scribbles, formulae, whatever it was, in some exotic language or one unknown to any man living, or the spidery hieroglyphics of the Void. I had literally no idea. It made no sense. It defied my brain to comprehend it. It churned my soul. Poked out its tongue. Intoxicated me and thrilled me but frightened me witless at the same time, as if I were standing on the edge of a cliff with no way down and no knowledge of getting there, but every ounce of me beseeching me to fly. I thought perhaps I should have ordered something a good deal more potent than honey and hot water.

I wondered at the path I had taken to get there. If I had turned back before getting to the East Cliff lift. If I had taken a different turning to the Old Town. But I could not look back. His eyes burned with a ferocity I could not walk away from, and, truth be told, could only envy. It was the kind of fire that had once burned in my own. I confess, I was as giddy as a schoolgirl.

My heart pounding hard, I said yes. "Yes. I will teach you."

He looked like all his Christmases had arrived at once. He was overwhelmed, and giggled almost uncontrollably. She made no sound at all. I noticed she had dark bags under her eyes. He went completely quiet, trying to devise, I think, some oath of allegiance.

He drilled out his cigarette into the back of his hand, hard, holding it there for some seconds, creating a black roundel of ash which he flicked away with his other hand, to reveal the stigma of a blister. "Do what thou wilt shall be the whole of the Law."

"*Thou* smells of the Bible," I joked. "And *wilt* is the last thing you want when it comes to sexual magic" Lamont laughed again, with tears in his eyes.

I took the same cigarette from the ash tray where it was smouldering and did the same to the back of my own left hand. "Love is all. Love under will."

He kissed Gisela full on the lips. I notice she stiffened and didn't seem to particularly enjoy it, but didn't recoil. The two of us shook hands. His eyes ablaze with delight, gripping my fingers tight, eyes unblinking, as if he never wanted to let go.

I immediately knew I was in the presence of an incredibly strong magician. One who, I could not yet know, would get only stronger as the weeks and months passed. The enthusiasm, and devotion, some might even call it a kind of love, bewitched me back then. I see that now. I gave of my knowledge freely and he absorbed it fully, ravenously, and without question, to begin with. I have never had such a focused and hard working pupil. Yet the truth was to dawn on me in a painfully slow, sickening wave, so much so that it took a long time for me to stop denying it. But in the end I could entertain no doubt whatsoever, that he had embraced the Left Hand Path. And now must be destroyed. Before he takes another soul. Before he becomes all-powerful and unstoppable. That is your purpose in coming here. Because, I swear by Nuit, Hadit and Ra-Hoor-Khuit, I cannot do this alone.

*
**

Dennis knelt to say his prayers, aware it was not much more than a shopping list he'd stuck to for years. Joan. The children. He hoped God kept track, like a teacher marking the register with a tick. What a preposterous image. He remembered when his prayers had been to preserve and keep his mother and father, but no amount of prayers can keep anyone safe and sound forever. Tonight the usual comfort felt bland and stale. He was tired. That was all. "*I cannot do this alone…*"

What had he said at the end of the conversation, as Crowley's strength faded, and a shadow passed over his face, a tremor of horror Dennis felt as though they had physically touched? He couldn't remember. Yes, he *had* been horrified—not only by what he'd been told, but by the sickly tableau that stayed with him long after he'd switched off the light and left the room, the tang of that oily, ruby red linctus he had spoon-fed Crowley before departing still lingering unpleasantly on his senses even now.

He got up from his knees and looked at the framed photograph of Joan he travelled with everywhere.

She looked radiant in it. Not a flighty movie goddess, but the real thing, come down from Olympus to mix with mere mortals. Marble skin. Strong brow and neck in the classical fashion. Straight nose. Hair in braids, the finishing touch to complete the resemblance, he always thought, to the head of Aphrodite of Cnidus in The Louvre. At which she would always respond the same way, which was to look at him as if he were completely mad. And that of course made him love her helplessly all the more.

He switched off the bedside light and climbed into bed, but lay sleepless on his back in the dark. Eyes open.

"I gave of my knowledge and he absorbed it fully...ravenously..."

He found that what he remembered had already become indistinct, the images in his memory insufficient to form a coherent story. Yet that was his business—stories. What was he to make of it? This stuff of a waking dream, already fading from his grasp? Or did he simply want it to fade? Perhaps he should have prayed for it to.

Crowley can't harm me, he thought, trying to persuade himself it was true. *He's as feeble as an injured bird. Those so-called evil eyes are weak and helpless now, the pupils shrunk, the shrivelled eyelids with barely the strength to twitch.* Yes, evil haunted the face—*haunted,* past tense—but that evil was pointed exclusively inwards, not out. All passion spent. That was the problem. That was why he'd got the letter. But harm from this *other*—that was something he couldn't so easily dismiss.

This new magician, whom Crowley feared. Whom Crowley wanted destroyed.

"Before he takes another soul..."

...Another?

Dennis heard whispers, which spooked him at first. The staff tidying up below him, of course. Empty bottles collected in the bar, nothing more. He wondered if Vernon indulged in night-time visits for the occasional secret tipple. Seemed the sort that might. Dennis could never understand men who had secrets from their wives, alcoholic or otherwise. Life was too damned complicated as it was, without added new levels of domestic subterfuge.

But lying in the pitch dark made him think of another husband and wife, and Crowley's honeymoon to Rose Kelly, a dipsomaniac, first in a long series of his neurotic women—and a tale the Beast had regaled him with vividly at the Hungaria. Having spanked her in a hotel in Cairo ("turning her from my wife to my mistress" as he so sensitively put it), Crowley had arranged a romantic dinner for two inside the Great Pyramid of Giza, at an opportune moment dismissing the servants and taking a candle to the King's Chamber, where he recited from the Goetia and blew the candle out.

Later, back in the hotel room, Rose had woken up with night terrors, screaming that a bat was caught in her hair. Crowley had tried his best to calm her, but Rose remained hysterical, or delusional, lapsing into a trance state as she began to hear voices over her left shoulder, informing him "They are waiting". She said she could see a hawk-headed king—though she knew nothing of the Egyptian pantheon. A few days later, on a visit to a museum, she led him straight to an ancient mortuary slab known as the Stele of Ankh-f-n-Khonsu (Later known as the 'Stele of Revealing') which depicted Ra-Hoor-Khuit, composite deity of the sun god Ra. The exhibit's number was '666'. The number of the Beast. A sign, if there ever was one.

Rituals in their hotel room led Rose, in trance, to declare that "the Equinox of the gods has arrived" and Nuit, goddess of the universe, pronounced "Love is the law, love under Will," which electrified Crowley as absolute confirmation of his theory of love as a transcendental gateway. He discovered the voice speaking through Rose was not Horus as he'd presumed but a deity named 'Aiwass'—a variation for the word 'yes' in Arabic, which again, Rose could not possibly have known. Crowley wrote down everything over the next three days, as Aiwass dictated *Liber Legis (The Book of the Law)*, the sacred scripture of his new religion and cornerstone of his future philosophy—that magic was the means by which to discover one's Will, or spiritual destiny: a quest that must be pursued above all else. And if that was blasphemy against current creeds, so be it. They were wrong. The truth had come from beyond the beyond, from the pyramids, from the shadows when the candle was blown out. And from it Aleister Crowley, with characteristic modesty, inferred he had been chosen as messiah of the new Aeon of Man. He was never the same again.

The next morning Dennis woke, un-refreshed. He lied to himself it was the mattress. He was used to the luxuries in life, and a paramount one was your own bed. He looked at the side table. *The Forbidden Lecture* was back on top of his Gerald Kersh. How on earth had that happened? He was sure he hadn't moved them himself, but he must have done.He pulled back the curtains, and it was certainly a sight worth paying for, he saw now. Panoramic views of the town, its Norman castle, to the south west, Eastbourne and Beachy Head. And below him, in tweed suit and plus fours, a solitary Crowley standing on the grass, outstretched palms and face turned up towards the sky. Dennis recognised the breathing and gestures as part of the tantric tradition. He knew a little of it, enough to feel like a crass amateur. He'd read about the wisdom of the East, had found it compelling, and appealing as a doctrine, but was too much the C of E choirboy at heart to learn too many new tricks. All religions, to him, pointed to a central goodness, whether through Jesus Christ, Buddha or Lao-Tzu. The Lord of Light had many faces and names, but the essential truth was the same, whether it came from the Bible, the Koran or the Zend Avesta.

As he came downstairs, straightening his collar and knotting his tie, Vernon was humming that the sun had put his hat on, whilst vigorously polishing the silver. For a fragment of time it was as if the chill conversation of the night before had never happened. The fresh breath of day banishing, if only briefly, pernicious night. Outside, he was surprised again at the picture of the paunchy rapscallion of a decade earlier now a stick figure, hands as yellow and mottled as branches of the trees, though his gestures were as beautifully modulated as those of a dancer. Dennis caught the odd word as he got closer. Joy…travelling the heavens…splendour… something or other abiding at its zenith, hail to the day…

"Master Therion" Dennis used Crowley's chosen magical appellation.

"Indeed" The old fellow only fractionally acknowledged his presence. "Liber Resh vel Helios, the adoration of the sun." Blissfully absorbing every ounce of sunlight into his pores, he brought his ritual to a close, hands in prayer to his sternum, Buddhist fashion, head bowed, lips touching his finger tips. "666 is a magical number associated with the sun, did you know that? Of course you didn't" Arms extended horizontally, then shaken the way a dog does after a rain shower. "The Great Beast, you see, is not evil. Revelation is entirely Gnostic and Kabbalistic symbolism. Its true message is that Christianity will be replaced by a new religion whose prophet is the Beast. We are entering the Age of Aquarius. In the zodiac Aquarius is a man, and that man is the Great Beast."

"So your mother was right all along."

Crowley smiled crookedly. "Ah, the chrysanthemums are out, I see."

Dennis looked behind him. Half a dozen plump white rabbits were dotted over the north eastern part of the lawn, lop-eared, noses twitching, giving the odd lolloping hop, looking very cheerful—if rabbits can look cheerful.

"Your magical assistants."

"Or stew, more likely."

Plus fours hanging on him voluminously under the tweed jacket and waistcoat, Crowley ambled off past the hutches and between a finely-trimmed privet archway, humming "Run rabbit, run rabbit, run, run, run…"

Dennis trailed after him.

The shrubbery-filled garden in late October had a windblown, scrubby attraction. Nevertheless he found memories surfacing of endless summer afternoons in his grandfather's idyll: lawns that seemed to encompass a whole country in one's infant imagination; climbing the mulberry trees; picking tomatoes in the tomato house, the most sweet and delicious tomatoes he'd tasted to this day; the two orchid houses; the far-off orchards; summer house ('Crusader castle' in other words); countless 'dens' of their own conception, even an archery target. His father rented a cottage at Churt, but there was no comparison. His grandfather's garden had been a small boy's paradise. Wooden swords. Lemonade. Bows and arrows. Playing soldiers.

"The flower beds brought much needed colour to the grey days of the end of the war, not unlike the owners" Crowley punctuated his thoughts with a wistful sigh. "You almost forget now what we'd known before it."

Walking alongside him, Dennis considered again how this once strutting bull was now reduced to the little gnome, an archdeaconish figure from a West End farce. He could hardly accept this was the same Great Beast who roared through life, thundering his mythic importance, with a whole organisation hanging on his every whim.

Side by side, the two followed the concrete path around the perimeter of the tennis court. Not surprisingly, it was devoid of players, also devoid of net. Dennis spied a man up a ladder against the side of the building, hacking at a rotten window sill with a hammer and chisel.

"You seldom see money change hands in this place," explained Crowley. "Household maintenance, gardening, that kind of thing, everything's done *quid pro quo*. Everyone mucks in and it all works out in the end."

His voice was a dry rustle like the wind raking the leaves. By daylight it could almost be said it had a caressing charm.

I visited their flat, a perfectly dingy place above a small shop in the Old Town. They had a young baby, a girl they'd named Astra Argenta, sweetly, after my organisation, the A□A□—still on the breast, but that made no difference to how we conducted ourselves. Sometimes the woman, Gisela, was involved, sometimes not. He called her *Frau Raab* or *mein liebchen* or *Fräulein* or *Marlene*. He'd say *Jawohl* and sometimes liked her to call him *Heinrich*. They were not married, but behaved as husband and wife.She fed the child without modesty, but I was used to that at Cefalù, where the babes ran around like rats. It invariably had a crust of green snot round its nostrils, a whine always rumbling in its belly ready to explode. Pretty enough thing, golden curls, piercing blue eyes like its father. Sometimes she would take it out in the pram to give us peace while we meditated or produced visions.

Our ritual explorations progressed. We moved forward in incremental steps, sometimes large ones. I gave Lamont a magical name: 'Frater Ein-Sof '—meaning The Infinite. He proved an extraordinary student, his single-mindedness staggering. Looking back at it, I should have seen the warning signs. He could shed humanity as most people shed a coat, and on a magickal level, I saw nothing in his aura. No colour. No brightness. It was like a beetle's carapace. Formidable—but for what?

Gisela would return to sheets of scribbles, dictation I had taken from Lamont's lips while he was under the influence of Enoch. The connections to my own work were uncanny, as if he had observed me since the day of my birth. I had no difficulty conferring upon him the status of Adeptus Minor and of Neophyte. Over weeks he escalated towards my own status of Master of the Temple, falling barely short of that of Ipsissimus, or Magus, the ultimate spiritual goal in the Tree of Life.

When I met him he'd already discovered Thelema, and lived by the essential nature of sex magic. The need to overcome the parental panic of enforced sin and to be free to encounter the cosmos for what it truly is. And that doorway is not outside the individual but within. Sometimes Gisela would return to find us both naked. I would take the passive part and Lamont the active.

"This is thy Scarlet Woman" he once said to me, using the name I used for the magical *shakti*. Her cheeks reddened to the tint of a luscious peach. She obediently began to undress but I said, "I'm afraid all I look forward to at this time of night is my Horlick's."

We laughed.

The gift was offered, but I sensed he was annoyed I refused it, though he seemed not to blame me, rather her. More than once I saw him talk to her curtly or kick her out of the way. It was not my place to come between a man and his wife. Buggery notwithstanding.

To be involved again with a core of magickal thinkers was energising. I wondered how long that could go on, because in my experience it always came to tears, to put it mildly. Perhaps man was not made to endure too much magick—as someone didn't ever say, and should have. But something changed, that day.

When Gisela had started to remove her clothes, I'd glimpsed a livid bruise on her shoulder, and a scar above one breast. These things did not often trouble me, but in her case, they did. Lamont would grab her in an embrace and kiss her violently, and while she gave no impression that she disapproved, her reciprocations were few and far between, and somewhat more lacklustre. A press of the lips to his cheek, while his fingers delved up her crack.

Perhaps the emotional electricity fuelled their carnality. Fantasy play. All humans have that, unless they are dead from the waist down. His assertiveness, her coyness. The frigidity an act to get his blood pumping all the more. It was not my business, or my inclination, to know, or be interested. But I was.

*
**

Dennis saw I-Ching sticks thrown down on the floor where Crowley must have left them. They'd come inside, retreating from a wind that had suddenly turned bitter. A draught from the window was like a gust from the North Pole. The housemaid must have opened it a few inches in an attempt to air his room. Not before time.

"Would you?"

Dennis closed and bolted the upper sash. Crowley was shivering and quite breathless, his chest heaving as if he had just completed a ten mile run.

"Do you need to rest?"

Hands shivering, Crowley opened the cardboard box Dennis had noticed the night before.

"No. I need to carry on...With help."

Dennis watched as he took out the syringe therein, dissolved a little scarlet pellet in the glass chamber as if it was the most natural thing in the world, rolled back his sleeve, and gave himself an injection, which produced immediate relaxation and satisfaction. The needle drew out of the puckered skin.

"Please," he groaned, at the sight of Dennis's unvarnished look of disgust. "It's on prescription. People assume it's for indulgence. It isn't. It's a medical necessity" He crooked his elbow on a ball of cotton wool. "I was given it years ago for bronchitis, long before it became illegal. Shook it for a while in the twenties. Encountered the storm fiends, naturally. Needed two doses of strychnine to put me right, and had to eat like a horse to reduce the craving. Fooled myself I could give it up at will. Cocaine was far easier."

The muddy look in the skull-face had vanished, and now that Dennis could see them, the eyes glowed. Not the glow of health, by any stretch, but a glow at least. Dennis was sickened, he wasn't sure whether it was with abject pity or total repulsion. Very, very probably both.

"I beat it for years, then this damn thing came back with a vengeance" Crowley patted his chest twice with a paw-like hand, an ungainly movement like that of a jointed string puppet. "I felt I was drowning in my own mucus" He coughed from deep in his lungs. What was left of them. "Nothing came near shifting it. Atrophine didn't cut the mustard. I got an inflamed chest, fibrillating heart…At my age it was simpler to register myself. My doctor in London prescribed a standard dose, between a sixth and a quarter of a gram. I'm up on that now, very much up, but here I am. Breathing. Just about."

He staggered to the sink and deposited the syringe there. Its glass tinkled against the porcelain.

"Dear old Magowan hands it out like a lamb. He knows the hell it causes when I don't receive my supply, by hook or by crook. And I'm always running out of damn needles. I say" He rounded on Dennis animatedly. "Are you going up to London any time soon?"

"I'm afraid not."

"If you are, for pity's sake, if you're near Wigmore Street, the John Bell and Croydon store, corner of Welbeck Street, is sure to have them. Number twenty. Half inch."

Crowley sank back on his divan, semi-pained, shut the no-longer-mysterious box and looked at Dennis, but Dennis said nothing.

"I know what you're thinking. No. As far as *illumination* goes, I prefer those darling cactus blossoms, *Anhalonium Lewinii*—mescal buttons. They delightfully loosen the girders of the soul. Bennett introduced us. One of the few things I have to thank the mad, misguided monk for, as a matter of fact."

"Is everyone misguided but you?"

"Without a doubt," said Crowley, scraping out the bowl of his pipe, and knowing whom Dennis was implying. "When it comes to magic, without the faintest shadow of a doubt."

*
**

One day, I left Lamont to his studies and visualisations and went out with Gisela, who wanted to wheel the pram along the sea front in the direction of St Leonard's. The baby was teething, and motion seemed to be the only reliable thing to lull it into slumber. She wanted to give us peace and quiet, but I impulsively decided to tag along. I needed a break from intense mental concentration, apart from anything else. I also wanted to talk to her. Alone. July or August, this was. The day was placid. Not a cloud in the sky. Even the sounds from the holidaymakers on the fun fair were oddly muted.

She told me Lamont was born in Aberdeen. Attending his grandfather's funeral as a boy, he'd found out his father was not his real father. His grandfather was. A man he idolised. He told her when his family moved to Wales he wished he could be left in the earth of Scotland with him, not dumped in this alien place where they spoke this alien language half the time. This information took me until we were approaching Warrior Square to extract, like getting blood from a stone. I'd met shy people before, painfully shy—Heidi Carr being the prime example—but Gisela Raab took it to the point of psychiatric. It positively made my nerves jangle, but I persisted as best I could, trying not to inadvertently say boo and watch Bambi take flight.

I asked how they'd met. She looked nervous as she inserted a dummy in the mouth of the grizzling baby before pushing the pram onwards.

"He will know."

"How?"

"He will ask and I will have to tell him" Her ice cream dribbled down its wafer cone onto her fingers. She threw it away and licked them clean. Mine was down to the last inch of biscuit. Not that I was a greedy beggar, I just hated getting sticky hands.

"Will he hurt you?"

"No," she said. I noticed her cardigan was pulled down to the white knuckles that gripped the rail of the second-hand pram. "He only does that when it's necessary. For the Work. To go beyond what is right and acceptable. To dare to do that without thinking of the consequence except for the consequence in your will. It's exactly what your books taught him."

"Is it?" I thought of my next question carefully. "What kind of a man is he, Gisela?"

"I don't know."

For all the talk of a German accent, I could barely detect one. Her r's were soft, and she had to watch her d's and t's—'hand' became *'hant'*—but I knew a rabbi born in the East End who was far more incomprehensible.

"Is he a good man?"

She hesitated. "I don't know."

I gleaned they'd met when he used to come into her father's sweet shop. He started coming in more and more often and her father said it wasn't for the Pontefract cakes. Then he asked her out. "Nobody asked me out before him because we were German. He'd sneer when he heard that. He'd say: 'Small Welsh brains, singing hymns and playing rugby. They've got no conception of the genius walking amongst them, the infinite power I carry within me. How easily I could smite them down.' I'd laugh because I thought he was joking. I felt sorry for him, too, because he'd been declared MU by the army. Medically unfit. Due to a heart murmur."

I felt I'd taken the cork out of the bottle, because now she started to talk it was as if she never wanted to stop.

"We'd drive up to the Brecon Beacons. Get away from people. Just the two of us. Sit in the car. He'd talk about the war, but not about the British winning. He didn't want them to win. He wanted the present day to end and the New Dawn to emerge. This is what he said he prayed for. For everything to be different, for the past to be burned away, picked off like the hard part of a graze to reveal the new skin perfect underneath."

She looked down, embarrassed.

"He liked to talk about Hitler very much. Hitler learned at the knee of powerful shamans, he said. Hitler was a magus. 'I would have made a good Hitler. Hitler knew about the power of sacrifice, and what needed to be done didn't worry him.' That was because the Nazis believed in history, he said, something the British have papered over with clergy and cathedrals. 'We've made ancient powers and wisdom anodyne, emasculated,' he said. 'This country is going to the dogs. There are those of us who'd rather go to the gods. The old gods.' He said there was a war to be declared that would put this war to shame."

He'd got on a train to London to join Mosley's lot. Didn't realise they were all in jail and the BUF was banned. Took it as a personal snub. Next he tried to join the Labour Party, anything for a soap box, but some old duffer in a moustache turned him away. Lamont thought the old duffer was suspicious because he hadn't joined up. He tried the Freemasons. They said he didn't have the 'necessary credentials'.

"He was hopping mad. He said they would pay for that. The next night there was a bombing raid. The Freemason's Hall was hit. He was ecstatic. The library in Ystrad was bombed too, the finest library in Wales, they say. The planes must have been aiming for the railway. His mam lived in a little house in Gelli. She said the books were scattered all over the streets and in the back yard and through the front window. Didn't matter to him. What mattered was they paid. He said it was his first truly successful act of magic. He said the sky was the colour of aleph, the flight into Egypt."

Looking back, I could see part of her, even then, held him in some rancid, unwholesome awe. To begin with, he must have offered her an exciting escape from the humdrum. Women, in my experience, can even think wolves wonderful creatures, while the wolf only thinks 'dinner'.

She said he always had pills in his pocket that made the world brighter. 'Up. Down. Shake it all about,' he'd say.

"I didn't like taking them," she admitted. "I said I was worried they'd do me harm. He said that's the whole point of taking them, because they did harm. We had to get strength from the harm. He said it was a test of how much harm we were willing to do to ourselves. We had to lose all that, our inhibitions, our grip on life and reality. He said reality was a massive rock weighing us down, stopping us from rising to a state of revelation."

I thought, well he seems to know all the answers.

"He read from your books to me out loud," she said, "but I didn't understand any of it."

"Oh," I said, with no great astonishment.

"He was annoyed with me when I didn't. It would make him angry so I pretended I did. He said he didn't care what I thought, that I'd be better off if I thought nothing. It was only sex he wanted from me, and that was that" Her shoulders shrugged. "He didn't want me seeing my friends or family either. Said I had to make a choice. Him or them."

"So it was him, I take it."

She didn't need to nod.

We paused and looked out at a battleship grey sea. Heads bobbed up and down. The freezing water torture of the English seaside. Foundation of the heroism of our island race, I'm utterly convinced. We'd have produced no Scott, no Nelson, no Wellington, without the hereditary directive to hurl oneself into numbing waves with goose-pimply skin, a wobbly lower lip, broken seashells cutting into the soles of our feet, and a double helping of intense and prolonged misery.

She took out a headscarf and tied it around her hair in a turban. The breeze had turned her hands as pink as mine. I offered her my gloves. She shook her head. The baby was fast asleep, and it almost seemed she could speak more freely because of it.

"He said I'd better make myself useful, so he got me to steal from shops. That was the one thing I was good for. He told me a man in Aberdeen once accused him of dipping his hand in the till, but he put a spike through his eye. It didn't bother him. He was always looking down at boring ordinary people who stood in his way. He always said people were nothing but pigs at a trough. 'They think they have power but they don't. They have nothing.' Once we went to see a film called *Shadow of a Doubt*. Joseph Cotten plays the murderer, Uncle Charlie. He says to his pretty young niece, who is also named Charlie: 'Do you think the world is a foul sty?' When we came out, Donald asked me the same question: 'Do you think the world is a foul sty, Blondi, eh?' I said I thought the world is a Hell, in a way. He said 'Good girl.'

"Once, up on the Beacons, we drove over The Bwlch, which everyone knows is terrifying because the road is narrow and winding and really close to the edge and it's a big drop right the way down. I asked him to slow but he just drove faster and faster, laughing. I thought he was trying to kill us both.

"Another time when we were up there, he told me to get out of the car and took me to a spot where there were clumps of gorse and stringy yellow grass and sheep droppings, and he said this was where he buried a child he'd killed. I didn't know whether to believe him or if he was just trying to horrify me by showing me that small pair of spectacles he kept in his pocket. He said he'd killed and buried lots of children. He asked if I wanted to go to the police. I said I didn't. He said, 'I'm the kind of person who takes what he wants. If you don't like that you can fuck off.' I didn't know if he was trying to shock me. He liked it when I was shocked and upset or crying, that was always when he liked to make love.

"Sometimes he would press my throat a little bit or quite hard; he enjoyed it more that way and I wanted him to enjoy it, didn't I? Once I went blank, though. I thought I might die. I was afraid he'd finish me. 'No, I want you alive,' he said. 'When I don't, you'll be the first to know about it.'

"It was my fault I bruise easily. He got me to have sex with other men. That was another way to get money, as he didn't want to work. It was beneath him. He didn't mind watching it as well, and, you know, well, sometimes satisfy himself while he did so.

"Then he wanted to make a child, but he said he wanted it to be a pure child of magick with a 'K'. He said your work had taught him that magick with a 'K' was about throwing off the chains of everything conventional, and that included the love that people felt for each other when they conceived" She sniffed. The sea air had caused her nose to run, and the rims of her nostrils were red. "There was no room for love in magickal sex" She stared into the pram as she spoke. "He asked if I was prepared for that, because that's where he was heading, and I said yes, if that's what he wanted, I did too. I didn't want to lose him. If he went, I wasn't sure anybody would fill the space he left behind. He said in order to transcend, it had to be an act of debasement or it would be nothing. If I was ready, it would be special and I would be special."

Trembling, she rolled up the left sleeve of her cheap cardigan for my benefit then pulled it down again quickly. The marks all over her skin were indescribable. I gave her my handkerchief to wipe her nose. She used it and handed it back.

"Thank you. He burnt me with a soldering iron. What else? Matches. Knife. Fork. Yes, made a real meal of it. All over. Razor blade. Lots of that. Backs of my legs. Above the hem line, you see. Careful, yes. I think I lay there for two days. Not moving. He said if I moved, it would just go on and on, forever. He starved me. Gagged. Tied. Bit me in places. I was almost grateful for the biting" The word caught in the back of her throat. "Then when he was ready he put me on all fours and wrapped me in barbed wire, put a leather belt round my throat and pulled hard, choking me till my face was blue as he put himself inside me."

There are those who might think this conversation would have given me pleasure. They would be wrong. There are people who might think they know me. They don't. Sadism between consenting parties is one thing. This was quite another.

I placed my hand on hers, on the rail of the pram. She flinched and I retracted it.

"Nine months later a child was born. We named her Astra Argenta after your…" She saw that I nodded gently. "He…he didn't want her baptised. He spat on her brow and pronounced her a whore. A harlot, just like her mother."

I had to turn my back to the waves. The salt of the sea air was making my eyes sting unbearably.

"He was so happy," she said, smiling. In that smile I saw the girl she once was. Innocent then—though innocent still. Her lips were dry and chapped. Unattended. Unkissed. "I don't think I've ever seen him so happy. Now, he said, his route to transformation and power had begun" She still did not look me in the eyes, and had not done for the entire journey. To her, I was hardly even there. A sprite. An elemental. Daimon of her daydream.

She turned the pram and started to make her way back to the

Old Town. I hobbled to keep up with her. She was still smiling but the smile was eerily fixed, unmoving.

"He quoted your words when he rocked her in his arms for the first and last time, and said them so many times I know them off by heart: 'For the highest spiritual working one must choose that victim which contains the greatest and purest force…a child of perfect innocence.'"

I stood in front of the pram, pressed down on it to halt it. I must have looked like a madman. "Those—those words, they are only my veiled attempt to allude to the methods of sexual magic. Blood. Death. Kill" I laughed—a madman again. "They, they are meant to convey—*semen—ejaculation—orgasm…*"

She looked puzzled. "Why did you use the words if you didn't mean them?"

"Because poetry and magic are always conjoined. A 'child' does not mean a *child*."

"It does to him," she said. "He calls it the Supreme Violation."
Supreme Violation.

The scene became a blur. Sky and sea one. I was convinced I would faint, or die of heart failure, and used the baby's carriage to prop me up lest I did. Could it be possible? Years before—many years before—befuddled, grasping, at the mercy of a spiritual block, I had written those same two words in my diary. *Supreme Violation.* It was as if either now, or then, Lamont had been inside my head. I remembered I'd written that it was an obscene idea, but of great antiquity. I'd been reading about the tantric holy ritual of the *panchatattva*—the imbibing of wine, eating meat, intercourse between castes; all five elements forbidden by Hindu doctrine— So, I wondered, in its proper context, could ceremonial violation be a powerful magical act? Could this, the knowing embrace of the forbidden, be the *exact* method to banish the dying god of the old Aeon—Jesus, Osiris, Adonis—to make way for the new?

Yes, I had thought it. I had *written* it. In the name of any god that was watching, or listening, I thought—*What have I done?*

Gisela wanted to move on, wanted to move past me, wanted to be rid of me, and tried to pull the pram away from me. I would not let her do so. She yanked it forcefully back. I did the same, jerking it forwards. The tug of war shook the baby awake. It began to wail.

To my astonishment, far from attending to it immediately as I expected, Gisela stopped shoving the pram and let it rest, and let her hands fall to her sides. She stared straight forward but I cannot say she stared at me. All I remember is that the smile was gone and the eyes were heavy with a burden I could not contemplate.

"One day we took a picnic up the Beacons," she said, deaf to the crying that was getting louder. "I laid out a nice table cloth on the grass and we had hot tea in a flask and tinned salmon sandwiches and rock cakes. I'm not a good cook but I did my best" Gazing absently into the pram, she rocked it gently with one hand. "He used a little bit of rock cake to get a sheep to come over. It was a lovely sheep, not grubby like most of them, but bright white as if it had just been washed. I was chuckling because he kept saying, 'Come on, come on, come on.' Then all of a sudden he was sitting on it like a bareback rider and that made me hoot even louder. He tied a pink bow from my birthday cake around its neck. I thought it was really funny, until he sat it up on its hind quarters and cut its throat in one slash of the kitchen knife and the blood poured out, and he held it upside down with it shaking and twitching, holding it by its back legs as it writhed around then gradually stopped, hanging there with its big pink tongue hanging out, not moving any more."

I could picture its staring eye, its stiffened hoof. Presiding in its death throes over barrenness as its life seeped into the earth, next to a woman kneeling on a gingham table cloth holding a flask of tea in one hand and a rock cake in the other. In my mind, the sky was gigantic and unforgiving.

I immediately recognised that what she had described was the *qorban* sacrifice of the Hebrews, the Turkish *kurban*, still practised in Greece as the *kourbania*—now passed off as a blood sacrifice in honour of a saint, but dating from pre-Christian, unChristian antiquity. Traditionally the animal is fêted, garlanded and decorated with ribbons. If Lamont had called upon the shepherd-god—shaggy, unkept son of Hermes—that day, I would not have been surprised. But she did not say so.

I could barely swallow. I still thought I might pass out.

"That is why he came here" I voiced my devastating realisation. "He had to prepare himself fully, because there would only be one chance to transform into the Godhead. Enoch. His true self. But he needed a Master to make him ready for that epiphany. Not just any master…"

The baby's cries were deafening now. Its poor little face was scarlet, its mouth shuddering. Gisela lifted it up, her cardigan arms enveloping it. Her tragic arms. Tortured arms and body. Every inch of her. Where? How many times? What had been *her* cries, over those hours, days of torment? I wanted to embrace her, hug her, but such an action would be terrible. If she wanted it ever, it would not be from me. I could do nothing. Say nothing. I *was* nothing. Standing there wrapped up in my bewilderment. Then, its face denting the softness of her breast, all was well. Silence, Contentment. Love. Yes, love. The simple attentiveness of mother to child was something that never failed to give me a lump in the throat and that occasion was no exception. I wanted to take over the job of weeping.

And would have, had she not pulled the pram to her, and might have rammed me in the stomach had I not stepped aside. But I caught her by the arm before she could speed away.

"Don't go. Please…"

"He will know that I have…"

"No. He won't. I will perform a rite of invocation of silence. He will never know this conversation ever happened. I promise."

She paused. "Thank you."

I took away my hand. "You must get the child, and yourself, away from him."

"It isn't possible. Don't you think I've…?"

"If you need money, I can find it. Take a train. Find a place of safety."

"Where?"

"Anywhere? Home."

Eyes shut, she shook her head in what looked like a spasm. "He would find me. I know he would. He will not stop, Mr Crowley"

She pushed the pram several yards back in the direction of her so-called home, that fetid temple. Then stopped and turned back, her offspring cradled in the crook of one arm, wearing a look in her eyes of what I can only call sublime resignation. "The Work is all that matters to him now. He is more powerful than ever. I can hardly touch him. It comes off his body, like fire, like electricity, like a disease. Only the most powerful magician could stop him" The babe in her arms had been soothed to the point of repose. Its gummy saliva had made the soggy imprint of a tiny mouth on the cloth of her blouse over her nipple. She knew I could see it and tugged the front of her cardigan closed. Her eyes were impossibly deep and impossibly sad. "Can you stop him?" I could only tell her the pathetic and inadequate truth, difficult though it was to come from my lips.

"I don't know."

The last sight I had of them both was as Gisela Raab walked away from me, pushing the pram, with her baby Astra in her arms, the top of its small, curly head just showing over the horizon of one of her mother's shoulders. Golden hair just long enough now to be tied in those two pretty bows of pink ribbon.

A brisk knocking echoed behind Dennis's shoulder. His back went rigid. He blinked, straightened his collar, cleared his throat. The door opened and a small middle-aged woman, presumably the afore-mentioned Miss Clarke, brought in a tray bearing what he soon could see (standing politely as a lady entered the room) to be a plate of tinned sardines liberally sprinkled with curry powder. Miss Clarke laid it across Crowley's lap. He leaned forward and she puffed up the cushions behind him pugilistically. When she'd done so, Dennis gave a smile in lieu of any thanks from Crowley. It was not reciprocated. The woman's face remained as intransigently sour when she left and Dennis sat back down as when she'd arrived.

"She's not overburdened with a bedside manner."

"She's an old witch," said Crowley, poking the tiny, slimylooking fish with a fork. "I see her cavorting past my window during the night on her broomstick, and told her so. She wasn't much amused. It was meant as a compliment" He placed down his cutlery implement and let out a sizeable exhale. "You have nothing to say?"

Dennis shook his head. He didn't wish to speak in case his words gave substance to what he'd heard—which he didn't want— or make him seem a fool, which he always tried to avoid. Crowley made a sound in the back of his throat, possibly meant to convey derision, but it trailed into a strangely musical wheeze rather like a quiet note from a flute.

"Good. Most people talk before thinking. The reverse is always preferable" Eyes closed, he lifted one leg onto the divan, letting his head sink deeper into the pillow, raising a palm to his forehead, where he left it.

"I tried to get through to his thinking, but he was closed off from me. Entirely focused" The chest rose and fell shallowly. "His will was strong, not only his mental willpower but his Will in the Thelemic sense. That sense of purpose I call the True Will. I tried to tell him that the path he was following was not Thelema and not Crowley, but he was no longer listening. I was no longer relevant to him. His interpretation of my words had long left behind my actual intention. I tried to tell him that the Great Work wasn't about sacrificing a life but the sacred elixir, the combined fluids of a man and woman, in orgasm. He quoted my own words back at me. 'Blood sacrifice is efficacious.' I didn't remember where or when I'd even said it. I said I'd only ever talked about sacrifice in jest. To shock people. He looked at me as if I was an imbecile."

Crowley prodded away the plate in front of him, without eating.

"What could I say? How could I argue? As my followers know, as the gentlemen of the press know, my morality is no morality. The road to excess leads to the palace of wisdom, but I've only ever required the sacrifice of one's wealth and utter obedience— physically and mentally. That's Crowleyanity. That's freedom. Find your limits and go beyond them. Then you will achieve true enlightenment, through the practice of ritual magic. And if you get there by mind-expanding substances, extreme sexual acts..." He swallowed drily. "But..."

Dennis's elbows were on his knees, forearms a V pointed at the floor. Head bowed until he lifted it. "He saw in his goal a divine purity," breathed Crowley thinly. "I could not shift him on it. He told me he was proud the baby had been conceived in perfect conditions. Necessary conditions. Necessary for him to go beyond the usual human limits...to abnegate and disavow love or pleasure in any form...to enact the *opposite* of love, and have the child born of that obscene union" His nostrils quivered. "The sacrifice is all, he said. It always was. I'd got it wrong."

Dennis watched him.

"He means to consume it, as Saturn consumed his own child."

Crowley's voice was reduced to a croak. "This is his destiny. Not to listen to Enoch, or to be the mouthpiece of Enoch, but to *become* Enoch, the All-Knowing Angel, in a final, irreducible act of total ego. Not in order to lose the Self, as the Buddhists aspire to do, but to *find* it, and make it All. Not to be nothing—as he has felt all his life—but to be *everything*. By harnessing all human civilisation finds repellent, the basis of every sin and crime—the very grammar and syntax that has taken us further and further from our true form as it was when the Cosmos came to being. All the forces of denial must be eradicated, one by one, so that finally the gateway to a higher plane of being can be opened, and he and the angel will be as one. Only then shall the World change forever."

"Dear..." Though he tried, under his breath, Dennis was unable to summon the name of his Creator.

"I realised then that I was no longer teacher and he was no longer pupil," said Crowley. "He was on the higher slopes and I was on the foothills, lost in a blizzard. He had taken me as his guide, only to surpass me, as he knew he must. Gradually, what I feared most of all came to pass—that he, not I, was the 'Ipsissimus' now. One day I heard the chill words, 'Master Therion, your work is done.'"

Listening, Dennis felt a shiver like an icy fingertip run down his spine.

"The balance shifted. I became sick. He became stronger.

Stricken, I had to take to my bed. He no longer wanted or needed me. I dreamt of the woman, Gisela Raab. I dreamt of the child, crying in its pram on the seafront. I saw the marks on her mother's skin. A battlefield of endless, heartless ravages. As I lay worsening through the summer months, I knew he got stronger even as I grew weaker. I knew his plan, but I knew I was too weak to stop him. I needed help."

Care Frater Scriptor—I beg of you, come immediately.

The words of the letter came alive in Dennis's mind. Hideously so.

A life is at stake—and not my own.

He looked back at Crowley, but Crowley's eyes were already on him, adding to a bilious sense of unpleasantness that was already turning his stomach.

"You must go to the police," he said.

"I?"

"*We.* What does it matter who?" Dennis's anger was rising.

"It matters a great deal," said Crowley. "We tell them what? What evidence do we have? A conversation over ice cream? And she will deny it. All of it! Even the scars on her body. I will tell you, St Peter will have nothing on her! Besides, they'd take one look at me— Hasting's most famous, *vilest* resident! For God's sake, man. You think they're going to believe The Wickedest Man in the World?"

"They'd believe *me.*"

"What?" Crowley yelped. "A peddler of tosh?"

"I take offence at that!"

"Oh, poor you! I'm *so* sorry" Crowley slipped the tray off his knees onto the bed covers. Tilted, the silver grey sardines slid in their oil. "Use your head for one instant, will you? If they *did* listen for one moment to our crackpot doctrines, and buy them wholesale, which is about as likely as flying to the moon, what do you imagine would happen the second they knock on his door? All we'd be doing is letting him know we are onto him, and he'd be gone, swift as the twirling-moustached genie through the trap door in the pantomime at the Theatre Royal."

"All right, we should bypass the law and go and confront him ourselves. Get the woman and her baby out of there…"

"Nothing would be more reckless and ineffective. It would only put mother and child in even more danger."

"Then what on earth do you expect to do to stop him?"

"I'd have thought that was obvious."

"No."

"Oh, please."

"Look, really—why exactly have you called me here?"

"Because you are the only person I know with the imagination and knowledge to know that this isn't insane. That there are people in the world who *believe* in this, and will *do* this."

"Because they believe in something…something so—"

"Yes!" hissed Crowley with organ-stop eyes.

Dennis rose and turned his back on him.

"I've read, God knows, I've *read* stuff to make the hair curl. Black magic. Voodoo. Obeah. Witchcraft through the ages. But *believe* in it? No, of course not" He found himself seething. Seething and trapped. "Whatever you are planning, count me out, right away. There's no way on earth I'll be involved in this kind of activity. I've always made it quite plain in my books I want no part of it. You have your beliefs. Fair enough. But I don't even begin to share your faith in any of it."

Crowley laughed. "You don't have to have *faith* in magic to make it work! You don't have to have faith in the internal combustion engine to know that a car works when you put in petrol, turn on the ignition, rev the accelerator and put it into first gear. My dear boy, it will *move*. The instructions, if followed precisely, result in the outcome. I've spent my whole life arguing that magic is an art that can be systemised like science. You don't need belief. But you do need the courage to use it."

"Because its misuse can be fatal. Thank you. My feelings exactly."

"Your feelings are irrelevant. Your *God* is irrelevant."

Dennis stiffened. It was the final straw. "If that is the case…" He took as many paces as it took to get to the door knob, and twisted it.

"People think that magic comes from some external cosmic force, some objective existence of angels who can impart knowledge," said Crowley. "The truth is that when magic works it unlocks an arcane, biological knowledge within our being. The demon or angel is only the key to what is beyond the door. Something that has always been there. Something that, by dint of sophistication and progress, through mankind's specious ambitions, we have lost."

"You make it sound almost rational," said Dennis.

"My approach to magic is entirely rational. Wait—"

"I'm sorry."

"Surely, as an intelligent human being—"

"I said I'm sorry." Dennis glowered. "As they say in the forces: 'Request denied.'"

"Yes well, these are *different* forces, my lad," Crowley said to Dennis's back as it disappeared across the landing towards his room. "I've done a great many things in this torrid life, I know— but I've never begged. I'm begging you now. *Help me.*"

Reaching his own room, Dennis felt compelled to look back.

Crowley was framed in the doorway to Room 13, his hands clinging weakly to the jambs, a dissolute ape gripping the bars of its cage, held up by them, the light of the room behind making a silhouette of him, a figure cut out of black paper.

"My heart is fragile. My body frail. My energy sapped. The new Magister Templi in the Old Town has seen to that" His bony knees sagged then straightened. His pinched face monkey-like. If it was skin he wore, it seemed an illusion. Dennis found his teeth gritted. His jawbones telling him not to speak. He had to defy them.

"Help you…how?"

"To invoke a demon," said Crowley.

Dennis's teeth relaxed into a chattering laugh, which ran long and hard until it dried up. He stared back at the old man, hard.

"You're serious."

"A child," whispered Crowley.

"I'm sorry. I simply…I can't do what you are asking. Not in any shape or form. You're wasting your time."

"I'm not strong enough. Not any more. Don't you see? That's what I'm trying to tell you. I can't. Not on my own."

Dennis wasn't listening any more. He was now inside his room and his suitcase up on the bed and thrown open. His pyjamas in a ball, his spare, unworn shirt flat, his spare shoes, the brogues, hairbrush, cologne—it took seconds, not minutes, to pack. He pressed down the framed photograph of Joan, a towel on top of it, the Gerald Kersh on top of that. The *Forbidden Lecture* he tossed onto the bed. Then, suitcase in his other hand, consigned it to the wicker waste paper bin in the corner. Good riddance.

Crowley was guarding the top of the stairs. Blocking his exit.

"Get out of my way, please."

Dennis brushed him gently aside, and descended, quickly, though not so fast that Crowley's disembodied voice from above didn't ring in his ears.

"So you can face the enemy, from a reinforced bunker under Whitehall, when it suits you. Well, what about *this* enemy?"

Dennis stopped at the half-landing—where Crowley himself had paused the day before so pathetically—and looked back at the goatish face leering with slitty eyes down at him.

"You're mad." He pronounced it, without emotion, as observable fact, and continued on his way, but if he saw it as his exit line, he was sorely mistaken.

"Wheatley!" Mottled hand crawled over mottled hand down the dark, polished banister rail behind him as Crowley descended one step, then two, the voice sibilant but bouncing off the wood panelling of the hall. "If we fail to stop him we are not only talking about one dead child. We are talking about his magical transform-ation succeeding. He will become a being and consciousness the like of which this world has rarely if ever endured. He will herald the New Aeon, yes, but in a way I never imagined. And he will be relentless. That's what I'm afraid of. And my fear trumps yours a thousand-fold."

Dennis felt a metallic belt tightening round his chest. Was it fear or was it sheer, unadulterated rage? He didn't know, but he *did* know he didn't want to look back and see Crowley's sickly, terrified, accusatory face looking down at him. He wanted to get out of there.

"Go to the police!" he shouted from the bottom step.

There. An end.

"I had you down as a man who didn't run from what he feared."

Dennis ignored that. He'd had enough. More than enough. He spotted a well-dressed couple entering the lobby from the driveway, Vernon greeting them in his patented unctuous but hospitable fashion. Dennis wondered if they knew what they were in for. He wondered if, more to the point…yes, they'd come by taxi. And yes, there it was outside, its engine purring.

"I'm sorry. I've wasted my time here."

He sidestepped the group. Vernon included. Vernon looked startled, mystified.

"Excuse me?"

No time to explain. What the hell *could* he explain?

"The station, please. Thank you."

Dennis threw his suitcase in the back seat ahead of himself, and, tie loosened, top button undone, could breathe at last. *Breath*—that precious commodity Crowley treasured so much. He felt he hadn't breathed, not properly, for an hour, and the cold October air as he rushed from hall to taxi, albeit thick with exhaust fumes, felt as fresh as menthol. The car reversed and did a three-point turn, crunching on the gravel. In so doing it meant Dennis had a full view back at the porch—Vernon, hands on hips, scratching head—and the side window, through which he could have seen the staircase if he wished, and whoever might be standing there, looking out, if he wished. But he didn't wish. He definitely didn't wish. What he wished for was to be home. Home to his wife and work and sanity, and away from this dangerous absolute bloody madhouse forever.

"I swear. It was as if I had wandered into the pages of one of my own black magic thrillers" He told Joan what had happened. "I half-expected an ab-human, red-eyed Malagasy to step out of the observatory!" He wondered if his levity fooled her that he wasn't at all shaken by the last forty-eight hours. It did precious little to fool himself. At least when he made reference to "this satanic 'Pinkie'"—referring to Graham's Greene's sadistic Brighton hoodlum—he knew his wife would get it, whereas Crowley's knowledge of contemporary fiction would have been non-existent. Not surprisingly, since he saw the entire genre as, what did he say—*vulgar?* Dennis had dithered over a bottle of Mumm's Cordon Rouge, but the taste of it—sour and cheap—reminded him of 'Shitty Bill' Inglis, that major in the RFA, nauseating sex maniac, and his pick-ups in that cheap flat overlooking Coram Fields. Instead he opened the Château Lafite 1899.

"Steady on," said Joan. "Do you really need to open two bottles?"

"If I need to find one to my liking, yes. Or are you going to tell me what to do with my own wine cellar?" By the look on her face, he sensed she might tell him what to do with his head, and that was to boil it. He winced. "I'm sorry" He still sounded sharp and it wasn't like him, she knew that, he hoped. Not at all like him. The pot was boiling over and that wasn't her fault in the slightest. He gulped another large mouthful. Needing to get a grip on things, he took a deep breath, and his voice was a good deal softer and more genuinely recalcitrant when he said it a second time. "I'm sorry."

Joan picked up the salt and applied it. The noise of cutlery where conversation should hold forth is the most depressing sound in the world. After a while he couldn't bear it. He was in the dog house so he'd better start barking.

Attempt number one. Try to make up for foul mood by giving wife compliment. "You look…"

"Oh, don't."

Shot down in flames immediately.

He was glad it was the cook and maid's night off. He hated when they were in the firing line of a domestic affray. He didn't know how the aristocracy could behave as though servants were invisible. Anyway, how often did he and Joan have tiffs? Almost never. Not as often as most couples, he was sure of that. But it always upset him when they did, and made him feel like a swine.

He walked round to her side of the table and filled her glass. Tinked it with the rim of his own. Silly gesture. Didn't raise a smile. Thought it might. He sat back down. Corned beef and piccalilli, not exactly the repast of kings.

"It's black magic and I refuse to get mixed up in it. The man's insane. Utterly. Anyway…all over. Finished with" He ate, as best he could.

"Do you believe there's a woman in danger?"

"What? She could just as easily go to the police as I can. It's simply none of my responsibility. None of it is."

He didn't mean to seem callous or dismissive but could tell that's what it came over as. She was simmering. Was she still angry at him for his being boorish, or his nonchalance, which, to her eyes, amounted to cowardice? Was he saying he didn't care? He didn't mean that, not at all. But she was incredible perceptive. Perhaps she could pick up that his chipper behaviour masked the fact that he was deeply rattled. That he wanted to scream and tear the paper from the walls, and it was all hidden, for the moment, behind a terribly placid smile.

Perhaps she equated fear as a weakness, as a lack of manhood, and it made him suddenly odious to her. Which made him think of the Savoy again. Of her friends who knew her Norman-French forebears and upper class credentials inside out. *She's far too good for you. You know that, don't you?* Joan saying to great laughter: *Of course he does.*

"I'm really not hungry."

She pushed back her dining chair and left the room, abandoning her champagne. He heard a door open and close.

He walked round and poured it into his own glass, then stood by the French windows looking out over the lawn, downing it, periodically returning to the bottle in the ice bucket for a refill.

Dancing Bacchus, the god of wine, stood, bunch of grapes held above his open mouth, layered with a sheen of blue-green verdigris by oxidation, modelled as a satyr with sprightly goatlegs astride its plinth. It struck him now, looking out at it by the thinning evening light, as a strange hybrid of his old profession and his new.

He thought of all the building and gardening he'd supervised, or done with his own two hands, to transform the place. The maze. The glade of forest trees planted, and a yew—not to mention his brickwork. Lilacs, laburnums, peaches, cherries. Now he'd finally achieved it—a perfect English home the equal of the Eatons' in *The Devil Rides Out.*

Grove Place was his Arcadia. God knows, he'd worked for it. He'd led an exhausting campaign of attrition against weeds in order to make the house habitable. Industrial quantities of Nippon ant killer against those little blighters. Ferrets commandeered to keep down the rabbits.

Ah, the chrysanthemums.

He took another mouthful, swallowed. Just the good side of corked. Hell.

Was it growing darker already?

Hard to believe they'd only moved in a year and a half ago. Felt it was rather fated as soon as they'd seen the place. Edge of the New Forest. Small, delightful town with the only thing going for it a high street connected to Nell Gwynne and 'Old Rowley'— subject of one of Dennis's novels. That sealed the deal, somehow, but really the house sold itself. Georgian. 1770. High ceilings. Tall windows. It begged them to restore it to its former glory. And Dennis couldn't wait to get the stone balustrade up with a row of Grecian urns. In 1946, Britain was rebuilding, and they were rebuilding this.

He couldn't see it now, but what he most valued was the four acres of land, and beyond it the four miles of fields and woods to the Solent, the sea, and the Isle of Wight with its Napoleonic forts, protection from bygone invaders. Derelict now. Abandoned, unmanned, but not forgotten. Protecting from an invasion of ghosts.

He hardly ever missed London, but he missed it tonight. He would have given his right arm for a glass or three of Pimm's followed by jugged hare and a nice Château Pape Clément at Rules. Instead of which he had a wife who thought he was an utter beast.

He went into the music room and, not needing the sheet music, played the *Moonlight Sonata,* hoping it would calm him. He was anxious that he wasn't calm already, and it was becoming a vicious circle—being worried about being worried. He needed what soothed the savage beast—or was it breast? He never knew.

"Why are you playing that?"

He'd thought that Joan had gone to bed.

"No reason. It just popped into my head. You always liked it."

"I don't any more" Joan tightened the belt of her dressing gown.

He closed the piano lid and crossed the room to the gramophone, attempt number two to lighten the proceedings. He put a record on the turntable and lowered the needle, trying not to think of a needle pricking skin. It played Cab Calloway's *Zaz Zuh Zaz*.

"Creepy Crowley" Joan rubbed her arms as if feeling a distinct chill. "I thought you hated him."

"I do. He's everything I despise in a man" He saw her expression change. "What's wrong?"

"I told you not to go."

"Did you?"

"Yes. When you showed me the letter. You chose not to hear me. Perhaps he's eradicated it now from your mind with one of those spells of his."

"All right. I'm listening now. What did you say?"

"I reminded you that when you came back from that lunch you said you never wanted to see that man again in your life. You said he'd emitted the most sickly aura of malevolence you'd ever come across in a human being. You said you felt as though you were sitting across the table from a dose of syphilis."

Dennis laughed. "I don't remember saying *that*" He sidled towards her, touched her sleeve. "Really, darling…" She moved away.

"Why did you go there?"

"I don't know. He seemed desperate. I was just incredibly curious as to why he would contact me, of all people."

"You were flattered by the attention," she said. "Even from the likes of him. Like a fag in public school given crumbs from the table of an older boy."

"Oh, nonsense."

"You'd no need to feel inadequate."

"Inadequate?" Dennis was pained. "To be perfectly honest, a part of me was hoping for some good juicy research, something that could be the basis of a book. Who knows? I might have got one."

"Instead of which——"

"Instead of which, I wish I'd never…" He sat on the piano stool and drained his glass. He wondered what else he had said about Crowley after that lunch, in his cups. Yes, worse for wear, but you know what they say——a drunk man speaks a sober man's thoughts. *In vino veritas* and all that. Had he blanked it out? Frightening, if so. Or had it stayed with him? Did he always, deep down, know that one day he would be beckoned by that crooked finger?

"His reputation precedes him," he said, expressly to mollify Joan, who was already heading back to the stairs. "You were afraid for me, as a good wife would be. But here I am. Body and soul intact."

She looked back into the room from the hall as if he was the most pitiful child.

"But it's not over, is it? You know it's not."

This time she really had gone to bed. He heard her footsteps on the stairs and the shutting of the door was unmistakable. He retired to his study. His monk's cell. Having dredged the champagne to its limit, he poured a glass of Graham's 1897 Port and lit up a Hoyo de Monterray, one of his steady supply from Benson & Hedges. He was soon opening a bottle of Imperial Tokay——the best year, 1806—— to take the edge off the sweetness of the port. Unfortunately it reminded him of that damnable lunch yet again. *What does anyone seek but a lantern in the Void?*

That's what his guest had said, and here he was, sitting alone in the gloom, with a book by Carl Jung on his desk for research. Research——ha! What would Jung have to say about voices in a Cairo hotel room? No doubt that one's holy guardian angel is merely the unconscious mind working a night shift. And Freud—— was he so different from Crowley, saying that we were wrong to treat our physical urges as shameful, didn't he say that was the root of all our neuroses and problems too? "We are given rules from birth, rules we are told must not be broken, but when does any teacher ever tell us to listen to our bodies and souls?" Wise words, courtesy of the Hungaria. Doors. Doors. So many doors that are closed, and nobody allowing us to open them.

"What rot!" he said out loud.

Squiffy, but not as squiffy as he would have liked, he placed the Jung on his bookshelf, between the 1928 edition of *Malleus Maleficarum* by Montague Summers and his beloved *Three Musketeers*. He ran his fingers over his first editions. Gazed at the thousands of other books surrounding him. His bastion. The porcelain figures of Napoleon and Marie-Antoinette, their glazes glinting in the shadows. The spoils of his travels displayed on the walls. Not only the crossed sabres of the Scots Greys, but a Benin fetish object and a kuba horn from Africa. Dominating one wall, a superb copy of *Witches at their Incantation* by Salvator Rosa, the grim tone of the oils matching the dark sea he found himself in.

He stared eye to eye at one of his favourite acquisitions, a carved devil. *The Devel Sasabonsam*. Blood-sucking creature in the rich folklore of the Ashanti of southern Ghana. The thing was said to be in league with witches, *abayifo*, and black magicians, *mmoatia*. Was that what he was in league with now? The very things his imagination tried to keep at bay? The enemy that had no name? Did Crowley have a power over him, a magnetic draw, only his wife could intuit?

"The Devel Sasabonsam," he said to the empty room, toasting it with the Tokay. Down the hatch.

He sat unable to move because he knew he now felt afraid to the depths of his being, and he couldn't shake it or explain it. A feeling he had been...(that was the word, that was the exact word)— invaded.

*
**

He tried to extract his hand but he daren't. A sweat broke out on his forehead. How on earth had he got himself into this situation?

With his hand inserted into 'The Mouth of Truth' *(The Bocca della Verità*, as in the famous painting)—the sculpted Grecian head, staring at him from its carved, colourless and unforgiving eyes, she whose duty it was to bite the hand off liars. He was sure she would bite down at any moment, but wait, he wasn't the liar. Why should he suffer? What had he done wrong? Couldn't somebody help him? Where was everybody? And if he lost his hand—his right hand—who would do the writing?Out of the corner of his eye he could see a beggar sitting in rags, trying to knot the cut strings of wooden puppets, making an awful mess of it. Dennis wanted to say, give it to me, let me do it, but he couldn't move.

Next he found himself in the house belonging to the Eatons, Cardinal's Folly, but the landing he stood on was identical to the one outside his bedroom at Grove Place. He could hear Richard and Marie-Lou, Simon Aron, Rex, and the Duke—his 'Modern Musketeers'—dining downstairs, laughing, out of sight—though he could make out the warm spill of light into the hall below. He longed to join them, as a log fire might lure a freezing man, but overriding that was his sudden fear their loud and spirited voices would wake a sleeping child. He heard a baby crying. Why wasn't one of them coming up to see what was wrong with it? Where was Nanny? The butler, Malin—why was he serving strawberries and cream? The child was Fleur, of course, the Eatons' young daughter. *Fleur d'amour* as her father called her when sweeping her up in his arms, or soothing her when she was frightened of a giant spider in the bath tub. Stop, Dennis wanted to shout loudly. Stop laughing, stop enjoying yourselves, and *do* something.

But he couldn't leave the overnight bag on the landing. What was he going to do with it? How did it even get there? It wasn't his. He would have to take care of it first, like he had to take care of everything. The infant's bawling continued unabated, reaching new heights of high pitched, strangulated hysteria.

He knelt down, unzipped the bag across the top and tugged the opening wide. It was packed full of newspapers, old editions that nobody in their right mind would want to keep or read, the kind you ate fish and chips from at the seaside, stinking of salt and vinegar and urinals. What was contained in the newspaper was soft to the touch; his thumb print reddened and he thought of an illegal meat delivery. He peeled back a wet corner. Saw part of a tiny, chubby arm and didn't know what it might be connected to, whether it was the obvious or something else made of blood and slime and spit. *Mummy make it better.* He wanted to touch it, lift it out in case it was still alive, but couldn't. A bright light shone from within, from the gaps he'd made between the sheets of newspaper, blinding him. *Put that light out!* Now when he inserted his hands the things he found were bones for a dog to gnaw. Some aged bulldog with leathery testicles. So many of them, so many, the bag was bottomless and they just never stopped. Enough to build a wall of bones.

Dachau. Buchenwald. Belsen.

The telephone woke him. For a minute he waited for the housekeeper to answer it, then remembered it was her night off. He pulled on his dressing gown and went downstairs, half-shut eyes not wanting to acknowledge the stark reality of the dead of night. Three o'clock was what the grandfather clock taunted him with. "Lymington three one five" His slur was testament that he had not yet committed to waking, and the dream, its detritus, had not yet fully retreated.

The operator put the caller through.

"Mr Wheatley?"

"Yes."

Vernon Symond's voice. You say it with a sigh. Remember? "I'm sorry to disturb you at this late hour."

Disturb? You are not the one who has disturbed me, old fruit.

Dennis rubbed his eyes. "What is it?"

"It's, ah…" He already knew. "It's Mr Crowley" The pause on the line was filled by a crackle. "He's taken a turn for the worse, I'm afraid. The doctor's just left, and…"

Dennis wanted to say something ghastly and cruel. He wanted

to hang up, but the man didn't deserve that. It wasn't his fault. He and his wife, Johnny, had cared for Crowley. God alone knew why, but they had. More selflessly than he ever would have.

"He...he has asked for you," said Vernon. "Expressly for you" Softly apologetic. "I couldn't..."

"No."

"We don't know how long..."

"I understand. Thank you," said Dennis. Unbidden, Goya crept into his mind. An image of AC dying, overpowered by another magician's power of malignant evil. The sabbat. The priest and the donkey. The Duke de Richleau, Marie-Lou's 'Greyeyes', facing the Goat of Mendes. The goat propped up in a bed in Hastings.

"Hello?"

"I'm here. I'm still here," said Dennis. "Tell him I will be down on the first available train."

He heard a door gently shut upstairs. It was the door to Joan's bedroom.

At seven o'clock the next morning, Joan, in her night dress decorated with Chinese dragons, walked in to find Dennis re-packing his suitcase. He looked up at her quizzical expression briefly before continuing, undeterred. "You remember what it felt like when Diana was all those miles away in Africa?" It was the only way he could think of to explain how he was feeling. "Your brother was out there with her, supposedly looking after her, fat lot of use that was. Scatty and vulnerable and letting herself open to anything and everything her so-called friends got up to, cocktails, strip poker into the wee small hours when anyone with an ounce of sense would know she wasn't up to it, then spending her days sick as a dog. Nobody giving a fig about her character or safety. And us, back in London, worried sick, unable to do anything to help her" He flattened his packed shirt with his palms. "The picture of her staggering, bleary-eyed, half-dressed. In a stupor, having the clothes pulled off her and put to bed by complete..."

"Dennis—"

"Joan" He batted her firmness back at her. Diana wasn't even his daughter, by blood, but at the time, he would rather have died than see her descend into that kind of moral squalor. Was he making his point? Was he getting through? "She was the loveliest girl, and those people were—were spitting on the altar."

Joan snatched his cigarette case from the bedside table and lit one as an act of aggression.

"And you're saying that poor woman in Hastings is vulnerable and in the hands of a monster."

He said simply, "I *have* to."

"Why didn't you *have to* yesterday?" His wife stood half-encircled by the bay window, next to a vase of fronds from the garden— nigella 'love-in-a-mist', miscanthus grass, celosia. Her back to him. The strong shoulders he adored. "You don't know what game he's playing. You don't know what's at stake."

"I *do* know what's at stake. That's the whole point. The life of a child," he said. "Not just the life of a child. If this man is a magician as powerful as Crowley claims, then we're talking about the fate of the country, perhaps even the world" He watched her cock her head, then blow a horizontal jet of smoke, one hand on her hip. He tried his best to keep the tremor of emotion out of his words. Bland words, perhaps, ridiculous words, possibly—he was often accused of both—but he never meant anything more in his life. "Look, I'm not strong. I'm not clever, but I *will* fight for what I love. To the death, actually."

"You said yourself. This is black magic."

"Not black. White. Used for good reasons, not selfish ones."

"But magic nonetheless" She turned to him. "Do you have any idea what you are opening yourself to?"

"I should do. I've written enough about it."

"Then listen to yourself."

"I am, and my Christian conscience is telling me to go."

"Christian? What's *Christian* about this—what he wants you to do?"

"Is that why you're afraid? Don't be. God is on my side."

"Don't be a bloody idiot!"

She drilled the cigarette to obliteration in the ashtray also on his bedside table. It was his habit to have a smoke or two before he rose. At this rate his case was going to be empty. She was pacing now, rubbing her upper arms as she had the night before, pacing so restlessly he wanted to put his hands on her shoulders in an effort to calm her, but he daren't.

"I simply don't trust him" Her voice tremulous. "What if that isn't *all* that's at stake? What if he isn't telling you the whole truth? I'd say it's fairly inevitable he isn't, as a matter of fact. He's a fake, a charlatan, a liar, a philanderer, a…a con man. The most lewd, repugnant, odious individual—"

Dennis barked a laugh. "You've never even *met* him!"

"Yes—I have."

Said in such a throwaway fashion that its shock value took a moment to fully sink in. He felt it like a bayonet in his guts.

"What?"

"I *have* met him" She was back at the bay window, looking out, if she was looking at anything. The one thing she was not looking at was him.

"What are you talking about?"

She ran her fingers over the dried-out, almost transparent, leaves of honesty—*Lunaria annua.*

"It was during the war, obviously" Why obviously? "We were living in Chatsworth Court. You'd still kept your office in Oakwood Court, ten minutes away. He was living in Jermyn Street, off Piccadilly Circus, just south of Piccadilly itself."

"I know where Jermyn Street is," he said.

"Nancy Cunard told me the landlady kept a spiritualist den in the basement. Crowley never paid rent, but still complained about the racket made by traffic and the crowds and bombs—as if Hitler might pay any notice."

"Spiritualists?" Dennis considered them ninety-nine per cent frauds, the rest irresponsible dabblers who laid themselves open to contacting something inhuman and uncontrollable. She knew how strongly he felt about the subject. He couldn't believe she would be so reckless as to—

"Please. Let me…" Another cigarette found its way to the cleft between her fingers. The silver Dunhill lighter—his—flared and was tossed down onto an armchair. She took a substantial drag. "Uncle Max provided the introduction."

He remembered, years before, being a fish out of water at a party of Charles Birkin's, instantly warming to a charming civil service type with a Wellingtonian profile. Been on the *Worcester*, like him. Fan of John Buchan thrillers, like him. In time, the Wheatleys were privy to the fact that Maxwell Knight was in charge of MI5's department B5(b), monitoring political subversion in all possible forms, part of its job being to infiltrate right and left wing extremists, though mystical oddballs needed keeping an eye on too, with their secretive and Masonic ways—at the core of which potential hotbed sat the redoubtable Aleister Crowley. Max, however, was a man of secrets himself, though married. Most ambivalently of all, he espoused an interested in the occult as well and wanting to police it. Poacher *and* gamekeeper. Some feared the Nazis wanted Armageddon, and some thought that by employing magic themselves, they could help defeat them. Perhaps 'M' was one of them, as well as 'one of them'.

"You know how he was for an esoteric debate," Joan continued. "He could talk the hind legs off a donkey about why we are here, whether a supreme being exists or not."

"Are you sure he wasn't drawn to Crowley's deviancy? He did lead a double life, as we all know."

"All murky and rather sordid."

"Is it?"

He knew Knight had roped in Joan with her socialite connections to keep an eye open for undesirables in the upper classes, and used her son, Bill Younger, to infiltrate the Oxford Union. It was through 'Uncle Max' she'd found work with 'Five' during the war. But Dennis questioned now what those conversations were in dingy corridors that he knew nothing about. What secrets she kept to herself.

"You remember Max's wife died shortly before we first met him? He used to come over to St John's Wood Park, a shoulder to cry on? It was around then. He said Crowley'd helped enormously. Gave him the key to understanding why. Why...suicide" Joan seemed desperately fragile, suddenly—as fragile as the gossamer-thin leaves beside her. "He said he brought them back in the most wonderful way. He said he explained everything."

"Darling..."

Joan flinched. She couldn't bear him speaking. It just might pull everything apart if she let it, and she couldn't.

"I was having the most horrid thoughts, you see. About Hubert. I couldn't help it. I thought they'd gone away, but they hadn't" Hubert Lachlan Pelham-Burn. Captain in the Gordon Highlanders. Died 1927—in a car crash. Dennis remembered she was Joan Pelham-Burn when he first met her. "Was he thinking of me when he died? Was I a good wife to him? Was he ever truly happy?" She sniffed, then clenched her jaw. "'Be strong,' everyone said. 'Be strong.' I always have to be strong. Why do I always have to be the strong one?"

A large, flat petal fell from the dried flower to the table top. She made a sound, somewhere between a laugh and a sigh.

"I expected Crowley to make me feel relaxed. Not a bit of it. Right from the start he made me feel ill at ease."

"That doesn't surprise me in the slightest."

"He offered me a glass of Pernod. I don't even like Pernod. He listened, a little, then he said: 'Do the dead *wish* to be called back?'—prying into my character in the most personal and intimate fashion. 'Why do you want to contact your dead husband? Do you miss his touch, his...'" She shuddered at the recollection of the word Crowley had used. It wasn't difficult for Dennis to imagine it too. His wife's lip curled with distaste. "'It's necessary to be completely honest with the spirit world.' He had no intention of helping me. I was a fool to think he might."

Dennis felt nauseated at the very thought of Joan in the physical vicinity of Crowley. The fly had stepped onto the web, and the fat, bloated spider must have been overjoyed at the prospect of toying with the wife of that successful young novelist—even, horrid thought, tempting her into his insidious orbit, where the tempting of Dennis had failed.

"As it was, he had a field day attacking you and humiliating me. No sooner had I stepped over the threshold than he rolled his eyes up and down me and said: 'I see Mrs Wheatley wears the trousers.'"

"Very witty."

"Quite. He took every opportunity for a cheap jibe, calling you son of a Streatham shopkeeper. I said it was none of his business, and in any case you were proud of the fact both your grandfathers were self-made men."

That phrase again, thought Dennis. Had Crowley used it deliberately at Netherwood? Of course he had. Nothing was accidental when it came to The Great Beast.

"I said you'd been caught in the slump. It wasn't your fault. You sold the company to avoid bankruptcy, even though it meant you were demoted to a quarter of your salary, but it didn't work out, so you applied yourself to becoming a writer. You got back on your feet, dusted yourself off…He said, 'And that's the reason you love him, no doubt. How enchanting. How English. How *absurd*.'"

Dennis could hear it coming out of the man's mouth. He was enraged now as well as sickened. He'd dragged his father's business kicking and screaming into the modern world, buying up private cellars, creating elaborate catalogues, putting on lavish events to court publicity and drum up sales, even opening a cigar room with Mervyn Baron. He'd worked his fingers to the bone building up a wider clientele, even employing Bino (Joan's brother, as it turned out) to lure in more customers with his charms. Yes, it had failed, but Crowley was dismissing all that graft with contempt? There again, did it really surprise him?

"I'd had enough," said Joan, with the kind of strength he knew her for, and loved her for. "He used workmen's words, gutter words."

"What did he say?"

She shook her head.

"Good God, darling, I've been in the army. No words can shock me."

"These might" She took another drag. "In any case, I don't want them to pass my lips."

"Why didn't you tell me?"

"How could I? I didn't know what you'd do. Or rather, I did know what you'd do. You'd ask me why I'd gone there."

"I'd have understood."

"No. You wouldn't have."

She sensed he had stepped closer, and stepped away, maintaining the distance between them. He wanted her to turn and face him. Dear God, why did she not *turn*?

"I, you see...I'd taken my coat from the peg. I'd put it on. I was facing the mirror next to the front door opposite the coat hooks. I said I was going now." She fuelled herself with another long inhale, and he could see the raised hand was trembling. The cigarette, trembling. The grey smoke a zigzag in the air above it. "He lifted my coat from behind and pushed me against the hall table, and pressed himself against my dress. I don't know if his buttons were undone but the shape...of it...hot and hard against my..." A laugh came from her lips. A laugh Dennis did not want to hear again in his life. "And I saw my face, my reflection, and I thought, 'Why aren't you doing something, you silly fool?'...but I couldn't move, because I didn't really believe what was happening—it couldn't be, could it?—and I smelt the Pernod against my..." She rubbed the nape of her neck, stopping halfway through a breath and swallowing. "He said he would happily ravish me." She adopted an astonishing state of composure. "He didn't use the word ravish."

Rage incinerated Dennis. Yet at the same time he was outside his body looking down at the scene, at this stupid man standing in his bedroom who is saying nothing, who had done nothing whilst his wife went through an abominable act of indecency—and held the horror within her all these years. What a feeble excuse for a man he was. Let him burn. Let him burn to a crisp.

He reached out a hand.

The thought of Joan, his darling, his rock, his life, being *touched*— by anyone, and of all people by *him*. It brought back all the unwanted touches, the kisses and fumbling below deck, in the monkish dark of *HMS Worcester*. He a cadet. Easy pickings. A 'jam'. One of the 'new shits'. His descent into Hell. How could *he* touch her now, and she not be repulsed?

"I called him a beast." Joan constructed the thinnest, bitterest of smiles. "He said it wasn't the first time he'd been called that particular appellation. As I stepped out into the sunlight of Jermyn Street, I heard him at the piano, playing *The Moonlight Sonata*."

She looked at Dennis full-on at last and he almost wished she hadn't. The image would never leave him. She held her eyelids wide open lest the tears bulging there demean her dignity by rolling down her cheeks.

Dennis turned away.

"He's a dangerous man," she said forcibly. "He *uses* people. He draws them to him then he tries to destroy them. Tries to destroy love. He gets pleasure from that."

She saw him take something from under his pillow.

A British Service Smith & Wesson .38 revolver. Everyone had them during the war, and nobody handed them back when it was over. As a memento, or 'just in case'. Just in case of what, nobody knew. Which is why, like him, they hung onto them.

"Don't," said Joan.

He checked. Six bullets. Placed the pistol in the suitcase, under his towel.

He didn't see himself from above any more. All he could feel was the unexploded bomb in his chest. And *she* was the one who touched *him*—why was *he* the one who shrugged her hand from *his* sleeve? Why was his anger paramount, not hers? He couldn't explain it, but he couldn't even look at her. He simply had to act. He had to kick a dog. He had to dig a grave. He had to pull a trigger. He was a man. That's what men did.

"Don't go, please. Stay. Dennis."

The suitcase left a rectangular shape dented into the bed covers. She was not the same any more, and he was changed, utterly. She had been debased. He could not live with that degradation. Not on his night watch in the mud with a rifle across his lap. Not while he had a shell in his gun and the wit to fire it. Not while he had any sense of duty left in his miserable body.

Worst of all, he lied to himself that he could neither embrace nor comfort her, for the hurt would overwhelm them both, and she did not need that. Not now. Not until he'd slayed the dragon. Become the person he needed to be. That was the excuse he fabricated for himself as he left Grove Place. Pathetic creature that he was, happy to leave her in tears.

He drove to Hastings this time, pressing his foot down hard on the accelerator, almost blind with rage the whole way. By the time he arrived at Netherwood, sitting there frozen, having difficulty unpeeling his hands from the steering wheel, he realised he had no real memory of how he'd got there, of the vehicles that he had overtaken, or had been passing in the opposite direction. None whatsoever. He couldn't recollect a single sign or turning. The entire journey was not so much a blur as non-existent, and that suddenly frightened him and got his heart pounding even harder than it was already. He'd driven like an absolute maniac and could easily have killed himself.

Dumping his suitcase at the top of the stairs, he immediately knocked on the door of Room 13. A young maid emerged carrying a chamber pot. She avoided his eyes. After the strong tang of urine wafted away, Dennis stepped into a fug of old age combined with Abramelin oil—which was said to be the oil which ran down Aaron's beard. Or was it just the sweet stink of ether? A spittoon sat on the floor within reach of the single bed, and there was evidence the doctor had been. He could see a supply of Veronal— he wondered if it was to replace the Liminal or to augment it—and the telltale signs of cocaine.If such a thing was possible, Crowley looked weaker and more helpless than when he'd last seen him. Shockingly so, in such a short period of time. The lolling, egg-shaped head seemed to be attached to his spindly neck like that of a puppet, and the hands akin to fleshless talons. *The Old Crow*, Dennis thought. What did Crowley always say when people pronounced his name incorrectly? "*Crowley as in 'holy'—not as in 'foully'. I am the Crow, not the Owl.*"

You are not even the crow now, old son, thought Dennis. *You are barely anything. Look at you. You are just an old, old man.*

And that produced in him an extraordinary and unexpected change of heart. He had arrived ready to punch Crowley in the face, or strangle him, or at the very least attack him verbally for what he had done to Joan. But now he was there he found he could do none of those things. Even the vitriol he had built up during the car journey refused to pour from his mouth. Somehow even that would have been tantamount to killing an animal in its death throes, or thrashing a defenceless and crippled child.

The Beast's claw hands threw I-Ching sticks down onto the tray on his lap. Six turtle shell rectangles with a solid line one side, a broken line on the other.

"I will do what you want, damn you," said Dennis. What the man had done to Joan was wrong, despicable and absolutely repellent. But there were more pressing matters—for now.

Crowley stared at the hasty hexagram he had cast. "Of course you will."

The highly appealing notion of throttling Crowley resurfaced, but Dennis supressed it. A huge act of restraint on his part. It made him aware there was another thing in the back of his mind, too, which was he didn't want to give Crowley the satisfaction of seeing the anger and distress he had caused, of thinking it some sort of perverse triumph.

Crowley fumbled amongst his accoutrements and slid in his dental plate. Dennis noticed his lower incisors were missing, probably extracted due to decay, the remaining teeth broken and heavily discoloured. It was a maw full of ruin, a street pitted and blasted to distraction after an enemy bombing raid.

"Be a good chap and send Miss Clarke up to help with my ablutions."

If that involved an injection for his asthma, Dennis was more than happy not to be witness to it. "I'll also grab a late breakfast."

"You'll do no such thing," wheezed Crowley. "It's bread and

water for you and me till this deed is done. Normally one would prepare for this procedure with a thirty day fast at the very least, but needs must when the Devil drives."

Dennis left the room sorely wishing he'd used a different expression.

*
**

"He wants to get up now."Miss Clarke frowned. "Is he well enough?"

"I have no idea."

Dennis passed her and entered the dining room, seeing that most of the tables had been vacated and cleared, and the serving tureens of hot food removed from the dresser.

"I'm sorry, we finish breakfast at ten," said Vernon. "I can ask in the kitchen if they'll—"

"No," said Dennis, picking up a dainty toast rack with three semi-burnt triangles on it, shortly before the crumb-laden table cloth was folded and pulled away from under it. "This'll do. With a glass of water, if that's all right" Vernon glanced at the waitress, who had overheard, and she immediately disappeared to get him one. "Thank you" To his surprise, the owner of the establishment was sitting at one of the tables, sticking gummy labels onto large metal film canisters. Presumably returning them to sender, somewhere in Wardour Street.

"We had a film show for the children last weekend."

Dennis read the hand lettering on the sticky tape around the perimeter of one.

"*The Wizard of Oz*" He remembered Judy Garland being whisked up in a tornado and the strange friends she found—lacking, what was it? The Scarecrow, a brain. The Tin Man, a heart. The Lion, courage.

"They showed it a year or so ago in Hastings, at the Ritz. Mr Crowley was very keen on seeing it at the time. I had to break it to him gently it was a children's film" Vernon smiled, broke off some tape with his teeth. "He said they'd stolen the title from one of his own books, *Liber Oz*. Adamant he could sue, but was 'helpless against the lawyers of Mammon'. He said he doubted that in Hollywood they even knew 'Oz' was Hebrew for goat, even though they're virtually all Hebrews themselves."

Dennis chose not to spoil Vernon's story, or AC's high dudgeon, but in fact, the Frank Baum classic was published a good forty years before Crowley's *Oz* saw the light of day.

"Apparently the housekeeper of Orson Welles contacted him— you know, the *Citizen Kane* chap? Said he was interested in magic. Asked Mr C to send one of his books. He did, but alas, heard no more."

"Well, the film industry is fickle" Dennis took the glass of water from the girl and nodded his appreciation.

"He did see *Spellbound*, though, he told me. 'Most disappointing. Not a single actual spell from beginning to end!'"

Dennis had been good friends with Alfred Hitchcock and his wife Alma before the war. The director had even asked him to write a scenario about the bombing of London. Dennis remembered how his cherubic face would light up, intoxicated by each new idea. He'd also bought the film rights to *The Forbidden Territory* to make with George Du Maurier playing the Duke. He loved the sledge scenes in the snow, the aeroplanes, the gunfight with the Reds, the mad dash to the frontier, but because of contractual wrangling it wasn't made with Hitch at the helm, and the poor old Duke ended up being Ronald Squire.

He dared not let the cat out of the bag that Hitchcock had made overtures more recently via his agent to adapt *The Devil Rides Out*, though he wanted to 'tone down the black magic' and keep it entirely psychological. "No Bela Lugosi moments. Nobody disappearing in a puff of smoke like Abanazer in a panto," and he wanted to change the setting to America. "They understand the Devil in California."

This wasn't a problem for Dennis, who remembered Crowley saying he'd attended black masses in New York and London alike— "in either case rather a bore unless you get a thrill out of blasphemy". Hitch's casting ideas were the stuff of dreams, though:

Basil Rathbone as the Duke de Richleau. Errol Flynn as Rex Van Ryn, the millionaire playboy. Robert Taylor and Barbara Stanwyck, the real-life married stars, as Richard and Marie-Lou Eaton. Hitch had even asked Dennis to meet them in September when they were passing through Southampton. He had, and was sold the moment he met them. But what of Mocata, the slug-like head Satanist with bald head and hypnotic eyes? It could only be that perennial Hitchcock favourite: Peter Lorre. As Crowley would say, 'another ghastly foreigner' in the Wheatley *oeuvre*. Dennis would have to admit, if pushed, he'd prefer Charles Laughton.

"Will you be going down to see the procession this evening?" Vernon stacked the film cans. "It's quite a sight. Not to be missed. And the first since before the war. Guaranteed to be spectacular."

Dennis had no idea what he was talking about, and out of the corner of his eye had caught sight of Miss Clarke returning from upstairs.

"He will see you now." She reminded him of that comical radio show again, *ITMA*, and its catch phrase: "*Can I do you now sir?*"

He went back upstairs, but Vernon continued as if he was still in the room.

"You'd think people would be sick of explosions. Quite the opposite. I swear, last year a crowd started queuing up at 6 a.m. outside a firework shop in Grand Parade, and by 8 a.m. it was seven deep down Grand Parade and up London Road. The man sold out his entire stock and had to bolt and barricade the door. The crowd were shouting 'We want fireworks! We want fireworks!' The door was battered down, all hell broke loose. It's a miracle noone was hurt. The things people will do for a bit of fun, eh?"

*
**

Crowley was sitting up now, dressed in his tweeds and plus fours, but Dennis couldn't tell if he'd got to that position by his own physical effort unaided. His thin legs hung off the bed. His head was bowed, his hands either side of him. He didn't look up, breathing in sighs like an old, broken bellows. "I have a pistol in my suitcase with six rounds in it," said Dennis.

"You seriously think you can Richard Hannay your way out of this one? You have no conception of what we are up against" One hand on the head board, Crowley hoisted himself shakily to his feet. "I knew a fakir in India who could catch a bullet in his teeth. I guarantee if you fired a revolver directly at Lamont's face he'll do the same."

Dennis laughed. "That's nothing but market square chicanery."

"Then he'd not only kill the child and the woman, he'd come for you, and your loved ones. Is that what you want?" Dennis couldn't hide his exasperation. "Have you not listened to a word I've said? He's a magician, and an incredibly powerful one. You can't stop him with brute force and a pop gun. He'll stop the bullet in the barrel. Or just as likely turn the barrel back at you."

"You're making it sound like some Walt Disney cartoon."

"I assure you, it is anything but." Crowley's semi-opaque eyes suddenly bored directly into his own. "The forces he manipulates are real. And the ones we must use against him are real too. If we have faith enough."

"So that's why I'm here? Because I have faith?"

"Partly, yes."

"Partly? What is the other part?"

Without breaking eye contact, Crowley shambled over to him, silently sliding his slippered feet over the carpet, and placed the flat of his hand on Dennis's heart.

"The blood pumping in your veins. It doesn't help anything or anyone. We need to slow down your *chittam*" Dennis recognised the Sanskrit word for mental activity, not that it did him any good. "But, most importantly of all, don't be ashamed of being afraid. This will likely be the most dangerous magical ritual you'll ever be involved in."

"No," said Dennis, removing the hand. "It'll be the *only* one."

A brisk knock reverberated on the door.

"Yes," said Crowley. "Come in."

"Miss Clark said you wanted to see me?"

"Yes, Vernon, would you be good enough to clear the room of all but the most essential furniture, please? That can go. That can go. The bed will have to go, obviously. I'm sure there's a place you can store it all, temporarily."

"Er…"

"Keep that. I need that. And that. Everything else…Basically what we need is a space of six foot radius, twelve feet in diameter. Minimum. I think we can do it, just about. And, oh, lift up the carpet. We need the bare floorboards. That isn't too much trouble, is it? And sealing tape, and a quantity of salt, if your wife in the kitchen would be so kind."

Crowley lifted a wrinkled khaki mackintosh from the hook behind the door. Dennis helped him insert his twig-like arms into the sleeves.

"Where will you sleep tonight?" asked Vernon, bewildered, when the other two had moved out onto the landing.

"We shan't be sleeping tonight," said Crowley, a sheaf of rolled up papers under one arm. "We shall be working"

When they entered the Dance Hall, a detached building on the south side of the house, they let in a flurry of dry orange and yellow leaves which quickly fell to the floor, scampering briefly like vermin, then dying as Dennis closed the door and Crowley bolted it. Dennis had been worried about the older man slipping in the muddy grass and going flying, but Crowley had seemed almost powered by a constant, stumbling tilt as he hurried down the lawn—*Oh dear! I shall be late!* Though no white rabbits this time—and in fact Dennis had had trouble keeping up. Now they were both panting, ludicrously, as if they'd run a sprint.A projection screen had been set up in front of a proscenium arch framed by moth-eaten red curtains. Not exactly Drury Lane, Dennis thought, and just about on a par with the average village hall. Folding wooden chairs arranged in rows facing the large white, expectant rectangle. Of course. The children's film show Vernon had mentioned.

"Did you enjoy the flying monkey scene?"

Crowley didn't look up from the bundles of paper he was unravelling on the billiard table at the back of the hall. "Reminded me of the Battle of Britain."

"Making fun of the bravery of those young men who fought and died for king and country is low, even for you."

"What has this country ever done for me? Nothing but ridiculed me and pilloried me. Certainly not even begun to try to understand me."

"Perish the thought, but perhaps the Second World War wasn't about you."

"Of course not. It was about the conflict of Good and Evil, the Forces of Light versus the Forces of Darkness, and for many that's a deeply reassuring world view, and to many the alternative would be unpalatable. They prefer not to consider that even Satan is a fallen angel. The *Daily Mail* tells them otherwise. Oh, I'm sorry. You were serialised in the *Daily Mail*, weren't you?"

Dennis's anger rose up again. Not just at the idle taunt, which was nothing, but remembering Joan and what had happened when he wasn't there to protect her.

"Anyway, we should be thinking about the enemy ahead of us." Crowley spread the sheets of paper over the green baize surface and Dennis couldn't help but be reminded of the Chiefs of Staff poring over maps in the War Cabinet. The idea that Lamont saw himself as some kind of Second Coming reminded him with no little irony that one of his more outlandish plans while working at the London Controlling Section of the Joint Planning Staff was the idea of spreading rumours in Germany of a new Christ figure as an alternative to Hitler.

"What rough beast…" He said idly, quoting Yeats.

"That fair-weather friend" Crowley bristled. "Jealous of me because I was clearly the greater poet."

"Obviously" Dennis had no idea that the animosities cultivated in the crucible of the Golden Dawn still cut quite so deep.

"As Lamont grows strong, I grow weak. I'm under no illusion about that. He hasn't finished me off yet, but time is of the essence. Even the most basic Abra-Melin ritual normally requires at least six months retirement from daily life, and constant prayer and meditation to your guardian angel. We don't have that luxury."

Dennis walked over to switch on the electric lights above the table, then returned to look down at the sheet Crowley was stretching out flat under the trio of lampshades. It was greaseproof paper, the kind they use for wrapping meat in a butcher's shop, daubed with a geometrical pattern in coloured crayon, a circle divided into segment annotated with symbols. Dennis instantly recognised it as an astrological chart.

"The residents often ask me to do them a 'horror' as they call it. I've done his. She couldn't tell me the hour of his birth but she could tell me the date, month, year."

"Scorpio. Not astonishing."

"It's imprecise, admittedly—but enough to show his auspices."

"And this is important because?"

"Because, like Hitler before him, he will be keenly aware of significant astrological dates, both general ones in the northern hemisphere such as the coming autumnal equinox on 30th November and, more importantly, pivotal ones relevant to himself. It's equally important to consider ours" He revealed two more sheets under the first and arranged all three side by side, using strategically-placed billiard balls as paper weights. "You were born on January 8th, within three days of the centre of the Sun's period in Capricorn. That sign is ruled by Saturn, and Saturn's number is eight—the same as your name, 'Dennis Wheatley', numerologically speaking. Saturn is a malefic influence, usually, but you have Leo in the ascendant. The Moon is in close trine to both Uranus and Saturn, the depositor of the sun in Capricorn. The sun itself is in trine to Jupiter. The result being the most favourable position, promising protection, wealth, fame. You're unconvinced."

Dennis wasn't aware his face was so easy to read.

"My wealth and fame are factual."

"So is astrology. If you extract it from the buffoons, it's as fundamentally true as mathematics. Why would we not be affected by the planets? Is a grain of sand on a beach not affected by the vast swell of the ocean?"

"Good point."

"I know. I won't bore you with my own. Suffice it to say that there's a Full Moon on 29th October at nine oh six. If we don't act before then, our chances of success diminish rapidly."

"The planets are no longer on our side."

"Inelegantly put, but correct" Crowley gathered the astrological charts towards him and rolled them up together in a scroll which he bound with a thick elastic band he had kept around one wrist.

"Which means what?"

"It means we have to act now, or not at all."

"Then we should discuss a plan."

"No. A plan is already in progress. You merely have to obey my instructions to the letter."

Dennis blinked, then laughed. He wasn't sure why. It was certainly not even remotely funny.

Crowley walked over to a blackboard, clearly set up either to instruct the children or for them to play with. He made wide arcs with a duster, rubbing out naive images of a ladybird and a caterpillar, the sweet hieroglyphics of a nature-loving infant, and the ubiquitous 'Chad'—which took him back to the uniformed young man he'd met on the train.

"Gisela came to see me last night, a few hours after you'd left. She didn't need to say she feared for her life and that of her child. I knew that to be the case simply by looking at her. The poor thing was on the very fringes of crumbling, and believe me I have more experience than most of women being on the fringes of crumbling" Crowley stared at the blackboard, took a stick of chalk from a packet layered with white dust. "I gave her a handkerchief with this written on it in black ink" He drew a triangle within three circles, with two crosses outside it, which Dennis vaguely remembered from either Frances Barrett or Lévi. "In the triangle I enclosed the name 'Choronzon.' On each side, three sacred names from the Goetia— ANAPHAXETON, ANAPHANETON, PRIMEUMATON…at the vertices MI—CH—EL, because she needs the archangel's fiery sword as protection."

"I don't understand a word you are talking about," said Dennis.

"Why would you? I would hardly expect you to grasp in an instant what I have been studying for over fifty years" Crowley completed the 'MI—CH—EL' and stood back and admired his handiwork. "I told her to slip it into her boyfriend's pocket when he returns from the pub at half past eight. That's the time he habitually returns, on the dot she says, wanting his supper waiting for him before he goes to bed. I told her in no uncertain terms, it's imperative he have it in his possession when we carry out our evocation. Her failure to do so would not only jeopardise our chances, but seriously endanger us. She understands that, but we can't risk her failing to fulfil her end of the bargain. We have to know she's done it before we proceed. I've given her some of my sedative to put in his booze when he gets home. He may or may not drink it, and she may or may not be too scared to carry it out for fear of getting caught, we simply don't know. But if she accomplishes those two things, I told her to get out of the flat—tell him she is going to take the baby to see the fireworks— and instead take herself to a room I've booked in her name at the Queen's Hotel on the seafront. She needs to be well away from the place when Lamont has his uninvited visitor."

After several swipes with the duster, the sorcerous circle on the blackboard was completely obliterated.

"That's the most dangerous part for her. If he intuits it's a ruse, and decides to go with her, it will all come crashing down on us. I have performed some rites to protect her, but they may not be enough. His attachment to her is strong, a psychic leash, and if it's tugged by us, we have no guarantee he won't feel it."

Crowley placed the duster back where he'd found it.

"Before we go through with the ritual, we have to be absolutely certain for our own safety she has carried out what I demanded of her. She needs to provide us with a sign. I gave her the handkerchief in an old cigar box. If she has, she will leave it, empty, on the steps of St Clement Church in Swan Terrace, near the High Street, by 9 p.m.—I want you to go down and fetch it. If it's not there, the plan is aborted. If it's there and it's empty, we will know what we have to do."

He looked at Dennis but Dennis's face must have appeared blank. "Does what I've said make sense to you?"

"No, to be honest."

"I'm not interested in your honesty. Will you do it?"

No other answer was possible under the circumstances.

"Yes."

A loud bang reverberated in the sky above the roof, followed by a piercing, prolonged rat-tat-tat, and he instinctively looked up, flinched and ducked slightly. Crowley did not respond, calmly returning the stick of chalk to its pack and putting it deep into one pocket of his mackintosh.

"Now we must cleanse ourselves in preparation. Not exactly the Roman *thermae*, Indonesian *okup* or Arabic *hammam*, but close enough. In the Islamic faith it's customary before prayer to perform *ghusl* for the full body and *wudu*, for the face, hands and feet" Crowley walked towards a door marked with the words STEAM ROOM. Another firework, somewhere more distant than the first pair, futted and pop-popped ineffectually.

"Who, or what, is Choronzon?" asked Dennis before following.

Crowley hesitated, without looking back at him, then carried on. "No...You must know. Of course you must know..." With a creak of the door, or of his own limbs, the hunched, brittle figure entered a narrow, white-tiled corridor. "Come along. Strip off. All boys together."

Crowley divested himself of his raincoat, tweed jacket, plus fours and yellow stockings, leaving them scattered on a low wooden bench. Dennis pretended not to notice the dots of blood on his white shirt sleeves. Crowley seemed to get even smaller as he undressed, tiny, bird-like, displaying the terrible toll of muscle wastage through inactivity common to elderly people. Rotating under the cold shower, his wet skin sagged loosely as if he were wearing that of another person, which in effect he was—that of his younger, larger self. He was unembarrassed by his nakedness while

Dennis, self-conscious about his body at the best of times, was hasty to wrap a towel around his midriff. The door shut heavily as they entered the small, boarded cabinet in the centre of which grey coals emitted a wave of heat. Crowley sat, then immediately rose and used a ladle to sprinkle water over them. The room filled with a thick steam, rendering Dennis's view of his companion as opaque as if through a wall of early morning mist. Within seconds he felt his skin exuding a layer of sweat, and before much longer it was running down his face and back in warm rivulets. He'd enjoyed a Turkish bath many times in London, but this felt different—the hot, dry air lacked any humidity, and very soon the breath in his lungs and throat felt on fire. On top of which, this was altogether too claustrophobic. Far too reminiscent of a padded cell.

Crowley, however, seemed to have no such misgivings—this thing was probably designed to help such ailments as his asthma, after all—and leaned back against the slatted wall, resting the back of his head against it as perspiration ran down his beard, neck and hairless chest. Dennis couldn't help observing healed scars all over his forearms, and several more criss-crossing his upper arms and torso. Old scars, perhaps decades old. He wondered what kind of ceremonies, to what kind of ends, demanded such actions, but, on consideration, thought it best not to find out.

"Have you encountered the shadow?"

"Only in the books of Carl Gustav Jung," said Dennis.

"Not in a book, in life. I have. Very much so. My quest to be a future *bodhisattva* or enlightened being led me there. My search for my divine nature. But what I met was pestilence" Dennis listened patiently as Crowley wiped his face and then his eyes with both hands, then leaned forward, elbows on knees. "Almost thirty years ago, I met Victor Neuburg, a talented medium and suitable apprentice. All too eager to suck at the teat of Crowleyanity and call me master. Happy to commit his life to magical philosophy and total obedience. I'd discovered sex could be in high praise of the gods, you see. Ecstasy a short cut to enhance and amplify what could be achieved magically. Heresy to the Golden Dawn, middle class nonentities who felt it incumbent on them to be judge and jury to my libertine ways. If they wanted to stay safely in their Rosicrucian rot, so be it. I knew the truth. That sex and magic were part of the same vision. I had to follow my own path, whether others had the courage to follow me or not."

"And Victor did."

The silent mist from the stones grew thicker. The two men sat swathed in clouds as they might be on the roof of the world, where many go to find enlightenment, and others plunge to their deaths, their frozen bodies littering the slopes for other climbers to find or trudge past in their quest for the peak.

"We were both desperate to leave real life behind, shrug off the deadening quicksand of family, friends, responsibilities, to embark on an adventure of pure mental power, wherever it might lead us… " Crowley stroked his bare upper arms. "We performed our rites in Paris, then subsequently Algeria. Victor shaved his head. I grew a beard. In the Muslim villages they took me as a prophet. No less than I deserved, I thought. We committed every sacrilege known to Man, and quite a few of our own invention. We were the kings and queens of Sodom. We explored *per manu, per os, per vas nefandum*— fuelled by copious doses of hashish and mescalin, wandering ever deeper into the Sahara. Day after day, night after night, without food or water, beyond exhaustion, buoyed only by the repetition of ancient chants. We worshipped with fire and blood and semen, and damn the world while we did so. Depravity was the order of the day and our aim was to escape. To cut the guy ropes. To float. We reached below civilisation, all civilisations, stuck our hands in the cracks, and the spiders crawled out."

Dennis listened in slow-baked silence, watching a glassy bead of sweat trickle down the line of Crowley's nose until it dropped to the floor.

"We continued into the heart of the desert, wearing only robes and reading the Qur'an. We reached Bou-Sâada. The sun blinded us. The rocks cut our feet to ribbons. Finally our brains opened. We did not read the great mysteries. The great mysteries read us. I stared into the stone and asked for guidance. Aiwass, my guardian angel, only spoke the last words of Jesus. *Eloi, Eloi, lama sabachthani?*

It frightened me to death that he might have abandoned me. But I couldn't give up. We had come too far. We had to see this through, come what may."

Salty perspiration ran into Dennis's eyes and he had to shut them. But that only made the mental images Crowley was painting all the more vivid.

"We built a circle in stones and waited for night. Again, we gathered the unspeakable names of God in the sand. With shaking hands we partook of the elixir sacred to Jupiter and attempted to reach what Dee called the 'accursed' 10th Aethyr. The colours of the camp fire kept changing. Intense yellow embers spat skyward, mocking our efforts, sending microscopic fireflies sailing up into the nothingness. We were those fireflies. Less than those fireflies. But we were unrelenting. Finally the path across the Abyss was within our grasp—but Choronzon guarded the higher levels. He whom Edward Kelly called 'The Mighty Devil'—the primal and most dangerous of all evil powers. With supreme arrogance, I called upon him to take form. 'This broiling beast and broken daisy,' I said, 'are at your mercy. Reward us with your hatred and indifference.' The demon replied through Victor: 'I bow to thee.' Meaning that it did no such thing. It would not let us through. The payment it demanded was our souls. And the only way we could offer that was in an act that you would call indecency" Crowley's eyes glazed over. "... But I will tell you, we achieved the bright light of holy ecstasy in Bou-Sâada. It was the last picking off of my old snake skin. The new snake wriggled free, and when it had, I heard the words that Adam uttered at the gates of hell, 'Zazas, zazas...'—and Choronzon entered, like a drug entering our veins. Victor was thrown from the circle. He fell on the ground, writhing and fighting a naked savage with frothing fangs and an undulating back. I could not breach the circle to help him. I drew my dagger but could only watch helplessly as he screamed. The gate to the 10th Aethyr closed. The demon Choronzon had abandoned us, as a wild creature leaves carrion in its wake."

Dennis looked down at the old man's hand. It might have been his eyes being affected by the intense temperature, but he was sure it was pulsating with a spastic tremor. Again, he wiped his face, from the hairless scalp to the tip of his tiny beard.

"I cradled Victor through the cold of what remained of night. He said not a single word. I felt the breathing in his chest rising and falling and feared at any moment it might stop. I could not move until dawn bled through the sky above the starkness of the dunes. In the morning I let him rest as I lit a bonfire to purify the valley of what we had called to earth, and gave thanks for our salvation."

"Dear God in Heaven," said Dennis, finally able to speak.

"Far from it."

The final stage of ritual purification transformed Dennis's mood, the cold water pouring down over his body reducing his temperature in a blissful instant. He'd thought if he stayed in the steam room a moment longer he may have exploded like a land mine, his innards decorating the polished pine a fetching shade of scarlet. Now, remarkably quickly, he felt human again, as long as he didn't think too much about what the hell he had just been told. If he could step out of the shower and roll into nice crisp linen sheets next to Joan, he would have been in heaven. But, as it was, he knew he had to face Crowley. It was not over. It was not even yet begun. "I was lucky to be alive and far luckier still to be sane" Crowley stood under the spray, head bowed. The water gave his skeletal back and pouched buttocks a silvery sheen. "When we returned to Europe, Victor had a nervous breakdown. His poor, sensitive soul had buckled under the strain. I believe he was treated by ET Jense, a Freudian. We never saw each other again."

Crowley switched off the tap, fleshless breasts hanging, ribs sticking out so sharply Dennis could have counted them. With displeasure he realised then what the old man's emaciated body reminded him of. Richard Dimbleby's words on the wireless came back, unbidden—at the time their calm precision only adding to the dawning horror of bleak revelation. The emptiness of the radio signal had been in some ways worse than the grotesque and appalling images of the liberation of Belsen from Pathé News. Gaunt faces behind wire. A hammock between two soldiers, swung onto the back of a lorry, containing a thing that used to be a man or woman. Disease-ridden clothes piled in mountains and scorched out of existence by flame throwers. The place and memory not so easy to burn away.

"He is the one we must evoke for our purpose," said Crowley. "Choronzon, 333, Noznoroch, Dweller in the Abyss. Lord of Tophet, the Hebrew Hell. The most terrifying, powerful being I have ever encountered. Voracious. Cruel. Unthinking. Yet it toyed with us. Wormed through our minds. But he has no will, no true being, so he can be manipulated. For a price. Any unprotected soul he encounters he will destroy with fire, in mockery of the flaming bush in *Exodus* that burned but was not eradicated. It is his way of saying he is more powerful, more merciless, than God Himself. It is he we must send to do our bidding."

"Marvellous," said Dennis, not without an edge of sarcasm. He grappled to find a sane person's response to such information. Perhaps Crowley already knew there was none.

"Evil forces are like fire, or electricity, they can be called up for man's purposes. You can bind and control them to an extent, if you're clever, but woe betide the person who doesn't know what he's doing."

"But you *do* know what you're doing" Dennis tried to make it sound like a statement, rather than a question.

"I've opened the gates of Hell once. I can do so again."

"And once this—this 'Choronzon' is unleashed, how do we prevent it turning on ourselves, if that isn't blindingly obvious?"

"No. Not at all. Good question. Dee and Kelly said Choronzon is held in check by Babalon-Astarte, Hierodule of Heaven, the third *sephirah* of the Tree of Life. It is she we must summon to appease him when he has completed our task. I will take care of that."

Dennis pulled on his Argyle socks and tied his shoelaces. Crowley sat next to him, face beetroot, arms, legs and body the colour of a parchment in the British Museum.

"But we must be vigilant. In his cleverness he creates the illusion your mind is your own. Remember at all times, Choronzon is entirely power. Power over those who are blind to it. And it is blind itself. Like the Hiroshima obscenity. It is menstruation and catastrophe, a blend of blood and bomb. Both an energy spectre and a Warrior Lord. Horror made flesh. Made fire."

"And you would still call him up a second time," said Dennis. "After what happened to Victor? Knowing the risk to your own sanity, and life?"

As he towelled his neck and armpits, Crowley did not answer, at least, not directly. "What we must remember, above all, is that when you hurl magic at someone who has the power to hurl it back at you, it can rebound. When you climb a dangerous mountain, it's wise to be strapped securely to another, in case the snow gives way underneath your feet. Without it, I plummet into the abyss. With you, I have a chance" Crowley's eyes, sunk in that waxy, time-ravaged countenance, blinked once and turned with infinite sadness to fall on those of the man sitting next to him. "You are my only *chela* now."

The Sanskrit word for loyal disciple. The hairs on the nape of Dennis's neck stood on end. He felt both unexpectedly touched, and, at the same time, and to an equal and opposite degree, a sense of being utterly and irrevocably condemned.

*
**

"Careful."Crowley brushed a smattering of small leaves from his jacket. He'd been so fixated on lighting his Meerschaum pipe that he'd veered into a privet hedge as they'd come out of the Dance Hall. Luckily Dennis had caught him by the elbow.

"Dreadful bore. Things in reality are blurred, you see, increasingly—but it's not altogether unpleasant, or inappropriate" Gouts of smoke issued from the bowl of the pipe as he sucked, making cavernous holes of already hollow cheeks. "A clouding of the eye. I forget the exact diagnosis. Magowan insisted I give up. Made no difference, so I risked half a pipe. Then I'm lost. I'm always lost" He pocketed his box of matches. Consigned the dead one to the flower beds.

Dennis offered his elbow, but halfway across the lawn Crowley needed to loosen a build-up of phlegm in his chest, and lapsed into the most wretched series of coughs. He waved away any attempt to help him and instead staggered to an old oak tree, which he leaned against with an outstretched arm, allowing, when he could, a grim, brownish string of saliva to dribble down onto the green tufts at its foot. He patted his mouth with the back of one hand, afterwards wiping its mottled surface dry with a voluminous white handkerchief as he looked up through the mesh of branches.

"The Tree of Life."

"Spreading where it will."

Dennis saw that the old man's other hand was placed close to a horizontal line carved deep into the bark.

"To be sure," Crowley mused, turning to rest his back against the trunk. "Loved by some. Detested by others. Betrayed by all and sundry…We should go inside."

"There's no hurry. They'll be emptying your room. We'll only get in the way. Take your time" Indeed, he could hear activity, and see it, in the upper window.

Crowley steadily caught his breath. "That ghastly woman, saying in her book I used black magic. I had to sue for libel. No choice after the *Express* made me destitute."

"I remember. His Satanic Majesty in the dock. You lost."

"Judge said I had no reputation to besmirch" Crowley grunted. "At least the world was reminded I still existed."

"Even if the costs flattened you."

"On the steps of the Old Bailey a girl of nineteen prostrated herself at my feet, saying she wanted to have my love child. The very definition, I'd say, of every cloud having a silver lining." The wizened face lightened impishly. "It would have been churlish to say no."

Dennis almost smiled. He saw a tennis ball near his foot and rolled it under the sole of his shoe.

"She gave me a son, you know. I named him Aleister Atatürk.

No baptism, on pain of death. Little mite came into this world on Mayday. Pagan approval in the bag. As soon as war broke out, they were both evacuated. Next I heard, they were safe in Yugoslavia, but we lost touch completely. She had no interest in a religious or mystical life, you see—either mine or hers. We parted company and that was that; an arrangement that suited us both. Then, wildly unexpectedly, she contacted me. Back in Blighty. Beyond a miracle. I was flabbergasted they weren't dead. Her voice on the telephone! The girl Pat. I was delirious. 'We're coming Thursday!' This was the middle of May, just gone, soon after his tenth birthday."

Dennis realised what he should have at first glance—that the line cut into the tree, now just below Crowley's shoulder, marked the height of a ten-year-old boy.

"They stayed two days. Left on the Saturday. It was the most joyous two days, I think, of my entire life."

The chill, autumnal air eked a tear from the corner of Crowley's semi-vacant, semi-perplexed eye. He stared up into the branches from a grey head as far from the colour of flesh as was the bark, seeming to be succumbing to the seasonal decay of the wood and leaves around him.

"I thought they were dead, you see. Both…dead."

Dennis picked up the tennis ball as he listened. He watched as the man he'd seen up the ladder and another man lugged a bed frame in the direction of the Dance Hall, but his attention was on what Crowley was saying.

"I wrote to the lad since. Trying to say the kinds of thing a father ought. I said his visit made me intensely happy, and that I was glad to hear he was reading, because with reading, well, oceans divide, clouds open, worlds appear. Don't listen to the masters on the subject of copperplate, I said, develop your own style of hand-writing. Listen to no-one—impress your personality on the reader in your own way. Resist conformity. Be yourself. Devote yourself to Latin and all other European languages will follow."

Dennis remembered vividly running away from home when he had Latin the next day, and the beating his father, eyes like granite, had given him with a belt. The experience didn't enamour him to the subject.

"Above all," continued Crowley, "know thyself. Learn chess. Chess teaches one everything about the human animal. Learn Shakespeare and the Book of Job. Grammar, syntax, logic. To write correctly is to think correctly. We are surrounded by blunderers in reason."

"Hear, hear," said Dennis, who then threw the ball in the direction of the tennis court, hoping it would clear the fence. It didn't, and fell ignominiously to the ground. "I'll never play for England."

Crowley broke out of his reverie. "I've never asked about your children."

Dennis sighed. "I have a son, Anthony, from my first marriage, a failure on all fronts. Not him, dear God, no—or her, for that matter. Me." He shook a cigarette into his hand and hunted down his lighter before realising it was back on the armchair in his bedroom at Grove Place where Joan had tossed it. Crowley offered him the matchbox, so he used it. "I was bored to tears pushing a pram. My idea of a holiday isn't the seaside and sandcastles, it's lobster at the Hotel St Regis in Paris washed down with a bottle of Cliquot '06." He blew smoke. "I liked the Turkey Trot and the tango too much."

Crowley understood exactly what he meant, and that made Dennis blush for the innuendo.

"And Joan?"

Dennis's jaw tightened. He tried desperately to show nothing. He didn't know why he had already told Crowley so much, but he had done. Now he was afraid what his avoidance of an answer might spark.

"She came along with four in tow. Adults now, the boys. Bill and Jack more like younger brothers to me. And Diana, Little Miss Woolly Head, she'll always be a disaster waiting to happen. We got her a job during the war as a filing clerk, but she got sacked after four weeks for high heels and furtive cigarettes. She's only interested in one thing." He didn't say what. It wasn't necessary to elaborate. "Dresses like the worst kind of shop girl. It makes me cringe."

Crowley did not give the kind of knowing grin Dennis expected. On the contrary, deep in more personal thoughts, he wandered from the oak tree towards something in the grass and, one by one, picked up three cricket stumps that had evidently been left by the children. He looked at them as though they were fascinating archaeological finds from a long lost dynasty, then momentarily looked up, squinting, at a break in the clouds.

"The I-Ching directed us to a small sea port, barely more than one street, thirty-seven miles from Palermo. A villa. Everyone hated it, but it faced the sea. The children ran around free, like chickens. Nut brown. No restrictions. No rules. No clothes. No gas. No electricity. No plumbing. Two Persian nut trees." He pressed the point of one cricket stump into the grass. "The throne of The Beast in the east. The Scarlet Woman's throne opposite. The main room I called the Whore's Cell." He pressed down the second a few inches away from the first. "Circle on the floor, altar in the centre. Soror Cypris—Ninette—had two children. I renamed them Hermes and Dionysus." He stuck the third stump in the ground, parallel to the other two. "Anne Léa popped out of her mother's womb. Not a well little thing from the start. One of the little boys said in French: 'Why she looks no bigger than a doll, a *poupée*. So 'Poupée' she was. We fed her on goat's milk, since goat's milk nourished Jupiter. Love is the law. Love under will." Crowley leaned on a garden fork abandoned in one of the plots. He needed it, like a shooting stick, to support him. "We gave solar salutations. Soror Cypris and Soror Alostrael fought like cats. Jealous bitches. Not so much a ménage as a morass. Never a dull moment. But she never got better, my Poupée…" He wiped his nose, which was running in the cold. "I watched her wasting away, as we all got filthy and mad. The I-Ching had predicted her birth. 'Dimunition.' So I constructed her chart. Saturn and the Sun both opposed Mars. It told us the end was near. Weeks. Days. I howled like some creature in a zoo. Painting, insomnia, heroin, cocaine…How could I clear my mind for the Great Work, when my baby…" He stuffed the handkerchief back in his pocket. "We tried sex magic. It was useless. I had to walk out. *Coitus interruptus.* Ha!—Doctor. Hospital.

And one day I came home to find her mother, Alostrael, alone, sobbing."

Dennis could see that hearing it afresh, in his own words, had torn apart something inside Crowley anew. Re-opened the most awful wound, the most terrible memory imaginable. He didn't know if he was strangely privileged to be included in such thoughts, or merely invisible.

The two handymen returned from the Dance Hall to the house. His back to them, Crowley swayed as if buffeted by the all too insignificant breeze.

"We went to our temple and immersed ourselves in twentyfour hours of fasting, supplication and prayers for her journey into the next life. Knowing, as we did, that a Thelemite's immortal soul completes its ordained task in its earthly body then quits this place, whether it has spent seventy years or…"

Dennis did not want to hear more, or to endure any more of the man's pain. Or watch him endure it either. He took two steps closer. Then two more.

"Let's go inside," he said softly. "I…I'll order some tea."

"Tea!" Crowley roared a laugh both appallingly loud and absent of mirth. "Oh, that's delightful! *Tea!*"

He grimaced at Dennis suddenly with an expression transformed from pitiful sadness to one of ferocious disgust.

"You really *do* understand nothing. What was I even *thinking* by inviting you here? If you had forty or fifty cuts on your arms I might *begin* to believe you are up to the job."

Dennis was so taken aback as to be speechless. He had not been spoken to as if he was an incompetent and stupid child since the perpetual conflicts with his father, and wasn't prepared to put up with it as an adult from anyone—nor did he have to. But Crowley was shuffling off in the direction of the house, already too far away to call back with anything but a shout Dennis was loath to adopt, now that he saw the two Sapphic ladies, the rock and the tree, standing over by the path to the tennis court, staring at him blankly, arm in arm.

How much had they heard? Crowley's parting outburst, or more?

He couldn't tell from their expressions. Were they shocked, or did they always look like that, pained and rather disapproving? What was he supposed to say? He hadn't the faintest idea.

To his rescue, a screech cut through the air and after four or five seconds the stick of a spent rocket landed amongst the ornamental ferns, still spouting a purple-grey tail of smoke. The two women redirected their stares accordingly. Dennis hurried over, picked it up and doused it in a water butt.

"Sorry." He had no need to apologise, but it was what Englishmen said when they didn't know what to say. "Sorry."

The two women went inside, making a point not to look at him, and that made him feel that they regarded him as shifty, so he smiled, whether they could see it or not. And as soon as they were out of sight, damn it all, took out his cigarette case, put one on his lower lip, realised he had neither lighter nor matches, and thought damn it all again.

The cigarette went back in its case as he watched the two men again, this time carrying a mattress—mottled with ancient, unidentified stains—to the Dance Hall. He nodded hello as they passed, and they did likewise, one mopping imaginary sweat from his brow. In no immediate hurry to follow Crowley indoors, he sat on a wall and watched them bring out the divan, the two straightbacked chairs, a tea chest full of books, and a mercifully empty but flowery chamber pot. To be honest, he didn't like prolonging situations of conflict at the best of times, and he didn't want to prolong this one with Crowley. What the man had said was obnoxious and horribly ungrateful—*Scars?* Where had that come from? Had he seen Dennis looking at them?—And *he* didn't know why he was there either. Come to think of it, why didn't he just fetch his suitcase, get in his car, and drive home? All he'd done was offer a modicum of sympathy, only to get his head bitten off.

Then he told himself to grow up and be sensible. The man had dredged up dark feelings about his daughter's tragic death. Was it any surprise the shutters had come down? Was it really any wonder anger had boiled to the surface, along with guilt, regret and unbelievable sorrow? And he was in the firing line—so what? Didn't

Crowley deserve a *little* more psychological understanding, rather than Dennis's selfish petulance?

Finally, a rolled-up Persian carpet, sagging in a slight V between the two men's shoulders, emerged and was stored with the rest of the furniture from Room 13, and Dennis decided it was time to gird his loins, go inside, and face The Beast.

*
**

The Spitfire-shaped cigarette lighter on the bureau in the lobby beckoned. Using it in passing, feeling the welcome rush of nicotine relax him as he inhaled, Dennis glanced into the lounge. The followers of Sappho briefly looked up from perusing guide books, a white-haired old gent he hadn't seen before sat immersed in *Hangover Square* by Patrick Hamilton, and Basil Radford was snoozing by the picture window overlooking the garden, his blanket an open copy of *The Times*, threatening to slide to the floor with every rise and fall of his gigantic belly—a scene of pure suspense worthy of Hitchcock himself.Dennis climbed the stairs and considered knocking on Crowley's door, but on reflection thought it best, and safer, to give him a bit longer to calm down and have the pleasure of his own company for a while. The door to his own room lay open and his suitcase sat on the bed. He remembered he hadn't yet unpacked. He closed the bedroom door after him, yet still felt there was precious little privacy in this commune of the dubious and displaced. Happily, at least the *Forbidden Lecture* was gone from the bedside table.

He took out his clothes and hung them in the wardrobe. Returning to the suitcase and taking out his pyjamas, he stopped dead, realising he'd forgotten to pack the framed picture of Joan. His heart sank like lead. She'd been taken away when he needed her close to him more than ever before. But what had he done when they last spoke, except force her away? God, he was an imbecile. It made him irrationally upset, not having her with him in some form, but there was nothing he could do about it now. He had to roll with that particular punch.

He looked down at the Smith & Wesson, sat as it was on a spare towel he didn't need since Netherwood supplied one— albeit like cardboard, over there by the sink. He shut the suitcase, lifted it to the floor and slid it underneath the bed.

Hang it. If the mountain wouldn't come to Mohammed…

He crossed the landing and knocked on the door to Room 13.

No answer.

He turned the handle and went in.

The space, completely denuded of clutter, seemed twice, if not five times, as large with the furniture absent, a bare stage set without the benefit of scenery added, waiting for the actors to populate it and bring to it some fakery of life. The curtains were drawn and the light was on, a single bulb under a flesh-coloured lamp shade, with a kneeling figure below it. Crowley, knees resting on a cushion, hammering a nail into a floor board, a ball of string and a footruler either side of him. Dennis noticed an opened box of white candles and two large bags of salt, as yet unopened.

"We don't know the extent of his powers of self-protection. We can only make our own as strong as possible."

Crowley didn't look up at him, and Dennis was relieved that he behaved as though their previous conversation in the garden had never taken place. Perhaps he had blanked it out, as he had blanked out, of necessity, the death of Poupée. Dennis did not know how any father could survive such a thing. He could forgive him, now, for behaving as he had—even if he couldn't forgive him much else. And if if the man couldn't bear to meet his eyes at this moment, he would allow him that, too.

Crowley tied the loose end of the ball of string to the nail and measured, with the ruler, a length from it of about six feet. He then knotted the far end to a stick of the chalk he'd pocketed in the Dance Hall, and pulled it taut before circumnavigating the room, bent over almost double, with his hand touching the floor, shuffling backwards, creating a chalk-marked circle as he did so. When it was done he straightened, wincing at the pain in his lower back, groaning and blowing out air.

"What's the time?"

Dennis looked at his watch. "Ten past three."

"Good. You have six hours before you collect the cigar box on the steps of the church. Use that time to rest. Purge your thoughts. Think only of the task ahead."

The task you very kindly told me I'm not up to, thought Dennis. But that seemed to be forgotten. As his father very quickly forgot his maniacal rants, but left the family around him nursing shrapnel wounds for days.

"Have you kept up with your meditation?"

Dennis frowned.

"You told me you were taking lessons from Rollo Ahmed."

"That was donkey's years ago. Yes, Joan and I had a few classes. But we were too busy with other things at the time to continue." He saw Crowley turn away, irritated. "I remember the fundamentals though."

"How to breathe."

"How to breathe. Exactly."

"I do hope you remember that, at least," said Crowley. "How to breathe."

He took the Oriental rug off a Chinese chest, the only article left behind on his explicit instructions. Dennis could not make out what was inside, apart from some silk and a couple of brass candlesticks.

"Leave me. There are preparations I can only do alone. The lesser banishing ritual to rid the workplace of any elemental or planetary forces. The purification of the temple…"

So, Dennis thought, this seedy little bedroom is his 'temple' now? Not exactly the Doric columns of Ancient Greece, or anything approximating the grandeur that was Rome. Just a tawdry attic with well-meaning communists in attendance, not nymphs and shepherds.

"Go. Meditate. Sleep. Pray to your God, if you must do. Then go to the Old Town, without fail. Come to me directly on your return. We will do this together. We *must* do this together."

Dennis nodded, in earnest, even as he saw an element of nervousness cross Crowley's eyes. He didn't want to call it fear— for the simple reason fear was the one thing he didn't want to see, but in a strange way it reassured him that the fellow was human after all, and he clung to that as he turned to leave.

"Wait." Crowley approached him and held out a stone, sixpence and red thread he took from a small pouch. "This is what we call a hag stone, for protection from a magician or the evil eye. It symbolises the coin that covers the eye of the dead, and red—the colour of blood, and the living body. It will protect you against any threats tonight before you enter the protection of the circle."

Crowley placed it in Dennis's jacket pocket.

"Thank you," said Dennis, half-expecting Crowley to say the same thing back to him, but he didn't.

Back in his own room, Dennis found he had been nursing the most intense, throbbing headache, and guessed it was probably due to dehydration. He poured water from the jug, drank two full glasses, and within seconds it had started to lift.He put his jacket on the back of a chair and set the alarm clock for half past six. That would give him plenty of time to get up and make his way to the town centre before nine.

He tugged the curtains closed—sacrilege when it was still broad daylight outside. The absence of Joan's photograph had taken the wind out of his sails; he still felt devastated, but had to put that to the back of his mind now. He needed to relax, and focus, if he could remember how.

He took off his tie, placed his shoes beside the bed, pulled his shirt-tails out of his trousers, and unbuttoned his shirt and cuffs. He stood with his legs set apart, arms at his side and for ten minutes, eyes closed, took in deep breaths through his nose and emitted long exhalations through his mouth.

He wished his head would clear quicker than it was, but at least it wasn't worsening.

He lowered himself into the lotus position, cross-legged, hands resting on knees, thumb and index finger touching. That much he did recall.

Crowley had sneered when he said that he and Joan had been too busy to study meditation properly, and that had made him tense, even tenser. He'd had work concerns, money concerns, family concerns, both of them had. It was called life. But of course the needs of normal life were merely objects of disdain for Crowley. Yet Crowley had done many things Dennis could be disdainful about. One thing in particular.

Don't.

Concentrate.

Concentrate on *not* concentrating.

He tried to remember what the West Indian had taught them when he visited Queen's Gate. All he could think of was Joan and him, cross-legged on the floor, getting the giggles like naughty schoolchildren. She never had qualms about expressing herself in the face of figures of authority—without bordering rudeness, ever: she was far too well brought up for that—and many men admired her for exactly that quality. One in particular had been swept off his feet by it. She spoke her mind as he never dared, and it was intoxicating.

Concentrate.

The yogic postures. Breathing techniques. He wondered now why they hadn't stuck at it. But Crowley wasn't much of a shining example either. He'd told Dennis in the Hungaria that, whilst Allan Bennett had studied under the guru Ramanathan, the Eastern ascetic life had proven a fork in the road for him. *Dhyana* didn't enable the advancement of the soul the way he believed satisfying the physical impulses did. It cleared the mind of material distractions, yes, but Buddhism, he said, was a kind of malaria he had to build up his immunity to. It was, to him, nothing more than a leisurely walk before gearing up to climb the challenging peak.

Now. In. And—out.

The control of breathing was a step towards going inward. Withdrawing from the external, Rollo had said. Directing all your intention on that elusive object called the Self—which is identical to the Absolute. Become absorbed completely in that, to the exclusion of all else.

He'd called on Ahmed to advise him on *The Devil Rides Out*, just as he had with Crowley. He remembered listening avidly to his tales of the devil-ridden jungles of Yucutan, Guyana and Brazil. Of Voodoo and Obeah, as well as occult practices in Asia and Europe, where Rollo had travelled extensively. By way of thanks, he'd put him forward to Hutchinson's to write a serious book on *The Black Art*—which turned out, splendidly, to be the best book Dennis had read on the subject. Now the poor chap was in prison for fraud, he'd heard—a pattern of dishonesty common to a lot of occultists, sailing close to the wind, pockets always empty, having little desire let alone ability to secure a stable way of life. It was always amazing to Dennis that those who shook hands with the Devil, presumably in return for riches and power, always seemed to get such a raw deal in the bargain. And Rollo had once said that his teeth had been knocked out by a demon. Damn. Dennis wished he hadn't remembered that.

Hell…This wasn't working.

Far from being able to clear his mind, his thoughts were going like the clappers. Devil-populated jungles. Voodoo. Demons knocking teeth out. Lord above…

His head was splitting. He stood up and drank another glass of water from the jug. Someone was tuning in a wireless set, far off, downstairs. A dance band, barely more than a ghostly drone.

He tried a different tack, and lay flat out on the bed with his arms at his side and his eyes shut.

The alarm went off, drilling into his spine.

He cricked his head up and turned to check the clock.

Incredibly, it didn't lie. Six thirty. He banged his hand down to kill the metallic rattle. In the silence, the dance band had vanished.

Three and a half hours he'd been out. Ye gods.

He felt he hadn't been asleep, but he must have been dead to the world.

*
**

A familiar voice, hushed yet sibilant, floated on the air from behind the door at the far end of the landing. Words as obscure and esoteric

as those of the shipping forecast."Bethor…Phaleg…Adonai…
Thetragrammaton…Berkaiac…Asaradel…Amasarac…"

It faded as Dennis descended the stairs. Rather than ask anyone
for directions, he found a street map of Hastings in the library and
pocketed it. Crowley's bread and water diet was making his stomach
contract in protest. He realised he hadn't eaten for twenty-four
hours—his last meal being the hideous Spam or whatever it was—
so he helped himself to one of the crusty bread rolls that were
already on side plates in the dining room. From the lounge he could
hear a boy of about thirteen playing immaculate Spanish guitar.
The guests seemed quietly attentive, except for a man in a vicar's
dog collar who slept the sleep of the just. He could hear their
applause as he left, fetching his double-breasted Air Force greatcoat
from the back of the car. He needed it. The temperature had
plummeted.

He couldn't see the moon but its presence, filtered through the
cloud cover, gave everything the artificiality of a film set. The sky
was a watercolour of grey, stilled turbulence as he walked along The
Ridge in the direction of the coast, passing St Helen's Lodge on his
right and the Borough Cemetery on his left. He resisted the
temptation to take Elphinstone Road, as according to the map that
looked like ultimately being at the mercy of twistier little streets, so
instead kept to The Ridge, high up, until he could turn into
Frederick Road which then became Old London Road, leading
downwards. Evidence of the pummelling of HE bombs from five
years of air attacks greeted him every step of the way. He thought
of the endless alerts. Fatalities. Injuries. Countless ordinary lives
devastated. It made him all too aware that towns outside London
suffered their own personal Blitzkriegs. Their own horrors.

It took fifty minutes to reach the High Street and the single chime
of half past seven drew him like a pilgrim to St Clement's Church,
near the elevated pavement leading up to Cobourg Place. He was
far too early to expect Gisela to have placed the cigar box on the
steps, but something made him look there anyway. There was
nothing.

He could hear a male voice crooning *You Are My Sunshine* inside the Jenny Lind and his spirits lifted, at first, at the thought that, after the hardship and grimness of the war years, people were doing their best to enjoy themselves. Who could begrudge them? It restored a vague sense of hope. In him, anyway.

He had time to kill, and it was too freezing to stand on a street corner, so he ensconced himself in The Royal Standard. The smoke tested his throat like a rite of passage and the floor was sticky underfoot, the air a fug of hope and malt, tobacco tins and that insular defensiveness peculiar to the English. Two years ago a man standing alone at a bar might be branded a spy. Now, amongst the talk of the dogs or football, never about wives or daughters, effeminacy was the abiding suspicion. He ordered a bottle of Watney's Pale Ale and a glass of water, well aware that ordering the water on its own in a pub like this might have been an offence punishable by death, though his explanation that he was fasting in order to carry out a demon-raising occult ceremony may have been amusing for a few seconds before he got his lights punched out.

He sat in a dim corner with the ale that would go untouched. He didn't know why it felt impossible to break Crowley's rules— maybe he *was* under his spell, as Joan had said. He knew one thing, though. He wanted to be out of this insidious murk he felt trapped in, but there was no going back, there was only the way forward. Part of him wanted to open the cigar box and find the handkerchief inside, so that he could report back to Crowley and the whole thing would be off—but what then? Was he supposed to tootle off home, happily, knowing that Lamont was still intent on his ritual of transformation? Would Crowley compel him to stay even longer, like some prisoner? He had no idea, and didn't want to think about it. He wanted to do what was asked of him and get back to Netherwood. Then at least he'd know and they could get it over with.

By eight o'clock The Standard had thinned out, and he noticed more and more men leaving in twos and threes, taking their glasses with them. He went with the flow—literally joining a stream of people of all ages moving steadily and noisily in great anticipation towards the High Street. The occasional cracker hit a wall like a gunshot. Each time it did, a gasp was followed by laughter. The traffic was blocked off. It couldn't have got through in any case.

He wanted to linger close to St Clement's for obvious reasons. People were jam-packed into the Jenny Lind, bursting out in small groups to grab vantage points before the parade began, all lethal elbows and spillages. Every minute that passed they were bolstered by dozens more, surging in from all directions.

A poor excuse for rain threatened to dampen the proceedings, but a still breeze drove the clouds inland, and the air crackled with fresh injections of gunpowder and phosphorus as if it was a car engine that needed igniting. Professorial grandfathers broke their constitutionals with an after-tea pipe, while harried mothers bustled to keep their excited offspring in check. Shop assistants, office workers, none would have minded getting soaked to the skin, you could tell, just so long as they got their bonfire. That was all that mattered.

We want fireworks! We want fireworks!

On the opposite side of the road he saw a chubby little girl with a Shirley Temple haircut sitting on a man's shoulders, his hands gripping her flesh below the knees. She was probably too young to talk, possibly too young to walk, but the joy in her face was inescapable.

He wondered if Poupée died simply of neglect in Cefalù, out there in that misbegotten place full of incapable, volatile and selfimmersed souls. If so, Crowley—if the man could admit the possibility—could surely never forgive himself. She had lived only months, and her father had been devastated. Perhaps that was why. For the first time in his life he couldn't avoid that he was at fault. It suddenly made complete sense that he felt so strongly that another child—another *daughter*—must live. Could it be true that, not before time, Aleister Crowley wanted to atone for his sins? Dennis could almost hear him deny it outright. What had he said at that lunch? "I *approve* of sins. Virtues are just the sins of the highly unimaginative." So dry. So cunning. Such a mask.

Eight chimes echoed from the church spire. The crowd shuffled tighter together, shoulder to shoulder on the narrow pavements as still more joined the throng. A dropped bottle smashed. A cheer went up. The anticipation was building rapidly—uncontrollably.

People were pointing to the far end of the street, where a strange glow illuminated smoke, colours shifting, one minute red, then green, then flickering yellow.

Dennis could hear them long before he could see them: the unmistakable rattle and thrum of a drum and fife band, growing steadily louder and closer. Soon he could make out, peering between shoulders and heads and hats, the distant intensity of flaming torches and banners held high on poles. The cacophony gradually metamorphosed into a recognisable medley of tunes in a wild variety of keys, augmented periodically by raucous huzzahs.

The carnival emerged from the smoke, a motley assortment of characters nameable and nameless. Pirates in black and white striped shirts and tri-corn hats, with red knotted neckerchiefs. Lifeguards. Basketwomen. Celestials. Garibaldian volunteers in their white shirts, white trousers, and feathered caps, brandishing fixed bayonets. Men dressed in the costume of the fair sex—hairy arms and moustaches notwithstanding—sporting rolling pins, hair nets and aprons, marching in step as straight-backed as the Navy cadets and boy scouts. All heralding what could only be called hugely impressive.

Under the lurid glare of the torches and to the cheering strains of the brass, the International Friendship League, dressed in various national costumes, showed off its giant cotton wool dove of peace. Soon afterwards the Fisherman's Society passed with a striking tableau of a minesweeper. The float belonging to the St Clement's Bonfire Society was bedecked with a Guy Fawkes effigy, tower-tall and swaying in the night. Grinning and painstakingly attired, the seemingly drunken giant stood a good fifteen feet from his boots to the crown of his hat, billowing in monstrous parachute-white trousers, a square-cut black coat, and white gloved hands strongly tethered by ropes to stop him flying away over the rooftops. Punctuated by the strains of the St John Ambulance Band, the Boys Brigade Band and the Winkle Club Jazz Band, other effigies glided by, one by one, including the Tsar of Russia, the Sultan of Turkey, the Amir of Afghanistan, and Cetowayo, King of the Zulus—any old tyrant or ruler worth shaking a fist at, or knocking the stuffing out of—all flanked by uniforms historical and eclectic, livid pancake make-up bathed in the light of Catherine wheels and raining splashes of bright shining stars.

Below each self-identifying banner, every section of the parade carried its own brightly painted dustbin like an inert mascot ahead of a regiment—into which jackie jumpers were lit and thrown in an offhand manner, setting off deafening, percussive rat-tat-tats like submachine guns, lighting up the faces of onlookers even as mothers pulled their children to their bodies, several of the little ones, and not so little ones, sticking their fingers in their ears—joy and delight matched only by a latent sense of mad, potentially harmful violence straining at the leash.

To Dennis it seemed raw and timeless, a visit from the past. He thought of the fire festivals that seemed essential to Mankind, whether primitive or civilised—it seemed to make little difference: there was something fundamental and unassailable about fire. From before history began to be written, bonfires had been lit to the gods, people leapt over them for fertility, people drove cattle through them, burned their evil influences in them, walked through them to prove their manhood. They were celebratory beacons or funeral pyres. We kept the home fires burning, but fire was also redolent of Mischief Night, the destructive forces of the dark that could be called up for entertainment but that could so easily get out of hand.

Granted, everything was cheerful and fun so far—no more than a vast, good-natured, slow-moving party—but Dennis couldn't shake the conviction that at any moment it could all tip over into chaos.

As a hundred-strong cortège of St Leonards Boys marched past carrying hurricane lamps, his eyes were unexpectedly drawn to a tall, shadowy figure with his collar turned up behind significantly shorter people on the other side of the High Street. The man's features were African, and for a peculiar moment Dennis was absolutely convinced he was looking at his old friend Rollo Ahmed—until the reflected flash of a squib made it clear this was a figment of his imagination. The dark-skinned man looked up at the chap in the RAF coat staring across at him. For second, no more, their eyes locked, before Dennis looked away.

Britannia passed in a decorated car, helmeted, her trident thrusting at a diagonal angle as if posing for a penny piece, protected on all sides by whiskery sailors carrying oars, to a jaunty, if unsurprising, rendition of her ruling of the waves. A man walked in her wake dressed as a red petrol pump, with the slogan *Restore the Basic Ration*, followed by a ragtag troupe of Red Indians, clowns and highwaymen.

When Dennis looked back, the African man was gone.

He heard a loud bang and a shriek. Yards away, on the opposite pavement, some brats had put a lighted cracker in a woman's handbag and sped away as it went off. A man, presumably her husband or boyfriend, tore after them, and a scuffle ensued. Someone fell to the floor and the man, kicking, was held back by the shoulders, the resultant scrimmage obscured by a ring of bodies. Dennis concluded that the young bloods of Hastings saw today as an opportunity to test their bravado. Perhaps if they'd gone to battle against Hitler five years ago they'd have felt it tested enough.

The coarse laughter of men, behind him. Out of the corner of his eye he saw the flare of a lighter.

"Excuse me. D'you mind? Thanks."

Nearly his last. Isn't that what they gave someone before an execution? A last cigarette? But not usually one from Burlington Arcade, he imagined.

"Thanks," he said again, after inhaling.

The lighter clicked shut and its owner turned back to his friends. Dennis looked at the bony lump behind his ear, the line at the top of his cheek where he stopped shaving. A tall blonde joined them. Her cigarette end touched the man's. When she took it out of her mouth it had lipstick like a bloodstain round its rim.

Gisela?

No...This one's hair was straight, not curly. And the man with his arm round her waist was calling her 'Mo'.

With a sudden buzzing in his ears, Dennis realised she could be here, in the crowd somewhere. He looked all round, desperately, at the same time knowing that he only had a vaguest mental picture of what she looked like—and for that matter, her boyfriend too. Either of them could be here, right in front of his eyes, or both of them could. Imagine she'd said to him she was going out to see the bonfire procession and he'd replied that he would come too? It wasn't impossible. It was horribly likely.

Dennis's eyes scanned the spectators for other blondes, blondes with babies, and for—what had Crowley said?—a man with a combed back wave, almost a pompadour? Then a terrible thought struck him. What if Crowley had happened to tell Gisela that *Dennis Wheatley* was helping him? Lamont might easily know what *he* looked like, the famous author of black magic stories, his photograph always in the papers. Suddenly the thought of a blade sliding coldly across his throat—as the lamb on the Brecon Beacons had felt it— made his mouth go dry and his scrotum shrivel. He was in a crowd of cheering and happy people, but felt as vulnerable as if he'd been dropped slap-bang into enemy terrain.

The clanging of cymbals didn't help.

Every face now seemed a villain. Guy Fawkes the least of them.

A windmill. A lighthouse. The Bisto kids. St George and the Dragon...

Chilled to his bones, Dennis shivered and looked in the direction of Marine Parade, where all the other pairs of eyes were pointed.

Lit by torches, the effigies rocked to and fro as they lumbered towards the sea, proud resilient monsters fated (and fêted) for destruction. The walk to the scaffold. To the Fishmarket, as he'd seen earlier—where busy hands of giddy arsonists heaped wood upon wood, intent on singeing Mr Fawkes' beard.

The bulk of the parade had passed him now. The Ore and Clive Vale Bonfire Boys peeled off towards the Memorial. Only stragglers left. Brats marching in parody or picking up defunct ordnance, sniffing the tubes of burnt gunpowder as if they were opium pipes, and drunkards waltzing in each other's arms. The crowd showed little sign of dispersing, though, and the Jenny Lind was as packed to the gunnels as it had been earlier.

The haze retreated further seaward, turning from white to green to crimson, slowly returning night to its natural palette, the only remaining music apart from the ghost of the blaring bands a stray concertina accompanied by a mouth organ.

St Clement's bell tolled a sonorous nine o'clock. Just for him, or it felt like it.

He remembered his mission and shivered again, but not at the cold. He tossed the cigarette and walked round the corner to the church steps.

He saw nothing. A sense of relief slowed him down.

Then he made out a small shape in the shadows beyond the wrought iron gates, pushed back so as not to attract the attention of passers-by. He reached through the bars, turned it on its side and lifted the object out.

A box of Corona cigars. The paper seal broken.

Inside…

Empty.

He shut it and put it under his arm.

Right…He'd be back at Netherwood by around ten. There was no point in hanging about. He re-traced the same route, starting by walking up the centre of the High Street, since the pavements were still host to huddled groups of people for whom the night was young. The climb was steeper than he remembered it coming down, and he was out of breath sooner than he would have predicted.

He was glad to be on his own, though, away from the threatening bustle at last. Had it been threatening, truly, or was that his state of mind? Now that he had a distance from it, he wasn't sure. Did he feel safer—yes, but no. Something irrational made him think that the silence was a cloak for somebody following him.

He turned and looked back.

The street was empty, on both sides. Not a soul in sight under the street lamps.

He took in the view, light-headed, getting his breath back.

The huge bonfire in Rock-a-Nore had lit up the buildings for miles around, and cast rippling yellow brushstrokes across the surface of the sea. Voices were far distant, but eerily carried by force of numbers. Hundreds of squibs went off in all directions, making him blink. He thought of sweethearts kissing on VE day—and how that moment of transformation seemed a fallacy now. There was no magic moment when everything was safe. All we could do, at best, was to fool ourselves with fireworks.

In Frederick Road he thought again that there was a presence following him—presence? Yes, *presence*—so much so that, this time, ridiculously, he was too afraid to turn around.

He told himself he was being silly, and kept on walking, his pace unaltered, thinking of that MR James ghost story of the deadly parchment returned to the magician's pocket without him knowing, so that the demon comes to him instead of the intended victim. He almost wanted to do what he did as a child when he was scared, which was to whistle, because if you whistled nothing could jump out and frighten you, and if you didn't look at the brick wall on your left with the street light behind you, there couldn't be a shadow there, sloping, lengthening, several yards behind your own.

He spun round, panting.

It was the African man with the turned-up collar. The one he'd mistaken for Rollo Ahmed. His face much blacker, he could see now—so black he was almost blue.

"What the blazes—?"

The man, seeing his anger, took a few steps backwards, then a few steps more, holding his hands up in surrender, palms far lighter than his face.

"Whoa. My mistake, fella. My mistake…"

Dennis could see his shoes were brand new, polished to perfection, as he kept on retreating down the pavement, before turning and walking away. Dennis watched him for a while, his chest heaving, waiting till the stranger was out of sight before resuming his climb.

He checked his pockets. Nothing there. No parchment scrawled with runic symbols. No piece of paper slipped in, unbeknownst. No handkerchief.

Only the hag stone. His protection.

Above him he could see no stars, as if the earth had grown a sullen carapace. The vast moon, a merest fraction away from full, looking remarkably like a hole cut out of black paper, as if the whole of space beyond it was an infinite surface of silver craters, a dry, never-ending, lifeless universe of which we were only given the most miniscule, keyhole peek.

Deep inside his pocket he clutched the hag stone in his fist, holding onto it tightly all the way back to Netherwood.

*
**

He hadn't thought whether the front door would be unlocked, but it was. He let himself in quietly. The whole house was still. The lounge and dining room deserted. Most residents were in bed, though he knew one, at least, who wouldn't be.As he hung up his RAF greatcoat he saw the telephone in the niche under the stairs and felt the sudden urge to hear Joan's voice. He lifted the receiver and asked the operator to put him through to Lymington 315. He waited and heard it ringing, then hung up before it was answered.

"Snifter?"

Dennis turned sharply. Vernon stood next to the optics.

"Er…No. Thank you. I need to keep my senses about me."

Vernon frowned, then added ice to the short he had on the go. "Mr C said not to be disturbed." He sipped it and smacked his lips, chuckling theatrically. "'Even if the screams of hell erupt from that room…' he said: 'on on no account open the door!'"

"You know our Mr Crowley." Dennis pretended to smile. "One for the highest possible melodrama." He began climbing the upstairs.

"Quite. Even so…What exactly…if it isn't too…?"

Dennis saw him craning his head round the corner of the bar.

"Let's just say Old Mother Clutterbuck is burning the midnight oil."

Vernon laughed. "He always was dedicated to his work. Well, I'll wish you goodnight." He raised his glass, hail fellow well met. "Sleep well."

Dennis nodded and forced a grin but was quite sure he wouldn't sleep well. He severely doubted he would be sleeping at all.

His knuckles tapped the door lightly. The landing, unbearably cosy with lumpy armchairs and landscape paintings, felt like a shadowy antechamber to the Pharoah's tomb. He entered to find incense dispersing rapidly, hanging in clumps in the dingy air, a thicker, darker, more acrid smoke rising from a censer, mingling to creating a soft, grey mist. Through it, on the floorboards, he could make out a perfect circle enclosing a five-pointed star drawn in white chalk: the most powerful of all magical symbols. Dr Dee's Star of Bethlehem, consisting of cabbalistic signs of precise significance and the names of Hebrew gods arranged between nine candlesticks. Pointing upwards, the star stood for God and was used for invoking good spirits—pointing downwards, the beard of the goat, the opposite. Which way was it pointing now? It was pointing at Crowley—a bag of bones perched on the corner of his Chinese chest, wearing only his grubby underwear, injecting into the map of veins on the side of his bare foot. The yellowing toenails were overgrown and curved like talons, just like those in Goya's etching *Who Will Pare Them?* The image took Dennis to the same artist's infamous painting of the witches' Sabbat, and the man-goat in adoration at its centre. As the needle was extracted, Crowley's eyes rolled and his jaw, and body, sagged. "*Apo pantos kakadaimonos*," he mumbled, slurring, though Dennis could not tell if it was gibberish or part of an incantation.

"Shall I come back later?"

Preposterous, but what else could he say?

Crowley shook his head. Just about managed half-opening his eyes.

Dennis stepped closer, hoping their blurred vision could focus on the cigar box he held out, and see it was empty.

It appeared that it could. Crowley's neck and shoulders cricked and he gave a nondescript gesture with one hand while the other fumbled to return the syringe to its box.

"If you wish to go, go now...of your own free will. But if you stay, know this. If we call upon the powers of darkness, we are vulnerable to them."

"You're a born salesman," said Dennis, trying to lighten the proceedings. A vain hope if there ever was one. He told himself his groaning chasm of a stomach was simply a hunger pang, and nothing to do with his all-consuming and entirely rational sense of foreboding.

The effect wasn't instantaneous. He could only watch as the substance worked its slow but visible rejuvenating magic. And it did seem rejuvenating, as if a corpse had come back to life, its cheeks slapped on a mortuary slab. Chop, chop. Work to be done. Look lively. Hands off cocks, on socks, as they said in the Navy. Crowley's skin was the colour of a death certificate. He wondered how many needles the man had left in him. How many weeks, come to that. How many days.

He placed the cigar box on the floor, next to a dagger made of papier-mâché, black with gold decorations—not used for cutting, he knew from his own researches, but for casting the circle: *As athame is to the male, the cup is to the female*—the phallus and vulva. He had no idea if Crowley had used it, or its purpose was reserved for the ritual yet to come.

When he looked up, through the mist of incense the ailing Beast was pulling on a white kaftan over his head. A sapphire gleamed on the third finger of his left hand.

"This is the robe and ring I wore in Bou-Sâada."

Around his neck he draped a necklace from which hung an amulet displaying the distinctive drop and spiral eye in imitation of the falcon.

"Horus-Set-Hather—god of healing and making whole. We will need his blessing. Seal the doors and windows, would you, please?"

Dennis found himself handed a roll of sealing tape and immediately did as he was bidden, running it around all the edges of the sash windows, cutting out every possibility of any atom of influence, physical or psychical, infiltrating from outside. It reminded him of doing a similar job in Earl's Court, putting all those crosses of tape across window panes to minimise damage during bombing raids. He wasn't quite sure whether it minimised anything, but they were told to do it and they did. After that, he sealed all four sides of the door, blocking out the last cracks of light from the landing, remembering the dread silence when the doodlebug's engine cut out and you knew it was falling, and it might be falling on you.

He turned back to see Crowley wheezing as he hobbled from candle to candle, lighting each in turn.

He remembered the four elements that had to be used at the four compass points, where Crowley was now calling on the blessing of the archangels. "Raphael. Gabriel. Michael. Uriel." A pinch of earth, a sigh of breath, a drip of water, a burning match...The flash of the cigarette lighter came back to him. The negro's face lit up by a skyrocket.

Crowley lapsed into an ugly, hacking cough, bending over double as it persisted. It seemed to go on forever, frightfully, and Dennis thought at one point he would bring his lungs up.

"You should sit down."

Waving a hand irritably, Crowley shook his head. Lit the last candle. Made the last sign of the pentagram in the air.

Dennis's belly growled again, and he realised for the first time that his teeth were chattering. He'd been frozen on the way back from the Old Town, even in his greatcoat, and there'd been a layer of frost on his car in the drive. The house had its heating on, but he was not yet warmed up. Yes, that was it. It must be it. His nose and fingers felt blue.

Crowley must have noticed. "Remember, the seventh and lowest Hell of Dante was not a roaring furnace but a place of ice." Dennis didn't thank him for that thought. Nor could he stop shivering. Crowley stood cadaverous in the candle glow. It wasn't just the flickering flames that danced, the very air seemed to ferment and flicker. "Do you want to know what I shall be doing?"

"I'd rather not, actually."

"Good. I'd hate to waste my spiritual energy on a lecture to the semi-ignorant. No offence intended."

"A little taken," said Dennis. "But I'll live with it."

It would all literally be Greek to him, he was sure, or Hebrew, or written in Dee's so-called Enochian language of the angels. None of which tongues he felt particularly fluent in, to put it mildly.

"Do you have a pen on you?"

Yes. Pen and notebook, always. The essential equipment of Dennis's trade. He took out his Waterman fountain pen from an inside pocket and took off the cap.

Crowley snatched it, walked away, and used its nib to drill a hole in the lower corner of a bag of salt, which he lifted, bent over, as it trickled out in a fine stream which he used to demark the outer circle. When he'd finished he placed the bag within, on its side, so that no more would run out, careful to leave the salt circle incomplete. Dennis knew that it would be sealed only when they were both inside it; a magician broke the perimeter of their astral fortress at their peril.

"The best use your pen has been put to in years."

Crowley straightened up, capped it and handed it back to him.

"Keep it. Write your memoirs."

"I already have."

Crowley slid it into the breast pocket of the younger man's jacket.

Dennis looked down at the pentagram on the floor, decorated as it was with the chalked symbols of the Olympic spirits who rule the planets. *Pentacle.* He corrected himself, remembering Crowley doing so at the Hungaria: "*Put a circle round it and it's a pentacle, dear boy, not a pentagram.*"

"Drawn with a stick in the dirt or carved in the most expensive marble, it doesn't matter a jot, the effect is the same."

"You *were* listening over pudding," said Crowley.

His smile disappeared as his back undulated. He hacked like thunder, worse than before, worse than ever, screwing up his eyes until he brought up a scrape of sputum like a cat with a fur ball. Dennis winced.

"Seriously. Should I call the doctor?"

Crowley shuddered, made a face. Gesticulated in the negative.

"Look, are you sure you're up to this?" He was thinking not just of the old man's safety but his own.

"I have to be."

Dennis sighed, and Crowley noticed his frown darken as he circumnavigated the circle, as he suspected it might. Dennis looked at him and looked back at the floor. He'd expected the standard words from *The Clavicule of Solomon* or *The Grimoire of Pope Honorius*— IN NOMINE PA + TRIS ET FI + LII ET SPIRITUS + SANCTI et cetera. Instead of which he read, as a slow, bilious wave rose up from his gut—MOLOCH + BEELZEBUB + LUCIFUGE +ASTAROTH + ASMODEUS + BELPHEGOR + BAAL + ADRAMMELECH + LILITH + NAAMAH.

"I'm sorry?"

"Don't be. The Holy Trinity has no place here tonight. Or anything holy for that matter. These are the ten evil Sephiroths under the supreme command of Sammael."

"Separated by…Good God—*swastikas?*"

"Absolutely. Not the Nazi anti-clockwise kind, but clockwise-spinning ones—the ancient sign of the radiant Sun—666."

If Dennis had laughed it would have been hollow and pointless. He was in far too deep to question anything now. And too weak to argue. He felt quite light-headed after his climb from the Old Town and his brain was pulsating inside his skull as he swallowed to wet his desert-dry throat.

Go, a voice inside was shouting. *Go, walk out, don't look back, get out of here.* Then he saw the woman wrapped in barbed wire. Then he saw the child with ribbons in its hair and knew he could do no such thing.

Crowley walked over to the censer and doused what was burning. It smelt like sage. He clapped several times sharply in the air, as if to frighten away birds. The final act of a banishment. A spiritual clean-up. Dennis didn't feel clean. He had the tang of fireworks still clinging to his clothes. Phosphorus. Charcoal. Sulphur. Brimstone.

Operation Brimstone.

The plan for the Allies to take Sardinia. Dennis remembered it well, in the bowels of Whitehall, in that poky office where all seemed impossibly straightforward and true. But perhaps this was the *real* Operation Brimstone. Tonight, in Hastings, at Netherwood, right now.

"Once we are within the pentacle," breathed Crowley weakly, almost inaudibly, "we will leave the confines of the body. Nobody and nothing can help you there. If Choronzon confronts you, say the four-letter name of God—Yahweh, and instruct the creature to kiss your hand and repent. Do this in the circle. Don't break it, any more than you would toy with an unexploded bomb. Is that clear?"

"This is madness."

"You've noticed," said Crowley. "But what is madness to the great unwashed is a door. If you don't acknowledge that, I have taught you nothing."

He picked up a large, flat stone carved in an intricate spiral pattern. He placed it at the centre of the circle.

"This is your pillow. It's your entry to the other realm. With a unicursal labyrinth you won't get lost, that's the trick. If you keep moving widdershins, anti-clockwise, you will always arrive at the sacred centre, and, more importantly, be able to find your way back."

"What?"

"Strip to the waist. Take off your belt and socks. And get rid of that tie. Or someone or something might strangle you with it."

Dennis did as he was told, while Crowley lapsed into a coughing fit even more debilitating than the one that preceded it, and, when he had recovered, shuffled to the coffee-making contraption bubbling away in the far corner. A flask of water had come to the boil. Crowley poured it into a glass stuffed with leaves and granules, stirring it with a spoon.

"Drink this. It'll relax you. Mint. Fennel. Cloves."

Dennis blew away the rising steam, gulped a large mouthful and swallowed.

"Disgusting."

The second was no improvement on the first. His face contorted.

"Finish it."

When he had, Crowley placed the glass on the floor and dropped a tea towel over it.

"Break it."

Dennis did so with his sole. Felt it give, then shatter.

Crowley bent down and picked up a jagged sliver between forefinger and thumb and, before Dennis could protest or even speak, had cut an X in the outer surface of his own left forearm, the blossoming red shouting against the tapestry of white marks already carved there. Not an ounce of pain, or for that matter ecstasy, dimmed his features. It was an action as devoid of emotion as the marking of a polling card.

He reached out and took firm hold of Dennis's left wrist with his own left hand, as if to read the time on the younger man's watch. He looked into his eyes as he handed him the same long, curved sliver of glass.

"Ten being the number of Mulkuth, the sphere on the Tree of Life where the initiate symbolically begins."

It was an invitation. One that Dennis felt impossible to refuse, even though nothing was stopping him, and his fear was undiminished. Perhaps it was that very fear that compelled him, made what he did inevitable but at the same time perplexing, even as he was doing it.

He drew the glass across his skin exactly as Crowley had done, making the same mark—the Roman numeral for ten—on his own left forearm, feeling a rush to his heart and forehead like wings lifting him, before tossing the piece of glass across the room where it broke, tinkled, fell. Neither man looked there.

When it was done, Crowley turned his back and tore a square from an old newspaper, licked one side of it and pressed it to Dennis's cut. The blood showed through in an X almost immediately, the coagulation holding it there while Crowley's wound merely seeped, dry and bubbly, the way the dead carcass of an animal might.

He stood back and gave the two-fingered sign of sacerdotal benediction, known in Rome as the *Mano Pantea*. Dennis was far beyond wondering at this stage whether such a thing was blasphemous or not, and happy to receive any benediction at all.

"Lie down, close your eyes, and keep them closed."

Dennis dropped to his hands and knees, then lay so that the back of his head rested on the labyrinth stone and the heels of his bare feet touched the rim of the inner circle. Crowley wasn't happy with the arrangement, lifted his legs by the ankles and shifted him six inches to the left. Dennis shuffled his rump accordingly until he seemed satisfied.

"I said keep them closed."

"Sorry. Sorry."

The candlelight dull through his shut eyelids, Dennis felt Crowley grab his arms, shake them loosely, then position them, wrists crossing over his chest, like a corpse in a coffin. Dennis tried to concentrate on his breathing—concentrate on *not* concentrating, as Rollo Ahmed had said—but for a moment felt Crowley pressing down over his heart quite hard, holding his hand there while he took several long breaths, before letting go.

"Shall I visualise something?"

"No. If the visions come, they will need nothing from you. Say nothing now, unless I ask you to."

As a blind man might, Dennis felt something change in the room, the movement of a loose flowing garment in the air, a step, then another as Crowley took his own position in the pentacle and—yes, that was it—he was pouring the final thin trail of salt to seal the circle, then exhaled as he lay flat.

The other man's body providing another radius to the circle, yet their heads only inches apart at the centre, Dennis could hear his breathing, the shallow rattle in his chest, the whistling hush of his almost-death rattle.

Weeks? Days?…Hours? *Minutes?*

His pillow was hard. He asked himself why he hadn't seen another labyrinth stone. Did Crowley not have one for himself, to find his way there, wherever they were going, and back again?

Oz, the great and powerful.

Where was he planning to go that Dennis wasn't? What had Joan warned him—he's a con man, you can't believe a word he says? He could hear her saying it, clearly.

"Repeat after me…Nuit, Hadit, Ra-Hoor-Khuit."

"Nuit, Hadit, Ra-Hoor-Khuit," said Dennis, like a child. "Apollo, Abraham, Adonai, Allah."

"Apollo, Abraham, Adonai, Allah."

"Keep your eyes closed," said Crowley sharply. "Nuit, Hadit, Ra-Hoor-Khuit."

His eyes *were* closed.

"Nuit, Hadit, Ra-Hoor-Khuit."

"Apollo, Abraham, Adonai, Allah."

"Apollo, Abraham, Adonai, Allah."

His eyes were closed. His eyes had always been closed, ever since he got here. What was he doing? What the hell was he doing, lying in a bloody candle-lit room with bloody Aleister Crowley? He must need his head examined. His head—pounding, clawing at the bone to get out, with that sickly smell of—what?

Bonfire? Burning? Brimstone?

No—horrible. Rubber. All round his mouth. No. Not imagining a mask over his mouth. Not imagining the smell of ether.

Keep your eyes closed.

No! He opened them. Nothing. Blackness. A hand covering them. He tried to lift his hands, to flail them, to punch, to struggle, couldn't.

"Nuit, Hadit, Ra-Hoor-Khuit."

He shook his head. The fingers parted. He saw the face, as if through slatted blinds. Saw Crowley over him, filling the sky of his vision, the cut-out moon of Crowley, the whole dry universe, holding the rubber mask down, holding it hard, the ether hissing.

"Apollo, Abraham, Adonai, Allah."

He tried to repeat it but couldn't.

The dentist swam back to his brain, mouth filling with blood. Short trousers, spitting up blood in the metal mirror sink. The vomiting feeling that stayed in your nostrils for days. Wanting to wail for his mother but being a man.

Joan!

He tried to move his head but it was weak, watery, drowning.

He was inhaling the world. The wink. The thumbs-up. The *Worcester.* His was the breathing out and taking in of the world. The gasp, the grasp, the aha, the father, the release of breath in acceptance, wonder, awe and...

"Nuit, Hadit, Ra-Hoor-Khuit."

Black, Minotaur-like forms walked in a line across a landscape.

They passed buckets to one another, in a chain, to put out the fires. Their hooves stood on broken bricks.

He heard whispers in the dark. A woman.

"Sshh…"

Joan?

"*Go to sleep. Sshh…*"

A droning sound, far away. A machine. A good machine or bad?

He was sitting cross-legged on green grass near Noël Coward's house in St Margaret's, overlooking the White Cliffs near Dover. It was a beautiful sunny day and the sea was powder blue, reflecting a perfect, cloudless sky—a sky free and unsullied by war. The lightest of breezes complemented the warmth in the air and the smattering of birdsong. They were enjoying a picnic, he and Joan, with Vernon and Johnny, the owners of Netherwood—old friends, very old friends. Johnny wore a flowery summer dress, garish, bright, and was shapely, or stood smoothing her thighs as if she thought she was, hooking her curls behind her ears, while Vernon, unattractive but confident, if not cocky, was bald, and gingery. Was it Vernon or was it not Vernon? He wasn't sure.

"Play the song, you know it's beautiful," said Johnny.

Dennis wound up the portable gramophone next to the Fortnum's hamper. Placed down the needle on the disc. It played Cab Calloway's *Zaz Zuh Zaz*.

A cork popped. They were getting squiffy on champagne. Johnny was staggering and well gone and they were all laughing, not at her but with her because she was a lark. She turned her back, fingers piling her hair on top of her head and, giving a sultry, jazz-singer pout, she jutted her backside to and fro, getting closer to Dennis's face.

"We're having a nice time. Aren't we having *such* a nice time?"

Laughing, Dennis lay back on the grass, his glass of bubbly resting on his chest. She slumped down next to him, propped herself up on one elbow and began fondling his penis through his trousers. He was surprised, but unresistant.

"Do you like that?" she said to him. "It's nice isn't it, eh?"

She was laughing. So was Joan and the husband, who had their arms round each other, watching.

"She doesn't mind. Look at her. We're just enjoying ourselves. That's all it is."

Johnny stroked his erection, undid his trousers, grinning, laughing, thoroughly tipsy. "No harm in enjoying ourselves, is there? We're all grown-ups here."

The smell of newly mown grass filled his nostrils, and he heard the sound of willow hitting leather. A cricket ball rolled right up to his hand. He looked up as a young man dressed in white ran towards him. The fielder stopped, picked up the ball, tugged the peak of his cap and stood, panting, with his hands on his hips.

"Sorry, old man."

Behind the cricketer, in the blue expanse of the sky, Dennis saw a distinctive shape passing overhead, and knew what the deep rumble was coming from. A Fokker bomber passing over, low, with a Spitfire on its tail, firing at it, all guns blazing.

"Put that light out!" An ARP warden was yelling. "Put that light out!" But that was his job, wasn't it, in London—as fire watcher?

Suddenly the lights did go out. All of them, and he was plunged into darkness, and he was terrified, and Hitler's bombs were dropping again on poor defenceless England. The record was scratched so his fingers spidered in the dark to find another one and put it on the turntable of the trench Decca. Gracie Fields sang "If you were the only girl in the world and I were the only boy…" What did she mean, if *she* were the only boy? He remembered seeing that show at the Alhambra, starring George Robey. But here he was now in the thick of the Blitz in an air raid shelter, the one he remembered building out of champagne cases and sandbags of cement. A woman clung to him. Her breath was warm, wine-tasting. He was still aroused, and his hand felt Joan's breast with an erect nipple inside her blouse.

"Not here," she said.

"Why not? Why not anywhere?"

Air raid sirens interrupted with fear, palpitations. She cut her finger on a nail. He saw the blood. He sucked it better.

"There, there."

"There, there." She imitated him, a tease, belittling him but not meaning to. He turned away to light the lamp. She snaked her arms round him from behind, slid her fingers between the buttons of his Wing Commander uniform.

The lamp glowed into life and he blew out the match. They were now in a church with hundreds of candles. Not a Christian one. Not English. Middle Eastern. Perhaps Istanbul. *The Eunuch of Stamboul.* Where had he heard that title before?

He was facing a golden Buddha. A naked woman was crouched on all fours with her face down in the Buddha's lap, as if sleeping. Her rump was stuck in the air and her anus visible, a red slash of flesh, semi-buried as her buttocks moved in slow, enticing gyrations.

The compulsion to enter was overwhelming. His heart thundered as if his life depended on it, and the Buddha, smiling inscrutably, seemed to be allowing it, facilitating it, encouraging it, blessing it.

And it was Joan, but not Joan.

And she was not dreaming, and not sleeping, but pleasing the golden Buddha with her mouth, giving horrid reason for that inscrutable smile as her head rose and fell, rose and fell. The smile unmoving, a constant, not even of pleasure but of knowing, of expecting, of power. The power to take and to have, and not even care. To care absolutely nothing, but to own.

And he was inside her, crying out invisibly, filling her, remembering those two girls in that brothel in Amiens, Mme Prudhomme's, swapping partners, taking turns in the dentist's chair, whose names he never knew, and was happy not to know.

Joan but not Joan's head pressed against the fat belly of the idol, hitting it over and over and over again as he thrust and kept thrusting, and didn't care.

He couldn't stop. He was a beast. A creature of hunger and no restraint. The thing was let loose now and it took what it wanted.

He couldn't pull out of her. Didn't want to. And his want was everything.

He was an animal and felt like an animal and smelled like an animal. He knew stables of old and stank of them. They were in his blood, seeping out, and he didn't care—an animal freedom was still freedom. He had a goat's freedom—horned, bearded, rutting, indiscriminate, promiscuous, immoral.

Was he goat or was he man? He didn't know any more. He was helpless.

He held her ribs and couldn't let go. His fingernails cut into her back. She made no noise and felt no pain. No ruin. Her head rose and fell like a wind-up toy. The hairs on the back of her neck were red, like the curls above them. Scarlet. *Scarlet Woman.* Babalon...

He looked up.

The Buddha was no longer the Buddha, or golden.

It was Crowley. The fat-bellied Crowley of 1934. Stark naked. Stroking the woman's hair as she obediently did her work down below. His grin broadening—not because he enjoyed it, but because he enjoyed what he saw in Dennis's face directly across the woman's back, right opposite him. His novitiate. His patsy. His fool.

A devouring light ate away everything. Incendiary bombs fell with a hiss and blinding sear of light. He heard a hot, gibbering natter above the crashing orchestra of the Blitz.

"Got change of two shillings?"

He said he hadn't.

"I could do with a smoke too. Play the game, old man."

He tried to spit out the taste of plaster-dust mixed with the tang of high explosives.

The church was gone now. They were in a bomb site. Hoses of water tackled the flames as best they could, plumes lit by the surrounding inferno. Outside, somehow, he knew the London sky was pulsating like a wound and—locked as he was in the physical act like two backstreet dogs on heat—he was desperate, in that heat, to get home before the big one dropped. Where was he? Holborn? Marble Arch? The side of the church caved in, a hundred tons of masonry curving like a bed sheet in the breeze then crashing into dust, a gigantic spiral of orange fire spouting from a crack in the road.

Under the fireworks in the night sky an ARP warden staggered in a gas mask, holding a little girl's doll. He clambered down from a pile of bricks and approached them. When he took off his gas mask it was a face Dennis recognised instantly.

"Gott mit uns," said Rudolf Hess, all sunken cheeks and deepset eyes. "Gott mit uns!"

Hess took out a pistol—Dennis's Smith & Wesson .38— checked the magazine was full, and placed it on the woman's bare back, resting it in the soft valley of her spine.

"The Docks've gone up," he said, now in a broad Cockney accent, before stepping back into the greedy shadows. "Gone up!"

Dennis heard a sob. Looked down.

The Scarlet Woman was Joan.

She had tears running down the one cheek he could see. Her eyes were tightly shut.

She was not enjoying it. He was not enjoying it either—but couldn't extract himself. He was enslaved. It was never-ending. An act of pleasure had become an act of insanity. He'd made a pact with the Devil. This was Hell.

"Stop, stop, stop," wept Joan. "Stop, please."

He couldn't. He couldn't release her. He couldn't release himself. He didn't know how.

Crowley stroked her hair.

Dennis felt a concussion as if he'd been thumped on the head. For several seconds he was deaf, then his hearing returned as a shrill, whirring noise. The doodlebug. Was it overhead yet? He had to wait until the engine cut out, then it would fall.

His rage boiled and he knew what to do. It was the only thing he could do. The thing he'd wanted to do all along.

He picked up the revolver.

He pointed it at Crowley's forehead.

The only way to end this…

To end Jermyn Street. The *Moonlight Sonata*. The face in the mirror.

To end the secret that she'd kept—the one secret, for all his years in intelligence, he'd never found out. To end the hurt. The horror.

His inadequacy. His failure.

His finger tightened on the trigger.

He never wanted anything as much in his entire life. A scream built up inside him like a storm, a house-lifting tornado in black and white. He felt tossed and carried helplessly by it.

Flying monkeys chattered in the sky above him.

Rudolf Hess stood on the Yellow Brick Road.

He stared down the gun sight at the red dot on Crowley's forehead where his bullet would enter his brain. Guru. Master. Magister Templi. Ipsissimus. The smug smile on his face, shattered at last. Sending the grinning Beast, 666, on the final journey—where?

He would pay, that was the important thing…He *had* to pay.

For Joan. For his love, his soul mate, his life. For what he did to her.

For the unforgiveable.

But outside, he could hear the horses, their high, bellowing screams…

And was back there again—taking ammunition from a depot up to the artillery at Passchaendale, his twelve wagon convoy hit by Howitzers minute upon minute, the animals galloping as chunks of brick rained down—as they rained down now. Outside the stained glass windows he knew lay Vlamertinghe and landscapes he would never forget. The endless line of wrecked, unmanned vehicles. The Overturned Gasometer, the Lunatic Asylum on the Ypres Road. The Menin Gate, where they were bombed night and day. Where he saw his first twisted dead body. Two weeks later the Mess had been bombed, and he faced the carnage of horses. Hours in the freezing mud putting them out of their misery with pistol shots.

He heard them now. Out there.

The same horror at St Roche—trying to get them into vans while the station was attacked. Men. Horses. Blood. Limbs…A train hit, men drowned in a volcano of hot coal and steam. And the lives… No. No more.

Not another life. Not one.

He would not become the enemy. He would not blacken his own heart for the sake of revenge.

He could pull the trigger—but he *would not*. Because he had a choice. Because he was not an animal. He was a man.

And then it came, as if summoned by those very thoughts—a great slug-black shape looming behind Crowley, as if it had been lurking there all along. The black man of the witch trials, the Shadow, priapic avatar of antiquity. He of the cloven hoof, whose horns stretch from one corner of the heavens to the other. It had no need of eyes.

And Dennis knew that this was what the demon wanted—Crowley's soul. That was its payment, and Crowley had known it all along.

And Crowley sat across the table of the Hungaria, with his white napkin tucked under his chin, delicately wiping each side of his mouth. The starched white table cloth between them. Looking up as if momentarily startled, the glass of red wine midway to his lips.

"No…You can't have him."

Dennis lowered the barrel of the Smith & Wesson. He threw it away into the dark, where it shattered as if made of glass.

He stared at Crowley and Crowley stared back, immobile. He remembered what the old man had said to him, but not all of it. He didn't know the four-letter name of God, but he knew how to pray to Him. Had since the nursery. Every night, kneeling beside his bed with his tiny hands clasped. He closed his eyes tightly.

"Our Father, who art in heaven, hallowed be thy name…"

Horse-heavy and glistening with sweat, the Minotaur's head loomed close to his. He closed his eyes but smelt the rancid stink of its horns and hooves and beard. Its skin was hard and leathery. Its pizzle engorged. The breath from its nostrils that of a slaughterhouse. The slaughterhouse of Europe.

"Thy kingdom come…thy will be done…on earth as it is in heaven…"

He felt blood oozing from the cut in his forearm. Something made out of mouth and teeth went in, and down.

"Give us this day our daily bread...and forgive us our trespasses...as we forgive those who trespass against us..."

He heard the tolling of fire-bells as the darkness shrank from him even as it embraced him. But wasn't giving in without a fight.

"And lead us not into temptation...but deliver us from evil..."

One succulent maw clung to him with its razor fangs. And even as it departed it gave him a glimpse of what he feared, the very thing he wanted that he didn't even understand. Freedom. And the demon could see through it and into him. Saw what it saw in all men. The question: *What am I?* And sucked upon it like a newborn, sucked on the terror of being ravaged, and the longing to be. His deepest desire, not to be himself, but to be Joan.

"For thine is the kingdom...the power and the glory...for ever and ever..."

His voice thinned to almost nothing, a scrape, a cut, Dennis opened his eyes.

"Amen."

The demon was gone. Crowley was gone. The golden Buddha sat, cross-legged where it had before, with its inscrutable smile intact.

"Joan," he hardly-breathed, and reached out his hand.

The naked figure under him moved, if fractionally. The back was not the smooth flesh of a healthy woman but the wrinkled and mottled skin of a skeletal old man. The head resting in the lap of the Buddha turned its hollow, aged cheek. The chin sported a wispy goatee below the curving slit of a smile.

It was Crowley.

***

Something vile clogged his throat and he woke, heaving his body up to a seated position then falling back on one elbow, his head over to one side, dry retching with his mouth wide open. With every jerk of his diaphragm and gagging gargle from the back of his throat, nothing came.His hand splayed out below him, breaking the solid white curve of salt. His mouth was full of the trench-taste of chlorine gas and he wanted to be rid of it. What he wouldn't give for a vermouth-cassis. The thought almost made him laugh. Laugh and cry, as his neck buckled and he tried to bring up the blockage without success.

To his shame he saw that his erection was now only beginning to diminish. He quickly tucked himself in and did up his fly buttons.

"And I thought the most I'd get out of you was a stiff upper lip."

Crowley's voice was barely a rasp. He had already left the circle, and was extinguishing the candles using an upturned tea cup. He wore a tasselled, lime green dressing gown, its belt hanging free so that the sides fell slightly apart, and in the gap Dennis could glimpse his dangling, hairless genitals, which resembled— and he didn't linger on the sight—the depiction of a shrivelled and decaying fruit made hurriedly out of not enough plasticine.

"A natural physiological reaction. Nothing to be ashamed of. I'm sure you've spilled your seed on many a lesser account."

On impulse, Dennis touched his own forearm. He felt no newsprint. Saw no X cut into the skin. No blood either. The wound simply didn't exist any more. If it ever had. He tried to hang onto memories—the sense of his flesh giving to the blade, the rocket-gush of pleasurable pain—that were already blurring, circling him like witches on broomsticks, mocking him with their insubstantiality.

The mist that had filled the room had mostly dissipated, except for the small black question marks of smoke over each candle as it went out.

"It wanted to take you," he said.

"It almost did."

Crowley extended a hand to help him up.

Dennis didn't take it. Instead he stood up of his own volition, but too quickly, the room swimming. A profound sense of vertigo washed over him and he rushed to Crowley's private bathroom, dropping to his knees at the porcelain bowl, where his system voided itself of pestilential liquid. The reek was unbelievable. He'd found dead badgers in the wood at Grove Place that smelt sweeter. Far sweeter. God in heaven, It might even *kill* badgers, this.

"What did you put in my damned tea?"

"Your tea was the one thing not damned. But encounters with

the superhuman can often unsettle one's stomach. You grasp for a rational explanation even now. Your head will recover, if your soul may not."

Yes, great, thank you.

Dennis closed his eyes tightly. He'd had the misfortune to catch sight of his own face in the mirror and wished he hadn't. He looked dug up, buried, and dug up again weeks later. That was being charitable. That was the obituary in *The Times* version. For some unknown reason he remembered something he'd read. How the Muse priestess of Helicon used two products of the horse to stimulate ecstasies—the slimy vaginal issue of a mare in heat and a black membrane cut from the forehead of a newborn colt, which the mare normally eats. He immediately took to the porcelain again.

Crowley gave him five minutes. Then ten. While he waited he emptied powder into a glass and poured water on top, causing it to fizz. He held it out to Dennis when he was ready. Dennis looked at the glass, at Crowley, then back at the glass, with no small amount of suspicion.

Crowley sighed and held up a bottle of Eno's.

Dennis took a sip, then drank it back more confidently— though how something from Boots the Chemists could help with the kind of infection received when touched by the blackness of a Minotaur, he wasn't sure. What was the medicine you could get over the counter to combat the effects of a darkness that sucks in the light?

He made a face, shuddered as the bicarbonate hit the crucible of his stomach, hoping and praying it would stay there. He looked down at the labyrinth stone on which he'd rested his head.

"Did we succeed?"

"Time will tell."

"Who were the others? There were others in the room."

"There are always others."

Crowley briskly tugged back one curtain then the other. The bright light blinded Dennis, who shielded his eyes as Crowley lifted the lower sash six or seven inches to let the remaining smoke disperse.

"Time for breakfast. I'm ravenous. Another side effect of magic,

I'm afraid. I expect you could eat a horse. Though hopefully Johnny hasn't let her standards slip quite that far yet."

Crowley crossed the floor, his bare feet scuffing the chalk rendering of the circle. Planets were smudged, lines of the fivepointed pentacle semi-erased. He tore the sealing tape from the perimeter of the door in one long, loud ripping motion, and scrunched it up in a sticky ball.

"Come down when you're ready." He knotted his dressing gown cord—a blessing—and Dennis saw that the skin on his arm was uncut, just like his own, though the old, white scars were extant. "No rush," he added matter-of-factly, pausing only to wrap a silk scarf round his neck and slide his feet into a pair of Persian slippers, before disappearing downstairs.

The landing was lit up by sunlight, a million miles from the outer sanctum of the night before. It also flooded the room Dennis now stood in, alone, but he didn't want to stay there a minute longer. Through the open door he could see his own bedroom, and, once he'd gathered his socks and shirt, belt, jacket, tie and shoes, like some gigolo escaping from a lady's boudoir after a tryst, hurried to it, closing the one to Room 13 after him.

He swilled his face and neck at his sink. It cooled him off, but not much else. The soap helped, good old Lux—*fiat lux*, let there be light—but his heart was still going as if he had run a marathon, or been in battle, been shot at, been maimed. Perhaps he *was* maimed, in some fashion he could barely contemplate or understand, and that made him feel more adrift. Hanging his head, eyes closed at first, then open, he watched the oily white suds congregate, viscous and repulsive, and ran more water, harshly, sweeping them away down the plug hole until they were gone. "*I took the passive role.*"

He looked down at himself and tore off his stained trousers, leaving them in a bundle on the floor, pulling on a pair of grey flannel slacks and a clean shirt from the wardrobe where he'd hung it, pressing in the gold cufflinks he'd put in his jacket for safekeeping. He left the jacket itself where it was and took out a dark blue V-necked pullover, plucked out fresh socks from the drawer of the dresser where he'd placed them, and sat in the wooden chair next to it to put them on.

Something caught his eye in the shadows under the bed.

He knelt on the floor, dragged out his suitcase, unlocked it, and opened it.

The Smith & Wesson .38 was there. Untouched.

Descending the stairs, he straightened his tie, tucking it in, his gesture to keeping up appearances, to feeling human, which he didn't feel at all, in spite of the Bond Street brogues. Sibelius's *Finlandia* was playing, scratchily, though it was the words of the old hymn *We Rest on Thee* that ran through his mind, from too many cenotaphs and military chapels:"*We rest on thee, our Shield and our Defender,*

We go not forth alone against the foe,

Strong in Thy strength, safe in Thy keeping tender,

We rest on Thee, and in Thy name we go…"

"Soldiers." Crowley looked up from his table with childlike glee, holding up a thin strip of toast before dipping it into a runny yolk. "The last egg. They pamper me. I don't know what I've done to deserve it. Kedgeree?"

"Don't."

Dennis felt the tea pot before sitting down. He took it that what was inside was a different concoction from the one that was still making his skull throb, but didn't want to risk even the most benign Lapsang.

"What happened?"

"In the astral plane?"

"In reality."

The ungainly, shy girl who had served them before served them again. Crowley saw the bruise of a love bite on the side of her neck.

"Ah, the lovely Dorothy. Who flies to Oz in her dreams, or Bexhill-on-Sea."

She looked as though she wanted to shrink to nothing. The remark was designed to embarrass her, and did, horribly. Dennis felt his own cheeks redden. He didn't want to compound the damage, so closed the menu and shook his head, enabling her to pocket her notebook and go. Her hair was pulled back in a pony tail and Dennis noticed, which he hadn't before, that she was a redhead.

"For sex magic to work, first there must be sex," said Crowley. By way of explanation, it appeared. Perhaps it was the effect of being drugged, but the cogs turned a little too slowly in Dennis's brain.

"Do I really have to spell it out? I see I do…" Crowley looked tired, but strangely energised. Another soldier dunked into the boiled egg, a yellow dribble running down the shell. "I couldn't work it alone, as I told you, many times. The truth is, the fact is, sadly, very sadly and regrettably, due to my…" He coughed, then coughed again, dislodging something slippery from his oesophagus. "My *years* of drug…abuse, use, whatever you want to call it—I am, not to put too fine a point on it, impotent." Crowley filled his mouth, scooping out the last of the white of his boiled egg with a spoon. "In the gross vernacular, I can't *get it up*, dear boy. My turkey neck's gobbling days are over. So that is why I needed you. Your *upstanding* commitment to romantic desire, so to speak. Your libido, to be exact. And don't say I lied to you. By omission, if anything, but barely that. I simply—what is the word—*withheld*. Something that you, my friend…"

Dennis battled a different kind of nausea. The mental kind. "You made me—"

"I made you do nothing. You did everything willingly. Anyway, the deed is done. You proved yourself up to the task. Very 'up' to it, I should say. My choice was vindicated." Crowley sipped his tea, pinkie finger raised.

The redhead returned from the kitchen and Dennis couldn't bear to look at her. He thought of the Scarlet Woman. Joan, but not Joan. The one that he had…He couldn't bear to think about it.

"Who was she?"

"Oh, someone who wanted to play with you. Don't worry. She only had intercourse with your mind. It isn't technically adultery, being on a plane beyond the physical. Your marriage vows are still intact."

Dennis looked sharply around him at the other residents, suddenly worried that everyone in the vicinity could hear what was being said, because Crowley didn't seem to be lowering his voice in the slightest.

"If you wish me to write an explanatory letter to your dearest, I shall. Rather like from a headmaster at prep school. Or would you prefer to explain the whole business to Joan yourself?"

My God, you're enjoying this. Every second of it.

The background noise became a fog, a symphonic cacophony of cutlery and crockery and politeness Dennis didn't want to listen to anymore. He didn't want the tea, and he didn't want anything in this place or from this vile creature, and wasn't compelled to, any more.

His chair scraped back with a shriek. He stood up. He'd been lied to. He'd been used. Hideously.

"Where are you going?"

"Home."

Guests looked up, necks twisting.

"Why? We should at least celebrate."

Dennis laughed bitterly. "Celebrate what?"

"Victory over dark forces, dear boy. What else?"

Dennis managed to keep his voice even—a feat he thought impossible even as he was achieving it. "It seems to me that the darkest of all forces is very much intact."

"Oh, really!" said Crowley. "I should hate to part on bad terms, after all we have been through."

"What *have* we been through?"

"There really is no need for raised voices. This is a civilised establishment, and Mr Symonds runs it with an admirable degree of decorum."

His face burning, Dennis really couldn't give a damn about that—or about being the victim, ad infinitum, of the kind of goading that clearly gave Crowley pleasure. Perhaps it was the only kind of pleasure he could have, nowadays. But that wasn't his problem, or his responsibility. It made him see the Great Beast in a new, despicable and loathsome light. Or rather, no light at all— only a horrendous and heartless darkness. And if half of the other guests—Arthur Askey, the rock and the tree—teacups half-raised, lips half-pursed, were staring at him as if *he* were the mad one, it didn't matter. They could go to hell. They could *all* go to hell.

He turned from the breakfast table and went to pack his suitcase and was going to get out of there, before he did something he really *would* regret.

"Dear oh dear." Crowley played to the gallery. "Mere mention of the word 'sex' and the English run for the hills." A smattering of laughter.

At the foot of the stairs Dennis, seething, found himself intercepted by a bewildered-looking Vernon.

"How much do I owe you? For the room?"

"Really. As I said, all we ask is…"

"I insist."

Dennis took notes from his wallet and flung them onto the open guest book.

By the time he came back down with his suitcase, Dennis had cooled down slightly, but not much. Crowley used his foot to push the chair out opposite him. "Don't rush away. Please. I have something to tell you. You seem frightfully out of sorts. I wouldn't like to see you getting behind the wheel of a car in that condition. Really. Don't underestimate it. Ritual practices take their toll. Sit. Eat something. You'll—"

"I'm not taking any more orders from you."

"I'm not about to give them. I prefer to offer enlightenment."

Dennis laughed hollowly, making his point, he thought, unambiguously.

"Don't you want to know the future?"

The shy girl took Crowley's empty plate from in front of him. Crowley smiled at her and stroked her bare arm with one extended finger. She did not react, which made it all the more despicable. Dennis could see now that he was shuffling a Tarot card deck—not his own design, 'The Book of Thoth' as he grandly called it—but the traditional Rider-Waite designs, well-thumbed and dog-eared. Some saw Tarot as fairground fortune-telling. Others, on a deeper level, as a kind of portable grimoire of knowledge, carrying both holy and impure spiritual forces, *Sefirot* and *Qlippoth*, as well as secrets of the larger cosmic process itself. Dennis didn't know about that, but he'd had it done many times, for amusement, over the years. He didn't count himself as superstitious, but at certain crisis points in his life he'd had his cards read and they'd turned out to be—what could he say? A godsend?…At any rate, uncannily accurate.

"It's the very least I can do. By way of…" Crowley let the sentence be incomplete.

Dennis left his suitcase in the hall. He returned to the dining room and sat down. It was almost deserted, apart from the fusspot stable girl and her reedy bride of Lesbos—*The Sporting Life* and *The Lady*—whilst Vernon's wife supervised her staff.

"How are you, lovie?"

"I'm very well," said Dennis quietly, blushing—though Johnny wouldn't have the faintest idea why. "How are you?"

"Mustn't grumble, sweetheart. Can I get you a fresh pot?"

"No, thank you. I'm going to be hitting the road soon. But thank you anyway."

"That's a shame. We've enjoyed having you. Haven't we, Vernon?" Johnny giggled girlishly, took the stale pot in her cupped hands, and departed, lipstick shining, sway in her hips, ladder in her stockings. The young waitress brought a glass of grapefruit juice and placed it in front of Dennis. He prodded it away.

"Get me a Scotch."

A fraction alarmed, she removed it.

Now it was just the two of them. Eye to eye.

"All systems of thinking reach towards the same answers," said Crowley, placing the deck face down between them. "Art.

Psychology. Science. All show reality in different ways. Tarot is just a different way of seeing. One day it might even be seen as the cornerstone of magic."

"Maybe you should do tea leaves, like Gypsy Rose Lee."

Crowley didn't let the insult ruffle his feathers. "If you're right handed pick up the deck with your left hand, and vice versa. Shuffle well, thinking of the question you want the cards to answer."

"What if I don't have a question?"

"Everyone has a question."

The waitress returned. He studied his malt and knocked half of it back in one.

"Now let the pack fall in two, side by side," said Crowley. "Then place one on top of the other, still using the same hand."

He looked at the top card, shrugged, placed it at the bottom of the deck, and laid out the traditional, cruciform, five-card spread on the tablecloth between them, a sixth card laid across the middle one, horizontally. The Celtic Cross.

"I doubt anything you can tell me will make a ha'peth of difference to the way I'm feeling at this moment."

"Let's see, shall we?"

Dennis drank the rest of the Scotch, resolutely fixing his eyes on Crowley, not the cards.

"The central position, representing the present. Nine of swords. Overactive mind, anxiety…"

Dennis couldn't argue with that insight, but you didn't exactly need psychic powers to glean that, Mr Crowley, did you?

"The negative crossing it—the ten of swords…a feeling of being defeated, short-changed, betrayed."

Oh, well done, how on earth did you work that out?

"On the left side is your past which influences you now. The six of wands. Success, accolades, achievement in abundance. It's good. It's very good. But that's in the past. Here, below, are the hidden factors affecting that, and it's the ten of Pentacles."

Bloody pentacles again.

"Financial success, strong business relationships. But these two are the important ones…"

Crowley's crooked finger pointed to the top.

"Your potential at this moment. Death. But as you well know, in the Tarot, death isn't death, death is change. Something ending. Lack of certainty. And here the future."

Dennis stared at this broken, yellowed fingernail as he tapped the card on the right. And stopped, rigid.

"What?"

"It's…"

"It's the Tower, yes," said Dennis.

"Crumbling…"

"I can see that."

"It's all collapsing around you at some point. You have success and money and fame and, still, you're at the mercy of powerful forces. The lightning. Electrical fire. Heavenly power. But the clouds are dark, not bright." Crowley frowned, swallowed. Fixed intently on the image on the card, he became troubled.

Dennis laughed, leaned back in his chair, shook his head. The act was good, but he'd seen it too many times before.

"That's enough. I'm going now."

"Yes, go. By all means, go." Crowley waved his hands in the air. "Get another reading from someone less…Good idea. I'm not the right person to…"

Dennis laughed again, but when he saw Crowley about to gather up the spread, he stopped him.

"What are you talking about?"

"No. Believe me. This was a very bad idea. You're right."

"If there's something bad about my family or loved ones, I want to know it."

"No. Nothing like that."

"Then tell me."

"It won't do you any good, I promise."

"I said: Tell me."

Crowley could see he meant it. He cleared the table of all the cards except the Tower. He squared it up using the flats of his hands, then moved it up and down with his forefinger.

"Are you sure?"

Dennis did not need to nod in confirmation. His eyes said it all.

Crowley held up the card next to his face, but Dennis wasn't sure now if he was reading what he saw in the card or the man who sat opposite him, into whose eyes he was staring—those limpid grey, hooded orbs that always seemed to be flitting between wisdom and malice.

"This tells me you will have great success in your life, from your novels, financially, literary success, comfort at home, it's all here. The adoration of thousands of readers…"

But?

Crowley paused. His lids flickered. His lips parted. It really seemed as though he didn't want to go on. His discomfort—no, his *sadness*—was palpable.

"But after your death, you see, that's the lightning striking…the Tower crumbles. It means that, like all artists, your time will come and go. Then, sooner than you think, everything you have written will be virtually forgotten. Within twenty years, few if any will even have heard of your name."

Dennis took a moment to absorb what was being said to him, then snorted his derision. It wasn't even worth the dignity of a laugh. It was pathetic. If this was Crowley's idea of enjoyment…

But, the thing was—Crowley wasn't smiling at all. In fact, Dennis could have sworn that his rheumy eyes glistened with tears.

"I'm sorry. I can only tell you what I see."

"And what do you 'see'?"

Crowley's milky cataracts lost focus, and what he saw, if he saw anything, was not seen by his eyes.

"I see that your vast popularity today, and for the next few decades, will barely outlive you. By the time you die you will have already turned into an anachronism to the new generation. A joke. They won't be interested in nasty goings on when the ball is over. Or semen splashed on the altar of the Home Counties as the Château Petrus Pomerol is quaffed. It will be a different world. A world that will leave you behind."

Dennis was almost taken in by it for a second.

Almost.

By that pained old mask of a face buckled with heartache, as if struggling with the painful duty of imparting his Cassandra-like prediction to the one who would suffer.

What utter bilge!

This was nothing of the sort. This was a clever actor—a con man and charlatan, as Joan put it—having his moment in the spotlight, finding absolute glee deep in his soul even as he delivered damnation. What was on show was nothing less than a sickness. But strangely, he no longer wanted to explode.

"You might not be The Wickedest Man in the World—I think a certain German corporal has the claim to that in recent times," Dennis said softly and carefully, wanting to be sure Crowley heard his exact words. "But I do think you are the most manipulative bastard in Christendom."

"Tut, tut." Crowley blinked in mock horror. "Language, Mr Wheatley. I thought language was your art form."

"You would test the language of a saint."

"Oh, I have, my dear boy. And often." He collected the Tarot cards with outstretched arms, as if gathering to his bosom a litter of diabolical pets.

"You expect me to believe—"

"Believe or don't believe. Your choice. But it's the price we paid."

"Price? What *price?*"

"The price the demon demanded, of course. And took. I told you if he did as we commanded, something valuable would have to be given in return."

"It *wanted* your *soul!*"

"My rancid soul is very small beer compared to a good man's heart. Not to mention his immortality." He wrapped the Tarot deck in a silk cloth.

Dennis was dumbstruck.

"You knew."

"Of course I didn't *know.* But I know now."

"Well, thank you for that. I suppose if the Devil promises me years of luxury and contentment in return for being forgotten in the annals of literary history, I daresay I will get used to it." He stood up, and Crowley did too.

"It wasn't my doing."

"Wasn't it? I think you know perfectly well this is *all* your doing. Every last bit of it."

"The forces of the cosmos are hard masters. They think nothing of what we hold dear." Crowley stuck to his tail. "My daughter Poupée died because she impeded my progress. Of that I have no doubt, now. My love for her was a distraction. They let me know that, in no uncertain terms."

"The very idea of that is obscene, even for you. You should be ashamed of yourself."

"That's the thing though, you see. I never am, am I? And that's what people cannot bear."

"You know, for a clever man, you talk absolute balderdash. For all your insight and enlightenment, what good have you done with your life?"

"You're quite correct. I should write ugly little potboilers."

"They are not…" Offended, Dennis jabbed an index finger at him. "… *little!*"

Crowley laughed.

"No, I'm serious. What have you achieved?" Dennis railed. "It's the same with anybody who gets involved in the occult or black magic. They do it for one reason and one alone—to inflate their shallow self-importance. In reality they're nothing but…but lonely minds or miserable, onanistic perverts, seeking validation for their insatiable and insignificant egos—finding in the fabrications of the ancients something they can use to lord over the gullible and equally mentally deluded."

Crowley's eyes bored into him. "The flaw in that plan being?"

"Life!" Dennis almost choked on his pent-up rage. "It excludes *life*, Crowley—and all that is good and proper about it."

"Oh…*Proper!*" Crowley rolled the word mellifluously on his tongue.

"Yes, mock—why not? You always had a hearty disregard for everything I believe in. My success, my reputation. It's everything you think ludicrous and pointless. That's why you've wanted to undermine and destroy it. And now it's blindingly obvious you got your thrill from duping me all along. God, you must have been laughing up your sleeve from the moment I fell for it, hook line and sinker. There is no woman in peril. There is no child sacrifice. No evil Satanist, is there? The only lamb to the slaughter was me. This is all about power, to you. Your pathetic plot to string me along, humiliate me, and get a high out of it in your vacant, impotent, empty life. Well, you've had your fun. The entertainment is over. Now if you'll excuse me, I'll be happy if I never see you again."

"I believe you said that the first time we met." Crowley watched as Dennis picked up his suitcase. "Do send my love to your darling wife, by the way. Saint Joan. Sweet thing. Wouldn't say boo to a goose. Consequently I can't stop imagining her opening her legs. I'm sure you're the same."

Dennis tried to control his simmering. "I'm definitely *not* the same as you—in any shape or form."

"I admire your certainty," said Crowley.

"I'm sure you don't."

"She entered of her own free will, you know. Sadly I didn't get the opportunity to enter her of mine."

Something clicked inside Dennis, some switch was thrown and he flew at Crowley, wanting to punch him on the jaw and not caring if he broke his scrawny neck, and he might have done, easily, had Vernon not already had his arms hooked around his, holding him back. And he felt a wave of shame even as his anger detonated, because it was the one thing he'd sworn not to do, and that was to give Crowley the satisfaction of a reaction. To show he had needled him sufficiently to light the blue touch paper. He hated that he'd accomplished that, and it made him hate Crowley more. He knew that he should turn the other cheek, as Jesus did. The Bible was his bedrock, but it couldn't help him now. He wanted to tear him to pieces.

The tree shot to her feet, hand to her mouth. The rock emitted a high, spaniel-like yelp. A tea cup rolled off their table and smashed.

"Mr Wheatley. Please!" said Vernon.

Dennis strained to be let at his opponent like a boxer in the ring. What did it look like? A thug? Frankly he didn't care. If he looked insane, perhaps he was insane in that moment, or perhaps he was finally doing the manly thing after all. But slowly the red mist lifted and he could see the folly of that course of action, and he could see not Crowley but some poor shrivelled husk of a man, deflated from his great days, with quivering jaw, feeble arms raised to protect himself, lapsing into a coughing fit, the sound of a wrench scraping against metal, bent double, fighting the phlegm, the last enemy, and thought of Joan and what she would think of him, and was the Englishman again.

Shrugging Vernon off him, he straightened his cuffs, and, wanting something to occupy his right fist, picked up his suitcase.

"In mirrors people see what they want to see," Crowley wheezed from behind his defensive napkin.

Dennis turned back to him, glaring.

"I prefer to look directly into a man's eyes and get the measure of what he's about. More of a measure than a whole bookshelf of words."

"Well, you would know."

"I do know," said Dennis.

And he knew he wasn't afraid any more. Because he knew that deep down he had what Crowley would never have. A strong marriage of equals. Of devotion. Of selflessness, of pride and of mutual support. That love—and it *was* love—was his bastion, and he was sure that Crowley even on some level envied him for that, though he could never, ever admit it. Perhaps that was the real reason he resented him and needed to belittle him. In truth, he represented everything the old man's despicable soul had always craved, but never found.

"Goodbye Mr Wheatley."

Dennis did not answer.

"Love is the law. You're supposed to reply: Love under will."

"I know what I'm supposed to do," said Dennis.

"Then there's hope for you yet," said Crowley, inculcating a smile.

*
**

He was grateful for the fresh, cold air. He lugged his suitcase into the boot of the car, took out his keys and walked round to the driver's side to get in. The smell of leather and the feel of the steering wheel gave him a foretaste of the most exhilarating escape, even before he turned on the ignition. Catching something out of the corner of his eye, he looked over his left shoulder. A figure was framed in the passenger window, against the ivyladen porch of Netherwood House. A toss up whether it was more like a scarecrow or a waxworks. Perhaps only fit for the bonfire itself, now. And he'd happily shove him there, given half a chance.

Dennis put the gear stick into reverse and revved hard, then turned the wheel in a right hand lock. The car almost clipped Crowley across the knees—and would have done, had Vernon not yanked the old man by the shoulders backwards a couple of steps. Dennis's wheels tore up the gravel in a spray.

By the time he had straightened the steering wheel and wrestled the gear stick into first, Vernon was rapping on the driver's side window. Dennis had no choice but to wind it down.

"Er…This is my…ah…"

Vernon handed Dennis a package wrapped in brown paper. Dennis knew from its size and shape exactly what it was. His play. Full of terrible dialogue and 'big boot' acting, he was certain. Soppy heroes and silly villains and endings and applause and a tipple at the bar before a taxi home, darling. Damn plays. Damn stories. He took it and dumped it on the passenger seat without a word.

"If you…er…"

Vernon backed away with the kind of unctuous gratitude Dennis abhorred, probably thinking the novelist a stuck-up, selfimportant type, and would tell all his friends so at the very least prompting. Well, so be it.

Dennis hastily wound the window back up, but realised Crowley was standing there, with his RAF greatcoat in his arms. Now Dennis remembered he'd left it on the peg in the hall. Before he could think what to do, Crowley had opened the back door and put it on the back seat. Now he was slowly returning backwards to the porch. Dennis accelerated out of the driveway onto The Ridge without looking right or left and without looking back.

For the next fifteen minutes, as he drove, he became increasingly disturbed by the thought of Crowley handling his greatcoat, touching the material with those odious hands, and slowly convinced himself that the man did nothing without some malevolent or self-serving intent; he'd done something with it, or put it there for a reason. He couldn't stand not knowing what, and thoughts of pockets and that MR James story came back to him, of runes and demons and witchcraft, and he started to imagine an aura of pernicious evil exuding from the seat behind him that he couldn't shake off.

He pulled into a lay-by off the main road, parked, and got out of the car. He tugged open the back door, took out his greatcoat and searched the pockets.

He found a sheet of paper, unfolded it, and read it.

FUCKING IS NOT AN ABOMINATION.
IT IS GLORY.

Refusing to let his anger rise yet again, he tore it up into shreds and threw it into the bushes, got back into his car, and drove home.

*
**

When he arrived, all he could hear were the damned rooks. Before he'd unpacked, or even taken off his coat, he fetched his Holland & Holland 10-bore, went straight out again and had a go at them. It made a hell of a noise, and the servants roused, Cook with her hands on her hips, black clouds of smoke drifting across the lawns from the nests in the tall trees. If Joan thought he had lost his mind, he didn't care.She moved forward, arms out, to greet him. He held up a hand and walked past her. Didn't want to be touched. He said the kick from the thing hurt like blazes. Made the excuse he was going to run a bath, but the truth was, he found the possibility of her tenderness unbearable. He'd driven in a complete daze, his thoughts all over the place, up and down, here and there, everywhere and nowhere. He felt beaten. Not physically, but mentally.

Minutes later he sat in the bath, bruised shoulder all colours of the rainbow but not really the cause of his pain, stuffing his knuckles into his mouth to stifle the sound of sobs that never came.

He didn't tell Joan what had happened, and never would. But what he did say, because he had to say something, eventually, wasn't a lie.

The following morning, breaking a horrible silence, he spoke. Crowley had been playing with him, had dragged him to Hastings for the sole purpose of belittling him, and now he felt foolish, upset and incredibly angrily. In fairness to her, Joan seemed to take that at face value—why wouldn't she? And if she hadn't, there wasn't terribly much he could do about it. He told her that, as he saw it, the so-called Great Beast, frail and pathetic now, had little more in his life than his fellow mummified guests, having alienated all his friends, and such games were his last breath. His last laugh.

Joan said nothing.

After breakfast, as he returned from inspecting the rooks— which were slowly returning in dribs and drabs, with plodding inevitability—he saw a bicycle at the front door, and a Boy Messenger in a navy blue uniform with red piping down the seam of his trousers standing beside it.

"Is that for me?"

"Mr Wheatley?"

"Yes."

A telegram. He could tell nothing from the address on the envelope, hand-written as it was by someone on the staff at the GPO—nine words for sixpence, and sixpence on top for Priority. He opened it and read it. Brief and to the point.

UNEXPLAINED FIRE IN HASTINGS OLD TOWN. ONE DEATH.—BAPHOMET

"No reply." Dennis folded it sharply. "You can go. Wait a

minute." He dug out a shilling and held it out. The boy took it, reluctantly.

"I'm sorry, sir."

"What?"

"Is it from the War Office?"

He must have delivered many an unwelcome notification to the bereaved concerning loved ones lost or missing in action over the past few years. What a thing for a mere whippersnapper on his push-bike to have to do. What an errand. It must have been something about Dennis's face that made the lad think he was one of them. "No, it's not from the War Office. Go on your way."

The youngster flicked a salute to the front of his pill-box hat and climbed onto his saddle. He must have been sixteen, but looked twelve.

Dennis opened the telegram and read it again.

Unexplained.

Did that mean the police were investigating it? If so, what was their conclusion? Did they think the cause related to the bonfire activities, a stray firework, even an unexploded bomb? If he wanted to know the facts, there'd be more in the local newspaper, but he didn't want to know more. He didn't want to be roped into Crowley's game any longer. He wanted the whole thing out of his head, not further in it. He wanted all memory of it cut out, the way a surgeon would cut out a malignant cancer to save an otherwise healthy body.

He had put the telegram on the fire and was watching it burn as Joan returned from shopping.

"I passed the Telegram Boy," she said, taking off her coat. "Anything important?"

"No."

"Telegrams are usually important."

"Well, this one wasn't."

He took himself for a walk, but he couldn't keep walking. He had to start writing sooner or later. His HB pencils were sharpened every morning. The pristine, untarnished eraser in its place. The question was, what to write? His mind was blank. Usually four pages of foolscap every day, rain or shine, was his objective. A book in seven months. Now it seemed an impossible task.

His secretary arrived at nine. He consigned her to deal with his post from the public. He had nothing else to give her, but his mail bag was always full.

Today would be different, he told himself. He'd needed some thinking time, that was all. Right…At ten o'clock he would start his new current novel.

All right…ten thirty, then.

Eleven. Eleven, without fail…

Yet he *did* fail. Hour after hour. Day after day. Failed to come up with anything even vaguely original—or, even more horrifyingly, anything at all.

Perhaps he should jettison the notion of being original, then, and rely on his old tried and tested formulae? Another Duke de Richleau story, perhaps? Or Gregory Sallust, his modern-day spy, bedding his way closer to a new, mentally-warped mastermind who wants to defile the world?

Even the thought of that bored him rigid. Heroes that saved the day. Villains with scars on their faces. Fakery, wasn't it? And historical romps, the dead lumber of the centuries, regurgitated from other people's books, was that any better?

Writing wasn't a beastly chore so much as something he had just completely fallen out of love with. Worse—he hated the very, imbecilic, thought of it. The very idea of scribbling away as he used to—ten or fourteen hours a day, until midnight or 2 a.m.— filled him with absolute dread.

He simply wanted to sleep. If he could curl up for his afternoon nap and never wake up, that would be fine. He could do that, just about.

It was all he was good for, what was left of him.

That, and slinking off, locking the bathroom door, feeling the flat razor against the skin of his forearm, pressing it down and holding it there, closing his eyes, and wondering what would happen if he gently pulled it towards him. Would it heal, would it vanish, or would he bleed?

⁂

Joan occasionally asked to read what he was working on. He'd tell her she would, when it was ready. When it was typed up in manuscript form. That was always the drill, she knew that. She didn't know, however, that he spent his days staring out of the window, hands in pockets, getting through cigarettes by the dozen without a thought in his head.Come November, everyone was enraptured by the Royal Wedding. Princess Elizabeth and Philip. The happy couple. Quite the fairy tale. All talk of the wedding dress. All eyes on Westminster Abbey. All ears craned to their wireless sets. While he put one foot in front of the other trudging the fields or cliffs in his RAF greatcoat, staring out across the Solent, but not really there at all.

Where was he then? Hastings. Netherwood. Room 13. The pentacle. The bonfire parade. All reduced to staccato images now, ones that were impossible to shake off or replace with new, more pleasant and far more desirable ones.

At social engagements he was regularly obliged to attend, he found himself drifting, rudderless, mentally absent, blocking out from his consciousness the plentiful evidence of his wife's deepening concern, wrapping himself in a sickly, self-absorbed cocoon.

When she could take it no longer, Joan had to break the deadlock, as women often did. Men as a rule being quite incapable of seeing beyond what was in their own thick heads most of the time.

"If you're not going to do something about this, then I shall. Call Dr Adams. Or I will."

Dennis protested that there was nothing wrong with him. Naturally he did. It was a stance that came naturally to all men.

Joan pleaded that she was worried. "I know someone in Harley Street."

He left the room, mumbling that, of course she did—she knew *everybody*.

Much door closing ensued.

They talked only when the servants had finished, and then only barely.

She suggested travel. A holiday. Somewhere in the sun, to recharge the batteries. He said he was far too busy. (That window needed staring out of, for God's sake.) But they both knew the pages on his desk were empty. He told her to take herself off with her friends instead. She refused to leave him alone. He insisted she should go and enjoy herself, it wasn't fair. She said she didn't care if it *was* fair, she wanted to be with him. Her words made him feel even more wretched. And if she had left the room, left the sight of him, which probably disgusted her, he wouldn't have blamed her. He was being monstrous with his silences, with this ghastly cocoon of his, but there wasn't a thing he could do about it.

As for bed, as in sharing a bed, the way a husband and wife should do, that was out of the question.

He wanted more than anything to reach out to her, to hold her, but she may as well have been a thousand miles away.

He read Crowley's obituary in *The Times*. Or rather, Joan did, aloud, at the breakfast table. The loathsome creature's health had deteriorated rapidly, and, in spite of daily injections of heroin that would have killed several horses, the attentive nursing of Johnny and Vernon, and the ministrations of the local surgery, the Great Beast had passed away on Monday 1st December 1947, with his son Atatürk and wife Deirdre 'Pat' MacAlpine at his side, as well as his old friend Lady Frieda Harris, who said he didn't recognise her at the end. It was reported there was no struggle. He simply stopped breathing, the final cause of death being ascribed to myocardial degeneration and chronic bronchitis.Hastings Borough Council denied permission for 'Perdurabo' to be cremated at Hastings Crematorium on The Ridge, a place he would have passed many times whilst walking. Instead, the funeral was held in Brighton the following Friday. Louis Wilkinson read Crowley's *Hymn to Pan* and excerpts from *The Book of the Law* and Crowley's *Gnostic Mass, Liber XV*, the OTO's central ceremony: *The Ecclesiae Gnosticae Catholicae Canon Missae*—symbolising, as it did, the sex act as a supreme magical rite. Interjections of "Io Pan" and "Do What Thou Wilt" occurred throughout the ceremony, causing those denizens of Fleet Street unable to understand the proceedings to label it a 'Black Mass'. Consequently, Brighton Council later placated ratepayers by promising such a blasphemous event would never happen again on public property.

AC had wanted no grave or memorial. It was later rumoured, nevertheless, that his ashes were shipped to the USA and buried next to a tree in Hampton New Jersey on the property of Karl Germer, Frater Saturnus, Crowley's successor as head of the OTO

True to form, the gutter press churned out the usual drivel, letting rip with regurgitated yarns of intercourse and abandon, heresy, cannibalism, tales that he had killed a cat when he was a child to test whether it had nine lives, murdered one of his coven, sacrificed babies, voted Liberal—whatever nonsense and truth they chose to print. Free to do so now he could no longer sue.

If they'd given him no respect in life, they gave him even less in death, and Dennis derived no pleasure from that. As usual, the scandal sheets were all too eager to make money from antics they claimed to deplore, yet were happy to run such stories endlessly for the base gratification of the sanctimonious but easily titillated British public. Sometimes Dennis thought society was run by savages, and this might be what he feared most. That the godless, in whatever shape or form, might get the whip hand.

Of course, he hated and could never forgive Crowley for what he did to Joan. It was deplorable and foul. But, when all was said and done, where was the man—and he *was* a man—in the grey area between satanic messiah on the one hand and misunderstood mystic and sex fiend on the other? Dennis really didn't know, even now. Yes, Crowley was a fraud. But *only* a fraud? He wavered between thinking the man's philosophy was profound or profoundly crooked; whether he was a true magician at all, or only a performer; a fourth or fifth-rate poet who put his own ego on a par with the gods, or someone who told a story so many times the lies convinced even him. Or perhaps he had believed them all along.

The following week Dennis received a cutting from the *Hastings and St Leonard's Observer* sent to him c/o Hutchinson's, his publishers, who forwarded it to his home address, with the attached note from Vernon, saying simply: "May be of interest."The enclosed article— really an interview with the Symondses about their most illustrious guest—contained very little Dennis hadn't read elsewhere. However, one paragraph, or section of a paragraph, jumped out at him.

Kathleen (i.e. 'Johnny') described how she and Mrs Thorne-Drury had followed the coffin to Brighton crematorium. "For such a world-renowned figure, it was sad to see only a few mourners turn up, perhaps only two or three genuine friends, amongst all the reporters from London. I remember a German woman at the graveside who placed red roses on his coffin after everyone had gone. Nobody knew who she was, nobody knew her name, and she disappeared soon afterwards."

Dennis immediately pictured a woman pushing a pram. Her hair platinum blonde under a headscarf tied up in a turban. The baby in that pram, its chubby hands reaching up to grasp something invisible.

"There was the most tremendous thunderstorm in the sky afterwards, as we drove back to Netherwood. Lightning and everything. I said: 'That's just how he would have wanted it!' And we laughed. Pat MacAlpine said it was the gods greeting him. Perhaps it was!"

Dennis didn't know if he wished Crowley to the gods or to Hell, but part of him wished he was somewhere united with his beloved Poupée, at last. For all his sins, he had loved her and grieved her with all his heart. That was the one thing he couldn't lie about. And as Crowley himself once said: "Every man and woman is a star."

"Dead," said Joan. "And his fantasies with him."Dennis was staring thorough the French windows at a lone rabbit on the grass. In

December. An individual, braving a harsh world. Mad, misunderstood, foolish, but strangely wonderful.

Run, rabbit, run, rabbit, run, run, run...

"He died as he lived. A charlatan and a monster." She folded the morning paper and passed it to him, knowing he would hide behind it, as he always did. Funnily enough, it helped her say what she wanted to say because she couldn't see his face. "He had power over women. He had eyes that undress you. Some men do." She warmed her hands on her tea cup. "They're like wolves with sheep. I expect he had women falling at his feet all the time. Or used to. Ones that have no respect for themselves. Or decency."

Dennis thought of the unnamed German woman at the graveside who had thrown a rose onto the coffin.

"Is that what you think of me?" Joan said. "That I have no decency?"

At first he was perplexed. He slowly realised that she took his brooding detachment for accusation. As if, all this time when he was inside himself, it was because he thought she'd done something wrong. Something bad. And this was his punishment.

"Is that what you think of me? That I have no decency?"

His face caved in.

"No," he said, before sobbing. "It's what I think of *me*."

She stood up and went to him and held his cheek against her body. He wrapped his arms around her waist and started weeping, like a child, like a babe in arms. The dam had burst, and he was unable to stop, even as her fragrance, Floris, Lily of the Valley, filled him, deliciously.

They held each other. Orphans in a storm. Clinging to flotsam to stop going under. But he wouldn't go under. Not now.

Finally he knew it was over.

He could begin again. Build himself up like he did the brick wall in the garden. Steadily. Surely. With patience. With care. Word upon word, sentence upon sentence, steadily, with faith and courage and the requisite foolhardiness.

He could do it.

He held a woman's body and that's what the little girl would be one day. Astra Argenta—the Silver Star—or whatever name she would choose to give herself. Fine, strong, beautiful, intelligent. Eventually with children of her own, no doubt. Gisela a grandmother, then great-grandmother. And so it continues. That is our *true* immortality. To be remembered by the ones we love. That is what mattered. Not words on a page. Not really.

Life was what mattered.

How you live it. The choices you make. The labour you choose. Whether you do good or ill towards others.

Whether you choose the right hand path, of understanding and tolerance, and vow to treat others as you yourself would wish to be treated, or the left hand path, of cruelty, selfishness, venal urges, and ultimate ruin. The path that can only drag down the human spirit. Never enrich it.

As for history, no one can know what it will make of our efforts, whether it will find them worthy or worthless. You can only play with the hand you are dealt, to the best of your abilities. To ponder where you were on the great roll call of literature was madness. There would always be Dickens. There would always be Shakespeare. There would always be Dumas. It was foolish to compare oneself to the greats of the past. Perhaps one's destiny was merely to provide excitement and distraction for ordinary people in troubled times. If so, there was no great shame in that calling. When all was said and done, all you could do as a writer, ever, was tell the stories you wanted to tell. Had to tell.

He looked down at the objects on the mahogany desk that had once belonged to Joan's father. The Chinese soapstone pencil box. The Wedgewood biscuit barrel; he never did lose his sweet tooth. The onyx ash tray. The crystal-sided ormolu-mounted box that had belonged to his mother. The Toby jug.Sounded like a nickname. Feller named Jugg. In the services, any chap named White was inevitably Chalky. Anyone called Clarke was always Nobby. He remembered 'Tubby' Dawson, one of his friends at the JPS. when he finally won his spurs as a Pilot Officer RAF in the Future Operations Planning Section. Dennis himself had been a soldier, a gunner subaltern, and a naval cadet before that, but neither pleased him as much as wearing the uniform of a Squadron Leader.

'Toby' Jugg

He saw a man, an airman, stripped of his RAF uniform and dignity, ravaged by mental torture. In a bedroom. A shapeless darkness in the corner of the room. The helpless terror of not knowing what was a nightmare and what was reality...

It brought back to him the pain, the gut-churning fear.

But he held it, as if in the palm of his hand.

We reached below civilisation, all civilisations, stuck our hands in the cracks, and the spiders crawled out.

Magic was transformation, but writing was transformation too.

Would it flow effortlessly from his fingertips? No. Was it a God-given gift? No, he didn't think so. It was hard work, he knew that. An act of immense, many would say deluded, faith in one's own ability. God was in the grafting. That's how he would put it, at any rate. No pentagrams. No pentacles.

He took the base metal of the page and managed to forge it into something new, in the blaze of that crucifer, his imagination, if he was lucky. Something that had never existed before. However paltry, however imperfect, however—yes—mediocre, even. It was still an incoherent wish, a dream, a nightmare even, made reality.

Writing was a magical act.

And there was grace in that. Because stories, and art, and music for that matter, be they about battling vast evil or something as tiny as a single kiss, were how we understood ourselves, if we could, if we dared.

He lit a cigarette.

The sunlight fell on him through the window, warming his shirt sleeve. He turned his face to it and closed his eyes.

After a moment he picked up a pencil and began to write.

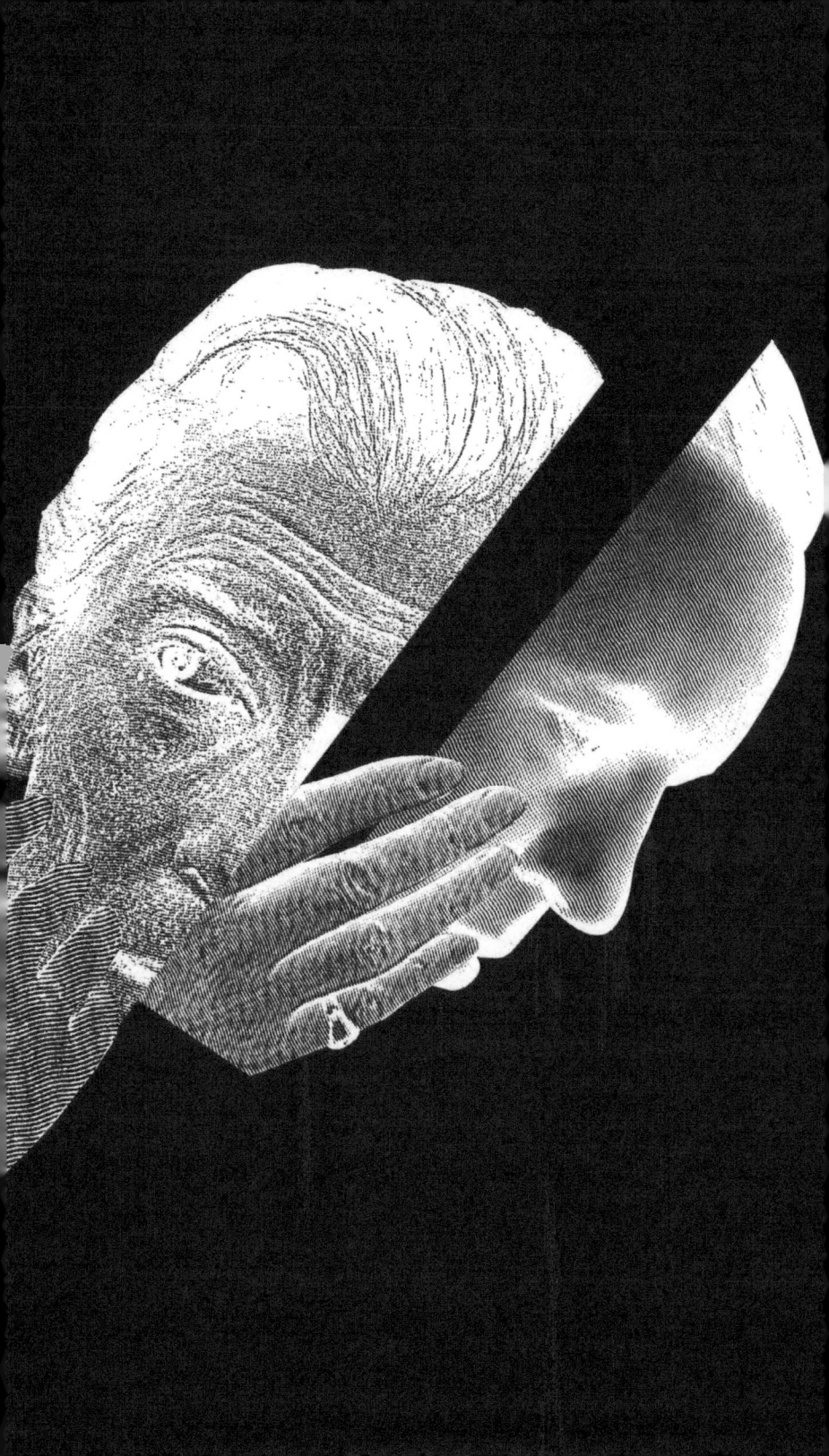

ACKNOWLEDGEMENTS

A T THE OUTSET I SHOULD POINT out that the novellas *Whitstable* and *Leytonstone* were first published by Spectral Press in 2013 and 2015 respectively, so I must put on record my huge debt of gratitude to Siobhan Marshall Jones and her team for enabling both to see the light of day. In particular, I have to thank Ben Baldwin for his marvellous covers, and my good friends Mark Morris and Stephen Gallagher for providing excellent Afterwords to the original editions.I should add that they appear with some minor revisions in the present volume.

WHITSTABLE It was a rare gift during the writing of *Whitstable* to have the encouragement of such genre luminaries as Jonathan Rigby, Simon Kurt Unsworth and David Pirie, as well as to receive their expert notes. Wayne Kinsey, Uwe Summerlad and Tony Earnshaw also pointed me towards crucial improvements, while Charles Prepolec and Anne Billson drew my attention to some outstanding interviews, particularly the documentary *Peter Cushing: One Way Ticket to Hollywood*, while John Probert and Thana Niveau alerted me to a Cushing classic I'd never seen. But I could not have written this story without the precious local knowledge given me by Whitstable residents Gordon Larkin and Brian Hadler. Thank you both.Whitstable Museum provided me with *Peter Cushing: A Celebration* and hosted the Spectral book launch to coincide with the centenary of PC's birth. It was sponsored by Whitstable's Harbour Books and presented by Victoria Falconer of Whit Lit, so thanks to all of them for making it a very special and memorable event.

Thanks are also due to Chuck and Julie Cartmel, for entertaining us in Kent, Tim Lebbon, ChiZine, Helen Marshall, Simon Barnard, Mark West, Peter Tennant, Jim McLeod, Geoff Nelder, Simon

Bestwick, Adam Nevill, David Sutton, *Fortean Times*, Sean Hogan, *Fangoria*, Reece Shearsmith, Phil Ambler, Geek Syndicate, Hereward Proops, Stephen Laws, James Everington, Dave Brzeski, This Is Horror, DF Lewis, Kim Newman, The Eloquent Page, Richard Wright, SP Miskowski, *Starburst*, Dan Reilly, Horror World, Gary McMahon, Andy Hedgecock, *Fear* magazine, Keith Brooke, Gef Fox, *SFX*, Nick Setchfield, Ian Berriman, Ebookwyrm, Stephen Jones, Gary Fry and Johnny Mains.

Needless to say, Cushing's two volumes of memoir, *An Autobiography* and *Past Forgetting* were invaluable, as were *The Hammer Story* by Marcus Hearn and Alan Barnes, *The Peter Cushing Companion* by David Miller, *The Peter Cushing Scrapbook* by Wayne Kinsey, and *English Gothic* by Jonathan Rigby. As always regarding gothic cinema, David Pirie's *A Heritage of Horror* was never far from my elbow. It was no great burden, either, to re-watch the AIP Hammer Films Production *The Vampire Lovers* (1970), directed by Roy Ward Baker from a screenplay by Harry Fine, Tudor Gates and Michael Style, based on the story *Carmilla* by Sheridan Le Fanu.

Naturally, it was to "the gentle man of horror" that this story was originally dedicated. I do the same here a second time, respectfully, and unapologetically.

LEYTONSTONE The germ for this novella was the well known and oft-repeated anecdote of Alfred Hitchcock, in which he recounted being incarcerated in a police station cell as a young boy on the instruction of his father. The point of this, the famous director said, was to teach him the lesson: "This is what happens to naughty little boys." (With characteristic laconic humour, Hitchcock suggested the same dictum for his gravestone.)I first explored the idea, tentatively, in my short story 'Little H', which first appeared in my collection *Dark Corners* (Gray Friar Press, 2006). To my surprise, the matter didn't end there. Over several years I began to be intrigued, then fascinated, by the notion that it was merely a jumping-off point. I didn't know whether it was the first act or final act of some larger drama, but somehow I felt in my bones there was far more to explore.

I must emphasise, however, that *Leytonstone* is a work of fiction. (In fact, readers with a passing knowledge of the director's life will notice several glaring inaccuracies: not least the absence of his siblings.) For those seeking, therefore, a thorough portrait of the real Hitchcock and his films I would recommend Patrick McGilligan's *Alfred Hitchcock: A Life in Darkness of Light*, which far from glossing over his 'dark side' rather puts such accusations in the context of the man and his long and extraordinary career. Other valuable sources of insight include *Hitchcock's Films* by Robin Wood, *Hitchcock on Hitchcock* edited by Sidney Gottlieb, and *Hitchcock's Secret Notebooks* by Dan Aulier. I'd also flag up (unsurprisingly) the classic *Hitchcock* interviews by Truffaut. Also, as an eclectic primer, the recent BFI compendium *39 Steps to the Genius of Hitchcock*; and, for sheer enjoyment, *Hitchcock at Work* by Bill Krohn.

Less obviously, but no less importantly, I must mention the inspiration of Dr Lenore Terr's articles 'Terror Writing by the Formerly Terrified' and 'Childhood Trauma and the Creative Product' as well as her book *Too Scared to Cry: Psychic Trauma in Childhood* (1990)—to my mind, essential reading for anyone interested in terror and its consequences.

My thanks must extend to Johnny Mains and Mark Morris, who both gave priceless words of encouragement when they were sorely needed, as well as to Gareth Jones, Dread Central, Lesley Manning, Ashley Thorpe, Anne Billson, Terry Johnson, Kit Power, Anthony Watson, Dark Musings, Jez Winship, Paul Simpson, SciFi Bulletin, Mick Garris, Barry Forshaw, Crime Time, Tim Dry, Neil Snowdon, Mark West, Phil Smith, Mytho, Barbie Wilde, Gary Fry and Christopher Fowler.

Last but not least, I am also deeply indebted to my friend Chris Smith for his encyclopaedic knowledge of a subject very close to Alfred Hitchcock's heart…Potatoes.

NETHERWOOD My longstanding interest in Crowley and, particularly, Wheatley (I wrote about the latter in *Black Static*, and *The Devil Rides Out* in *Horror: Another 100 Best Books*) was fuelled by a project commissioned by BBC Drama, so, off the bat, I must first thank Kate Harwood, Manda Levin, Lisa Osborne, Esther Springer and Anne Pivcevic for their trust, involvement and pertinent questioning. With weary inevitability, the fruit of that particular labour withered on the vine. I nevertheless gradually found a new seed growing in my mind, using two of the same characters. Soon it seemed to me to share things in common with my previous explorations of practitioners in horror and the macabre—and so the third in *The Dark Masters Trilogy* was born.With a title— *Netherwood*—firmly set, by spooky coincidence while researching I found a non-fiction book in a dingy bookshop in Hastings Old Town, literally sitting on top of a pile, as if waiting for me. *Netherwood: The Last Resort of Aleister Crowley, by 'A Gentleman of Hastings'* proved a treasure trove, and the writing of my own *Netherwood* would have been impossible, or severely diminished, without it. I'm indebted beyond words to its authors—Anthony Clayton, Gary Lachman, Andy Sharp and David Tibet.

Whilst the above-mentioned is the definitive account of The Great Beast's last days, writings on (and by) both Wheatley and Crowley are, of course, numerous. However, for the factually curious who would like a *little* further reading, I'd recommend the following:

The Devil is a Gentleman: The Life and Times of Dennis Wheatley by Phil Baker is brilliantly evocative and a wonderful read. The definitive (if unflaggingly sympathetic) biography of Crowley is, arguably, *Perdurabo: The Life of Aleister Crowley* by Richard Kaczynski, the hugely impressive result of decades of meticulous research.

There's much illumination to be had, also, from other portraits, such as *Aleister Crowley: The Biography* by Tobias Churton; *The Magical World of Aleister Crowley* by Francis King; *The Great Beast* by John Symonds; *Aleister Crowley: The Nature of the Beast* by Colin Wilson; and *Aleister Crowley: The Black Magician* by the poet C. R. Cammell (father of film-maker Donald Cammell, codirector, with Nic Roeg, of *Performance*—a film almost Crowleyesque in its heady mix of sex, drugs and magical transformation. For completists, Donald Cammell also played Osiris in Crowley enthusiast Kenneth Anger's *Lucifer Rising*.)

I should also name-check 'Necromancy in the UK', by Leon Hunt, an essay in *British Horror Cinema* edited by Steve Chibnall and Julian Petley, Crowley's own *Magick* edited by Symonds and Grant (1973), Wheatley's own non-fictional *The Devil and All His Works* (1971), *Churchill's Storyteller* by Craig Cabell (on Wheatley's WWII activities), and a book on the history of the Bonfire Societies of Hastings, *Kindred Spirits* by Tony Streeter.

My personal thanks must go to Charles Wood, Kate Wood, Rod Anderson, Hastings residents Martin and Alison Levinson for showing us around and introducing us to 'bonfire'; to Andrew Cartmel (for the voice recording of AC); to the lovely Guy Adams (for a copy of Wheatley's *Stranger than Fiction*), and the equally lovely A.K. Benedict for a wartime map of the bombing of Hastings.

Most of all I must salute my readers: Gary McMahon, Ray Cluley, Neil Spring, Kit Powers, Peter Engelmann and Johnny Mains. You helped more than you can know.

To Pete Crowther, who gave my pitch the thumbs-up, Nicky, Tamsin, Mike, and everyone at PS for working so hard on this book, and to Pedro Marques whose design work you hold in your hands—what can I say? Big hugs.

Finally, I should point out that, though the ceremony of demonic invocation described in the pages of *Netherwood* was written in conjunction with a practitioner of ritual magic who wishes to remain anonymous, certain details have been altered to make its efficacy, I'm assured, impossible.

Nonetheless...don't try this at home, folks.

Stephen Volk
Bradford-on-Avon, June 2018
www.stephenvolk.net

Note: For further information about the background to, and writing of, these stories, I happily refer the reader to my three interviews with Kit Power, available on Jim McLeod's admirable *Ginger Nuts of Horror* web site: www.gingernutsofhorror.com